D1272103

Saving Grace

Saving Grace

RYAN PHILLIPS

© Copyright 2004 — Ryan Phillips

All rights reserved. This book is protected by the copyright laws of the United States of America. This book may not be copied or reprinted for commercial gain or profit. The use of short quotations or occasional page copying for personal or group study is permitted and encouraged. Permission will be granted upon request. Unless otherwise identified, Scripture quotations are from the King James Version of the Bible. Please note that Destiny Image's publishing style capitalizes certain pronouns in Scripture that refer to the Father, Son, and Holy Spirit, and may differ from some Bible publishers' styles.

Destiny Image Fiction

An Imprint of

Destiny Image® Publishers, Inc.

P.O. Box 310

Shippensburg, PA 17257-0310

ISBN 0-7394-4308-9

For Worldwide Distribution

Printed in the U.S.A.

This book and all other Destiny Image, Revival Press, MercyPlace, Fresh Bread, Destiny Image Fiction, and Treasure House books are available at Christian bookstores and distributors worldwide.

For a U.S. bookstore nearest you, call

1-800-722-6774.

For more information on foreign distributors, call

717-532-3040.

Or reach us on the Internet:

www.destinyimage.com

Dedication

To Betty Cavan…who taught me the basics.

To Irma Henderson…who taught me to love other people's stories.

To Chris Tysh…who taught me to write my own.

Acknowledgments

Thank you to everyone at Destiny Image, especially Don Milam, for believing in Grace and me. Thank you for the opportunity. Thank you for the experience. Thank you for the journey.

Thank you, Mom, for your good advice, never-ending patience, and unconditional love. *Saving Grace* would not be the same without you. I would not be the same without you.

Thank you, Father God, for Your grace and mercy. You are my beginning and my middle and my end. You are all my reasons. You are my only purpose. You are my everything.

Endorsement

Saving Grace will heighten your sensitivity for administering God's grace more effectively to those who are struggling with life's challenges. It is a romance novel so well written that you can easily forget it is fiction.

Ryan Phillips has an imagination beyond her 22 years. After Grace's mother is killed in a plane crash, she realizes she could go where she had never been, into the arms of our Savior "Yeshua," where He was always waiting for her. This will be a must read for the thousands of youth in our Y2P youth protégé program.

—Alena Edmondson, Co-Founder
Christian Business Network
Christian Business Network Entrepreneur Training Institute

Contents

Chapter One

"Oh! Oh! Careful! You're gonna scratch it," I warned my best friend, Trina. I put down my end of the huge, cherry-stained oak desk and leaned forward to make sure the left corner was still intact.

"Grace, for the love of God, shut up and keep moving," she snapped.

Under any other circumstances, her attitude would have caused a spat, but she was exhausted. We'd been hauling furniture up three flights of stairs since early this morning. My legs were about to give out, my lower back throbbed, and I smelled like I'd never heard of deodorant. Two hours ago, I would've given anything for a chilled bottle of Perrier, a steaming hot Jacuzzi, and some Epsom salts; now I'd settle for the floor and a pillow. But we still had two sofas, a love seat, and a curio to tackle.

"Don't get cranky, now. *Pleeeeaaassseee*," I begged, trying to keep the mood light.

"Trust me," answered Trina, still holding up her end of the desk, "*this* is not Cranky. But if you don't pick up this oversized slab of wood and keep stepping, you'll meet Cranky's cousin, Peeved, real quick."

I couldn't help but smile. Trina's always had a way with words, especially when she's irritated. When we were kids, her brashness hurt my feelings, but as the years went by it became part of what I loved about her. Now I couldn't imagine living without her in-your-face honesty.

"Okay, okay. Here we go, ready?" We managed to get the desk up the last set of stairs, through the door, and into the second bedroom before we both collapsed onto a couple of unopened boxes.

"It really is a gorgeous loft," she managed between breathless pants.

I was so winded all I could do was nod. *It really is wonderful*, I thought, as I surveyed the spacious area. I love this loft. I could have never afforded anything this extravagant in Detroit, especially not downtown. It's practically all windows, with glossy hardwood floors that bounce sunlight all over the place. The kitchen has new appliances; there's central air and the master bathroom has one of the most elegant hot tubs I've ever seen. The other bedroom, which is on the opposite end of the loft, has delicate looking French doors that lead to a balcony. It offers a great view of Beale Street. I decided to use the smaller room as an office. It lets in the most sun, and I write best when there's lots of natural light.

"Explain to me again why you didn't hire professional movers to do this?" Trina asked, while handing me a glass of ice water. I was so busy soaking in my new surroundings that I hadn't even realized she'd gotten up for drinks.

"Because," I answered, after taking a swig of water, "last time I moved, half of my stuff ended up missing, and the other half was so banged around it wasn't even worth keeping. I figured it would be better to do the work myself. That way, I could save my money and my furniture."

"Right. So, when you figured it would be better to do it yourself and save money, you were really thinking you would just enlist my services for free."

"Something like that," I answered, with a sheepish smile. "Anyway, don't act like you haven't enjoyed this little bonding experience."

"We could have bonded at the massage parlor over a couple of cappuccinos and a mud bath," she answered. "This, my sweet manipulative friend, is not what I call bonding—this is what I call manual labor."

"Don't even start," I warned her, as I finished off the water and set the glass on the windowsill. "This was your idea. I wasn't thinking about moving to Memphis until you came begging."

"The nerve," she gasped dramatically, trying her best to feign offense. "You know your eyes teared up and your bottom lip hit the floor the minute I told you that Darius wanted me to move with him to Tennessee."

As usual, there was a ring of truth in both of our stories. Darius is Trina's high school sweetheart. They've been on and off now for nearly nine years. Their relationship is complicated. I stopped trying to understand it a long time ago. Despite all the rotten things they've done to each other, she's never happier than when they're together. So when he landed a marketing job in Memphis, it was pretty much a given that Trina would follow. There wasn't really anything tying her to Detroit, except me.

I really did cry when she decided to go with him. Ever since we were in middle school, Trina has been my source of strength. She's the only person in my life who's never let me down. The thought of living nearly eight hundred miles away from each other had us both sobbing at the rate of two boxes of Kleenex a day.

"This is so stupid," she'd declared, wiping away a tear with the back of her hand. "I'm just going to tell Darius that I'm staying. I mean, who is he to expect me to just uproot myself and shuffle my life around because it's best for him?"

As much as I had wanted to be selfish and proceed in ripping Darius apart for wanting to be close to the woman he loves, I couldn't, not because I gave a rat's tail about Darius, but because I knew Trina would be miserable. She'd been waiting for years for some sign of long-term commitment from Darius, and he finally asked her to live with him. The only problem was he wanted her to live with him in Memphis.

"No, come on now, you've been waiting for this way too long. If you pass it up now, he may never offer it again."

"Yeah, but at what cost?" she'd asked. "I'm going to be the same person in Tennessee that I am here. Why, all of a sudden, am I good enough to live with him now that he's moving?" She'd made a good point, but no amount of rationalizing would make her happy once he was gone. As much as I wanted her to stay, I would never put her in a position where she felt like she had to choose between Darius and me. It just wouldn't be fair. And then it hit me—

"You know what? I could move to Memphis with you."

"What?" she'd asked, looking at me as if I'd just offered to mop her kitchen floor with my tongue.

"Why are you looking at me like I'm crazy?" I asked. "Think about it. We could have so much fun. It's not like I have to be in Detroit to write, and I have more than enough money saved."

I could see it all starting to sink in, as the wrinkles on her forehead disappeared and a slight smile emerged.

"Oh my God, Grace, you're moving to Tennessee with me!" she squealed, pummeling me to the floor.

There really wasn't anything wrong with my life in Detroit, except that I was living with my mom and I was completely bored. I'd graduated from college and my writing career had taken flight when Taylor and Dotson, a major publishing house, signed my children's book series *Simon and Eddie*. Writing was fun and I freelanced here and there, but something was missing. I wasn't sure what I wanted to do with the rest of my life. I'm still not sure. I'm in the middle of what my mother has tritely dubbed a "soul searching" phase.

"You're trying to figure out who you are, Grace, and there's nothing wrong with that. Just don't use your search as an excuse to become lazy."

That, to me, is a crock. I'm twenty-seven years old. I know exactly who I am. I'm a short, chunky, manless, almost over-the-hill black chick, who only has one true friend and a moderately successful children's book series to show for her nearly three decades of living. It's never been an issue of not knowing who I am, but rather one of not knowing where I belong.

I'm taking steps in the right direction, though.

I love Memphis. I've always heard legends about southern hospitality, but who would have thought it actually existed? I was born and raised up north, where everyone has a "you mind your own business and I'll do the same" mentality. Having lived in Detroit for nearly fifteen years, where smiles are expressly reserved for important people, like your boss, your in-laws, and your neighborhood drug dealer, I had to polish up my manners quickly. At first it was kind of eerie seeing perfect strangers stopping to exchange pleasantries. But in these few short days, I've found myself smiling and greeting like I've lived here my whole life. The move was a good thing; I needed a new environment and more importantly, I needed to be near Trina. As much as I made it out to be a favor to her, we both know I was suffocating in Detroit. At times, our friendship was the only thing that kept me going.

Over the past several years, it seemed like every aspect of my life had fallen to pieces. My only constants were Trina and my writing. I'd been looking for a chance to escape for some time. I just never expected that Darius would open the door that would allow both Trina and me to enter new chapters of our lives.

"Earth to Grace." Trina waved her hand in my face. "Girl, you better snap out of it. We still have some major stuff to lug up here."

"I know, here I come," I answered, practically slinging myself off the box and into a standing position.

"Don't quit now; if we're lucky the curio and love seat will fit in the elevator. Gimme a sec, though, I gotta go to the little girls' room."

"That's *so* much more information than I needed to know."

I had just started unloading a couple of the many boxes strewn across the floor when I heard a light rap at the door.

"It's open," I shouted. It was probably Darius coming to pick up his beloved. *Well that's too bad*, I thought. *You're just gonna have to wait. There's no way I can carry the rest of that stuff up here by myself.*

A few seconds later there was another rap.

"Darius, just come on in, my hands are full," I called over my shoulder. I heard the door open, followed by some heavy footsteps.

"Don't bother getting comfortable," I said, my back still to the door. "We've been slaving up and down those stairs all day, and we could use some brute strength right about now to get the rest of that stuff up here." I continued stacking books and little knickknacks onto the bookshelves. "She should be out any second."

Just then, Trina emerged from the bathroom. "Oh, hi," she said somewhat awkwardly. "Are you a friend of Gracie's?"

I whirled around, completely confused. Standing sheepishly in the doorway was one of the finest looking men I'd ever seen. His chocolate skin was flawless—dark and rich like the color of cognac. His big brown eyes were surrounded with delicate long lashes, and he had a wide stately nose that gave him an air of importance. His lips were striking. They were full, almost pouty, and perfectly round. He had a killer smile with a perfectly placed dimple on each side of his face, and his small, orderly dreadlocks fell just past his shoulders and were neatly pulled back with a rubber band. He had a broad, nicely built torso and even through his tee shirt, I could tell that his arms were toned and muscular. His khaki shorts stopped just past his knees, revealing two of the biggest, sexiest calves I'd ever seen. He had to be at least six feet, three inches, which explained his massive tennis shoes and enormous hands.

"I'm so sorry," I said, dumping an armload of books into a nearby box. "You're not Darius."

"No," he answered, with a warm smile. "But if you're still looking for some brute strength, I think I can be of some assistance."

His voice was baritone deep, but kind. I noted that he didn't have the customary southern drawl.

"That's so nice of you." I walked over, brushing the dust from my hands and onto my already filthy shorts. "I'm Grace."

"Nice to meet you. I'm Mike. Or Michael. Mike is fine," he stammered, as he reached out to shake my hand.

He's nervous. That's so cute.

"I live three floors above you."

"It's nice to meet you Mike, Michael, Mike," I teased. He made a feeble attempt to laugh. "This is my friend, Trina. She's just here helping me get situated."

"Hey, how's it going?" she asked, with a small wave that resembled the wax-on, wax-off move in the *Karate Kid* movies.

He nodded. "Here," he said, handing me something rectangular, neatly wrapped in aluminum foil. It was warm. "It's banana nut bread."

A gorgeous man who can bake? Wave the red flags, this is too good to be true.

"That is so sweet of you," I said, coyly. "A brute who can bake? I'm impressed."

"Oh, don't be," he responded, with a wave of his hand. "My mother made it."

"Oh."

Ding! Ding! It is too good to be true. He's still breast-feeding. There's nothing more pitiful than a mama's boy. "So you live with your mom?"

"No, actually, she lives down on the second floor. She saw you moving in—said you've both been working hard all day and decided to bake you a little something in case you got hungry."

Okay, so he doesn't live with her, but the fact that they live in the same building on different floors isn't any less alarming.

"Well, when you get the chance, please thank her for me," I said, reverting into formal mode. There was no point in flirting; this guy had obvious Peter Pan issues. I didn't have the time or the energy to play tug of war with any man's mama.

"I will definitely do that," he replied.

"We've been moving in all day. I'm surprised we haven't bumped into her," I said, putting the bread down on the kitchen counter.

"Yeah, she lives in the front of the building. She just happened to see the moving truck parked around the corner when she was out walking her dog. She wanted to introduce herself, but said neither of you were anywhere to be found. You must have been using the service elevator around back."

"The *what?*" Trina shrieked.

"The service elevator," he repeated. We both stood there, speechless.

"Nobody told you about the service elevator?" he asked.

I shook my head, absolutely dumbfounded.

"Then how did you guys get all of this stuff up here?" he asked.

"The stairs," Trina answered, through clenched teeth.

I could feel her glares burning holes into the back of my head.

"Wow," he said, smirking. "I don't know if I should feel sorry for you or be impressed."

"You can feel sorry for her," Trina said. "Because I'm through."

With that, she stomped off towards the bathroom. If it weren't for Mike's presence, she probably would have tried to sock me. Of course, if it weren't for Mike, Trina and I would be none the wiser about the service elevator, and I would still have my moving buddy. He must have been reading my mind.

"Don't sweat it," he said. "We can have whatever's left up here in no time."

"Are you sure you don't mind?" I asked. "I think I can coax her back."

Just then we heard the spray of the shower coming from behind the bathroom door.

"Well, then," I said. "Let's get started."

He wasn't kidding. All of the remaining furniture easily fit into the service elevator. We had everything situated in the apartment in less than an hour.

"I don't know how to thank you," I said, looking up at Mike. *My God, he's so handsome, and he hasn't even broken a sweat.*

"It was nothing," he shrugged.

"Can I get you anything to drink?"

"Water would be good, thanks." I was washing two mugs that I'd wrestled from the bottom of a moving box when someone knocked on the door.

"Could you get that for me?" I asked.

It was Darius.

"Hey, Grace. You didn't work my baby too hard, did you?" he asked.

"No comment," I said.

"Better to plead the fifth than to lie, right?" Trina asked teasingly, as she emerged from my bedroom swallowed in my favorite pair of sweats and a wrinkled tee shirt.

"Hi, sweetie." She threw her arms around his neck and gave him a quick peck on the lips.

"Darius, this is my neighbor, Mike. Mike, this is Darius, Trina's boyfriend."

"How's it going, man?" Darius asked, his arm still wrapped around Trina's waist.

"Not bad," Mike replied. There was a brief, awkward silence. Mike turned to me. "I'm gonna head on up."

"Oh, you don't have to," I said.

"Yeah," Darius agreed. "Trina and I are on our way out."

"No, it's late, and I know you're tired," he said, heading toward the door. "But if you need any help putting things away or hooking stuff up, I can come by tomorrow."

"Thanks," I answered. "But I think I can manage from here."

He nodded and walked out the door.

"You're a quick one, aren't you, Grace?" Darius asked with a wink. "You haven't been here a week and you've already dug your claws into some poor, unsuspecting farm boy."

"Don't even go there," I said, unwilling to listen to anything he had to say about my personal life. "I wouldn't have even needed his help, if 'Little-Miss-I'm-Through' hadn't up and quit on me."

Trina shot me a don't-make-me-hurt-you look and went to my room to get her things. By the time they left and I'd eaten, taken a shower, and cleared things away enough to make a bed on the floor, it was well past midnight. As I lay there trying to unwind, I surveyed my new home. The chill of anticipation traveled up and down my spine. This was the change I needed. I tried to map out a plan for the next day, but all I really had to do was return the U-haul truck I'd rented. The rest of the day was mine to spend as I wished—obligation-free. I felt like a load had been lifted from my shoulders. As my eyes grew heavy with sleep, I was confident I'd made the right decision to leave Detroit, and put my past behind me.

There is a lot to be said for escape. My mother's always tried to keep me from escaping, or running, as she calls it. She's always encouraged me to stare life's dilemmas straight in the face and to muster up the courage to accept whatever consequences may come. I've marveled at her strength and practicality—two qualities I spent the majority of my teenage years trying to mimic. But somewhere along the way, I stepped back and started dissecting her words of wisdom and I found that, while they were true, they weren't universal.

My mother and I have always been, and will continue to be, two completely different people. She's realistic and sensible; I'm a dreamer. She's organized and plans for the future; I'm spontaneous and work best in a crunch. She's resilient—almost everything rolls off her back, and I'm hyper-sensitive. She's happy alone, and I long for companionship. So when my first and, thus far, only love cheated on me, she wasn't able to give me the type of support I needed. The entire incident—both my ex-boyfriend's betrayal and my mother's lack of understanding—devastated me in a way I'd never before experienced.

I was twenty-one then, a senior in college, and life was wonderful. I belonged to a plethora of organizations and clubs that kept me busy and feeling useful, and a few top-notch publishers were interested in *Simon and Eddie*, which was, at the time, nothing more than a concept. I wasn't really looking for a boyfriend—a first for me. I had actually managed to find other, more productive ways to occupy my time. But apparently, Stanley had been looking for someone like me his entire life, or so he said.

I vaguely recognized his face on the breezy autumn afternoon when he first approached me before class. He introduced himself as the guy who sat behind me in Conceptual Physics, but since there were nearly 120 students taking the course—who all sat behind me because I made it a point to sit in the front row—I couldn't distinguish him from any other. After a few seconds of awkward silence, I asked him if he needed notes. After all, it was cold, I was late for class, and he was way too cute to actually be interested.

"No, no," he answered, laughing nervously. "I, um, well, I've just seen you around and thought, you know, you looked interesting."

"Interesting?" I asked, not sure where he was leading and whether or not I should be offended.

Words like *special*, *unique*, and *interesting* bugged me. They're safe words people use to be polite. They're words that a babysitter would use after spending the entire day with a kid who resembled Satan's spawn. "Oh yeah, that Johnny has a unique sense of self-expression," she'd say, after Johnny had scribbled a string of profanities across the wall in permanent ink. When what she really meant was that he was by far the worst child she had *ever* encountered and that she would strongly suggest immediate psychotherapy for his obvious anger issues.

"I'm sorry," Stanley continued. "That wasn't what I wanted to say. I've been noticing you since the beginning of the semester, and I've wanted to approach you, but I didn't know your name, and I still don't. I'm not really sure what made me come after you just now. Anyway—"

"Grace," I offered, trying to end his aimless babbling.

"I'm sorry?" he asked, a little jolted by my abrupt interruption.

"Grace. That's my name. You said you didn't know my name. Now you do."

"Right," he said with a smile, revealing the most beautiful white teeth I'd ever seen. "It's nice to meet you, Grace. I'm Stanley."

I remember the confusion that came over me as we stood in front of Baker Hall and continued to exchange pleasantries. I just couldn't understand what it was about me that struck his fancy. On a campus with tens of thousands of females, most of whom were thinner and more attractive, what was it about me—little, round Grace—that he found appealing? I would remain bewildered by it throughout the entire four years of our relationship.

He was the type of guy that I'd always pined for, but assumed I could never have—attractive, popular, suave, charismatic, and intelligent. There were times when all I wanted to do was stare at him and soak in every curve and feature of his face. He didn't have the classic, chiseled look I'd always been drawn to; he was more doughy and huggable, with rich mocha skin, smooth and inviting. His almond-shaped eyes were huge and glossy—two beautiful dark seas, a perfect balance of mystery and intrigue. He had thick, shiny eyebrows and lashes so long they put mine to shame. When he smiled, his entire face glowed, and revealed the tiniest crow's feet in the corners of his eyes, giving him an air of warmth and wisdom. His straight, pearly teeth were surrounded by two fluffy pillow lips that ached to be kissed. He was clean-cut and well-groomed; his face trimmed low, his goatee neat and spruce, and his clothes always pressed. It would be months before I discovered the painful measures he took to look like a GQ model every day.

His beauty regimen consisted of weekly visits to a barber and manicurist. He bought at least one designer outfit per month, and he sent all his laundry to be dry-cleaned, a habit that produced an exorbitant weekly bill. At first glance, he just seemed to be a well-dressed guy. I never would have guessed that his appearance was almost an obsession. He was a covert pretty boy, who prided himself in looking great, while masking the effort behind it. Still, none of that mattered. In fact, it was endearing, and in no time at all, he'd swept me off my feet and stolen my heart.

Whenever I was with Stanley, I felt something I hadn't known I was missing—camaraderie.

Having spent the majority of my life in affluent neighborhoods, ensconced in the crème de la crème of private schooling, I was frighteningly aware of my race at an early age, and of how it separated me. There just weren't very many black families in my neck of the woods. There was Trina, but she had earned a scholarship to another private school out by my grandparents' house. So until the bell rang at three o'clock, I was forced to fly solo in the race department.

As a child, I would stay up for hours past my bedtime, pleading for God to be merciful and make me white. I wanted the long flowing hair and colorful eyes. Brown skin seemed so uninteresting. Of course, I never woke up looking like Barbie, but I was still lucky enough to make friends, lots of them. And for many years, I tricked myself into believing that race wasn't a factor in my world. When I looked into the mirror, I was just one of the girls, wasn't I? I concentrated on not noticing that when we went out, I was often the only dark brown face in the group. I was happy pretending that everyone was colorblind, the same way a drug addict pretends he's not addicted. But in the end, it was all an elaborate case of denial, a desperate need to sweep reality under a rug so I could keep moving and living—so I could breathe.

My imaginary world came crashing down around me as I grew older and my interests began to turn to the opposite sex. I wanted to flirt and date like the rest of my peers, but there were no takers. The weekends gradually became lonelier as one by one my friends paired off with the typical hormone-driven, zit-infested, pubescent high school boys, while I, for the first time, was forced to acknowledge that being black made me different. I tried to combat the sting of rejection by immersing myself in black culture. I read dozens of books about black icons such as Sojourner Truth, Frederick Douglass, and Rosa Parks. I stopped weaving my hair and started listening to rap and old-school rhythm and blues. Trina disapproved, but tried to write it off as a phase.

"What's wrong with rap?" I asked her, after she turned off my stereo and flipped on the television.

"It's not the rap, it's you."

"What's wrong with me?" I asked. "Is it a crime to embrace my culture?"

"No, Grace, embrace it, but don't let it define you. Look at you," she said, pointing. "Baggy clothes and head wraps? We've known each other our whole lives and this is not you.'"

"People grow and change," I offered.

"By all means, grow, change, but do it naturally. Why are you trying to cram yourself into some sort of mold you've made up in your head? I'm not what people would consider your typical black girl, but I'm not ashamed of who I am."

Everything she said was true, but Trina didn't understand. She was thin and beautiful, and she exuded confidence. She was vice-president of her class, captain of her softball team, and envied by everyone she knew, including me. Guys, both black and white, drooled over her every movement. How could she even begin to understand?

"So, I'm not allowed to explore my heritage?" I asked, trying to avoid her question.

"Whatever. You're so pigheaded. You're not even trying to listen to me."

I was certain we were about to get into an argument when the expression on her face softened.

"Look, I'm glad you have this newfound curiosity. Just don't totally change the Gracie I love."

I saw her point, but it was like we were looking at each other from opposite sides of a great precipice. My sudden interest was much more than curiosity. I wish it were as simple as a quest for knowledge or some sort of innate pull. But it was much more contrived than that, much more desperate. I was panicked because inside I knew I was drowning. And somehow I thought I could stay afloat by embracing the culture I had denied for so long. It was a life jacket of sorts—a last resort I was certain I'd never have to use. I figured just the notion of belonging to something would keep me from drowning in my loneliness.

A sense of belonging can be a powerful thing, and even more potent when you don't have it. No one had coached me on what to do when being black drew a line in the sand and forced me to stand behind it, while my peers explored life's limitless offers. Up until that point, my life had been rose-tinted—a harbor of delight. Now I was scrambling for anything that would make me feel like more than an outline—more than a minority. I tried to get my friends involved by lending them my rap and R&B and teaching them how to braid hair. At the time, I couldn't see that for all my ethnocentrism, I was still seeking their permission to be black. It was like I was saying, "See? Isn't this fun? It's not so bad. I'm not so bad." And while they were polite and tried to feign interest, the fact remained that being black was my burden to carry, not theirs.

Eventually, it all became tiresome, and I remember the exact moment when I stopped trying to explain my skin color, the night I quit searching for validation from others. It was during my freshman year in college. Our Student Arts Council was hosting a poetry reading. They'd managed to reserve Coffee Underground, a popular little restaurant across the street from the student union and hired an up-and-coming local band to attract a broader range of people. When I heard they were soliciting talent to read original short stories and poems, I was ecstatic. It was the perfect opportunity for me to express myself in what I thought would be an open environment. I planned to show off my talent while educating the masses. My suite mates were supportive when I announced that I would be reading, and even promised to attend.

When I entered the room, the lights were dim, and the customary tables and chairs were replaced by an array of mismatched couches with oversized pillows. In the far right corner was a small bar that served free soft drinks and liquor. Sprawled throughout were tables lavished with all sorts of hors d'oeuvres, and in the center of the room was a square, makeshift stage, a stool, and a microphone. The room already was filled close to capacity, and outside the line of people waiting to get in was wrapped around the block. It was a typical college gathering, mostly white faces, practically everyone sporting flip-flops and shorts and looking bored. I'd become accustomed to that scene, though, and I found myself instantly at home, but still jittery with the anticipation of what was to come.

All in all, the audience was warm. They offered gracious applause after each reading, even for the short Asian girl, who'd lost her place twice and finally folded under the pressure and walked off the stage and straight out the door.

"It'll be great. You'll see," I kept telling myself out loud. "You'll be up there for less than sixty seconds. What could possibly go wrong?" And then I heard my name filtered through the speakers.

"Grace? Is Grace Naybor here?" a petite, trendy brunette chirped pleasantly. As I stood before hundreds of blinking eyes, my stomach churned. I introduced myself, gripped the microphone, took a deep breath and recited the poem from memory.

"I want to be white,
With skin so light and pale
Unhampered by the sun.
Smooth and pastel
Innocent and pure
Like freshly fallen snow.
Uninhibited and too beautiful to touch.

I want silky, shiny hair.
The kind that slides
Through your fingers
And lays dramatically against your back.
The kind that flows
From side to side when you
Shake your head.

I want to be emaciated.
A frail shell, with rib bones
That protrude from beneath
My skin to greet the world beyond.
I want pelvic bones that poke
Through my skirts and thighs
That never speak.

I want green, no, blue eyes
The better with which to see this culture

I want them gray or hazel, even purple.
Any color than dark brown.
Any color than what I am.

But if this should happen,
When I went home,
They wouldn't know me.
And they wouldn't braid my hair
In beautiful corn row designs.
My nappy hair that doesn't flow.

There'd be no room in my concave
Stomach and mute thighs for
Food that speaks to my soul like
Comfort collard greens
Black-eyed truth
Cornbread fairytales
Macaroni rituals
Fried chicken lovin'.

And when they looked into my eyes,
My big chocolate, almond, dark brown
Eyes,
There'd be no recognition
Because blue, green, hazel and even purple
Don't come with this history.
And aren't privileged to know its secrets.
Or feel its pride."

I'd delivered it more passionately than I thought I could. It almost seemed like performance poetry, my voice rising and falling methodically with each syllable. Even to my own ears it sounded powerful—convincing. But as the last word fell off my tongue, I was greeted by silence. And when I opened my eyes, I was staring at what was unmistakably a room of irritated people. I was too shocked to be humiliated.

"Thank you," I concluded, with a sheepish smile. Five or six people made a futile attempt to start a round of applause and that was it. The chipper brunette rushed back on stage and quickly reclaimed the microphone.

"Okay, thanks, Grace," she said, blatantly embarrassed for me. "And next up, we have Adam Ulmer. Adam, are you here? There he is! Let's give him a hand."

I took that as my cue to step off the stage. At first, I thought it might be my imagination. Maybe the audience just *looked* upset. But I was pretty sure my poem wasn't well received. I was crushed, desperate to leave. As I grabbed my bag and headed for the door, I overheard two young men standing next to a tray of finger foods.

"I can't stand it when they turn everything into a race issue," said finger-sandwich-guy-number-one, between bites.

"I know what you mean, man. It's like you can't go anywhere without having all that 'my-life-sucks-because-I'm-a-minority' bologna shoved in your face. Like nobody else in the world has problems."

"I know. It's like, get a life already."

I left before I could hear any more, before anyone could see the tears streak down my face. I walked the twelve blocks home, angry, crushed, and defeated. It finally dawned on me that I had to live my life for myself, and just be grateful for any true friends I may meet along the way. And so I stopped forcing myself to read boring books and listen to music that I didn't really like. I even went back to wearing weave and hair extensions. Because in the end, I figured, people will make of me what they will, despite how I may want to be perceived.

For the next three years, I allowed myself to just be one of the girls again and enjoy life. I joined clubs, volunteered, tutored, and organized. My schedule was too packed to notice any inner voids. For the first time I felt like I was truly happy—or at least satisfied.

And as fate would have it, when I finally stopped looking for a boyfriend, Stanley found me.

Part of what I loved about him was that he accepted me for me. He was willing to offer me friendship and love with no strings attached. He didn't label me for being privileged or well-spoken, because he was, too. We'd both grown up in well-to-do families and went to all-white, private schools. We both struggled to identify ourselves, and to fit into our mismatched environments. He felt the shame and sting of rejection from black kids who refused to associate with him because they assumed he had a superiority complex, and he had also experienced the bite of rejection from white kids who wouldn't be bothered with him because they couldn't get past the color of his skin.

Just like me, he'd felt the frustration of the race tug—too white to be black and too black to be white. We were happy together. I was happy. I spent the next four years on a perpetual high. Stanley became the center of my universe. If he wanted it, and I could give it, it was his.

At the time, it never dawned on me that he rarely paid for anything or that if he did, he'd ask to borrow at least twice that amount a few days later. I never realized how he managed to forget all our anniversaries and every major holiday.

"I'm sorry, baby. I'm really bad with dates," he'd say, after it became embarrassingly clear that he'd forgotten Valentine's Day. Or, "Christmas came around so fast, I didn't realize it was that time of year again." He'd lie to me right after I handed him his extravagantly wrapped gift. In hindsight, there were many telltale signs throughout the relationship that he was scandalous and shady—mysterious pages, random disappearances, and hour-long, late-night trips to the convenience store around the corner. I guess I just chose not to see the signs. Even when I did drum up the courage to question him, he always had reasonable, irrefutable explanations for everything. By all accounts, he appeared to be a perfectly behaved boyfriend. Then, finally, it all unraveled.

I wasn't trying to be a 007 that morning when I discovered he'd moved on to greener pastures. I'd popped over to his apartment to see if he wanted to go to breakfast. Never in my wildest dreams did I expect to see him prancing around his small kitchen in his boxer shorts fixing coffee for an incredibly slim, incredibly attractive woman, who was sporting nothing more than his terry cloth robe and slippers. When he saw me, he looked shocked, irritated, and amused all at once. He offered no explanation or apology; he didn't even scurry to his bedroom to put on some clothes. He just sat there watching me watch him and his guest in horror.

"I don't understand," I whispered pathetically, my voice unsteady.

"Was I supposed to meet you this morning?" Stanley asked, completely unmoved by the situation.

"Are you crazy?" I asked, ignoring his question, my voice rising as the initial shock was replaced with unadulterated fury.

"Is *he* crazy?" asked his nameless sleepover guest, who had by now perched her waif of a body on Stanley's old leather recliner. "You're the one bursting into bedrooms uninvited." I glared at her as she crossed her little legs, removed the twisted towel fastened to her head and shook out her damp hair.

"Who are you?" I asked in a tone that was really saying, "Get lost."

"I don't really think that's any of your business," she said nastily.

"Well, that's where you're wrong, because I have a right to know who's messing around with my man."

"Your man?" she asked, hardly able to conceal her amusement. "And how long has Stan been your man?"

The question annoyed me in many ways, but the fact that she'd called him Stan really did me in. For as long as I'd known Stanley, he would never let me call him Stan. He even cringed when his mother used the abbreviation. So what made towel girl so special?

"Four years," I spat, hands on my hips. I knew she couldn't have been expecting that. Most people were surprised at our relationship's longevity. Just as I'd expected, she pursed her lips, looked over at Stanley, and waited for an explanation. Ha! One point for me.

"Come on, Grace, it's been four years *off* and *on*," Stanley said desperately, while making sure to avoid his other girlfriend's angry glower.

"Off and on? Have you lost your mind? Stanley, you're full of it. We separated once for, like, what?" I asked throwing my hands up in exasperation, "a half a day, and that was two years ago." He looked at me blankly as if I was speaking a foreign language. "God, I don't even know who you are."

"You've been with him for four years and you don't know who he is?" asked his little friend.

"Shut up!" I shouted. "You don't exist to me and you certainly don't matter. So, shut up."

"Watch it!" warned Stanley.

"Are you defending her over me?" I asked incredulously. "I can't believe this."

"Look, she has a point, Grace. We've been together for a while, off and on that is, and you didn't even know I was ready to move on."

"And that's my fault?"

"I'm just saying that you're too consumed with *your* life and *your* problems. It's like your universe revolves on a Grace-tilted axis. I need someone who can understand and appreciate me. Beth gives me that." Ah! So, she had a name. Beth. It rhymed with death. How convenient.

"Whatever," I replied, as if I didn't care, when really I had a million questions running through my mind, a million insults and retorts. But none of it mattered, because Stanley wasn't worth fighting for. The situation was bigger than I was emotionally capable of handling. And nothing could have made it better. There was no explanation, no excuse, no justification that could have mended the situation, which meant that questions would have only led to hurtful information. I didn't want to be the proverbial cat that curiosity killed. For self-preservation, I needed to walk away, and so I did. I turned and walked out the door and away from Stanley for good. He didn't chase after me or try to call. I'm sure he went on with his life and never gave me another thought. But he's permanently etched in my brain. He's proof that sometimes, unfortunately, dreams do come true.

Once in my car, I made a beeline for my mom's house. It was instinct, like emotional autopilot. If I had actually stopped to think, I would have u-turned right in the middle of the highway and headed home or to Trina's. But I was too shell-shocked to think rationally. I was like a little kid who'd skinned her knee. My instinct was to run home and let Mommy make it all better. But my mother was never that type of person, not even when I was a child. She didn't dab on peroxide or hand out Band-Aids and kisses. She could barely get off a conference call long enough to throw me a dishtowel and a couple of ice cubes. She had just enough time to nag, but never enough time to coddle. In short, she was and has always been inaccessible. When I walked into the house she was tying up a trash bag in the kitchen. As usual, she looked hurried and unavailable.

"I wasn't expecting you this morning," she said hastily.

"Yeah, you're not the only one," I replied, already feeling a huge sob swell in the back of my throat.

"What does that mean?" she asked, not bothering to look up from the overflowing wastebasket. "Did something happen?"

After years of trying to find the right time to bring up difficult subjects with my mother, I'd found there never was a right time–mainly, because she had very little time to give. The best thing to do was just dive in and tell her before something of more importance claimed her attention.

"I went to pick Stanley up for breakfast and I caught him with someone else."

"Good Lord," she said shaking her head. "How do you find these boys? Really, Grace, you're like a magnet."

"Her name's Beth," I said, my voice quivering and my eyes filling with tears. "He said she understands and appreciates him. He wants to move on."

"Consider it a favor," she replied, finally looking up from the overstuffed trash bag. "Are you crying?" she asked, obviously irritated. "Why? It's not like Stanley was some sort of catch. He's a bum. Honestly! You can't be that desperate for companionship. He's not worth fretting over."

"It was four years of my life, Mom," I said, tears rolling down my face.

"Oh, honey," she sighed, as she walked over and gently grabbed my shoulders. "You've really got to stop with the melodramatics. He was a small portion of your life for four years, not your whole life. This is the type of thing that happens when you try to make some silly boy the center of your universe. You're an adult now, Grace. You've got to learn how to prioritize, or you're going to keep getting burned like this." And with that, she gathered up the trash bag and headed for the back door. "Oh, and Grace, now that you know what some of Stanley's extracurricular activities are, you should make an appointment with Dr. Griffin. Just because you're upset doesn't mean you shouldn't be responsible."

That was it. That was all she had to give, and we never talked about it again. She never asked any questions, and I never offered any information. It was as if it had never happened. I would be lying if I said her response didn't add another layer of devastation to the incident. I would have loved it if she'd hugged me, even handed me a tissue and told me I didn't deserve what he did to me. I would've appreciated it if she had, for once, allowed me to be the victim. But she was too strong, too hurried, too occupied to sympathize with my trauma, and I was too ashamed to let her see me broken.

My mother is an interesting character—a unique mix of brazen business woman and makeshift mommy all rolled into a stout, 5′2″, high-waisted, big-busted package. She's all work and no nonsense—the type of person who could actually use a few more hours in the day. Motherhood was not on her "to do" list when she got pregnant. But after toying around with the idea of aborting me, she decided she could manage to pencil me in for at least the next eighteen years, and that's exactly what she did. For as long as I can remember, I've been this obligatory thing in the back of her mind, or that's how I've felt, anyway. It's like when you wake up the morning after one of the worst days of your life, and you know something is wrong, but you're too dazed to remember exactly what. So, you sit there until you get your bearings and then it hits you that just yesterday, a systematic array of things happened to make your world come crashing down. And just like that, your momentary morning bliss is erased and replaced by disappointment, depression, and regret. I am my mother's daily reality check—the unexpected rain cloud that looms over what had all the makings of a sun-kissed life. I'm not sure what was the most devastating part of her becoming pregnant. Was it the fact that she never loved my father? Or was it the issue of having to rearrange her carefully planned trip up the corporate ladder? I suspect the thing that really irked her was that she'd become another statistic—another single, black female who'd been knocked up and left to fend for herself.

From childhood, my mother had always been the antithesis of her surroundings. She'd stuck out among her siblings and classmates as the one who actually had a chance to get out of the ghetto. She graduated at the top of her class and was vice-president of a prestigious marketing firm by thirty-one. Living in a Chicago high rise, with a closet full of furs and a bar stocked with the finest of wines, her life, for a brief moment, was perfect. She was anything but ordinary. That's when her friends decided that she needed a handsome man to complete the equation. What they forgot was that good looks minus intelligence and compassion equals disaster or, in this case, my father.

They met on a blind date. My father was attracted to my mother's money and my mother was attracted to my father's flashy smile and sense of style. It was as superficial as a relationship could get. At that time, they were both shallow, self-serving people who were playing host to each other's parasitic appetites. The relationship was mutual—my mother used my father as a big, bright bow to sit atop her perfectly packaged life and my father used my mother for every quarter, nickel, and dime he could sneak. When they made love for the first time, it wasn't really love. It was just the next step in the natural progression of a relationship. My mother freely admits that she only had sex because she thought it was time.

"All my friends were doing it and I figured it was bound to happen sooner or later," she told me casually a few years back.

"So, you weren't in love? You only had sex because that was the day you decided you were going to lose your virginity?"

"Something like that. As foreign as the idea may seem to you, Grace, everything isn't always romanticized. I didn't have time to create some dreamy scenario. I had priorities."

Leave it to my mother to pencil in losing her virginity. But that's just the way my mother is. Looking at the rest of her family, I can't really blame her for the way she's turned out.

The nagging she got from my Grandma Doria, who just needs to be unhappy about something. She's a short, sixty-five-year-old woman with a bad attitude, who gets fatter by the month. Her philosophy is that nobody can do anything right but her, but she acts like she's too helpless to do anything for herself. She carries a bell around the house, so that she can beckon the nearest person to do her bidding. I didn't realize how bad she'd gotten until I stayed at her house over the holiday.

Grandma's cleaning lady, Mary, an older black woman who straightens up the house once a week, came over at eight in the morning. At noon, Mary was just starting the upstairs bedrooms. My grandmother would let her clean an area, and then would go behind her with yellow post-it notes and mark anything that wasn't to her satisfaction. This process of clean and inspect would go on three or four times, until the room was up to my grandma's standards.

I could tell Mary was both tired and irritated, so I offered to help her with the upstairs vacuuming. My grandmother was livid.

"I pay good money for her to clean up around here. I don't need you causin' no confusion," she hissed, yanking the cord to the vacuum cleaner out of the wall. She grabbed my elbow and dragged me downstairs.

"I was just trying to help," I informed her, removing my throbbing elbow from her firm grip.

"She's been cleaning this house for three years now and ain't never needed help. Sometimes, you just gotta let things be, Grace. Even if you don't understand them. It's not your place to go fixin' every little thing you see. I pay Mary good money, and I want it done right. However long it takes her to do it is up to her. I got all day."

"What is the big deal?" I asked. "Mary was grateful for the help."

My grandmother looked at me sternly.

"You just remember that this is my house," she said, wagging her finger in my face. "What I say goes. End of story."

As with most of the times I encountered my grandmother's wrath, I had dozens of quips lined up on the tip of my tongue, but all I did was shrug my shoulders and head for my room. It's not that I was afraid of her, but I'd witnessed her hypersensitivity firsthand. I'm not sure if she's really sensitive or just a master manipulator, but whenever someone out-snaps her or makes a concrete point that she can't refute, her feelings get hurt and she starts crying. It's both amusing and pathetic. Like the time we all started teasing her about how cheap she is. We didn't mean any harm, we just thought it was funny that she insisted on washing out her freezer bags when she had six or seven unopened boxes in the basement pantry.

As a matter of fact, she'd built another kitchen downstairs—cabinets, refrigerator, and all. My grandmother could feed her entire block for months if it came down to it. The cupboards, both upstairs and down, were stocked with every type of canned and dried food available. I wouldn't be surprised if some of it was inedible by now.

God knows she used to freak out when I would come over with Trina after school and try to grab a snack. I was lucky to sneak two slices of bread and a cup of tap water before she started complaining about having to feed me and half the block. If I had my druthers, we would have gone to Trina's house, but her aunt was still at work when school got out and she didn't trust us to be home alone. My mother didn't trust us to be by ourselves either, so we were forced to spend the afternoons at my grandma's. It was a conspiracy to keep us miserable and hungry.

Anyway, after just a few minutes of teasing, she burst into tears and went into a fifteen minute monologue about having to live through the Depression and how a trauma like that is insurmountable.

"If any of y'all had to go through what me and mine done suffered through, you wouldn't harass me so. You'd respect me 'stead of mockin' me," she whimpered, with tears running down her cheeks. "Is it such a crime to wanna make sure your family will always have what you didn't?"

It was a rhetorical question; she didn't even breathe before starting up again.

"It'd be a diff'rent story if I made y'all fend for yourselves. But naw, I never turn none of you away when ya tromp in here unannounced and sit down at my table, eyes wide, tongues hangin' out, singin' 'bout mama what you got to eat. Y'all grown and still my door is always wide open and my table is always set for ya. Ain't none of y'all offer a dime to help pay for all you eat and got the nerve to bring yo kids, too? But do I complain? No, because I love you. All of you, and I want your bellies to be full, like mine never was."

Looking at her stout, nearly two-hundred-pound frame, you couldn't tell that her stomach had gone without. She didn't look like she'd missed a meal in her whole sixty-plus years of living, but of course I couldn't say that. I just nodded with the rest of the family and apologized. How it is that someone can be so ruthless, but crumble at the slightest bit of teasing, I'll never know. That's just Grandma Doria.

My grandpa Mearl is a character himself. When I was smaller, I thought the sun rose and set on him. But as I got older, we grew apart. I still can't figure out if he turned into a jerk over the years, or if he was always mean and nasty, and I was just too young to realize it. Whatever the case, we can't relate to one another. Recently, I've noticed how he's taken to blatant criticism.

I stopped by the house with my cousin one day last summer to pick up a package for my aunt. He was sitting on the couch in the living room reading the paper. We said hi, and as we headed downstairs to the basement, he said, "You know something, Grace?"

I turned around, waiting to hear the rest of his thought. He looked me up and down and nodded slowly. I didn't know if he'd stumbled over some sort of epiphany, or maybe discovered the secret of life. From the look on his face, it seemed he was about to dispense some priceless jewels of wisdom.

"What?" I asked.

"You're gettin' fat," he said.

He didn't mean to be harsh or spiteful, just honest. I wanted to slap him. More than anything I was irritated, but not because it wasn't true. I knew I was heavy, but did he honestly think I hadn't noticed the twenty pounds I'd put on after the Stanley mishap? What good was telling me supposed to do? By the time I came up with a response, he'd already gone back to reading the sports page. I looked at my cousin, who just shook her head.

I'm pretty sure my grandfather has an entire list of things he can't stand about me. But as a man who struggled to get everything he owned, I think he mostly resented how easily things came to me. Namely, how my mother lavished me with nice gifts. I'll be the first one to admit I've been spoiled, but I'm an only child—it comes with the territory. I didn't see how it was really anyone else's business what she gave me. But, when she bought me a brand new SUV the summer of my eighteenth birthday, he had a fit.

"Well, don't you have the life?" he spat, when I walked into the kitchen.

"Excuse me?" I asked, unsure why he had an attitude.

"All you do is eat, sleep, and go to school. You don't have a job. Haven't made yourself useful all summer. But you still got that truck outside. Just for doing nothing. Now that must be livin'."

I couldn't tell if he was joking and wasn't sure how to respond.

"Grandpa, I do have a job," I said tentatively. "I've been working at the bookstore for almost two years."

"That ain't a job. Not a job that can pay for that fancy truck you got out there." The car was a graduation gift, and he knew that. What was his problem? I figured he was just in a bad mood and decided to keep it light.

"Yeah, that's true," I said. "I guess it was just Mom's way of showing me how proud she is."

"Proud of what?" he asked sourly.

"I don't know. Maybe the fact that I don't drink or do drugs, I've been on the honor roll since the second grade, and I don't have any kids running around?"

He was starting to get on my nerves.

"All you did was graduate from high school. It ain't like you created a cure for cancer. You need more than a high school degree to make somethin' of yourself these days," he lectured. "You need to go to trade school and learn you some sort of skill."

"I don't want to go to trade school, Grandpa. I want to go to college and then write books."

He just rolled his eyes.

"Write books, huh? That ain't a job, either, if you ask me. Sittin' around makin' up stories ain't gonna pay your bills."

Well I didn't ask you! And who cares what you think anyway? You probably can't even read! That's what I wanted to say. But all I did was nod and say, "Well, to each his own, right? Anyway, mom supports me and thinks I can do anything I put my mind to."

"Yeah, okay," he said, bored. "Or maybe she's just raising you to be worthless." That stung. Yes, it was unfair, but mostly it made me feel like nothing.

When I recounted the conversation to my mother, she just shrugged her shoulders. "He's old, what can you do?" she asked, unconcerned.

"Nothing, I guess. It just really hurt, that's all."

"Well, maybe it was a good thing for you to hear. Gives you some incentive to prove him wrong."

"Are you serious?" I asked, irritated at her apathetic response and implication that he may have a point.

"Oh, come on, don't turn into a dramatic teenager on me now. Really, Grace, what difference does it make? You know how he is. If it bothers you that much, then stop putting yourself in a position to get burned."

Of course, it was my fault. My mother would never let me be the victim. "Other people aren't my responsibility, honey, you are," she'd explained to me when I was sixteen, after I accused her of never taking up for me. "I can't correct other people, but I can always make sure that you've done the right thing."

"It doesn't matter," I said, unwilling to let my crabby grandfather bring me down.

"Exactly," she said, already turning back to her computer. "There are always going to be situations you can't control and people you can't change. So forget about it." She tapped away on her keyboard. She was right. He was just a grumpy old man and there was no point in letting him get the best of me.

Five years later, after *Simon and Eddie* was picked up by Taylor and Dotson and contracted to become a series, he didn't even bother to show up at my release party.

"Where's Grandpa?" I asked my mother, who had retreated to a quiet corner to check her voicemail.

"I don't know, honey," she said, holding up her hand to motion that she wanted me to stop talking so she could hear her messages.

Unbelievable, I thought. *Why did you bother to come? We both know work is way more important.*

I managed to find my grandma sitting at a table talking to someone I'd never seen before.

"Hey, Grandma. Is Grandpa here?" I asked.

"No," she said "He was tired, but he told me to give you this." She handed me a yellow envelope that had my name scrawled across it in red ink.

"Thanks," I said, taking the card. I wanted him to be there, to officially prove him wrong. I hadn't forgotten what he'd said to me that day in the kitchen. I wanted him to acknowledge that I wasn't useless, that I wasn't the failure he expected me to become. His opinion shouldn't really matter, but he was the only male role model I'd ever had, and somehow I'd convinced myself that I needed him to be proud of me. Maybe he's embarrassed, I thought. *Maybe his pride won't let him apologize in person.*

My fingers trembled slightly as I tore open the envelope. On the cover of the card there was a pudgy black baby in a diaper, sucking on a bottle of milk. On the inside he'd written: *Congratulations. Twenty-three and still being fed by a silver spoon. What're you gonna do when all your words have been said and there are no more stories to tell?*

Chapter Two

I've been in Memphis for four months now, and life is good. I decided that my new life in my new pad deserved a new me. So I mapped out a self-improvement plan by listing my most important goals. Okay, so I could only think of two, but they were big ones, and they'd require all my attention and massive amounts of effort.

First, I wanted to lose weight—a lot of it. If I added my "freshman thirty," plus the extra twenty I put on after Stanley, and the ten I gained just from the stress of moving, I needed to shed a good sixty pounds.

Second, I wanted to establish a career. Writing children's books was gratifying in its own way, but I wanted to write something that appealed to a more mature audience. I wanted adults to be able to relate to my writing. I was actually thinking of trying my hand as a journalist. None of that hiding behind bushes for hours trying to snag an interview, either. I wanted a syndicated column—my own personal slice of the pie that would set me apart from the average columnist. I had majored in English, so I was sure that if the right people saw my stuff, I had a good shot at snagging a column in somebody's magazine.

I didn't feel pressed to get a job, though. I was still receiving pretty decent checks every three months from Taylor and Dotson, and I always had part of my trust fund to fall back on. My transformation, I decided, was going to happen leisurely. I was running on my own timetable now.

I wasn't sure how to get started on the whole weight loss issue. I've been chubby my whole life, but my weight hadn't become an actual problem until college. It's not that being heavy didn't give me an inferiority complex as a teenager. The extra weight made me feel like school was more of a cruel house of mirrors than a learning institution. Each reflection revealed unfixable imperfections and permanent scarlet letters that managed to encompass me, branding me as hopelessly flawed. Of course, it was mostly in my mind because nobody ever teased me outright. In truth, I had plenty of friends. Besides Trina, I belonged to a clique of fellow misfits—at least until they started dating—and we comforted each other with assurances of being better off in our own world of binge eating and video watching. But secretly, or maybe not so secretly, we all daydreamed about what it would be like to live on the other side, where we were carefree, beautiful, and desirable.

I remember when Cynthia, one of my close friends, went to fat camp, unbeknown to the rest of our group, the summer before our junior year. The following fall, she returned as Cindy. The lumpy, plus-sized-wearing wallflower, whom I'd grown to love and admire over the past several years, had turned into a sleek, long-legged knockout. She'd arrived at a place we fat chicks had only dreamed of. All of a sudden, she was sporting the latest Puma gear and perfectly highlighted bob. Where she once had a plump, flushed, jolly face, she now had sharp, high, stately cheekbones. She looked harder, confident, almost arrogant, basking in her newfound world of boyfriends, stretch halter tops and celery stick lunches. Never once did she remember from whence she'd come. She was intoxicated by her instant status. And while I never begrudged her the happiness and acceptance, I spent the remainder of my high school career envying her and that chance meeting with lady luck that had granted her the euphoria I hadn't yet experienced.

In college, I completely abandoned all self-control and refused to go near a scale for almost two years. I could see the pounds creeping on, but I was so busy living it up that I didn't have time to address it. I think I've hidden the extra weight fairly well up until now, though I was slightly depressed when I couldn't fasten my size fourteen Gap pants. If I didn't get it under control soon, I'd have to start shopping at plus-size stores. So, I bought a couple of cases of Slim Quick and resolved to get up every morning and walk for an hour, or until my legs couldn't take it any longer, whichever came first.

I'm not going to lie and say that I decided to lose weight to be healthier. I wanted to turn heads. For once, I wanted to be the woman who makes men look twice, and who drives other women crazy with envy. Selfish motive? Yes, but a wonderful incentive.

I was up every morning by 8:00 and out the door by 8:30. At first, I stuck to the park nearby, which offered two different paths. The first, a straight sidewalk, void of any litter and lined with every type of flower and shrubbery you could imagine. It paralleled a busy street and provided a spectacular view of the Mississippi River. The second, a windy, impromptu path in the grass created, I assumed, by various joggers and bikers who wanted to enjoy their jaunts outside, away from the spastic clatter and smog of the city's buses and cars.

Each route was roughly three miles long and offered drastically different views of the area that were easy to appreciate. But after the first few weeks, both paths, in all their scenic glory, became monotonous. So I ventured out of the park and into the neighboring streets. Unlike larger metropolises, downtown Memphis was manageable and welcoming. The streets weren't congested with blazer-wearing, cell-phone chatting businessmen who didn't know how to say excuse me. The motorists followed the speed limit, taking care not to terrorize pedestrians, and the construction sites were minimal.

I walked without a destination, looking through shop windows, and taking in the uniquely blended smell of fresh bread and orange spice that wafted outside from a quaint little tea store on the corner of Third and Main. It wasn't just exercise. It was a time of escape—no soul searching, no deep, sentimental introspection, just a clear mind, my old Keds, and a sense of adventure.

One morning, while I was out on one of my walks, I came across the local YMCA. I hadn't really given much thought to joining a gym. Trina had suggested it once when I started complaining about the heat, but I was so pleased with my results that I didn't see the point. I'd lost eight pounds in just under a month, and could fasten my jeans without lying across the bed and sucking in my stomach.

"I'm not saying you aren't doing a great job," Trina assured me. "I'm just saying that eventually, you're gonna want to start toning, so that you don't look flabby. And most gyms are air-conditioned, so you wouldn't have to sweat to death."

It wasn't so much that I didn't want to tone as that I didn't want to work out in front of dozens of fit people. But spring was quickly turning into summer, and I didn't know how much longer I'd be able to stand up against the Memphis heat. *No big deal*, I thought to myself. *If you decide to join, you'll just come early in the morning and wear baggy sweats.*

When I walked into the Y, I was met by a blast of cool air. A few feet away from the door, a young man was seated behind an information desk. He was smiling and motioning for me to come over.

"I saw you standing outside: I was wondering if you were gonna come in or if I was gonna have to go out there and get you," he said pleasantly. He had a mature warmth about him, though he couldn't have been older than twenty. His red hair was tossed all over his head and his clothes were wrinkled. If he didn't smell like heaven, I would have assumed he had just rolled out of bed and come to work. He had freckles all over his face and crisp green eyes.

"I'm Jason," he said, extending his hand.

"Nice to meet you," I said. "I'm Grace."

"Well, Grace, do you think you'd be interested in joining the Y?"

"I'm giving it some serious thought," I answered.

"Well, what are your long-term fitness goals?" His tone was so professional that it didn't match his appearance. It took everything I had not to laugh.

"I'd like to lose about fifty pounds. Originally, I was shooting for sixty, but since I've started walking, I've already lost eight."

"Well, congratulations," he said. "Do you think your success has been mostly due to diet or exercise?"

"I'm not sure. I try to eat less and drink a Slim Quick every morning, but I think maybe the exercise is what's doing the trick."

"I'm not sure if you know this, but many weight-loss drinks are not as healthy as you think. Take Slim Quick for instance. It's very high in sodium and carbohydrates."

"I thought carbohydrates gave you energy?" I countered. Of course, I would find out Slim Quick wasn't all it was cracked up to be *after* I'd stocked my cabinets with at least a month's supply.

"Well, yes, some carbohydrates are good for you. Do you know the difference between complex carbohydrates and simple carbohydrates?"

Look at me, I'm fifty pounds overweight—do I look like I know anything about health? I wanted to ask, but he was too nice to scare off like that, so I just shook my head and tried to look interested.

"That's okay, no problem, that's why we're here. You see, Grace, complex carbohydrates are good for you; they give your body fuel to create energy. But simple carbohydrates just turn into sugar. They're empty calories. You want to avoid those simple carbs if you can. You see where I'm coming from?"

I nodded.

"Tell me," he said, motioning for me to sit down in the chair across from him. "Have you ever considered a personal trainer?"

"No, not really."

"We offer several different packages that include monthly fitness assessments, daily one-hour training sessions with a personal trainer, and weekly weigh-ins. Now, I know the prices may seem a little steep," he said, handing me a sheet of paper that listed each trainer's hourly rate, "but I guarantee you'll be happy with the results. We'll have you slender in no time."

He was so sweet, and I didn't want to interrupt his pitch, but honestly, all I heard was "blah, blah, blah … we'll have you slender in no time." Still, as he kept on talking, I envisioned myself with a small waist and no double chin.

I was sold.

"Great, sign me up." After nearly thirty minutes of filling out forms about my weight history and family health, I was finally assigned a personal trainer. His name was Don Stiner, and I was officially his eight o'clock client.

"You know what?" asked Jason, shuffling through all of the paperwork. "Don should be here now; let me take you upstairs and introduce you. That way you'll know who to look for tomorrow, and you can check out the facility."

I followed him around the corner to the elevators.

"Our cardio and weight training are both located on the second floor; there's an indoor track and practically any kind of workout equipment you could imagine," he explained, as we stepped off of the elevator and onto the second floor. I noticed there were mostly older white men there, but I did see a woman nearly twice my size huffing away on a stationary bike in the corner. She was dressed in a purple sweat suit, and she looked like she was about to die.

If she can do it, I know I can, I thought to myself.

"Don! Don!" Jason called out across the room. For a second, I didn't know who I was looking for, and then I saw him—the most beautiful specimen of a black man I'd ever seen. I swear, I heard the Hallelujah Chorus in my head as he approached us, smiling. He was tall, maybe 6′2″, with a shiny bald head, and a perfectly trimmed goatee. He had beautiful eyes and a decent smile, but the thing that did me in was his body. He had muscles on top of muscles, especially in his arms and shoulders. His thighs were also nice and tight. I could tell he had muscular legs just by the way they were bulging from beneath his sweats.

He was so dark and scrumptious that I could have taken a bite out of him right there, but instead I just smiled back.

"This is your new eight o'clock," Jason informed him.

"Great," he said enthusiastically. "Too bad I have a client in about ten minutes, or I'd take you now."

"Well, tomorrow's another day," I said.

Over the next few weeks, I got to know Don a little better. I found out, to my great disappointment, that he was married and that ten months earlier his wife had given birth to his first child, Chloe. I could tell he was a loving father by the way he talked about his daughter. He couldn't mention her name without smiling. He flipped out when I told him I was the author of *Simon and Eddie*.

"You're serious?" he asked.

"As a heart attack."

Even though he was married and off limits, his obvious dedication to fatherhood made him even more attractive to me. There's nothing more endearing than a loving father. I envied his daughter in a small way. I wished my father had been as passionate about me.

I was surprised at how freely he opened up. After a short time, it felt like we were old friends.

"Marriage isn't easy," he confessed. We were running side by side on the treadmills. "As much as I love Chloe, if I had it to do over again, I don't think I would marry my wife."

I was so winded, all I could do was nod.

"When I married Laura, I thought we were going to support each other, you know? I thought we would help each other fulfill our dreams. But now," he said, shaking his head, "all she does is tell me to get my head out of the clouds. When I told her I wanted to apply for the Shelby County Fire Department, do you know what she told me?"

"What?" I wheezed.

"She said that I needed to find a job more on my level. Can you believe that? What's that supposed to mean? I'm thirty-two and in the best shape of my life. I think I would make a great firefighter."

"Of course," I sputtered. I only had forty-five seconds left, and then I'd be able to concentrate on what he was saying. I understood exactly where he was coming from, but I could still sympathize with his wife's perspective. A couple of years ago, my uncle applied to be a firefighter in Detroit. He had to go through an extensive series of mental and physical tests, only to be laid off eight months later. So I understood why Laura wanted Don to shoot for a more dependable line of work. But I also remembered the depression that swept over me every time my grandfather said I'd never support myself with a writing career. If I had listened to him, I wouldn't have mustered the courage to submit my manuscript for *Simon and Eddie*. I would still be wondering if I had what it took to be a writer.

As the treadmill slowed to a halt, I dabbed my sweaty forehead with a towel, and turned to Don, who was looking down at my chart.

"Listen," I said. "You only live once. If it means that much to you, Laura should find it in her heart to support you. I know you're married and you have an obligation to your family, but you also have a responsibility to make the most of your life. We all have to be a little selfish at times; otherwise, when it's all said and done, our lives won't be anything more than a series of regrets."

I felt a little guilty telling him to go against his wife's wishes. The last thing I wanted to do was start trouble in someone else's relationship. But judging from the look on his face, I'd told him exactly what he'd been waiting to hear.

He wrapped his burly arms around me and gave me a tight squeeze. "You really are something else, you know that? You always know just the right thing to say." I'm not sure if I was imagining things, but I could have sworn his lips brushed my neck as he released me. "Maybe we can chill some time—as friends," he said.

"What do you mean?" I asked, a little nervous. "We hang out every morning, five days a week."

"No, you know what I mean. Outside of the gym. Maybe we could catch a movie or something."

It's not that I didn't want to spend extra time with Don. He was attractive, smart, and funny, but he had a wife. And as much as I wanted to believe there was no chance of anything happening between us, I didn't trust myself not to pounce at the chance to be with him if the opportunity presented itself.

Going out with a married man wouldn't just make you a skank, I told myself. *It would also make you a home-wrecker*. I looked into his expectant eyes. His big, beautiful, brown, hopeful eyes. *Say no! Say no! No!*

"Sure," I said. "I'd like that. I could always use another friend."

I woke up to sunlight streaming through my bedroom window. I looked at the clock; it was a quarter past nine. *Ohmigod, I'm late*, I thought. I almost started to panic, and then I realized it was Saturday. I had plans to see the new Kevin Spacey movie with Don tomorrow afternoon. I wondered if Laura knew he was going to be out with me. All the way home from the gym yesterday, I wanted to kick myself for saying yes.

But as the day wore on, I realized I wasn't forcing Don to do anything. *He* invited *me* out, not the other way around. I wasn't out to steal any woman's man, but if Laura insisted on pushing him away by stomping all over his pride, I certainly wasn't going to let him go to waste. I decided to just go with the flow and if it ended up that something more than friendship evolved, so be it.

I was rummaging through my closet trying to find a decent outfit for tomorrow's outing, when the phone rang. I looked at the clock—10:30. It had to be my mom; nobody else would have the gall to call me before noon on a Saturday.

"Hello?"

"Grace?" someone whimpered on the other end.

"Trina?"

"Yes," she sniffled.

"What's the matter?" I asked, alarmed. Trina, as small as she is in stature, is tough as nails. She's the type of person who makes other people cry. So when something manages to get under her skin, it's usually pretty big.

"Da- Da- Dari-us thinks mo-oo-oving in t-to-get-ther was a mis-ss-take," she sputtered between sobs.

Oh, here we go! As much as I loved Trina, this whole break up to make up thing they were doing was getting tiresome. Twice last week I had to go get her in the wee hours of the morning because she and Darius got into an argument and he wanted her to leave.

Before we even came to Memphis, I had my doubts about Trina moving in with him. Darius has always been the type of person to shove favors back in your face. I tried to get Trina to secure a job for herself in Memphis before she left Detroit. That way, in case anything happened, which it almost always does with the two of them, she'd be able to support herself.

"Oh, Grace, don't be silly," she'd said. "Darius makes more than enough for us to live on."

"I know that," I told her. "But it's not like you're his wife. He's not obligated to share it with you."

"Why are you being so pessimistic?"

There was no talking to her when it came to Darius. There wasn't any subject that made her jump to her defenses quicker.

"Please don't misunderstand me," I'd said soothingly. "It's not that I don't trust that Darius will take care of you." Okay, so I lied. "It's just that I think you should be able to take care of yourself in case anything happens. Secure your independence."

"Look, I know you mean well, but everyone isn't like you, Grace. Some of us don't want to make it on our own."

I don't know when her housewife gene kicked in, because when we were in college, all she wanted to do was be a successful child psychologist.

"Once I establish my career, then I'll marry Darius. I have to build my life around what's best for me, and that is a good paying job, not a man," she'd once told me. Now, fast forward five years later, she hasn't even tried to put her degree to use, and she's bawling on the phone over some loser who gets off by tugging on her heartstrings.

I sat down on my bed. "Did you guys get into another fight?" She couldn't even answer me, she was sobbing so hard.

"Trina?"

Sniffles.

"Where's Darius now?"

"G-gone."

"Okay. I want you to get dressed and pack an overnight bag. I'm coming to get you."

Sniffles.

"Did you hear me?" I asked.

"Y-y-yes."

"Be ready," I said sweetly. "I'm gonna throw on some clothes, and I'll be right there."

When I pulled up to the house, about twenty minutes later, I was shocked by what I saw. The front door was ajar, Trina's clothes were scattered all over the lawn, and one of the front windows had been shattered. My first instinct told me to call the police, but before I could find my cell phone, she walked out of the house with a small overnight bag and her purse. She looked tired and frail. I could tell by the scratches on her face that this time the fight wasn't just verbal.

In the nine years that they'd been messing with each other, I could only recall one time when Darius hit Trina. We were at a bar with mutual friends. It was the weekend before finals and instead of pulling all-nighters, we decided to let loose and have some drinks. Everyone was a little tipsy, but Darius was plastered. We all tried to ignore it, but the more he drank the louder and more vulgar he became. Eventually, it got to the point where people at surrounding tables were asking to be seated somewhere else. Trina, sensing everyone's embarrassment, quietly suggested to Darius that he'd had enough.

"What did chu shay to me?" he asked, practically shouting.

"Maybe you shouldn't have any more," she whispered into his ear.

"Iy'll deschid when Iy've had enuff," he said, leering at her.

"Okay, honey," she said, glancing at the rest of the table. "Well, then just give me the car keys."

"Fer what?" He could barely hold his head up.

"So I can be sure you get home safely."

For a second he just sat there and looked at her. I could tell he was steaming. Then, abruptly, he stood up and grabbed her by the elbow. He yanked her so hard his chair fell backwards and hit the floor with a loud thud.

"Get up!" he demanded.

"Whoa man, take it easy." Fred, a lanky white guy in my Biology class, stood up in Trina's defense. "She was just trying to help."

"Mind chure own bissness," Darius spat. Just then the bartender walked over to our table. He was a short, middle-aged man with his hair pulled back in a ponytail. Following close behind him was a huge black guy; I could only assume he was the bouncer. Neither one of them was smiling.

"Sir, you are disturbing the rest of the patrons here, and I'm going to have to ask you to leave." The bartender was polite, but firm. Darius stood there, swaying. He looked around at the whole bar, which at that point had fallen quiet. All eyes were on him. He nodded, took a step back and then hauled off and back-handed Trina right across her face. The blow hit her with such force that she flew backwards out of her seat and landed on the floor, flat on her back. Before I knew it, the bouncer had Darius pinned to the floor and someone had shouted, "Call the police!" I ran over to Trina, who was staring up at the ceiling, completely dazed. Her lip was bleeding and her left cheek was beginning to swell.

"Trina? Trina, look at me." Her eyes moved slowly from the ceiling to my face. And as our eyes met, a tear rolled down her cheek.

And now, evidently, history was repeating itself. Darius wasn't good enough for Trina then, and he isn't good enough for her now. Still, despite her pain, she'd be back in that house before the weekend was out. All he had to do was call her in a few days with some sob story, and she would go running back to him. Just like she bailed him out of jail the morning after the bar incident. He was an albatross around her neck and she couldn't see it. But she was grown; I couldn't make decisions for her no matter how badly I wanted to jump in and fix it. All I could do was love her and wait for her to see, in her own time, that Darius was a dead end.

By the time I'd calmed Trina down and gotten her back to my place, she'd pretty much told me the full story. When Darius had come home from work night before last, his behavior had been strange.

"I had made dinner, set the table, put on some music. I figured we could have a nice, romantic night in. But when he came through the door he blew straight past me and got in the shower. No hello, no kiss—nothing."

"What happened when he got out of the shower?"

"He put on clean dress clothes and said he was going out with some people from work. He didn't even give me a chance to respond before he went into his whole 'don't smother me' speech. I was livid—but only because he hadn't bothered to tell me earlier that he was going out. If he had called me, I wouldn't have spent all afternoon cooking."

I wanted to grab her shoulders and shake some sense into her. Why did she feel like she had to justify her anger toward him?

I just nodded.

"So, that's what I told him. I wasn't trying to nag, but I just thought it was really unfair of him."

"And then?" I asked.

"And then he told me it wasn't his problem if I didn't have a life." Her eyes started to well up with tears, and her voice cracked. "So, I told him it's not that I wanted to keep him from having a life, you know?" She sniffled. "I just wanted us to spend a little more quality time together."

"And what did he say?"

"He said he was too young to have a child my age."

"What does that mean?"

"That's what I asked. He said I was more of an obligation than he was ready to handle. He told me I was like a baby who needed constant attention. That I'm too dependent on him."

It took all of my strength not to mention the conversation we'd had back in Detroit about her dependency. I knew that saying, "I told you so," would not be the sensitive approach.

"That made me even angrier because he's the one who told me not to work," she continued. 'No woman of mine is going to work.' That's what he told me. Does he honestly think I *like* sitting around the house all day with nothing to do but scrub the toilet and wash his dirty underwear? I'm an educated woman with a degree; I have dreams of my own. I only stopped working because I thought that's what he wanted."

Finally, she was really getting angry. How much more of this was she going to take?

"So what did you do?"

"Nothing. Before we had a chance to finish the conversation, the doorbell rang. It was some dumpy, bottle-blonde broad, wearing a tight pair of capris and a tiny belly shirt. I'm telling you, Grace, it looked like someone had to stuff her into those clothes."

"Well, what did she want?"

"She was the 'people from work' he was going out with."

My face was getting hot. Dragging her down here, away from her aunt and job, only to cheat on her within the first few months was one thing. But having the audacity to invite the other woman over to their house to flaunt her in front of Trina was a new low.

"He told me not to wait up and then he left."

"Why didn't you call me?" I asked. "We could have gone out, or talked."

She shook her head, "We're not little kids anymore. I made a choice to be with Darius, which means I have to suffer through the rough spots."

I appreciated the fact that she wanted to deal with Darius on her own, but as I looked at the bruises on her face, I couldn't help but wonder if I could have somehow prevented her from getting beaten. If she had just called me, I could have gotten her away from him.

"Rough spots? Trina, look at you, this is more than a rough spot. It's abuse. I understand relationships are hard work, but how much do you think you're obligated to go through before it's okay to walk away?"

"Please don't chastise me."

Her whole body was shaking. What was I thinking? She needed someone to listen, not to criticize.

"You're right," I said, wrapping my arms around her. "I'm sorry. Just try to calm down." She laid her head on my shoulder, and I rocked her gently. She was so fragile. The guy had traumatized her.

"Do you want to tell me the rest of the story?" I asked. I wasn't trying to force her to relive what had happened, but I would be lying if I said I wasn't curious about the scratches on her face, all of the clothes in the yard, and the broken window.

She took a deep breath and continued. "By three the next morning, he still hadn't come home. I wasn't sure what to do, so I paged him. I heard a beep coming from the laundry basket, and I realized that when he'd changed his clothes, he'd forgotten his pager. So, I felt around the hamper until I found it. He had four new pages besides mine, and they were all from the same number. I don't know what came over me, but I needed to know who he was messing with, you know? I wanted a name, some sort of explanation."

"That's perfectly understandable," I assured her. "Any woman in your place would have felt the same way."

She grabbed another tissue and blew her nose. "So, I dialed the number. Can you believe it? I dialed some woman's house at three in the morning. I had no idea what I was going to say. After four rings I got an answering machine. It was some cheery lady's voice telling me I'd reached the Calhoun residence and asking me to leave a message. So, I introduced myself and told her, whoever she was, that I didn't appreciate her messing around with my man. I asked her how she could sleep at night knowing she was breaking up someone's happy home."

I caught myself smiling just at the thought of her ranting on some strange woman's answering machine. "Good for you," I said.

She managed to muster a tiny smile. "About five minutes later the phone rang. It was Joseph Calhoun. He got my message and wanted to talk to me about Darius and his wife, Janet."

"Oh, my God," I gasped, cutting her off. "She's married?"

"It gets worse. She's Darius's boss. She runs his whole department."

"But that doesn't make sense," I thought aloud. "Why would she page him from her home number if her husband was there?"

"Mr. Calhoun said he'd come home early from a business trip because his last meeting was canceled. He wasn't due back in town for another two days."

Well, that clears that up, I thought.

"So, was he upset?"

"I'm not sure. He probably was, but over the phone, more than anything, he just seemed tired." I felt sorry for the guy. He was a victim, just like Trina. "They've been married for eight years and have two kids," she added.

"He told you all of that?" I asked.

"Oh, yeah, we talked for almost two hours. I found out all sorts of things about her."

"Like what?"

"Like this isn't the only affair she's had. He wanted to leave the first time, but she begged him to stay, so they agreed to marriage counseling."

Figures, I thought.

"Well, what happened when Darius came home?" I asked, jumping ahead.

"That's just it, he didn't come home. He called me Friday afternoon from work and apologized profusely. He swore nothing happened. Said he had a little bit too much to drink and fell asleep on Janet's couch. But he was obviously lying, because I'd spent two hours talking to her husband, who was waiting for her at home. I'm guessing they went to a hotel or something. I just stayed quiet. Then he asked, 'You believe me, don't you, baby?' And that was all I could take. He thinks I'm so stupid." She was talking loudly now, forcefully. I could see the hurt in her eyes. "He thinks he can tell me anything, and I'll believe it."

I just sat there and listened. But inside I knew that Darius *could* tell Trina anything and make her believe it. That's how their relationship had managed to last this long. Years ago, Trina closed her eyes and decided to love and trust Darius with blind faith. He lied to her and mistreated her because she let him. She'd made him out to be something more than he was. She'd convinced herself he was a good man.

"Well, did you answer him?"

"Yeah, I told him I believed him, but that Joseph Calhoun probably wouldn't."

"Are you serious?" I was surprised by her forwardness. After all of these years, she'd finally found her voice. I knew she had it in her. She managed to speak her mind to everyone else; Darius should never have been an exception. I was so proud of her. "What did he say?"

"Nothing. He hung up in my face. I didn't hear from him for the rest of the day. I was too upset to really care. But at around ten o'clock that night, I started to worry a little. He hadn't come home or tried to call and I couldn't beep him because I still had his pager. So, I called Janet's house. I just wanted to talk to Joseph and see how he'd handled it. Truthfully, I kind of wanted to know if Janet had come home, or if she and Darius were out together."

"Did you reach him?"

"I let the phone ring a good six or seven times, and right when I was about to hang up, a woman answered. I couldn't think of anything to say, so I just held my breath. I knew it was Janet. She asked, 'Who is this?' But I was too nervous to speak. Then she said, 'It doesn't matter; I know who you are. Let me ask you a question. How do *you* sleep at night knowing you broke up *my* happy home? You better hope we never cross paths, you meddling little twit, because if I ever get my hands on you, not even God will be able to save you.' Then she hung up."

"She actually had the nerve to be mad at you?"

"Yeah, but I really wasn't worried about her. At that point, I knew the cat was out of the bag, and that Darius was probably on a rampage."

"You should have called me, Trina. If you knew he was going to be out of control, you should have let me come and get you." She looked up at me and nodded. During the course of telling the story, she had stopped crying and sprawled out across my bed.

"I didn't shut my eyes once the whole night. I just sat at the dining room table and waited for him to come home."

"And did he?"

"Around seven this morning he kicked the door in. He was wearing the same thing he had on when he left two days before. His tie was draped around his neck, and he reeked of liquor. 'What're you trying to do to me?' he asked. I told him I wasn't trying to ruin his life, but that I needed to know the truth. He walked over to me, got right in my face and said, 'You want to know the truth? The truth is that I don't love you. I don't even like you. I only asked you to come with me so I could get some free cleaning and a few hot meals out of you. If I'd known you were gonna be this much trouble, I would have left you in Detroit and hired a maid.'"

Her eyes were starting to tear up again. I wanted to assure her that everything was going to be fine. I wanted to make her smile. But I knew from personal experience that nothing I could say would make it better. There are no words to describe the pain of betrayal. After I'd discovered Stanley's relationship with Beth, I thought I was literally going to die. I'd only given him four years of my life; Trina was nearing ten with Darius. She was in a delicate place, and I didn't want to say the wrong thing, so I just rubbed her back and handed her some more tissue.

She took another deep breath, dried her face off on my duvet, and went on. "Then, all of a sudden, he yanked me off the seat by my hair. I kicked him in the shin, and that's when he punched me in the jaw." That explained the huge bruise and scratches on the side of her face.

"How did all your stuff end up on the front lawn?"

"I'm not quite sure. He was cursing and throwing things. I was really scared; I'd never seen him in such a rage. So I locked myself in the laundry room. I could hear things hitting the floor and glass breaking, but I was too afraid to open the door to see what was happening. Eventually things died down, but I never heard the car start, so I wasn't sure if he had gone or if he was waiting for me to come out. After about an hour, I realized the house was empty. That's when I called you."

"I'm sorry I wasn't there for you."

I really meant it. While I was flirting with Don and obsessing over my own insignificant problems, the one person who meant the most to me was locked in a laundry room, fearing for her life. I looked over at Trina; she had a fat lip, and her eyes were puffy from crying. I felt hot tears spring to my eyes, just at the thought of losing her.

"Oh, sweetie, don't cry." She sat up and hugged me. "I'm okay. Everything's okay."

Here I was crying like a baby and she was the one who'd just been to hell and back.

"You must be exhausted," I said, wiping away my tears. Her eyelids were at half-mast and she hadn't slept a wink since Thursday.

"Yeah, I'm pretty beat," she admitted. I looked over at the clock; it wasn't even noon yet.

"I have an idea," I told her. "Why don't you sleep for a couple of hours, and if you feel up to it later, we'll go to the mall, maybe rent some movies and order in. It'll be just us."

"Okay." She was grinning. "That sounds like fun."

"You know you can stay here as long as you want," I said, as she slipped underneath my duvet.

She nodded. "I don't know what I'd do without you. I love you."

I squeezed her hand. " I love you, too."

Trina and I headed to the mall at around three that afternoon. It was less than a mile away, so we decided to walk. The sky was overcast and there was a nice breeze, so we didn't have to worry about the summer heat.

I really enjoyed spending time with her. We used to be inseparable back in Detroit, but after we moved to Memphis, Darius and daily chores took up most of her time. Up until now, I hadn't noticed how much I missed her. We strolled down Main street, window shopping and admiring the unique charm of downtown Memphis. There was no rush, so we bought frozen yogurt and kept a leisurely pace. We reminisced about our childhoods and told the same old stories we'd told first as kids and then again as teenagers and now as adults. For some reason, they never got old. Even though we always knew the outcome, each story seemed as fresh and new as when it first happened.

She had me cracking up with an uncanny imitation of Stanley. She recounted the horrible Beth fiasco with such animation that by the time we were standing across the street from the mall waiting for the light to change, I was crying with laughter. I marveled at her strength. I knew she was hurt, that Darius had finally cracked something inside of her. But she was still able to make light of life. As much as she loved Darius, and as unsure as she was about their future, she managed to push aside the drama and let herself enjoy the day.

Earlier, Trina had agreed it would be best to stay with me for a while, but almost everything she owned was spread out all over Darius' front lawn. We threw out a couple of options while we waited in line for a cookie at Mrs. Fields.

"We could drive by and see if it's still out there," she suggested. I was thinking the same thing, but the thought of running into Darius made my stomach flip.

"No," I said. "I don't want to be anywhere near him right now. Maybe you could call and make arrangements to go pick up some things while he's out."

"Please!" she scoffed. "I don't have anything to say to him. I'd rather go naked."

"I have a better idea."

"What's that?"

"Shopping spree!" It was just what we needed to brighten up the rest of our day. Shopping always cheered us up.

"I can't," she said, her face dropping.

"Why not?" I asked. "You deserve to be spoiled right now."

"Spoil myself with whose money?"

"Mine," I announced, without missing a beat.

"You know I can't do that, Grace. It wouldn't be right."

"You'll pay me back when you can," I said, even though I knew I wasn't going to take a dime from her.

She cracked a smile. I could see her excitement building.

"Well, maybe just a couple of outfits and a pair of pajamas. Nothing excessive."

Two outfits turned into three pair of jeans, a skirt, two pairs of shoes, a couple of tank tops, a sordid array of Victoria's Secret lingerie, a load of Mac cosmetics, two pairs of flannel pajamas, a decent size bag of Godiva chocolate and a book on how to know if you're dating a loser. We had a blast, and I could tell that Trina's spirits had definitely lifted. Especially after two guys tried to pick her up in Abercrombie & Fitch.

"If the dark-haired one looked like he was legal, I might have given him a chance," she said, after they'd left. I was amazed that she was so flattered by their advances. But then it dawned on me that she'd become so accustomed to not being appreciated by Darius, she could no longer see what a catch she was. He'd completely stripped her of her confidence.

It wasn't until we got to the food court that we realized we had no transportation home. The shopping spree was an impromptu treat. We hadn't planned on buying so much. There was no way we could carry all our new goodies a mile to the loft.

We got smoothies, sat down, and debated our options.

"I say we suck it up and trudge home," she said.

"Yeah, well, if I was in great shape like you, I'd be all for that, too."

"Oh, come on, you work out more than I do. What about your morning walks? I'm sure you trek three times the distance we're talking about."

"Yeah, but not with twenty pounds of clothes strapped to my back and a shoe box tucked under each arm."

"Fine, you want me to stay here while you go back and get the car?"

"No, I don't like that plan." I couldn't stand the idea of leaving her behind. "Why don't we call a cab?"

"This is Memphis, Gracie, not New York." She was right. Even if I could locate a taxi company, it would take forever for one to get to the mall.

"Okay, then. You win. I'll suck it up."

"Good girl!" She clapped. We finished our smoothies, gathered up our packages, and walked outside right into pouring rain. As we spun around to run back inside, I slammed straight into some guy carrying a bag from Taco Bell.

"I'm so sorry," I said, and looked up to see Michael, the handsome mama's boy who'd helped me move into the loft. I'd seen him around the building several times since then and we'd exchanged pleasantries, but I still hadn't really gotten to know him.

"Hello," he said, a big smile spread across his face.

"Hey, Mike, how are you?" I asked.

"Pretty good. Here, let me help you with those." He bent down to pick up the packages I'd dropped.

"I'm really sorry," I said again.

"Don't be silly. There's no harm done. I'll help you to your car." He offered to take some of the bags I was carrying.

"Actually," I said. "I walked here with Trina." I pointed behind him in her direction. She had run back into the mall to escape the downpour and was looking at us through the glass door. He turned toward her and she gave him the wax-on, wax-off wave. He nodded.

"From the loft?" He looked confused.

"Yeah, it was a nice day so..." my voice trailed off. There was really no way to explain the situation. "What can I say? Poor planning."

He burst out laughing.

"Well, I'd be more than happy to give you two a ride home," he chuckled.

"That would be wonderful," I said.

"Just wait right here; I'll go get my truck."

I motioned for Trina to come over. I didn't want to keep him waiting when he pulled up.

"Who was that?" she asked. "He was pretty hot." She'd been so mad at me on moving day when she found out about the service elevator, she'd completely forgotten about Mike.

"You remember him." I tried to jar her memory. "He lives three floors above me. Banana nut bread? Service elevator?"

"Oh! Right! What was it—Mitch?"

"Mike."

"Has he always looked that sexy?" she asked.

I chose to ignore her. The last thing she needed was a man.

"He's going to give us a ride home," I said.

"Well, wasn't that perfect timing?"

I was surprised to see Mike pull up in a shiny, expensive-looking SUV. I don't know why I assumed he drove something a little more understated, like a pick-up truck. He just didn't strike me as a flashy guy.

"Ladies," he said, opening the door and giving a little bow, as if he was our butler. Trina giggled and hopped into the front seat.

"This is a phat truck," she told him, once he'd finished loading our bags into the back and had settled into the driver's seat.

"Thanks. Where to?" he asked in a mock British accent.

"Home, Jeeves," Trina teased back.

We rode in silence for a few minutes, until I noticed that something was stinking up the truck.

"What's that awful smell?" I asked, as we stopped at a red light.

"Hey now, be nice." His lip poked out. "That's my dinner." Trina held up the soggy Taco Bell bag.

"You're not serious." Trina's nose scrunched in disgust.

I almost asked him why he didn't just get his mom to cook him dinner, but on second thought, I figured he might find my question offensive. I kept my mouth shut.

"We can do better than this," Trina said.

Oh, please, Trina, don't, I pleaded silently. I tried to ignore all the signs, but she was definitely flirting. She was probably just on the rebound, but I could tell by the way she was giggling and batting her lashes that something about Mike had struck her fancy. And when Trina wants to win a man , the first thing she does is invite him over for a hot meal. I have to admit, my girl can throw down in the kitchen, and any other time I wouldn't be opposed to her entertaining Mike, but I had my date with Don tomorrow and I was hoping to get to bed early.

"Leave the man alone," I said, subtly trying to prevent a late night dinner party. "Maybe that's what he wants to eat."

"Nonsense," she said. "Nobody actually *wants* to eat this stuff." She turned to Mike. "Why don't you let me fix you dinner tonight? You can consider it a thank you for driving us home."

"Oh, I don't know," he said looking at me through his rearview mirror. "Grace looks a little tired, and I wouldn't want to impose."

"She's not tired."

Trina turned around in her seat and looked at me, hopefully. I didn't have the heart to disappoint her. She'd been through so much over the past couple of days. And chasing after Mike would give her something to concentrate on besides Darius.

"No, I'm not the least bit tired," I lied. "Really, you have to taste Trina's grilled salmon. She's a wonderful cook. Don't cheat yourself out of a once-in-a-lifetime meal."

Trina smiled and winked at me.

"How can I pass that up?" He turned into the loft parking lot.

"Give us a couple of hours. Say … eight?" she chirped, practically bouncing up and down in her seat.

"I'll be there."

I had a better time than I'd expected. Trina outdid herself. For the main course, she whipped up smoked mackerel, garlic mashed potatoes, and steamed asparagus with a decadent lemon pepper sauce. And for dessert, we had raspberry sorbet with whipped cream and chocolate syrup. I was shocked when I saw everything laid out elegantly on the table. I didn't even know I had those ingredients in the house.

"Grace wasn't lying," Mike said to Trina. He got up and started clearing the table. "You really are a great cook."

Trina smiled. "Put those down," she scolded gently, taking the dishes from him. "Grace and I can do this. You're our guest. Relax."

I didn't budge. Far be it from me to turn down help cleaning the kitchen. Besides, I was tired and my belly was full. I didn't want to do anything but crawl into bed and go to sleep. Trina took one look at me, and knew I'd be little help.

"I'll be right back. Don't go anywhere." She laughed playfully, and headed to the kitchen with an armful of dirty dishes.

"So, Grace," Mike said, turning to me. "How do you like Memphis so far?"

The last thing I wanted to do was make small talk. I heard dishes clattering as Trina rinsed them off and put them in the dishwasher. *Hurry up*, I thought.

"It's really nice," I answered. "I don't think I'd want to live anywhere else." It was the truth. My entire life I'd felt out of place in Detroit. I wasn't tough enough—coarse enough—to fit in with people up there. Everything was rushed—too fast-paced for me to find my niche. But in Memphis, life was slower, people were nicer. Nobody condemned me for speaking differently or taking things at my own pace.

"It's always good to hear that," he said. "I didn't know you and Trina were roommates."

"Yeah, well, it's a newly-formed arrangement," I said, without elaborating.

"Things not working out with her boyfriend?" he asked. "I couldn't help but notice the huge bruise on her face."

I felt like he was prying, and I made it a point never to tell anyone else's business.

"How's your mom?" I asked, changing the subject. He didn't seem to notice.

"She's great," he told me. "I saw her earlier today."

Isn't that a shocker, I thought.

I'd almost cried when I moved back home after graduation. The thought of being around my mom all day, every day, practically sent me spiraling into a depression. I had no idea how he could handle living mere floors above her.

"Did you remember to thank her for the bread?"

"Yeah, she was glad you liked it."

I guess we had nothing left to say to one another because an awkward silence settled between us. *What is taking her so long*, I wondered. The kitchen had gone silent a while ago. I looked over at Mike, who was studying me with such intensity that I felt goose bumps creep up my arm. He was making me nervous. I smiled and looked down at my jeans. I brushed away imaginary lint and silently willed Trina to come back. Finally, she came through the door carrying a tray with a pot of coffee and three mugs. I noticed that she'd neatly pulled her hair up into a ponytail and applied a fresh coat of lip-gloss.

"Sorry I took so long. I thought we would all enjoy some coffee. Maybe play a game of Scrabble?"

Great! Just great. I looked at the wall clock. It was almost ten. If I drank coffee now, I'd be bouncing off the walls all night and end up flat for my date with Don. I couldn't get out of it, though. Trina had already starting pouring the coffee and Mike had excused himself to use the restroom.

"Isn't he sweet?" she asked, after the bathroom door closed. There was a dreamy expression on her face. I didn't have the heart to tell her I thought he was a little weird.

"Yeah, he's something," I said.

"What's wrong?" she asked. "I can tell something's not right."

"What are you talking about?" I dismissed her allegations with a wave of my hand.

"Don't even try it. You've been quiet all evening. Is it Mike? Just tell me what you want. Because you know I would back off in a heartbeat if you told me to."

She couldn't be serious. I wouldn't pursue him for all the rice in China.

"Don't be ridiculous," I said. "I think he suits you."

"Me, too." She had a dopey grin on her face. "I mean, he's handsome, articulate, and funny. What's not to like, right?"

I agreed. In spite of his freakish attachment to his mother, he had a great sense of humor. I found myself completely captivated by the stories he told over dinner.

"Right," I answered.

"Then what is it?" she asked again. "Why have you been so distant tonight?"

"It's nothing. I just have a big day tomorrow and I'm a little tired. I don't think I'm really up for coffee and Scrabble."

"Oh, but I *need* you," she whined. "Just until midnight. Pllleeeaaassseee?"

"Why do you *need* me? You look like you're doing fine."

"Yeah, but he hasn't really warmed up to me yet. Just play a couple of rounds with us. Come on, a few more hours up won't kill you."

"Just till midnight?"

"Yes, I promise. I'll loosen him up in the next couple of hours and at the stroke of midnight, you can leave us here, go into your room, and turn into a pumpkin."

"Deal! But no coffee. Otherwise you may have to scrape me off the ceiling when you wake up in the morning."

It was nice to see Trina hanging out and conversing with a man other than Darius. It had been a while since I'd seen her laugh so much. I was grateful to Mike for that. I decided to make a real effort to be nice to him. He couldn't be all that bad. In just one evening, he'd managed to restore some of Trina's zest.

Over the years, she'd lost her natural spunk—the exuberant confidence that drew people to her. I remember how she used to stand up to Darius—remind him how there were plenty of guys who would love to be in his place.

"You are not indispensable," she used to warn him. I think part of her strength came from growing up in the roughest neighborhoods in the toughest cities. She lived in Detroit just as long as I did and before that in New York with her aunt. When we were kids, she used to carry pepper spray and a whistle wherever she went. By the time she was a senior in high school, she'd taken practically every self-defense class offered in the state of Michigan. If I weren't her best friend, I'd be scared of her. I had to practically hog tie her to keep her from causing Stanley bodily harm after she'd found out what happened between us. That's how she used to be—fearless.

Trina and I met in middle school. She'd gotten into Westminster Academy on an academic scholarship after she scored in the ninetieth percentile on a standardized test. Nearly every private school in Detroit and the surrounding cities offered her a full ride. I'd like to think they saw in her what I always knew was there—the potential to be extraordinary. In reality, they were probably just trying to fill a quota.

Being the only two black females in the Academy, we had this magnetic pull toward one another. For a while, people thought we were related. But that myth was put to rest when she was kicked out after one year for cursing at a teacher. The truth is that Trina and I come from drastically different backgrounds. Her father passed away when she was three and a short while after, her mother decided that she lacked a maternal gene and signed away her parental rights. Nana Earnestine, Trina's grandmother, adopted her just before she was to become a ward of the state. But not even a year later, Nana passed away from heart complications. Trina's father's sister, Arlene, agreed to take her in. I don't really know what was going on in Trina's head then. When all that happened, neither one of us knew the other even existed. But for whatever reasons, she started to act out. By age eleven, she was sexually promiscuous, dabbling in drugs, and flirting with anorexia.

Arlene felt that if she didn't get Trina out of New York, the girl would end up raped, beaten or dead. So, with a thousand dollars in a cigar box, two suitcases full of clothes and little Trina in tow, she jumped on a bus to Detroit and left New York behind.

"All I saw was that my baby girl was losin' herself. We had to get on out of Queens," she told me a few years back over a cup of coffee. "Wasn't nothin' there for us but the gutter."

Looking at Trina now, sitting across from me playing Scrabble, she doesn't resemble the problem child I grew up with. Over the course of our friendship, her wild streak peaked and then gradually disappeared, leaving behind this beautiful, articulate woman, who has just the right mix of love and determination. If I hadn't been the one to hold her hair back after her vodka binges all through high school or been the one who gave her the four hundred dollars to get an abortion after Darius told her he wouldn't stay if she kept the baby, I would think she was just as innocent as I used to be.

I spent a lot of my spare time cleaning up Trina's messes. She used to show up at my dorm room at the crack of dawn, reeking of booze. It was always the same request— "Can I stay with you tonight?" And no matter how late it was, or what I had to do the next day, I'd get her undressed, showered, and tucked into bed.

My mother's never liked Trina. She still calls her "that trouble maker." But I've always gotten along famously with Arlene. In some ways, I wish my mother was more like her—warm and affectionate. She thinks I'm Trina's guardian angel.

"She didn't start acting like she had some sense until she met you," Arlene told me at my high school graduation.

"I don't know what I was thinking," Trina told me once. "In hindsight, I wasn't trying so much to numb the pain as I was trying to create an illusion of control."

It was all psychobabble to me. I never doubted her pain, but she was also too stubborn for her own good. I'm sure a swift kick in the pants when she was a kid would have resolved a lot of her issues.

"How much control can an eleven-year-old have?" I asked, trying to imagine how many times over my mother would have killed me if I had even thought about pulling any of Trina's stunts when I was her age.

"You don't get it," she answered, dismissing me with a wave of her hand. "You've had a privileged life, Grace. You like to pretend you have all this drama to deal with, but you really don't."

"How would you know?" I asked, my face hot with irritation.

"Because I've known you since you were twelve. You're spoiled rotten. You've never had to go without any of life's luxuries, much less the bare essentials."

I wanted to retort, to come up with a million examples to prove her wrong. I knew I'd always had a pretty easy life, but that didn't compensate for love. I used to be so jealous of Trina and Arlene. They ate dinner together every night and spent hours telling jokes and talking about their days. Her house was like a fairyland to me. I would make up any excuse to spend the weekend there. It never occurred to me that it was a sacrifice for Arlene to feed me. Most nights we'd have Ramen noodles and some sort of vegetable. It wasn't until college, when I learned the joys of budgeting, that I realized

Ramen noodles were a low-cost wonder. It was probably all she could afford. Still, I remember wishing for poverty so that Mom and I could be like them.

"Grace, it's your turn."

I had completely zoned out. I looked up at the clock; 11:30—close enough.

"You know what, guys?" I hoisted myself off the floor. "It's way past my bedtime. I'm gonna have to say goodnight."

"Maybe I should go, too; it *is* getting kind of late," Mike said.

Instant disappointment spread across Trina's face.

"No, no. Finish the game. Stay as long as you like."

When I got up around four o'clock to go to the bathroom, I could hear Mike's low rumbling voice coming from the living room.

Go 'head girl, I thought to myself, with a smile.

Chapter Three

I woke up around ten that morning. The house was dead silent. "Trina?" I whispered, cracking open my bedroom door. She was usually up by this time, but I knew she'd had a long night. I wasn't sure if Mike had stayed over, and I didn't want to disturb them if they were still asleep.

There was no response.

I slipped on my robe and tiptoed into the living room. Everything was in its proper place, and the blankets and pillow I had given her were folded and neatly tucked into the far left corner of the room. She wasn't there. *Did she go up to Mike's place?* I wondered. As much as I admired her ability to bounce back after a fall, I didn't have a good feeling about her being alone in some guy's apartment—even if it was Mike. She barely knew him.

I noticed a yellow post-it stuck to the door. Good girl—she'd left a note.

Morning sleepy head! Gone to church with Mike. Will be back later this afternoon. Love you.

Church? I didn't know what to think. I knew for a fact she hadn't stepped inside a church since her grandmother died when she was nine. One night, when we were younger, I tried to get her to pray with me.

"What for?" she'd asked.

"I don't know. To ask God to bless your family and stuff."

"That's a load of rubbish. I'm surprised you don't still believe in Santa Clause," she snapped. "God doesn't exist. All you're doing is talking to yourself."

I didn't argue with her about it because I didn't get what prayer was about, either. I wasn't brought up in a religious family. My grandparents called themselves Christians, but that was it. My mother and I only went to church on Mother's Day, Easter, and Christmas. We usually arrived late and left early. It was my grandma who'd convinced me to pray every night before I went to bed.

"You should say a little prayer every night, just to get all the day's worries off your chest. That way, tomorrow you can start fresh," she'd told me. I followed her advice all through elementary school, but by the time I was a teenager, I didn't see the point. Most of the time, I just asked for things I never got, like long hair or a puppy. God was obviously too busy. It was more effective to beg my mom.

I read the note again. *She must really have it bad for him*, I thought. I remember when we were seventeen, and Arlene found Trina's diaphragm—she nearly had a heart attack. I guess she had convinced herself that Trina and Darius weren't having sex. When Trina came home from school that day, Arlene gave her an hour-long lecture about fornication and living in sin. They had a huge blowout and Trina ended up staying at my house for a couple of nights.

"I'm not like her," she told me. "I don't believe in sin. I believe people should do what feels right. I love Darius and what we do behind closed doors is nobody's business. I mean, it's not like I was a virgin before I met him. You would think she'd be proud I'm taking the proper precautions."

I didn't have anything to say on the matter. I was still a virgin at the time. Pregnancy and contraceptives weren't even in my realm of thinking. My biggest worries were trying to secure a date to junior prom and figuring out how to combat the latest outbreak of blackheads that had sprouted across my forehead practically overnight.

I never told Trina, but I was always more on Arlene's side. She and Darius were like wild jackrabbits. They got it on anywhere, including Arlene's house. It's not that I cared that they were sleeping together, but sneaking Darius in through her bedroom window and having sex with him right under Arlene's nose, when she'd specifically told her not to, just seemed devious. Arlene worked two jobs to support Trina, and she didn't have time to check up on her and make sure she was following the rules. A part of me always felt like Trina took advantage of Arlene's trust.

"I don't need her pushing her self-righteous morals on me," Trina ranted. She wasn't the least bit put off by my silence. "If she wants to go to church and chant with all the rest of those losers, that's on her. I can't believe she doesn't see what a waste it all is. What has God done for her? She works twelve hours a day, six days a week, so she can barely afford a raggedy house in a rundown neighborhood. I couldn't care less about what she imagines God thinks about me having sex. This is my body and my life."

I continued to sit there and listen. She stopped pacing back and forth and looked at me. There was a sort of pleading in her eyes.

"Sex feels good," she continued. She had lost the authority in her voice. It almost sounded like she was trying to convince herself that she was telling the truth. "Darius makes me feel good. He makes me feel loved." She let out a deep sigh and slid down to the floor. "That's more than I can say for her God."

I looked down at her post-it note for a third time and wondered if Mike knew what he was getting himself into.

I was supposed to pick Don up at one o'clock. That gave us just enough time to get to the Peabody Place, find a decent parking space, and grab some refreshments before the movie. At ten to noon, the phone rang.

"Grace? It's me, Don."

Oh, God, I knew it! He's going to cancel. This can't be happening, I thought. I looked over at the clothes I'd laid out on my bed. I picked a cute purple and black sundress. It was low-cut and showed the perfect amount of cleavage—just enough to be sexy, but not enough to look trashy. I'd planned on wearing it with a black cardigan—just in case the theatre was cold—and black, strappy sandals. I was going for a casual, yet alluring sort of look.

"You're not going to be able to make it," I said. It was a statement more than a question.

"No, I'm coming," he said quickly. I couldn't help but notice that he sounded nervous. "I was just calling to ask if we could meet there instead." Friday, at the gym, I'd offered to pick him up. They only had one car and his wife, who was a nurse, worked Sunday afternoons.

"Okay," I answered slowly. I wasn't sure why he was acting so strange. I heard a baby crying in the background. It must have been Chloe. "Look, if it's a bad time, we can always reschedule."

"Don't be like that. Some stuff just came up last minute and it would be easier for me to meet you there."

"Around what time?" I asked.

"1:30?"

The movie started at 1:45.

"That's kind of tight."

"True, but I was thinking maybe it would be better if you got there before me. Just in case, well, you know..." He let his sentence trail off. Yeah, I knew. God forbid anyone should see us together.

"No, I *don't* know," I answered, just to be difficult.

"Come on, Grace. You know I can't risk anyone seeing me out with another woman. They wouldn't know how to interpret it."

No kidding! I don't even know how to interpret it.

I knew I didn't have the right to be upset. I shouldn't be going *anywhere* with him; he's a married man. But I couldn't help but feel a little hurt at the fact he was trying to hide me. Ever since I'd agreed to go out with him, I'd been trying to tell myself it wasn't a date. But deep down, I'd managed to get my hopes up.

"Well, do you think maybe we can grab a bite to eat afterward?" *Don't sound so desperate*, I scolded myself.

"Uh, I don't know. Let's play it by ear," he answered. Just then I heard someone call his name. It was a woman, and she didn't sound happy. "I gotta go," he whispered.

Before I had a chance to say "bye," he'd hung up.

No he didn't, I thought. I stared at the receiver in my hand. For a split second, I had a mind not to go. I even hung the dress back up and put away my curling iron. But by half past noon, I started to feel guilty. I couldn't have him searching for me all over a dark theatre only to realize he'd been stood up. What would he say tomorrow morning when I showed up expecting to work out? That would be nothing short of awkward. I decided to give him the benefit of the doubt.

I spotted him as soon as he walked into the theatre. I'd almost given up hope. When he hadn't shown up by 1:40, I went ahead and bought my ticket without him. I picked two seats in the center of the room so that I'd be sure to see him when he arrived. But as the lights dimmed and the coming attractions popped onto the big screen, I started to think he'd changed his mind. Excitement shot through my body when he walked into the dark room. He stood there a minute scanning the vast row of seats, most of which were empty. I stood up and waved so he could see me.

"Hey," he whispered, sitting down next to me.

I smiled.

"I'm sorry I'm late." He gave me a feather-light kiss on the cheek.

"It's okay," I said quietly. "Is everything all right?"

"It is now." It was a corny line, but I couldn't keep myself from smiling. He looked great in his maroon polo shirt and jean shorts, and his cologne smelled so good it made me light-headed. He discreetly took my hand as the movie started. Looking down at our entwined fingers, I felt—in spite of his present circumstances—that we had a special connection.

"I'm glad you made it," I said, leaning in closer to take in his scent.

"Me, too."

"Have I told you how beautiful you look?" Don and I were waiting for a pool table to open up at Jillian's.

"Yes, several times, actually," I said flirtatiously. "But I don't mind."

"You don't, huh?" He wrapped his arms around me from behind. His muscular torso gently rested against my back.

"Nope. You can tell me as many times as you'd like." I let myself lean into his strong embrace. He made me feel so dainty and protected.

"You're beautiful," he whispered into my ear. He was so close, I could feel his lips brush my hair. I hadn't felt this euphoric in ages. Don was the first man since Stanley to make my heart race.

So far, things were going better than expected. Halfway through the movie, he'd slipped his arm around me and pulled me close. I let my head rest on his shoulder and placed my hand on his thigh. After a few minutes in that position, he cupped my chin in his hand, turned my face towards his and delicately planted a kiss on my lips. I couldn't believe that someone his size could be so gentle. He caught me off guard and for a second I didn't respond. He had started to pull away when I slipped my hand around the back of his neck and pulled him even closer. He tasted like butterscotch and mouthwash.

I let myself lean into his warm embrace. Up until that moment, I hadn't realized how much I'd missed being held by a man. There was an overwhelming satisfaction in knowing someone wanted me. It was a sensation I hadn't felt in a long time.

Don held me tenderly, slowly running his fingers through my hair, only stopping occasionally to caress my neck. All too soon the movie credits were rolling and the house lights came on.

I was almost thirty and still having make-out sessions at the movies. The mere thought had me feeling like a schoolgirl, but that's what made Don so enjoyable to be around. He made me feel carefree. Most of all, though, he made me feel like I was the only person in the world who mattered, and I relished every minute of it.

After the movie, we went to dinner. The conversation was okay. He mostly complained about his wife and how unhappy he was. At points, I wanted to change the subject, but I didn't want to seem insensitive. It's not that I didn't feel sorry for him. From everything he'd told me, Laura sounded like a controlling nag. She didn't respect the fact that even though they were married, he still had personal goals and aspirations. But what did he expect me to do about it? In my mind, Laura was only a problem if he made her one.

Periodically, he would reach across the table and tell me how much fun he was having.

"You make me forget all about my problems with Laura," he said. "When I look at your beautiful smile, I forget she even exists."

I wanted to believe him, but he brought her up so much that I felt like she might as well have been sitting in the booth with us. Why did he ask me out, if we were just going to talk about his wife the whole time? I was his date, not his therapist. As he began to tell me all the reasons he resented his in-laws, I started to wonder if I'd made a mistake.

This man has a lot of baggage, I warned myself. *He's making this too complicated.*

He must have sensed my apprehension, because he changed the subject mid-sentence.

"Can you play?" he asked, pointing to the game room behind me.

"What? Pool? No! I'm horrible at it."

"Well, then, let me teach you a little something." He flagged down our waiter and asked for the check.

"Number seventy-nine?" I looked down at the yellow ticket stub in my hand. "That's us," I told Don, who had his arm wrapped protectively around my waist. We'd been waiting almost twenty minutes for a pool table.

The heavyset woman behind the hostess's podium looked hot and irritated. When I asked how long before a table might open up, she looked me square in the face and asked, "Do I look like a psychic?" I was surprised by her attitude, an uncommon rudeness in Memphis.

"Excuse me?" I asked, ready to tell her exactly what she *did* look like.

"We have somewhere to be in a couple of hours," Don jumped in before I could reply. He lied. The only place he had to be was home by the time Laura got off work at ten. "We thought maybe we could get a couple games of pool in if the wait wasn't too long."

She looked at me and then back at Don.

"I can't make you any promises. We charge by the hour, and there's one party in front of you. Shouldn't be too long."

"Thanks," I snipped.

"Don't mention it." Her tone was dry and indifferent. "Don't forget to take a number," she said to Don, with a noticeably sweeter voice.

"Seventy-nine?" she shrieked again. Her shrill voice yanked me out of my thoughts.

"That's us. Right here," Don said, gingerly prying his arm from around me. He walked over and got our balls and two cue sticks.

"Okay, let's see what you got," he said, after he set up the table.

"You break," I told him. "I need chalk." I picked up the small blue cube sitting on the edge of the table and rubbed it against the tip of my pool stick. He bent forward and spent a few seconds positioning himself. I could tell by the way he was studying all the possible angles that he wasn't a novice. He took his shot; two solids went into the left corner pocket.

"Your turn again." I stalled for time.

"No, it's okay. We're not playing a real game. I just want to see how you shoot."

"I told you, I don't know how." I didn't want to seem like a poor sport, but I felt ridiculous standing there with a huge stick in my hand.

"Just try," he prodded me.

I bent down and tried to find the easiest ball to hit.

"No, hang on a sec," he said, just as I was about to take my shot. "Are you right handed or left handed?"

"Right." A small smile popped onto his face. "What? You're holding your cue stick in the wrong hand."

If it weren't for the dim lighting, I'm sure he would have seen me blushing.

"Wouldn't you rather grab a cup of coffee and find a nice quiet spot to talk?" I asked, backing away from the table.

"Come back here," he said playfully, grabbing my wrist. He pulled me so close our noses almost bumped. "Let me show you."

He turned me around so that we were both facing the pool table. "Hold it like this," he whispered into my ear, while he rearranged my fingers. "There. See how you support the stick with your hand?"

I was too flustered to say anything so I just nodded. I could barely concentrate on what he was trying to show me.

"Try to get that one in," he said pointing to a white and orange striped ball just in front of the right corner pocket. I obliged, my hip bumping against his belt buckle as I bent forward. He didn't move. "Good, now line it up." He leaned over me. We hovered over the table with his chest pressed against my back. I couldn't keep myself from shuddering.

I swallowed hard. "Okay, now what?" I asked in a whisper.

"Now, just relax and shoot." His voice was deep and soft. He kissed the back of my ear before he stepped away to give me space.

"What was that for?"

"Good luck."

I took the shot, but missed. I didn't even come close. "This definitely isn't my sport," I pouted.

"Aw, it's okay," he soothed. "I'm sure there are other, more important, things you're good at."

"Other things, huh?" I asked. He leaned in for a kiss.

"Yeah." His breath tickled my cheek.

"Like what?"

"I don't know." I felt his hands travel down my back. "We'll just have to find out."

I got home at quarter to nine. After a few more tries at pool, Don and I bought some frozen yogurt, found a bench, and talked until it was time for him to go relieve the babysitter. The conversation went much smoother than it had at dinner. We talked about everything from our childhoods to sports. He didn't mention Laura once.

We held hands as he walked me to my car. He gave me a little peck on the cheek.

"Thanks for a wonderful evening," he said. I stood there expecting him to kiss me more passionately, but he just smiled and waited for me to get into my car. I have to admit, it was anticlimactic. I was hoping for a more sensual good-bye. Still, I wasn't disappointed with the evening.

I caught myself smiling the entire drive home. I could hardly contain my excitement as I unlocked the door and walked into the loft.

"Where in God's name have you been?" Trina sat at the kitchen counter reading.

"Excuse me?"

"You aren't so grown that you don't need to leave notes if you're planning to be out all day," she snapped. "I wrote *you* one before I left this morning."

"Ah, yes. Before church. How was that?" I teased. "I hope your snoring didn't disturb the rest of your pew."

She wasn't smiling.

"Gracie, I've been sitting here for hours worrying about you." Her face softened. "You didn't tell me you were going to be out this late. I didn't know what to think."

"I'm sorry. I was in a rush. I didn't even think to leave you a note."

"Don't forget next time," she demanded.

"So, seriously, how was church?" I asked, trying to migrate into friendlier territory. Her face lit up.

"I had the best time," she confessed. "It's nothing like I'd imagined."

"Tell me about it." I really wanted to recount every last detail of my date with Don, but I figured it could wait.

"Well, it all started last night. After you went to bed, Mike and I got to talking. He was telling me all about his mom and what he does for a living. Really, Gracie, he's nothing like you'd expect."

Little did she know, I had no expectations. I hadn't given Mike a second thought since I moved to Memphis. I didn't know the first thing about him and truthfully, I didn't care. He seemed nice enough, but he lacked personality and intrigue. I had him pegged as a mama's boy within the first five minutes after he'd stepped into my loft. I needed a man who could captivate me. Someone who was more of a challenge. Someone like Don.

She continued, "He went through a lot as a kid, you know? His dad died when he was seven and his mother abandoned him and his two little sisters when he was ten."

"What do you mean, she abandoned them?"

"She left the apartment one day and never came back. They were there by themselves for a week before someone found them."

"That's kind of odd," I said. "Seeing as how his mother lives two floors below me." I was starting to get the impression that Mike was a pathological liar.

"No," she corrected me. "That's his adoptive mom. All three of them, Mike and his two sisters, became wards of the state. They were separated and placed in foster homes. Anyway, by the time he was in high school, he was dealing drugs for extra cash and dabbling in petty theft. You know, a bike here, a purse there."

Great, I thought. *She's moved from Darius, the woman beater, to Mike, the petty thief.*

"A crook that goes to church," I said wryly. "That's priceless."

Trina's eyebrows furrowed. It was obvious she didn't appreciate my flippant take on the matter.

"Look, you asked me to tell you about church. That's what I'm trying to do. If you weren't interested, you could have just said so."

"I *am* interested—in the church part. All you've talked about so far is Mike and his sordid past."

"Well, if you'd stop interrupting me, maybe I could get there."

"My deepest apologies," I said with mock sincerity. "Please do continue."

"He got caught trying to steal spare car parts out of some guy's auto repair shop. It wasn't his first offense, so he was looking at quite a few months in jail."

"So, he's a convict."

"Nope, ends up the guy wouldn't press charges. He offered Mike a deal. Told him if he worked off the cost of the window he'd smashed to break into the shop, that he was willing to forget the whole thing. To make a long story short, Earl ended up taking him in and changing his life."

"You've lost me. Who is Earl?"

"Oh, he's the man who owned the auto repair shop. He and his wife Lani ended up adopting Mike a year later."

"He's a lucky guy," I said.

"That's what I thought at first. I mean, what are the odds, right? But Mike said there's no such thing as luck or coincidence. He believes that God sent him to Earl and Lani that night."

"God sent Mike to rob car parts from an innocent couple?"

She had to be kidding me. I wondered if someone had slipped something in her communion wine.

"No, it's bigger than that. You have to try to see the larger picture." She was so excited her hands were flailing as she talked. "It's all a ripple effect. If Mike hadn't broken into the shop, he never would have met Earl and Lani. They never would've adopted him, which means he probably never would have finished high school or gone to college. Without his college education, he would never have had the skills to pursue his art career."

"He's an artist?" I interrupted.

"Yeah, he's an illustrator or a cartoonist. One of those, I'm not really sure. My point is that even after all of the wrong turns he made, he believes God still had a purpose for his life. Think about it. He was on his way to jail. If it weren't for Earl and Lani, he never would have discovered God's love and been born again. Instead of fulfilling God's purpose for his life, he would still be out on the streets trying to think up his next big hustle."

Born again? She was starting to scare me. One night of Scrabble with the guy and he'd managed to turn her into a Bible beater.

"Is this where the church part comes in?" I asked. She'd been talking for twenty minutes easy, and I still hadn't heard one thing about church. I could tell she was annoyed that I was rushing her. But I had to be at the gym by eight the next morning and I still hadn't told her about my date.

"Church was fascinating. It was in a huge auditorium. There had to be thousands of people there. Everyone was so friendly. The music was contemporary. I didn't know there would be a full band and orchestra. People were dancing around in the aisles and crying. At first, I was a little freaked out when the woman next to me went limp and fell back into her seat. But Mike told me not to worry. He said she was overcome by the Holy Spirit."

"And you believed that?" I asked. It all sounded so unrealistic.

"I don't know. But the part I *did* believe was the sermon. I felt like the preacher had prepared the message just for me. He talked about some woman at a well, who had been married five times and was shacked-up with some guy who wasn't her husband. Jesus stopped at the well because he was tired, and asked her for a drink. It was a big deal back then, because he was a Jew and she was a Samaritan. They weren't even supposed to talk to each other. But Jesus didn't care what nationality she was or what her past was like. He just wanted to offer her salvation."

I glanced down at my watch. *Is there a point to all this?*

"Now, she didn't know He was the Son of God," she continued. "But *He* knew who *she* was and He still loved her. He never judged her, not once, despite all her mistakes. He saw her for who she was, spoke to her, counseled her, and offered her everlasting life in heaven."

"That's it? I don't get it," I said. "What's so special about that story?"

"I guess I feel like that could have been me."

"What could have been you?"

"I could have been the woman at the well. You know? Like maybe she's a metaphor for people who are trying to live normal lives and pretend like they don't have all of these skeletons in their closets."

"That's not you," I assured her. "You *do* have a normal life."

"I know that's what it looks like, but so far, I feel like my life has just been a random series of mistakes."

"That's a little bit dramatic, don't you think?" I couldn't help but note how much I sounded like my mother.

"I guess. It's just that I had such a different vision for myself. I always said I wasn't going to end up some desperate woman, who put playing house with a man over her own personal dreams. But look at me." She threw her hands in the air. "That's exactly who I've become."

"Don't be ridiculous." I said. "Life is *supposed* to be a series of trial and error. Everyone has to learn to roll with the punches. You live and learn and try not to repeat the same mistakes."

"You're missing my point. What I'm saying is that maybe God meant for Arlene to be my Earl and Lani. You know, maybe He was trying to reach me through her, just like He sent Jesus to talk to the woman at the well. Only I was too busy doing my own thing. I ignored His mercy and in the process screwed up my life."

"I think you're being a little hard on yourself, Trina. You were just a kid when Arlene took you in. You were trying to deal with your mom leaving and you didn't really have anyone to trust."

"Yeah, but Mike's mom left *and* he was separated from his sisters. Look at him. Look at what he's done with his life. He's accomplished so much, and he's only thirty-five."

"That may be true, but you said yourself that he was a bad seed for a while."

"But he was still able to recognize a blessing when he saw one. Instead of straightening myself out when we left New York, I got more rebellious." She looked so glum.

"If this is the effect going to church has on you, my suggestion is that you find something else to occupy your Sunday mornings," I said.

"I felt the same way as I sat there listening to the pastor preach, but then he told the congregation that just like the woman at the well, any one of us could receive forgiveness and the promise of eternity in heaven, if we just confessed our sins and asked God into our lives."

"Confess to whom?"

"To God. Then the preacher had everyone repeat this thing called the Sinner's Prayer, where we asked God to forgive us for all of our sins and to enter our hearts so that we could be born again in Him. It's kind of like a second chance, I guess."

"And you prayed the prayer?" I asked.

"Yeah. In the middle of it I started sobbing. I just couldn't control myself."

"Did Mike say anything?"

She shook her head.

"He gave me some tissues and just rubbed my back."

"That was nice of him."

"Yep. Then the pastor asked anyone who'd said the prayer for the first time and meant it to come down front."

"Oh, God, Trina, you didn't."

"Why are you being so difficult about all of this?" she asked. I could tell I had hurt her feelings.

"I'm not. It's just... I'm not."

"It's just what?"

"Nothing. It's just that I thought you didn't believe God existed."

"There was a point when I didn't believe in anything but my own personal gratification. And for a while, that seemed like it was working, but look where it's gotten me. I'm twenty-eight with no job, no house, no money, no purpose. I feel like I'm just stumbling around blindfolded letting life happen to me. I *have* to believe there's something greater out there—that I was put on earth for more than to just chase after a man who's busy chasing after other women and to bum off my best friend."

Her eyes started filling with tears. She was serious.

"So you went up front and then what?"

"Well, it wasn't just me. Maybe fifteen or twenty people got up. I met this woman named Jackie. She's our age—really sweet. She was crying, too, so I gave her one of my tissues. They escorted us to a small room in the back of the church and we prayed some more—talked about baptism and spiritual gifts that we could use to help the church. Look," she said holding up the book she'd been reading when I first walked in. "We all got one of these." It was a little red Bible.

"They gave you a Bible?"

"Yeah, and a list of seven Bible verses. We're supposed to read one each day of the week."

"You're really into this, aren't you?"

"I can't tell you how excited I am. I also signed up for Bible study. It meets on Tuesdays and Thursdays."

"How are you going to get to church every Tuesday and Thursday?" I felt irritated that she assumed she could have my car whenever she wanted it.

"Oh, that's what's so great about it. I signed up for Mike's Bible study."

"Mike's going to take you?"

"No, no. It meets upstairs at his place."

"So, what? Are you a *Christian* now?"

"Do you have to say it like that?" she asked.

"Like what?"

"Like it's some sort of disease."

I didn't answer her.

"Is this how it's going to be now?" she asked.

"What are you talking about?"

"This," she said, pointing at me and then to herself and then back at me again. "You turning your nose up at me because I'm into something that you don't agree with."

"I don't disagree," I told her. "People need different things in their lives. If this is what you think is missing in yours, I'm not going to discourage you."

"Thank you." She hopped off the bar stool she was sitting on and walked over to give me a hug.

"And to answer your question, yes. I am a Christian now."

"Well, I hope this makes you happy," I said.

"Funny that you should mention what makes me happy," she said with a knowing grin. "Because *you're* making someone happy yourself."

"I'm not surprised," I sad with an arrogant tone. "I have that effect on a lot of people."

She laughed.

"No, seriously, though. Have you ever noticed how Mike looks at you?"

I recalled the way he stared at me the other night when he came over for dinner.

"I haven't paid much attention," I said. "Besides, I thought you had a thing for him. The way you were giggling and batting your lashes, I thought for sure I'd be going to pick out china patterns with you in no time."

"I did like him that way. I mean, look at him—he's the whole package."

"So, what's the problem?"

"Nothing, except that he has the hots for you."

Before I could think twice, I burst into laughter. Mike barely knew me. We probably had nothing in common. I regained my composure.

"He told you he has the 'hots' for me?"

"Not in those exact words. He told me he thought you were beautiful and that he admired your confidence."

Me? Confident? Too bad he wasn't around for the last twenty-five years. I've only recently made peace with myself and who I've become. And that's only because I don't feel like I have any control over the things I want to change about myself. I just am who I am.

"Well, that's too bad for him," I said. "Because I've already met the perfect man. And we just had the best day together."

Trina's eyes grew big.

"Shut up!" she squealed. "When? Why are you just now telling me?"

"Well, you've had a rough few days and I didn't want to concentrate on me. Besides, I did tell you a little about him."

Trina's face drew a blank.

"What's his name?"

"Don."

"Don? Isn't that …"

It was my turn to squeal.

"Yes," I said, with a huge smile on my face. "And he's so amazing."

"But I thought he was married."

Oops! I'd forgotten that I'd shared that with her.

"Well, he is, but it's complicated. His wife doesn't appreciate him. She nags, and well, you know how it goes. He's really unhappy and wants a divorce. He's already talked to a lawyer and everything," I lied.

Trina looked disgusted.

"Don't look at me like that," I pleaded. "It's not as bad as it sounds."

"You have no idea how bad it sounds," she said. I could hear the repugnance in her voice. "You are unbelievable." She started to gather up her Bible and the rest of her papers that were scattered all over the counter.

"C'mon. Can I at least tell you about the date?" I asked.

"I don't want to hear anything about it," she snapped. She didn't even bother to turn around.

"You've got to be kidding me!" I was surprised by the volume of my voice. "I sat here for forty minutes listening to you drone through Mike's sob story and how he made you see the light, and you won't even bother to listen about my day?"

She kept shuffling papers.

"I don't necessarily believe in the healing powers of church and all this finding God mumbo-jumbo, but at least I listened."

Trina whipped around. "You're comparing going to church to having an affair with a married man? Who has, didn't you say, a baby girl?"

Did I tell her all that? I wondered. I talk way too much.

"Why are you being so judgmental? You don't even know the whole story." I could feel the veins in my neck popping. I was shouting so loud I didn't recognize my own voice.

"What's there to know? You're just another Janet. Women like you don't care who they hurt. Everything is about you and *your* wants. Never mind the lives you have to destroy to get what you want, right? I can't believe how selfish you are!"

What was I thinking? I'd totally forgotten about Darius and Janet. I should have never brought it up.

"Trina, this is different than what happened between you and Darius." I softened my tone and lowered my voice.

"Yeah, it always is." She turned off the kitchen light and headed for my office.

"Where are you going?" I didn't want to go to bed with things so heated between us. I already regretted shouting at her.

She flipped on the lights in the office, and stood silhouetted in the doorway. "To finish this reading, and then to bed."

"It's still early. Please don't go to bed like this." I felt a sob swell in the back of my throat.

"I have an interview tomorrow. I need to get some sleep." She was calmer, but still angry.

"An interview?" I tried to sound as interested as possible. All I wanted was for her to come back so we could make up.

"Yeah, a group of us went to lunch after church. Mike introduced me to a friend of his who's a social worker. He knows an adoption agency that needs a child therapist. I have an appointment with the director in the morning."

"Wow, that sounds fantastic. Tell me more."

"Look," she sighed. "I don't want to talk about it, Grace. I don't have anything to say to you. I don't even really want to know you right now."

She closed the door. My tears fell freely as I stood there in the dark.

Chapter Four

I woke up every hour on the hour all night long. I rehashed the argument in my mind until it was so familiar that I became detached from it. In just a few short hours, anger turned to regret, regret to confusion, confusion to self-pity, and self-pity turned to an oppressive numbness that I couldn't shake. I hoped my words weren't haunting her like hers were haunting me. How could she say she didn't want to know me? The idea of losing her friendship made me so uneasy that I writhed in the bed.

By seven the next morning, I was even less clear about what had happened than I was the night before. The sporadic rhythm of raindrops beat against my window and when I opened my eyes, I saw that it was dreary outside. Gray clouds replaced the rays of morning sunlight that usually streamed through my window. There was a chill in the room.

On an ordinary day, I would wake her up, fix us a cup of coffee, and listen to her plans for the day. But for the first time ever, I was unsure of where we stood with one another. We'd fought in the past, but never like this. Up until recently, I'd never had the courage to cross Trina. There was always a hierarchy in our friendship, and she was the boss. It was an unwritten rule—Trina's needs and problems were always addressed first. In high school, I had no time for my own issues because I was busy dealing with hers.

I snuggled deeper under my covers and tried to pinpoint exactly what had caused our dispute to spiral out of control. It wasn't entirely my fault. Yes, I could have taken her whole church thing more seriously, but she shouldn't have just up and ended the conversation when I told her about Don. I mean, the audacity. Didn't her whole boring story about the woman at the water fountain revolve around the idea of not judging people? Anyone who knew half of what I knew about that girl would think she was pure evil. I've wondered myself, but I never judged her, not even when I was the one stuck cleaning up her messes.

I'm not saying that I don't see where she was coming from. I know that at first glance, my relationship with Don, if I can even call it that, seems a little off kilter. But *he* sought *me* out. It would be a completely different story if I were trying to force myself on him. He's unhappy with Laura. It's obvious, and their breakup was in the making way before I came along. Divorces aren't cataclysmic and love is rarely a one-time thing. People get together and grow apart every day. Everyone should be able to make as many mistakes as it takes to find that certain someone. All of us aren't lucky like Trina. Most people don't get saddled down with their high school sweethearts. And besides, look where ten years of submission and compromising got her—beaten, dumped, and if it weren't for me, homeless.

Still, I felt empty knowing there was such a large rift between us. I thought our friendship was virtually indestructible. All I wanted to do was walk across the living room, knock on her door, and apologize. I didn't want to even consider what it would feel like to go about my day knowing that the most important relationship in my life was in turmoil. But a precipice of principle had been formed. Why should I try to make amends when I don't feel like I'm wrong?

As I brushed my teeth, I debated how I should approach Trina and our awkward situation. If I was lucky, she'd thought about it last night and had cooled down. Maybe she saw how irrational she was being. Why should my relationship with Don have any affect on my friendship with her? Darius wasn't my first pick for *her*, but I never used him as the catalyst for an argument.

I slipped on my sweats and sat down on the edge of my bed to tie my shoelaces. Part of me was excited about seeing Don. He didn't call me after our date last night, and even though I had his number, I didn't want to risk having a run-in with Laura—even if it was over the phone. Just thinking about his soft lips and cute lopsided grin made me smile. I wondered how things would be between us today at the gym.

Since everyone at the Y knew he was married, I was sure I couldn't count on any grand, public displays of affection, but just seeing him and hearing his smooth, gentle voice would be enough for me.

I glanced up at the window. It had stopped raining and there was a hint of sunlight trying to push through the heavy gray clouds. *See there! Things might turn out differently than you expect*. I felt my mood lighten. I was taking things with Trina way too seriously. It was only a spat. With a little space, we could reconcile our differences in no time. Trina wasn't one to hold grudges, and I would be sure to make myself available to her when she was calm enough to talk things out. In the meantime, I decided, I would be cordial so as to avoid any more confrontations.

I went to the kitchen to grab a piece of fruit and was on my way out the door when I decided it would be best to tell Trina that I was leaving. I could've just left her a note, but maybe taking the initiative to speak would act as a symbol of peace. She would know I wasn't mad at her, and I would be able to assess what she was feeling toward me.

I gave the office door a light rap. "Trina?"

There was no answer. I looked down at my watch. It was only 7:46; she was probably still sleeping.

I knocked harder. "Hey, Trina?"

Again, no answer. *There's no way she's still mad at me*. I'd prepared myself for the possibility, but I didn't think it would actually happen. Deep down, I hoped she would be just as eager to patch things up and move on as I was. I threw all my brilliant strategizing out the window. We had to talk, even if it meant that I was going to get to the gym a little late. Nothing was more important than Trina—not Don, not pride, not principle.

"Trina, I don't want to keep going like this," I said, opening the door. "Let's just talk it out like we always do." I was about to dive into an apology for not making more of an effort to understand her interest in God, when I realized I was talking to myself. She wasn't there. My first instinct was to panic. The last thing I wanted was for our fight to send her running back to Darius.

I glanced around the office; there was no sign of her things. Even the comforter and pillow she'd been using were gone. There's no way she would have moved out like that. It's just not her style. Especially if she was mad. She wouldn't leave without telling me why and giving me one last piece of her mind. I walked across the room and checked the storage closet. An overwhelming sense of relief came over me when I saw her little overnight bag and all the new outfits we'd bought neatly placed in the corner.

I sat down behind my desk and tried to figure out where she could possibly be. She did say she had an interview, but that couldn't be until after 9:00. I checked the desk to make sure she hadn't left a note. Nothing. It seemed so out of character for her to go somewhere early in the morning without letting me know what was going on. *If she's trying to make a point, this is not the way to do it*. Giving me the silent treatment and trying to avoid me by sneaking out at odd hours was only going to wear on my patience. I wanted to confront our issues—talk things out like mature adults. But I wasn't willing to grovel.

I looked up at my computer; it was covered with a thin layer of dust. I had barely gotten any writing done since I'd moved to Memphis. There were too many distractions. That had been the one positive aspect of living with my mom—I always had a quiet place to write. From an early age, writing had been my cure for everything. If I was teased or picked on, writing made me quippy and wise. I could reconstruct situations on paper and come up with cutting words and witty repartees that I never had the courage to say. If I got an unfair grade, I could go home and manufacture a universe where my teacher was dying of some never-before-heard-of disease, and I was the genius who discovered the cure. Writing reversed my world and shot me into a parallel universe where I was adequate. It gave me the courage to be more than the underdog.

I hadn't forgotten my other goal to start a career in journalism. I still wanted to get my own column. And I still had plans to write a few sample articles and send them to some local papers. I'd just been too preoccupied lately with more pressing matters.

I tried to count the pressing matters that demanded my time. There weren't any. I didn't have anything to do but go to the gym for an hour and then come home, watch talk shows, and daydream about Don. I didn't know if I was becoming lazy, or if I was too scared to find out if I had what it took to be a journalist, but I suddenly realized how empty my life was. Instead of finding ways to make myself useful, I filled my vacant schedule with self-indulgent forms of amusement like pedicures and antique shopping. Stanley was right; my life revolved completely around me. *You're the worst type of person there is*, I told myself. *You're too self-involved*.

Just then I heard Trina's key in the front door. I jumped up and rushed to the living room. She was standing in the doorway, soaked. Her hair was plastered to her cheeks, and her tan sweatshirt had turned dark brown in spots where the rain had soaked into the fabric. Her yellow parka was bundled up and crammed under her arm. I could tell she was cold by the way her fingers trembled as she closed the door and locked it.

"Good morning," she said, turning in my direction.

"What happened? Where have you been?" My heart was beating so quickly that I could barely catch my breath. Even though I'd been sitting down trapped in my own thoughts, I felt like I'd just finished running a marathon. The tables had completely turned. I knew now how she'd felt last night when I forgot to leave her a note.

"I went across the street to the park. I wanted to sit by the river and have my daily devotional."

She wasn't smiling and she was trying to avoid making eye contact. She was polite, but not friendly. Her attitude, however didn't concern me right then. I wanted to know why she had to go outside to have a devotional when there was a perfectly *dry* spot for her here.

"But it's raining." I pointed outside the huge bay window in the kitchen. Her wet clothes were starting to make a small puddle around her feet, where she still stood in the entryway.

"Yeah, but it wasn't when I got up."

"Well, why is your parka under your arm instead of on you? I know it's cold outside.

She removed her parka from underneath her arm and started to unfold it. She unwrapped her little red Bible and a spiral notebook and held them up.

"Didn't want to get them wet," she explained.

"I was up pretty early. I didn't hear you leave."

"I tried to be as quiet as possible." She stepped into the living room and placed her things on the end table next to the couch. "I left a little before 7:00. I couldn't sleep."

This was the perfect opportunity to get a discussion going. She was waving the white flag—wasn't she?

"Me either, I confess." Hot tears sprang to my eyes. I hadn't realized how stressed out I'd been over the whole incident.

"Don't cry," she said. It was the kindest I'd heard her voice since our fight. She lifted her soggy sweatshirt over her head and kicked off her sneakers. "Sit." She sat down on the couch and patted the cushion next to her.

I obeyed.

"What are you thinking?" she asked.

I wiped my tears onto my sleeve.

"I don't know," I admitted. "I hate it when we fight. I don't want anything to come between us. I should have listened when you were trying to tell me about church and Mike. I can see that this is special to you. I mean, look at you. You're getting up early in the rain to go spend time with God. I respect that."

She nodded.

"It's not that I wasn't excited for you," I continued. "It's just that I was so hyped up about my incredible evening with Don, I couldn't wait to tell you. It was selfish of me, and I see that now. I know I frustrated you. And things just snowballed. I was shouting, which was uncalled for, and you said some things you didn't mean, and before I knew—"

She interrupted me. "Hold on a second, Grace. I didn't say anything I regret. Everything I said to you last night, I would say again this morning."

"What?" A fresh batch of tears started to form in my eyes. "How can you say that?" My voice cracked.

"Well, are you still planning on seeing Don?"

"What does that have to do with us?"

"There you go," she said, shrugging her shoulders, as if my question was the simple answer she'd been waiting for.

"What do you mean, 'there you go'?" I felt like the wounds from last night's dispute were being reopened.

"I don't want to hurt you," she said, standing up. "And I know you aren't used to people opposing you, but I'm not going to tiptoe around this issue and pretend like it doesn't exist."

"What issue?"

She raised one eyebrow and put her hand on her hip.

"I don't have time for this little innocent game you're trying to pull. Any woman who's conniving enough to sleep with another woman's husband should be able to handle the truth in its rawest form."

"Who said I was sleeping with Don?" I felt my tears dry as my hurt feelings turned to anger. What type of person did she peg me for? I wasn't a whore. It was only one date, for pete's sake.

"Well, where do you think dating leads? Don has a wife and a child. Do you really think he's looking for the responsibility of a girlfriend? He's just bored and wants to release some of his pent-up energy. I don't care what he's told you or promised you. When you get boring, he'll be on to someone else, but no matter what happens, he's never leaving his wife. It doesn't matter whether he loves her or not, she's his security blanket. And there's nothing you'll ever be able to do to change that. There's nothing you can offer him to keep him from going home at the end of the day."

"You're projecting what happened between you and Darius on me and that's not fair." I was determined not to lose my temper.

"I'm not projecting, Grace. What happened with Darius and Janet is not unique. This big secret romance you're drawn to is not something new or special. There are married men and women all over the world looking for other needy men and women to fill their idle time."

"Well, if you would just listen to me for two minutes, you'd understand our special circumstances. We're friends. He confides in me. He made a mistake when he married Laura. He admits that freely."

She rolled her eyes.

"I'm serious. He wants to leave her. How can you say men never leave their wives? It happens all the time. Darius left *you*." I was trying to avoid the subject, but since she was so bent on paralleling our situations, I felt like I didn't have a choice but to bring it up. It didn't seem to faze her.

"Darius left me because I got to the point where I wouldn't let him walk all over me anymore. Do you think Janet's the first person he's slept with behind my back?"

I didn't answer.

"Well, she's not. I've found countless names and numbers. I convinced myself that as long as he came home to me every night, I had nothing to worry about. I was more concerned with having a warm body next to me in bed than a good heart. It's only when I decided to rock the boat that he cut me loose. And you know what? It's the best thing that ever happened to me."

"That's you, and this is me."

"That's true. You have to live your own life and make your own mistakes. But I don't have to sit around and watch you stumble."

"What about all the years I watched you stumble, literally? I never once walked away. I've practically carried you our entire friendship. You've been boozed up, drugged up, knocked up, and beaten up." I ticked off each offense on my fingers to emphasize my point. "And I've always been there. I let you make your mistakes and I never made you pay with our friendship."

"That was my past. I won't let you hold it against me. Nobody asked you to do all that. Maybe if you hadn't been there every single time I fell, I wouldn't be the way I am now."

"And how is that?"

"Weak!" she shrieked, with such force that I jumped. "I'm almost thirty and I can't stand on my own two feet. I'm not blaming you. I have to be accountable for my actions and decisions, but . . ." She stopped and let out a big sigh. She sat down on the loveseat and looked up at the ceiling. She tried not to cry.

"Trina," I started, but she shook her head and motioned for me to be quiet. I waited for her to go on.

"I'm a weak person," she continued. Her voice was slight—almost a whisper. "I'm way too old to be this dependent. This," she struggled to find an appropriate word, "crippled." She fidgeted in her seat a little and then crossed her legs. "You've been there for me when I burned all my bridges and was flat on my face. At the time, your help seemed to be the only thing that kept me going. But now, when I look at myself, I hate what I see. And I wonder, how did I get here? And all I can see is that after every disastrous decision I've made, you or Arlene or Darius have been there to sweep my messes away. And that the cycle repeated itself until finally there was no more room under the rug. So now, instead of being a confident woman with a bright future and a firm head on her shoulders, I'm this pathetic, underachieved nobody, who's wasted nearly half her life tripping over the same mistakes, because she knows no matter how many times she falls, someone will show up with a broom."

"So, you would've preferred that I didn't help you? Then what would have been the point in calling me your friend?"

"Sometimes not helping is more help than you think."

"So when you got pregnant, I should have let you drop out of college and lose your boyfriend? That's the type of help you want?"

"Maybe you *should've* made me fend for myself. It was my choice to have sex. If I had gone through with the pregnancy, maybe I would have learned what it means to love someone other than myself—to get up and be responsible for more than just my own happiness. And it's not like Darius ended up being Prince Charming. Maybe things wouldn't have had a chance to get so complicated if I had walked away sooner."

I was trying to stay open to what she was saying, but the more I tried to understand, the less she made sense.

"Where is all this coming from?"

She shook her head. "You wouldn't understand."

"I'm smarter than you think." I was getting irritated. "Try me."

"It's something I read in my devotional book last night."

I should have known.

"It was about plants that grow in different environments."

This sounds even worse than the water lady story.

"Basically, when a plant grows against a wall it may look strong, but it's not, because the wall protects it from the elements. When a plant isn't given the chance to weather things like strong winds or harsh sun or rain, it doesn't grow strong roots—it's weak. So while it might look good, when hard times come, the plant dies and is washed away. But when a plant grows out in the open where it's got nothing to lean on, it develops deep, sturdy roots. And no matter how harsh the elements, it won't die."

"You care to interpret that, Mr. Miagi?"

She ignored my attempt at humor. "People are the same way. Sometimes we need to brave the world and get knocked around a bit so that we can develop character and worth. It may seem like the honorable thing is to keep on shading someone from life's scrapes and bruises, but in the end, you're only enabling the person to stay feeble. And one day, no matter how hard you try, you won't be able to protect that person from some major crisis, because it'll be bigger than even you can handle."

"But you're not a plant. You're a human being. Plants may not need walls, but people need people."

She closed her eyes in frustration, her jaws clenched together.

"You're not even trying to understand me."

That was it. I'd about had it. She had no idea how hard I was trying to understand. I wanted more than anything to pick up what she was putting down, but she was talking in riddles, and I was sick of it.

"I'm trying my hardest to work with you, Trina." I tried to control the volume of my voice. "But I need you to speak in plain English. Call a spade a spade. You want me to not judge? Fine! But don't make me sit through some mythological story about an old hag at a well. You want me to back off and let you work through your own traumas? No problem! But just say that. Don't sit there and spew some Gandhi, Zen-like bull about plants and walls."

Her eyes bugged. I couldn't tell if she was shocked or furious. Just because she had fallen apart over Darius didn't mean she was a pushover. Trina was only soft when she wanted to be.

I braced myself for her reaction. She stood up and walked toward me. *Oh God, please don't let her take a swing*. She reached past me and grabbed her sweatshirt off the table.

"Where are you going *now?*"

She ignored me, swept her damp hair up in a clip, and headed for the front door.

"Hey!" I yelled. I reached out for her arm, but she snatched it away before I could get a firm grip. She glared at me for a moment.

"Don't ever put your hands on me again."

She was so close I could feel her hot breath on my face.

I took a step back. "Too bad you couldn't muster up some of that confidence a few days ago, when Darius was smacking you around and throwing your stuff all over the lawn," I spat.

She didn't flinch. We stood there for a moment glaring at each other.

"You're a pathetic human being," she said.

Surprisingly, the words didn't sound malicious, just matter-of-fact. Before I had a chance to respond, she snatched the rest of her things off the end table and marched out of the loft.

I was nearly a half hour late. Don was sitting at his desk reading something on his computer screen. His eyes lit up the instant he saw me. It was comforting to see a friendly face.

"I thought you decided not to show," he said, getting up. It looked like he was going to hug me, but he reached out and gave me an uncomfortable pat on the back instead.

"I know, I'm sorry." My gym bag fell off my shoulder and hit the floor with a thud. I braced myself against the open door and tugged off my sweat pants.

"I'm not," he said. He looked down at my legs. I followed his stare and realized that my spandex shorts had rolled so far up that he couldn't see them underneath my oversized tee shirt. I ignored his overture and pulled them down.

"Let's just try and make the most of what time we have left." I knelt down and rummaged through my bag and dug out my bottled water. "All set," I said, and then noticed his disappointed face. "What's wrong?"

"You're kind of giving me the cold shoulder."

I'd only been there three minutes and already I'd managed to offend him. I was on a roll.

"I've just had a bad morning, that's all, and I hate the idea of not training today." I felt flustered just thinking about my last two encounters with Trina. I tried not to cry, but the tears were already on their way. I closed my eyes, took a deep breath, and controlled my voice. "It has nothing to do with you, I promise."

"Hey, hey. Come on now," he said. My eyes were still closed. I felt his arms wrap around me. He kissed the top of my head and rubbed my back. I was surprised. Why was he being so openly affectionate at work, of all places?

"Everything okay in here?" I heard a female voice ask from behind me. I sprang away from Don and turned around. It was Kathleen, a stocky white woman with red hair and blond roots. She had a striking presence because she was so large and masculine. She wasn't ugly, just massive. Her square jaw and broad shoulders were even more pronounced than Don's. She managed the staff on all four floors. I didn't know her personally, but I saw her every single morning and Don had told me a little bit about her. There was a picture of her along with a little testimonial in the hallway by the elevator. She used to be over three hundred pounds and a diabetic. One day, she resolved that she was going to lose weight, so she changed her eating habits and started exercising. When she got down to one-hundred-sixty pounds, she didn't need to take insulin anymore. Eventually, she got into weight training. She won a few amateur bodybuilding competitions and says that now she's dedicated to helping other overweight women meet their fitness goals.

"Yeah, everything's fine," he answered calmly.

"You okay, hon?" she asked.

I knew I looked like a wreck. My hair was matted to my neck because it had started raining again and I'd forgotten my umbrella. And even though I didn't have a mirror, I'm sure I had mascara running down my face. I'd decided to put on a little bit of makeup this morning, since Don and I were more than just friends now.

I nodded and made a futile attempt to wipe my face. "Gained two pounds," I explained, feebly.

"Oh, sweetie, that's nothing. Probably just water weight. Lighten up on your sodium intake for the rest of the day and I promise you, those two pounds will be gone tomorrow."

I was surprised at her delicate, cheerful voice. I just assumed that since she looked like a man, she'd sound like a man. I thought back to Trina's story about cutting people slack and not judging.

"Thanks," I sniffled.

"Maybe you shouldn't work her anymore today," she told Don with a knowing nod, and closed the door behind her.

He gave me his swivel chair and sat down on top of his desk. "What's going on, Grace?" He sounded more like a father than a boyfriend.

"Nothing." I wanted to vent to someone, to get some advice, but there was no way I could talk to Don about it. How could I even begin to explain that my best friend and I had fallen out, in part, because she knew he was married?

"Look, if this is about yesterday or me not calling last night, we should talk about it. I don't want to see you like this. I know it can't be easy for you to watch me go home to someone else, but you have to believe you're on my mind all the time and that when I'm with her, all I do is wish I was with you."

He wasn't even close. The only time I thought about Laura was when he brought her up. I glanced over at him. He had an odd look on his face. His eyes seemed sad and the wrinkles on his forehead gave him a semblance of concern, but his lips were turned up ever-so-slightly. It was a disconcerting mixture of worry and amusement. If I didn't know better, I would have thought he was stroking his ego with the idea that I was falling to pieces over him. His presumption irritated me beyond belief.

"This has nothing to do with you," I said curtly.

His smirk faded. He cleared his throat and folded his big arms across his chest.

"I'm not saying it does. I just hate to see that beautiful face of yours all streaked with tears. I want you to feel like you can tell me anything that's on your mind."

He waited. I guess he was expecting me to spill my heart. I looked over at the little clock on his desk.

"I only have fifteen minutes left in this session. Should I hop on the bike or something?"

"No, you're not in any shape to work out today."

"I'm fine," I said. "See." I sat up and tried to look perky. Anything would be better than sitting there trying to convince him that nothing was wrong.

"You might think so, but trust me, you aren't. I can look at your baggy eyes and puffy face and see you didn't get enough sleep. Exercising is fifty percent mental. You have to be vamped and ready to put everything you've got into these sessions. How are you planning to give me your all, when half of you is still at home, moping over something you don't want to talk about?"

I shrugged. It wasn't even nine and my mind had already shut down for the day. I was too whipped to answer complex questions.

"Don't worry," he said. "I'm not going to count this as one of your sessions for the week. Everyone has off days. You've been here, on time, every morning for almost three months now. I'm not gonna penalize you for having a bad day. Maybe we can meet this Saturday to get you back on track. Laura has to work and Chloe's going to be at my mom's. We could get in a light workout and spend some time together afterward—go bowling, catch another movie, or maybe go back to your place for something a little more intimate."

It was all I could do to focus on what he was saying. I was in a daze. I'd already decided to go for a long walk to clear my head before heading back home. I continued to mute Don out until it was time to go. He was so engrossed in whatever he was talking about, he didn't notice my inattentiveness. My foot tapped nervously against his metal desk. At five till, I put my sweat pants back on and draped my bag over my shoulder, continuing to pretend I was listening.

"I have to run," I said when the clock struck nine. He looked bothered that I'd cut him off so abruptly.

"I'm sorry. I don't mean to be rude, but I just remembered I have to be somewhere in an hour, and I want to go home and clean up first."

"Okay," he said slowly. "May I ask you something?"

"Yeah, shoot." I stood there shifting my weight from one foot to the other, the way toddlers do when they have to go to the bathroom. I stared everywhere—at the filing cabinet, the spotted shaggy carpet, the bulletin board overrun with memos. Everything seemed out of place, including me. I couldn't stand still. The walls closed in on me. All I wanted was to get outside, where I could breathe.

"Do you feel like this is a mistake?"

"No," I said, running my fingers through my hair. "I mean, do I feel like *what* is a mistake?" My lungs were about to explode. I could hear my own heart beating. It was an obtrusive thumping in my ear, matched only by the sound of my spastic, shallow breathing. My mind involuntarily retreated into my body. I could barely hear his response.

"Us. You know, me and you being…close."

"No, no. Don't be silly." I headed for the door, breathless. "I gotta go. Tomorrow, okay?"

I didn't wait for him to say goodbye. I dashed to the elevator and pushed the button. No time, needed air. I spun around and bolted out the emergency exit into the stairwell and took the steps two at a time all the way to the first floor. I ran past Jason, who was behind the front desk, and burst out of the huge glass doors, into heavy rainfall.

I could hear Jason calling after me. "Ms. Naybor? Ms. Naybor, you forgot to pick up your membership card!" I couldn't turn around. Instead, I gulped greedily at the air, willing my respiratory system to work. I stumbled to my car, got inside, and let out a blood-curdling scream. My tears mixed with rain and sweat as they slid down my cheeks and dripped off my face onto the steering wheel. *What is going on?* I asked myself over and over. How could life seem so perfect one day and so devastating the next? *What have I done to deserve this?*

I parked in front of a local coffee shop and walked to the park four blocks away. It'd been weeks since I'd visited the walking paths that had started me on my journey to self-improvement. It was still pouring outside and my thin tee shirt and sweat pants were soaked inside and out, but I didn't care. The cool rain felt good against my skin. My pores soaked up the water and invited the opportunity to be refreshed. I walked the entire three miles around the deserted park. I took my time. For once, the jaunt wasn't meant to serve as an escape from my everyday life, but a time of solitude when I could really assess the person I'd become. I examined myself, tried to see the Grace everyone else saw. If I was really the pitiful human being Trina claimed, I wanted to figure out how I'd managed to become such an awful person. I wanted to pinpoint the problem and fix it so that life would go back to normal, so that *I* would go back to normal. But by the time I rounded the last corner, my emotional malaise hadn't dissipated. My clothes felt heavy as they clung to my body. I crossed the street and headed to my car. I didn't want to go home, but the sky had grown dark and I could hear thunder in the distance. I had nowhere to hide.

Trina was still gone when I got home. As much as I hated the situation we were in, I was relieved to have the loft to myself. I tromped to my room, leaving behind a trail of wet footprints. My shoes and socks were so full of water that I produced a loud squishing sound with every step. I pulled my shoes off and threw them in the sink to dry. Then I drew myself a hot bath. I had a pounding headache and my nose was stuffy. I hoped the steam would help me breathe.

By the time I'd slipped on a pair of flannel pajama bottoms and a tank top, and dried my hair, my muscles were aching. Goose bumps traveled up and down my arms. I turned down my bed covers and headed to the kitchen to make myself some peach tea. But my throat was so sore, I could barely get half a mug down. A sharp pain shot through my neck each time I swallowed. I gave up on the tea and climbed into bed, propping myself up with pillows, and turned on the television. The last thing I remember seeing before I dozed off was the weather update on the twelve o'clock news. Memphis was expecting heavy thunderstorms for the next two days. *Perfect writing weather*, I thought, as I closed my eyes.

When I rolled over and looked at the clock, it was after five. I'd slept all day. I was freezing, but my neck and back were covered in sweat. I had a fever. One of Trina's favorite bands blared from the radio in the office. I wondered how long she'd been home. I wanted to talk to her, to ask how her day had gone, but I was scared. There were already too many hurtful words between us. Which words would mend the tear in our friendship? Earlier this morning when I tried to resolve things, I only made them worse. It would be best for me not to confront her until I was sure I could understand what she'd been trying to tell me. Somewhere in the course of our friendship, we'd grown up and grown apart. I wanted us to grow together again and accept whatever changes came as a result, but before I could tell her that, I needed to repair myself. I needed to hone in on the parts of my personality that needed work and decide whether or not I was willing to change.

I got up and rifled through my medicine cabinet for something to alleviate my cold symptoms, and found nothing. I rarely got sick, and never felt the need to stock up. The only thing I had were some over-the-counter generic painkillers that I took for cramps. I was debating whether to ask Trina if she would mind running to the drugstore for me when I heard a knock on the door. I waited to see if Trina was going to get it. Whoever it was knocked again. She probably couldn't hear over the music blasting from her stereo.

I pulled on a sweatshirt and went to answer the door. It was Mike with a guy I'd never seen before. His friend looked to be in his mid-thirties. He was short and white with a receding hairline. His glasses were speckled with raindrops and his black trench coat was soaked. Mike was wearing a baby blue dress shirt and black slacks. His dreadlocks hung loosely around his face. He was holding a bouquet of white roses.

I love white roses. They are, by far, my favorite flower.

"Hey," he said, with a broad smile. "How come you're not dressed? Our reservations are at six."

I felt like I was in the twilight zone. I didn't remember making any plans with Mike.

"Excuse me?"

"This is Ronald," he said, introducing me to his friend. "Ron, this is Grace."

"Nice to meet you." Ronald extending his hand. "I've heard a lot about you. All good, of course."

"Nice to meet you, also." I shook his cold, wet hand.

"You don't look too good," Mike pointed out. "Coming down with a cold?"

"Seems that way," I answered. I was so congested that all my words came out through my nose.

"We can always reschedule for another night," he offered.

"I'm so sorry, and maybe this is just because I'm sick, but I don't remember us making any plans."

"Didn't Trina tell you?" He looked confused. He obviously had no idea that Trina and I were in the middle of our own personal WWIII.

"Tell me what?" I asked, trying to sound as if the mix-up was just a lapse in communication. Mike looked at Ronald, who just shrugged his shoulders.

I smiled.

He tilted his head and looked at me sideways. "Are you joking?"

"I wish I were. I hate being the last one to know things."

Mike just stared at me, studying my face. I knew he knew something wasn't right. He saw straight through me. The concern in his eyes nearly brought me to tears. He was genuine, unlike Don, who was more concerned about being chased than he was with my well-being.

I fumbled for an explanation. "I've been sleeping all day. You know, the cold and all. I guess she didn't want to wake me." My chin started to quiver and I felt my eyes become moist.

"Yeah, I'm sure that's it," Mike said gently. Ronald didn't seem to notice the solemn undertone of the conversation.

"Well, better late than never, right? We're celebrating Trina's new job. She's now the Director of Child Psychology at Home Sweet Home," he announced.

"Home Sweet Home?"

"Yeah, it's a child placement service. The program works hand in hand with the Memphis foster care system. They try to find the most compatible foster parents for children who belong to the state. The idea is to make the experience as trauma-free as possible for the kids. You know, make sure siblings don't get split up and things of that nature."

A feeling of agony swept over me, and my fingertips started to tingle. Under normal circumstances, she would have told me good news as soon as she got home, whether I was asleep or not. How could things have gotten so bad between us? The new job was a big deal. It would be the first time since she'd graduated that she'd be using her degree. For a few years after college, she'd worked for a temp agency to help support herself, but mostly, she'd lived off Arlene and Darius. Ever since I can remember, she'd wanted to be a child psychologist. And despite our present circumstances, I was ecstatic for her.

"Wow," I whispered. "That's unbelievable. She must be beside herself. How did all of this happen?"

"God's timing, I guess," Ronald offered. "Mike introduced us at church and she mentioned her interest in psychology. I knew a friend who knew a friend. You know how these things go. She was in the right place at the right time."

"We made plans to take her to dinner at The Pier," Mike explained. "I made the reservation for four. I just assumed you'd be coming."

All I could do was nod.

"There's still time for you to change," Ronald said. "We were going to leave a little early because of the rain, but we can wait."

That's when I realized that they were still standing in the outside hall.

"God, I'm sorry. I don't know what's wrong with me. Come in, come in." I stepped aside.

"That's not necessary," Trina said, behind me. "I'm all set."

"Hey, beautiful," Ronald said, spreading his arms open for a hug. Trina walked over and embraced him. "Congratulations!"

She looked fantastic in her wide-leg silk slacks and red lace top. Her hair was pulled up in a French twist and she had two tasteful diamond studs in each ear.

"Trina," Mike said, once she and Ronald had separated. "Would you rather take a rain check and go another time when Grace is feeling better?"

She turned to me, one eyebrow up. "You're sick?" she asked. Her tone was one of irritation, not sympathy.

I shook my head. I didn't have the nerve to speak. It was the first thing she'd said to me since informing me that I was a pathetic human being.

"I'm fine," I said quickly, without looking at her.

"Please," Mike jumped in. "You sound horrible. I would feel bad leaving you here like this."

"Fine," Trina snapped. "I'll stay. We'll go another time. Is that what you want?"

I thought she was talking to Mike until I looked up and saw her glaring at me. She couldn't have sounded more inconvenienced if she'd just come out and said that I was ruining her special evening. I wasn't used to her treating me so cruelly. After all these years, I finally knew what it felt like to be on the wrong side of Trina's wrath. She was merciless. I bit my lip to keep from crying.

"'Course not," I whimpered, blinking back tears. I rubbed the back of my neck and coughed a little. All three of them stared at me. Mike was concerned, Trina was furious, and Ronald was either oblivious or confused. I was humiliated and hurt, but I refused to break down. "Have a great time. And congratulations on that new job." I glanced up at her, our eyes locked for a split second, and then she looked away.

I patted Mike on the shoulder. "See ya." Without another word I turned and headed for my room. Trina let out a massive sigh.

"Grace," she called after me, but there was no use in turning around. If she invited me to go, it would only be because she felt sorry for me. She didn't want me there and as much as I wanted to take part in her celebration, I wasn't going to force her to include me.

I kept on walking. "I'm gonna get some sleep," I said to no one in particular. Before anyone could say anything else, I stepped inside my room and closed the door. I could hear Trina and Mike's muffled voices. A low wail escaped my mouth as I slid into bed and pulled my duvet over my face. I'd already spent most of the past few days crying. My eyes were sore, but the tears kept coming. They slipped off my face and pelted the sheets.

I was so busy trying to suppress my sobbing that I didn't even hear Mike enter my room. I felt my duvet slowly glide down until it was no longer covering my face. I looked up to see Mike kneeling beside my bed.

"Hi," he said, kindly. He reached for the lamp.

"Please don't," I murmured. Even though it was still early, the room was dark because of the gloomy weather. I knew that it wasn't too dark for him to make out my face, but I couldn't stand the thought of him seeing me all disarrayed under bright lights. The shadows were comfortable.

"Gracie, what's wrong?" No one but Trina ever called me Gracie. I liked the way it sounded coming out of his mouth. His deep voice wrapped around my nickname and made me feel decent again. His big hand cupped the side of my face. He felt so cool.

"It's complicated," I cried. There was no point in pretending I wasn't upset. My tears were dripping all over his hand. He reached up and grabbed a tissue from the box on my nightstand and dabbed my cheeks dry.

"You have a fever," he said gently.

I nodded.

"Sometimes things seem worse than they really are when we're sick."

I waited for him to go on.

"Don't overwhelm yourself," he advised. "Trina loves you. And whatever is going on between you two will get fixed in time. Every friendship is tested now and then. She's not going anywhere, trust me. Just concentrate on fixing what you have control over."

"What's that?" I whined. He was smiling. I could see his two perfect dimples beaming at me.

"Getting better," he answered. "Do you want me to bring you anything? Food? Medicine?" He was sweet. I remembered the other night when Trina said he thought I was beautiful.

"Something that would bring my fever down and stop these muscle aches would be great." I felt uncomfortable sending him on an errand, but Trina obviously wasn't going to help me.

"You got it." He started to get up but then knelt back down. "Hey, would you mind if I prayed over you?"

"Now?"

"This is as good a time as any." No one had ever offered to pray for me. As a child, I'd given up on the whole notion of being able to talk to God, but I knew that at this juncture in my life, prayer could only help.

"Okay," I agreed. He cupped my face in his hand again and closed his eyes.

"Father God, we come before You and ask for You to do a work in Grace's life. I don't know the exact circumstances, Lord, but I can look into her eyes and see that she's grieved. I believe that she and a dear friend are struggling through a hard time in their relationship, and it's taken a toll on her mentally, physically, and emotionally. So, I want to lift Grace up to You right now and ask that You grant her peace. Help her to understand that You know everything and not one thing happens to her that You don't know about and can't handle."

I watched him as he prayed. He looked so serious, so passionate. More passionate, in fact, than I'd ever felt about anything.

"I also want to lift up this cold to You, Father. You have the ability to heal and restore. Touch Grace with Your mercy and completely restore her health. I know that Satan is busy in this household," he continued. His voice became firm, almost authoritative. "And I bind all the spirits that are trying to cause confusion and dismay. And I loose a spirit of peace and harmony. I bind the spirit of infirmity in Grace's body and loose a spirit of healing. Satan, you have no authority here. Leave, now! For God promises that what we bind on earth will be bound in heaven and what we loose on earth will be loosed in heaven."

I had no idea what he was talking about. All I knew was that he was praying to God and yelling at the devil. Ordinarily, my first instinct would have been extreme alarm, but a strange sense of peace came over me while he was praying. It was the first time since Sunday night that I didn't feel burdened. I closed my eyes and continued to listen.

"Lord, I pray a hedge of protection around Grace and Trina. Please restore what the locust has eaten. We thank You for Your mercy and Your love. In Jesus' name we pray, Amen."

"Amen," I repeated.

"How do you feel?" He brushed a strand of hair from my forehead.

"Better."

"Good." He stood up. "We shouldn't be too long. An hour, two at the most."

I nodded. "Mike?"

"Hm?"

"Thanks for being here. I mean, you don't even really know me and you don't have any reason to care, but you've been such a sweetheart tonight."

He put his hands in his pockets and shrugged, looking flattered.

"It's nothing," he said. "And just for the record, I know you better than you think."

"How do you figure?"

"Well, for starters," he bent down and picked up something off the floor. "These are for you."

It was the bouquet he'd brought with him. I just assumed they were for Trina. "A little birdie told me they were your favorite."

When I got up to go to the bathroom, it was just past nine. I noticed a stream of light coming from underneath the door, but everything was quiet. *She must have forgotten to turn off the lights when she left.*

I started toward the kitchen when I noticed a bottle of Nyquil on the dining room table. It had a little piece of paper attached to it.

Didn't want to wake you.
I will check up on you tomorrow.
Feel better, Mike

An instant smile spread across my face. I'd never met a man as tender as Mike. And to think, all this time I'd had him pegged as boring and predictable.

"Gracie?"

I turned around. Trina was sitting on the living room couch in the dark.

"Can we talk? Are you feeling any better?"

I put down the Nyquil and walked over to loveseat and sat across from her.

I wasn't sure how to respond. I didn't know how to approach her anymore. The last thing I wanted was to say the wrong thing and increase the widening gap between us. I decided to keep my answers short. How could I screw up if I didn't talk?

"Yeah, thanks."

"I owe you an apology," she started. "I didn't tell you about the job and I should've. I was trying to be hurtful, which was wrong and immature of me."

I nodded.

"And I should never have said what I said today," she continued. "You're not a pathetic human being. I love you, more than I love anyone else in the whole entire world. I want you to know that."

"I love you, too. And I'm sorry for saying what I said about Darius beating you. I was just angry—not as if that excuses it or anything. I didn't mean it, though."

"I know you didn't."

"I don't understand what's going on between us," I confessed. "I have an idea, but Don is not an issue because I don't want to see him anymore. And I respect your decision to become a Christian. We've dealt with much tougher issues than this. Why are we starting to fall apart now?" *So much for the short responses.*

"First of all, I don't agree with the whole Don thing. I can't tell you how angry I get when I hear you try to justify seeing a married man."

"But–"

She held out her hand and shook her head.

"I don't want to know anything about it. If you've really decided not to pursue things with him, then I'm proud of you. But he's not the big picture. We've got much more serious problems in our friendship, and I know you can't see them because you don't know any better. But I'm in a different place now. And I can't sit back and pretend like everything's okay."

"I understand that, but why do we have to throw away fifteen years of friendship? Why can't we work at whatever is wrong?"

"Who's throwing away anything? That's never going to happen. We'll probably always be in each other's lives. But I think we need to reprioritize our friendship."

"What do you mean?"

"For the longest time, we've been the backbone of each other's worlds. You've been my center and I've been yours. And I'll always love you for that because without your strength, I might not be here today."

"So what's wrong with that?"

She sighed. "The problem is that you aren't supposed to be the center of my world and I'm not supposed to be the center of yours."

"I don't understand. We're more than best friends; we're like sisters."

"I know."

"Well, how is it wrong to establish close relationships? I just can't believe people were meant to go about life completely alone."

"We're not. But everyone who crosses your path isn't necessarily supposed to be a part of your life."

"But I'm not just someone who crossed your path."

"I know. It's not you, it's me. I've put you where God is supposed to be in my life. I call on you for everything. I've never had to suffer any consequences or face any dilemmas, because you've always been there to bail me out. But look at what's happened in just the few days that I mustered up the courage to venture out on my own. I went to church, found God, landed my dream job, and met a man I really like."

"Who?" I asked.

"Ronald." I was surprised to find myself relieved. I was expecting her to say, "Mike."

"Really? He didn't strike me as your type." I'd never known Trina to date interracially. I didn't have a problem with it, but for as long as I'd known her, she'd been attracted to tall, dark, coffee-colored men with broad shoulders and deep, suave voices. Ronald was the exact opposite.

"I know! That's my whole point. Everything is different for me now. Ever since I made the decision to put God first, my whole outlook on life has changed."

"I'm happy for you, Trina, I really am. But why does that mean our friendship has to be different?"

"Because I need to surround myself with people who think and believe what I think and believe. When I'm around you, I feel like I can't be open about my faith. And that's hard for me because I've never been more excited about anything. I have to take you off the pedestal I've put you on for all these years and find the proper place for you in my life. I'm not saying that you're not my best friend. You know me better than anyone else. I'm just saying I think we should spend less time together and more time meeting other people. I want to get to know other young Christians, and I don't think you'd really feel comfortable in that crowd. You need to find what works best for you."

I felt like I was being dumped—only the nip of rejection from Trina was a hundred times worse than it would have been from a guy.

"I can't say that I fully understand, but okay. I want you to be happy. Even if that means backing off."

"There's something else," she said. "I know we haven't really talked about living arrangements. But I don't have anywhere else to go. With this new job, I could have enough saved in a few months to get a place of my own. So, I was wondering if we could agree on rent..."

I couldn't believe she actually thought I would ask her for rent, much less to move out.

"I told you once before, Trina. You can stay with me as long as you want—rent-free. If you want to move out in four or five months, that's on you." I resented being treated like her landlord instead of her closest friend.

"I was pretty sure you wouldn't mind, but you never really mentioned anything about me moving in. So, I wasn't sure how permanent this arrangement was."

"This *arrangement*," I said, "is still a friendship to me. Go explore the world, Trina. Meet new people, reprioritize as much as you need to. But just remember I'm here with open arms like I've always been. Nothing's ever going to change that. Nothing."

Chapter Five

The phone rang just as I was sticking my bagel into the toaster. I picked up the cordless on the kitchen counter and looked at the Caller ID. It was Don. He'd already called six times this morning. He was probably irritated with me because I didn't bother to go to the gym. When I woke up this morning, I realized the last thing I needed was to see him. Twenty-four hours ago, all I wanted—all I could think about—was Don. But today, my wants and desires didn't seem as clear as they had been. My attraction to Don wasn't as strong. His marital status seemed less like a temporary roadblock and more like a dangerous liability. It was as if a spell had been broken and for the first time in months, I'd been shocked with a bolt of clarity that plunged me back to reality.

I couldn't avoid him forever. We had a contract. I'd already invested hundreds of dollars in Don's ability to transform me into a sleek, breathtaking beauty. The irony was that now that my dumpy, oversized body was starting to take on a noticeably leaner shape, I was falling apart emotionally. Before I met Don, I wouldn't have considered looking cross-eyed at a married man, much less making out with one in a dark movie theater. I'd been so flattered by his attraction to me. But all of sudden, the way he handled me that night on our date made me feel cheap. It hadn't occurred to me until now that he spent more time trying to lock lips than getting to know me.

Did he even know my last name?

For the first time since I'd acknowledged my mounting attraction to Don, I tried to put myself in Laura's place. It wasn't hard. All I had to do was look at Trina—except that Laura's situation was even more complicated because she and Don were married and had a baby. I'd never seen Laura or spoken to her.

I couldn't pick her out in a crowd, but I knew she didn't deserve to have her husband snatched away.

I'm not gullible enough to think that if I decided to end my little fling with Don, he wouldn't just find another woman to feed his narcissism. But no matter who he roped into his sick little game, there would always be two unchangeable elements in his life: Laura and Chloe. I wouldn't allow myself to be the other woman—the person who's so unhappy with her life that the only way she can find any sort of solace is by making someone else's life just as miserable.

But I'd created an awkward situation for myself. There was no way I could continue to train under Don. I needed a personal trainer with whom I could be comfortable. There was too much sexual frustration between us. But I'd already paid for six months worth of sessions. I was either going to have to find an excuse to switch trainers or start going to a different gym.

I grabbed the cream cheese from the refrigerator door. The phone rang again. A pang of irritation shot through me. I looked at the Caller ID. It read: *Life Sketch* and listed a local number. *Life Sketch* was a huge illustration company based in New York. My agent had tried to get one of their artists to illustrate for *Simon and Eddie*, but at the time there was a seven-month waiting list. One of their people ended up referring us to another, smaller firm out of Pennsylvania. I didn't know they had an office in Memphis.

At least it wasn't Don. I pushed the talk button.

"Hello?"

"Grace?" It was a familiar deep voice.

"Yes. Who's this?"

"Mike."

I bit the inside of my cheek and tried to contain my excitement.

"Hey, how are you?"

"Blessed," he said. "I was just making good on my promise to check up on you."

I thought back to his little note that was attached to the Nyquil.

"Oh, right! Thank you so much for the medicine, and the prayer," I added. "I slept really well last night."

"I'm glad."

I waited for him to say something else, but the only thing I heard on his end was faint music.

"So, you work for *Life Sketch*?" I asked.

"Why do you ask?" There was a hint of alarm in his voice.

"Just curious. My Caller ID said *Life Sketch*. Trina told me you were a cartoonist or something. You must be really good to work for such an esteemed company."

"You're familiar with *Life Sketch*?" He sounded genuinely surprised. Why wouldn't he? Even though we were neighbors, we didn't know each other that well. He had no idea I wrote children's books.

"Yeah, I'm not as dumb as I look," I teased.

"No, I didn't mean it that way."

I laughed. He was so serious.

"I was just playing with you," I assured him.

He let a sigh of relief.

"The thing is that *Life Sketch* is a behind-the-scenes sort of thing. Usually only people in the business know about us."

"Well, did it ever occur to you that I'm in the business?"

"You draw?"

"No, I write children's books."

"Are you serious?"

"Yep."

"Anything I've heard of?"

"Probably not. My main claim to fame is a children's series called *Simon and Eddie*. It's kind of a small world, actually. We tried to get *Life Sketch* to do my illustrations, but I got put on a waiting list and was eventually referred to another firm."

"I remember," he said quietly. It almost seemed like he was talking to himself.

"You remember? That was almost three years ago. How long have you been working there?"

"Well, I don't really work there."

"You don't?"

"Well, I do and I don't." He wasn't making any sense.

"That's like being sort of pregnant," I said. "Either you are or you aren't."

"I'll have to take your word for it."

I smiled. He was cute when he was being witty.

"So, what do you do for a living, then? Other than *sort of* work for *Life Sketch*?"

"I own my own company."

"Really? What's it called?"

He cleared his throat. I could hear him shuffling papers.

"Hello?" I said.

"What are you doing today?" he asked. It was obvious he wanted to change the subject. That was fine. I was still a stranger. If he didn't want to talk about his personal business, I wasn't going to pry.

"Nothing, why?"

"Are you hungry?" I looked down at my bagel and jabbed at it with my finger. It was hard. My taste buds were shot because of my cold and my throat was still sore. Anything would be better than a stale bagel.

"Famished," I answered.

"I have just what you need."

"What is it?"

"It's a surprise." His cheerfulness was endearing. "Are you dressed?"

I glanced at my shorts and baggy shirt.

"Pretty much," I answered. Mentally, I was frantically going through my closet. Hopefully, I'd have enough time to change. Maybe give my hair a little bump and shave my legs.

"Great. I'll be down in ten minutes."

"Be down?" I asked. "Where are you?"

"I'm at home."

"But I thought you were at work."

"That's one of the perks of being your own boss," he answered. "Just be ready; I'll see you in a few."

I connected the dots as soon as I hung up the phone. Mike was Michael Cambridge, founder and CEO of *Life Sketch, Inc*. I knew from my own research that *Life Sketch* was a fairly new corporation, nine or ten years old. The company had two main objectives. First, it provided quality cartoonists, animators, and illustrators to the publishing industry. Second, it employed hundreds of artists (some of whom, without *Life Sketch*, would have gone unnoticed) and acted as sort of a union for the art world. The artists were contracted at a reasonable rate that was non-negotiable. At the end of the day, everyone went home happy. It was a unique concept, one of the first of its kind.

I dumped my bagel in the trashcan and headed for the bathroom. I studied my reflection in the mirror. My eyes looked tired, my face less friendly since I'd started losing weight. My cheeks used to be round and jolly even when I wasn't smiling. Over the past couple of months, they'd flattened. I looked older and wiser, less enchanted with the world. I pulled my hair back in a haphazard twist and clipped it down. A few stray strands fell against my cheek and framed my face. I tucked them behind my ear.

I opened my makeup drawer and started to pull out all of the bottles and compacts, powders and concealers that it took to make my skin appear smooth and flawless. I had hundreds of dollars' worth of cosmetics and creams, all designed to cover my imperfections and hide the real me. It was an illusion that had started so innocently. I just wanted to hide a spot here, disguise a bump there, and before I knew it, I couldn't leave the house without masking my entire face in layers of foundation, eyeliner, blush, and lipstick. The whole concept was an elaborate head job that millions of people around the world bought into. It was one more way for the masses to pretend they were better than they really were.

I thought about Mike. He was probably a millionaire. But he lived in a small loft and ate Taco Bell. He bought me Nyquil and wiped away my tears. If Trina's story was accurate, he'd gone from an orphan bound for jail to one of the wealthiest businessmen in Tennessee. How did he stay so humble?

I swept all my makeup back into the drawer. I didn't want to hide from Mike. Even if we just ended up becoming really good friends, I wanted him to know and see the real Grace. Not the person I thought everyone wanted me to be. I changed into a pair of old jeans and slipped on a lightweight cotton shirt.

I was tidying up the living room when he knocked on the door. I opened it and there he was, standing in front of me with a dopey grin on his face. He was carrying a plastic bowl covered over with aluminum foil.

"Mister Cambridge," I said, with a snotty British accent. I bowed dramatically and shuffled aside so he could come in.

He smiled sheepishly. "So you figured it out, huh?"

"What can I say? I'm a smart cookie."

"So, does this mean no soup?" He held up the bowl.

"You could tell me that you were Donald Trump's long lost son and I wouldn't turn down a hot bowl of soup. My throat is killing me." I took the big bowl and headed for the kitchen. He closed the door and followed behind me.

"It's not just any soup."

I grabbed a couple of bowls and two spoons.

"It's not?"

"Nope. It's my mother's world-famous chicken soup with rice. Guaranteed to stomp the cold out of anyone in less than a week."

This man was such a paradox. On one hand, he was a successful artist and businessman, intelligent and discerning. On the other hand, he was this big kid who lacked the poise and sophistication you would expect from a man who probably had millions of dollars sitting in his bank account.

"What's your story?" I asked.

"What do you mean?"

"I mean, how did you get here—to this point?"

He looked amused.

"It's simple."

I sat down and leaned in closely so I wouldn't miss a word. It's not everyday I learned the secrets of a rich entrepreneur.

"I just called you up and asked if you were hungry," he said.

He chuckled at the contorted look on my face. His shoulders bobbed up and down, his entire body shaking with laughter.

"Very funny. You know what I'm trying to say. How did you become who you are?" I got up to grab a ladle and some crackers while he unwrapped the bowl.

"How does anybody become anything?" he asked.

"I don't know. It just seems like your circumstances are so much more extraordinary than most."

He looked at me strangely. It didn't dawn on me that maybe Trina had told me all that stuff about him in confidence. "Not that I have the slightest clue what your life's been like."

He smiled that cute lopsided grin of his. "It's okay," he said, taking the ladle from me and pouring two big scoops of soup into each of the bowls. "It's not a secret. I'm not ashamed of my past. All the things I went through were just stepping stones to get me where I am today."

I handed him a spoon and a napkin.

"Grace?" He reached for my hand and looked as if he wanted to confide in me—as if he felt a connection with me and wanted to pour out his soul.

"What is it?" I took his hand.

"No, I mean, do you want to say grace—over the meal?"

I felt like a complete idiot.

"Oh! No, I'm not really good at that sort of thing. You should do it."

"Okay." He bowed his head and closed his eyes. Unlike last night in the darkness of my room, I did the same.

"Dear Heavenly Father, we just want to thank You for this food You have been gracious enough to set before us. Thank You for another day that we're alive and able to praise Your holy name. Please bless this food that it may give us strength to go about our day and do Your work. And I want to give You special thanks for bringing Grace into my life and affording us the opportunity to fellowship with one another. In Your holy name we pray, Amen."

"Amen." When I opened my eyes he was looking at me with a slight smile on his face. He didn't drop my hand.

"So, you don't have any regrets?" I picked up the conversation we'd started before we paused to say grace.

"It's hard to explain. There are things I've done in my past that I'm not proud of. You know? If I had a chance to do it over again, I'd make drastic changes. But then I think my life wouldn't be as full as it is now."

"Kind of like only being able to appreciate the sun after the storm?"

"Yeah, that. But also, I just wouldn't be this happy or feel this fulfilled because I wouldn't have discovered my purpose—my reason for being on this earth."

I nodded.

"I don't know how much Trina's told you about my past."

"Not that much really, just the highlights."

"There's no point in denying it. I was a hellion."

It was hard to imagine that the accomplished, thoughtful, well-groomed man slurping soup in front of me used to be a troublemaker.

"That's hard to swallow," I confessed.

"No, really, I was stubborn—hardheaded." He balled his fist up to emphasize his point. "My teachers labeled me incorrigible. I didn't stay with a single pair of foster parents for more than a month before they kicked me out and sent me back to child services."

"And things changed when you met Earl?"

"You know about Earl?" he asked.

"Trina," I shrugged. He nodded.

"My whole life changed after I met Earl, but not right away. I hated him at first. I only stuck around so I wouldn't get sent to 'juvy.' I remember the night I broke into his shop. It was in the middle of December. I didn't plan on stealing anything. I mostly wanted to get out of the cold. And I hoped to find food. I'd been on the streets for almost two weeks. When I found out my foster family was sending me back to the agency, I snapped and ran away. I was tired of being bounced around. Something breaks a kid when he feels like he's constantly being discarded."

"You think all those families were wrong for giving up on you?"

"No. Let's face it, not everybody is blessed with the patience to deal with a troubled kid. I had a hard personality. I would push and push to test how far a person's love extended. It devastated me and my sisters when my mom walked out. The only way I could make sense of it was to believe she just didn't love us enough. I was too young to realize she was only human. Sometimes we make our parents out to be superheroes. You know what I mean?"

"I know exactly what you mean."

"We're so dependent on them, we don't realize they're just like us, only older. She was depressed. She had three kids by three different men and she was struggling with her own demons." His eyes were shadowed with sadness. "Anyway, I spent half my childhood angry at my mom for abandoning us and the other half feeling responsible. My solution was to push people away before they had a chance to leave me."

"Makes perfect sense." I lowered my spoon to gather another mouthful of soup before I realized the bowl was empty.

"What'd I tell you?" He picked up the ladle and poured me some more. "It's good stuff, isn't it?" He looked so proud of himself and his mother's soup.

"I have to hand it to you, it's delicious." I wasn't lying. Despite my stuffy nose, I enjoyed every savory spoonful. It was full of carrots, peas, rice, chicken, and celery—way better than the canned kind.

"So, you were cold and hungry with no place to go..." I prompted.

"Right. So I roamed up and down these vacant streets in the wee hours one morning until I spotted Earl's car repair shop. There were a dozen other buildings I could have gone to, but I chose Earl's because his side door, the one that led into the alleyway, was mostly glass. I figured I could break one of the panes and walk right in. It was a Saturday and no one would be back until Monday. My plan was to bum around there all the next day. You know, keep warm and figure out my next move. What I didn't know was that Earl and Lani lived above the garage. Years later, Mom told me they'd actually watched me walk up the street, go down the alley, and break into the building. Anyway, I had my backpack with me and when I got in there I decided to steal a few engine parts and try to hock them later for a couple of bucks. After I'd stuffed my bag, I found a sofa in the back and started to doze off. Then out of nowhere, I heard squad cars screeching around the corner. Lights were flashing all over the place and a swarm of cops were waiting outside, shouting for me to come out with my hands up. I was petrified. I think I wet my pants."

A giggle escaped my lips. He raised an eyebrow at me in good jest.

"Sorry, keep going."

"The cops searched my bag, found the car parts, and hauled me off to jail. I stayed there two nights and then on the third day someone posted my bail."

"Earl?"

"Nope. Mom."

"Your mother? I thought she split years before."

"No, not my biological mother. Lani. She and one of the police officers on duty sat me down in this little room and told me that if I worked off the cost of the window I'd broken and the cost of the car parts I tried to steal, they wouldn't press charges."

"Was that even legal?"

"I don't think so, but I was sixteen. I didn't know any better."

"So, you went to live with Earl and Lani?"

"Not right away. At first Earl would come and pick me up from child services every morning at seven. I would work until one or two in the afternoon and then Lani would take me back. After a couple of weeks, I'd work until closing and then stay for dinner before I went back. Eventually, I started sleeping over and only going back on weekends. After about three months, Earl told me that I'd worked my debt off. I burst into tears. He pulled me to him and gave me a huge bear hug. I can still remember how good it felt to be touched after all those years."

"None of your other foster parents hugged you?"

My heart ached for him. Since I can remember, I'd been complaining about my mother and how she chose her profession over raising me. I reminded her of it every time she made me mad, but at least she loved me enough to hug me—to kiss me and rub my face. As a child, those were my favorite moments, when she came home from a business trip and scooped me into her arms and planted kisses all over my face. Those were the moments when I felt truly loved.

He shook his head. "You'd be surprised," he said. "A lot of people only go into foster parenting for the money. They'll hug and kiss on their own kids all day long, but a foster child is nothing more than a monthly paycheck."

"That's so sad."

"It really is. But God blessed me with Earl and Lani, who couldn't have cared less about the money. Turns out they'd already made arrangements to take me. After Earl calmed me down, he told me he had something to show me. We went upstairs to their apartment, and he took me to my new room. They'd cleaned it up—new carpet and furniture, fresh paint. That was beginning of a new season for me." He tilted his bowl up and slurped the last of his soup.

"More?" he asked, reaching for the ladle. I easily could have eaten more, but that would make my third bowl. I didn't want to seem like a pig, but the soup felt good going down and there was plenty of it left. Mike must have been able to sense my internal conflict. He filled my bowl up before I had a chance to answer.

"Can't have you getting too skinny on me." I could have kissed him for even insinuating that I was thin. Maybe I'd progressed from chunky to thick, but words like slender, skinny, and thin did not apply to me—not yet anyway.

"Look at me," I said, patting my bulging stomach. "I have enough meals stored up here to keep me alive for months."

"I think you look great."

My heart skipped a beat. I tried not to smile too broadly.

"I would think someone like you would go for really petite women."

He raised both eyebrows and grinned.

"Someone like me?"

Perfect! I thought. *I should have just kept my mouth closed. How do I explain my way out of this one?*

"Yeah, you know," I said, swaying my head from side to side. "The dreadlocks, the jaw, the muscles." I pointed to his head and then his chest. He let out a hearty laugh. I was extremely uncomfortable. I could feel my face flush with embarrassment.

"What's wrong with my jaw?" His eyes were full of good humor. He enjoyed watching me squirm.

"Nothing's wrong with it. You have that square, chiseled jaw that women fawn over."

"Women fawn over square jaws?"

"Oh yeah, square jaws are up there with six packs." I can't believe I just said that. He howled and nearly choked on his soup.

I was surprised by the satisfaction I felt just by making him laugh.

"What about you?" he asked. His chuckles died down.

"What *about* me?"

"You said *most* women like chiseled jaws and hard abs. But what do *you* look for in a man?"

It was a tricky question. I didn't want to be obvious and name off certain characteristics that I knew he had, but if I listed qualities he didn't possess he might think I wasn't interested. I decided to be as honest and vague as possible.

"I'm not sure." I thought about Don and Stanley. "All the things I thought I wanted turned out to be exactly the opposite of what I needed. I guess the real question is, what do men look for in women? Maybe if I knew that I wouldn't be so confused."

"You obviously have some idea of what you think men want."

"How do you figure?"

"Well, you're not dropping weight just for the fun of it, are you? I mean, you assumed I was only attracted to smaller women, so you must think that most of what men look for in a woman lies in the outward appearance."

"Doesn't it?"

"I don't know. Maybe for some men."

"But not for you?"

"What can I say? I'm not most men."

I smiled.

"You're the first person who's noticed so far," I said.

"What?"

"My weight loss."

"Well," he said, picking up his spoon. "What do I know? I'm just your lowly neighbor, but if you ask me, you're the perfect size."

"Really?"

"Yeah, like my mom always says, 'Nobody wants a bone but a dog'."

"My grandma used to say that all the time."

"Smart woman."

"Yeah. Smart and over three hundred pounds. I just figured that expression was something she made up to make herself feel better."

He shook his head and laughed.

"You're something else." He gazed at me with an unmistakable look of admiration. I glanced over at him and our eyes caught. He was so gorgeous, I could have looked at him all day. I tried to get the conversation rolling again.

"So, you feel like *Life Sketch* was your calling?"

"Yes and no," he said, reaching for a cracker. "When I started out, I was twenty-two, just graduated from college, and looking to illustrate Christian children's books. All I wanted to do was glorify the Lord through my drawing. But it was hard to break into the business—even with a degree. Most publishing houses already had their favorites. They weren't willing to take a chance on new talent. I tried to freelance for a while, but I wasn't making any money. I decided to teach art instead, but God had other plans. Less than a week before I was supposed to start teaching, Earl died in a car accident."

I gasped. That was the last thing I expected to hear. "I'm sorry."

He nodded solemnly.

"He was on his way home from Bible study. It was around nine." His voice was low. "One of those big eighteen wheelers crossed over the median and slammed him head on. The car burst into flames before anyone could get to him. We found out later the driver had been drinking and fell asleep at the wheel. We got a big settlement. I wanted my mom to have it all, but she insisted on giving it to me. With the money she got from selling the shop and what he left to her in his will, she was able to buy a house out in Germantown, and that's all she wanted."

"So that's how you got your business off the ground," I guessed.

"Exactly. I can't tell you the miraculous events that happened to catapult *Life Sketch*. Within three years, I went from a tiny office in downtown Memphis to my own warehouse in lower Manhattan."

"Yeah, I was wondering about that. Why are you in Tennessee when your business is based out of New York?"

"About five years ago, my mom had a stroke. She fell on her living room floor and was there for two days until a friend of the family stopped by to check on her, and realized something was wrong. When the hospital called me,

I was beside myself with panic. I could only get bits and pieces, because there's only so much they're willing to tell you over the phone. All I knew was that she was severely dehydrated and that the entire left side of her body was partially paralyzed. But what got me the most was when Diane, a close friend of hers, told me that every time she woke up, she called my name. She needed me to be there and I wasn't. I was hundreds of miles away and I couldn't reach her because there was a major snowstorm in New York, and the airport had shut down. I had to wait nearly a week before I could get down here. I'd never felt so helpless. The only thing I could do was beg God not to take her before I had a chance to say goodbye."

His voice cracked. He looked down and shook his head. I reached out and rubbed his arm.

"Remember when you asked me if I had any regrets?" he asked.

"Yeah."

"In all the years that I knew Earl and loved him as my father, I never called him 'Dad.' He didn't try to force me. We talked about it once and he told me to call him whatever I felt he meant to me. He was the only father I ever knew and if it weren't for him, I'd probably be a drug-addicted bum sleeping on a street corner somewhere. That's my biggest regret—never thanking the man who saved my life by giving him the title he so rightly deserved."

"I'm sure he knew. Seeing you grow into a handsome, bright man was thanks enough."

"Yeah, but still I felt like my pride had robbed me of something I couldn't get back. I wasn't gonna let that happen with Mom. By the time she got out of the hospital, I'd sold her house and bought the loft downstairs. After some physical therapy, she regained most of her muscle use. She kept trying to get me to go back to New York. I think she felt guilty, like she was holding me back or something. But I couldn't do it. So, I bought my place upstairs and set up a home office. Every now and then I fly up there for budget meetings and to oversee our major accounts, but for the most part, the business runs itself."

"You must be pretty on top of things, though. You've got hundreds of clients and you still remembered my book from three years ago."

A strange look crossed his face.

"If I tell you something, do you promise not to get mad?"

My heart raced.

"Is it really bad?"

"It depends on how you look at it."

"Okay," I said slowly.

"*Simon and Eddie* wasn't put on a waiting list. We have more artists than we can use."

"So then why did your guys refer us to another firm?" I wasn't mad yet, just confused.

"We use a process. There's a team that only deals with the manuscripts. They read the material and decide if it's up to the company's standards. If it is, it goes through to the next step and if it's not, it's sent to me. I read it and if I don't feel like it's something that I want *Life Sketch* associated with, I wait-list it. And another team finds someone who's willing to pick it up."

"Right. So, what you're telling me is that my work wasn't good enough?" My tone had changed. The problem wasn't so much that my series was rejected; the bigger issue was that the man who'd personally deemed it as substandard was sitting at my kitchen table telling me so to my face. It was a poke at my pride.

"Don't get angry, please. I remember reading it. That's how good it was. I can still remember the story from three years ago."

"Of course! It was good, just not good enough to bear the precious *Life Sketch* label," I hissed. I felt bad showing out in front of Mike. The man had brought me soup and just spilled his whole life story. But something had come over me. I felt so inadequate. Here he was, this big-time artist turned business pro, and all I had was a measly children's book series. But as if that weren't bad enough, my books weren't even good enough for his company's illustrations. I grabbed the bowls and spoons and took them to the sink.

"Gracie." Just hearing him call me that turned my anger and humiliation down a notch. "Please let me explain." I could feel his eyes staring at my back.

"I'm listening," I said. Without turning, I rinsed the bowls.

"*Life Sketch* is a Christian organization. I admired your writing style and thought you really had a gift for reaching out to kids, but I couldn't illustrate for *Simon and Eddie*."

"Why not?" I turned around, leaned against the sink, and folded my arms.

"Because *Simon and Eddie* are wizards who use sorcery to solve their problems, and that's not material I feel comfortable attaching my company's name to. It wasn't an issue of talent or quality. It was an issue of morals."

"It's not like they're transvestite gang-bangers that smoke reefer and rob old people. They're just kids who discover they have magical powers. It's make-believe. What's wrong with creating a world where kids have the power to change who they are and make things happen for themselves?"

"I know that's what it seems like. Trust me, I do. But to me, *Simon and Eddie* is just a clever way to package witchcraft and sell it to kids. It takes away the evil aspect of demonic activity and makes it socially acceptable."

"That's how you look at it because you're an adult, but these are kids we're talking about. It's not that serious. To them, it's just another way to escape the pressure of real life."

"Come on," he said, throwing his head back. "Be realistic. If you really believe that, then you obviously have no idea how impressionable children are. You don't think that some kid read one of your books and believed that he could become a sorcerer and wield his world through the power of magic? Voodoo, sorcery, witchcraft—those are real, and they're dangerous."

He had a point. I hadn't looked at *Simon and Eddie* in that light before. When I first decided to write a children's book, my main objective was to create a story that would envelop children, regardless of race or sex, and encourage their sense of empowerment and imagination. Making the two main characters sorcerers opened up my plot possibilities. It was easier to create wild adventures when the boys could just wave a wand and change their circumstances. It never occurred to me that some kids might actually begin to believe in the power of black magic.

But I wasn't willing to admit that to Mike.

"So, you wait-list people whose work doesn't meet your religious standards?"

"I wouldn't say that. Most of our clients don't even target Christian audiences, but their product doesn't conflict with my main mission for *Life Sketch*, and that is to glorify God and ultimately to lead people to Christ."

"Well, if you feel so strongly about it that you would turn business away, why don't you just tell people like me the truth? Why get our hopes up?"

"When I first started, that's what I did, but most people had the same reaction you had. Let's face it, nobody likes to be rejected, no matter what the reason. In the beginning, we just had disgruntled would-be clients, but after a while, people started suing. We had nearly ten discrimination suits one year. One lawyer even called us unethical. So a friend of mine came up with the system I told you about, and that's what we've been doing ever since. Besides, I think more than half our business comes from people who've heard that there's a long waiting list for *Life Sketch* artists, and that some of the biggest names in the industry get turned away."

"I don't know what to say."

"Will you at least come back over here?" His voice was cute and pouty.

I rolled my eyes, dried my hands off on a dishtowel, and sat back down.

"I think we'd make a great team," he said.

"You mean my writing and your drawing?"

"Yeah. Think about it. We could produce some quality stories. Something adventurous but still inspirational."

It was an intriguing idea.

"Maybe," I said nonchalantly.

"You're not upset, are you?"

"No, it's just that I was thinking about trying my hand at journalism. My own column would be ideal."

"Really. See? I didn't know that about you."

"No one knows. It's just an idea. I don't really have any formal training, so I'm not sure if anyone would hire me."

"If it's meant to be, anything can happen. Some of my best artists at *Life Sketch* don't even have high school degrees. A lot of the time it's about raw talent."

"Yeah, you're probably right."

"So, tell me more about you."

"There's really nothing to tell. Trust me, my life sounds like a fairytale compared to yours."

"Great! I love fairytales," he said. He smiled, propped his head up with one hand, and waited for me to talk. He looked like a kid waiting to hear a bedtime story.

"Well, what do you want to know?"

"How did you become the person you are?" He mimicked my question to him.

"That's too broad." As much as I appreciated his openness, I couldn't bring myself to tell him my whole life story.

"Okay, give me one defining childhood moment. Something that changed your outlook on the world forever."

I gazed up at the ceiling and really searched myself.

"I've got it," I told him. "But it's kind of—weird."

"There's nothing you can tell me that would make me think less of you. Just be honest. Come on, *I* was with *you*."

"Isn't is funny the things we remember? How insignificant moments stick with us; and sometimes we can't even remember momentous occasions?" I grabbed a fistful of air to indicate something slipping through my fingers. "I've learned some of life's greatest lessons from the most unassuming people in the most unlikely places."

"When I was younger, I used to love to go to the doctor's office. It was an odd source of delight, but there was something about the doctor, and nurses, and the bright colorful walls and posters that flooded me with excitement. The doctor's office seemed like a welcome escape from my dreary reality. Does that make any sense?"

He nodded. "Yeah."

"The people there doted on me and rewarded my bravery and cooperation with candy and stickers. At home and at school, I was expected to be a certain way, act a certain way, look a certain way, without any incentive."

"What kid wouldn't want to go to a doctor who gives her candy?"

"It was more than just the candy. I loved how nothing ever changed. I could always count on the same routine, in the same place, with the same people. I would hold my breath as I walked into the waiting area. Everything was so bright. All of the reds, greens, yellows, and fuchsias evoked feelings I didn't experience anywhere else. And it didn't hurt that the place was always packed with all types of toys that just seemed to beckon to me."

Mike didn't interrupt when I closed my eyes and tried to picture the office in detail.

"Framed posters hung on the walls, many of cute little animals with slogans printed across the bottom like, 'If you can dream it, you can do it,' or 'Don't worry, be happy.' Even though I saw those same posters year in and year out, each time I read them, I felt a renewed sense of empowerment. They made me feel gigantic. You know? Bigger and better than the rest of the world."

"What else?" he asked.

"Next to the sliding glass window was a small television that played Disney movies. And huddled on the floor, a half dozen curious kids peered at the screen, engrossed in a fantasy world as they waited their turns to see the pediatrician.

"I never sat on the floor with the rest of the kids. I was mature for my age—too mature. I sat in one of the multicolored chairs in the back. I'd watch my mom pick up a magazine and cross her legs and I'd mimic her exact movements, taking care to be just as refined."

"I can imagine," he said, smiling.

"I'd look at the glossy pictures of expensive cars and skinny women. After that got boring, I'd toss the magazine aside, sit back in my chair, and watch the movie. Eventually, my mom complained about the time. I was only eight and even I knew the doctor always ran behind schedule but we'd go through the same routine every time. First, she'd sigh loudly and look at her watch. Then, she'd ask other patients what time their appointments were supposed to be. And finally, she would walk up to the plate glass window, knock, and ask the attendant how much longer they expected her to wait. It didn't matter if the answer was ten minutes or an hour. She'd shake her head in disgust and inform whoever had the unpleasant fortune of dealing with her that her time was as valuable as the doctor's, and that tardiness was unacceptable. It was embarrassing.

"Once, after my mother had finished her tirade and settled back into her seat with a new stack of magazines, I noticed an elderly couple sitting across from us. The man looked oddly disgruntled. When I smiled at the man, he pursed his lips and looked away, sourly. The woman stared at her hands, cupped in her lap. I examined the two of them for quite some time, even though I knew it was rude to stare. I remember thinking how out of place the old pair seemed in a pediatrician's office."

"They could have been there with their grandkids," Mike offered.

"True, but that didn't occur to me back then. A young black woman who was gazing lovingly at the infant cradled in her arms caught my attention, distracting me from the couple. I wondered if my mom loved me like that when I was a baby. I was about to turn back to the movie when the old man backhanded his wife across the mouth. It was such a clean, swift movement, that I wasn't even sure it had happened. I looked up at my mom to see if she had witnessed the same thing, but she just shifted uncomfortably in her seat and kept on reading."

"That's weird. He hit her out of nowhere?"

"Out of the blue. I don't know if anyone else saw it the first time."

"The first time?"

"Yeah. I watched the old couple for a few more minutes, but nothing happened. I'd almost convinced myself that I was seeing things when he hit her in the mouth again. That time, my stomach turned. I knew it wasn't my imagination, because the loud smack I heard when his hand slammed against her lips echoed in my ears. The young black mother I'd been watching just a few minutes earlier and another couple gathered their kids and left."

"Did anybody say anything?"

"No. The old woman, who'd been statuesque until that point, started to cry. But she didn't lash out. You'd think she'd stand up for herself in a public place. But she simply opened her purse, pulled out a tissue, and patted away the blood on her bottom lip, keeping her eyes lowered the entire time."

I pantomimed her actions exactly as I saw them that day. "As a child, I couldn't verbalize the range of emotion that swept through my body. I think it was fear, anger, shame, and nausea, compounded by the tears of a stranger."

"You were that in touch with your feelings as a little girl?"

"No, no," I shook my head. "This is all in hindsight."

"I was gonna say, you were more emotionally mature as a kid than most people are as adults."

"At the time, I felt physically sick. When the old man slapped her a third time, it took all my strength not to leap to my feet and dash to the nearest exit. I could have gone, even without my mom's permission. She would have understood, but I couldn't make my muscles work."

"You were probably petrified."

"No. It wasn't fear. It was that I couldn't bring myself to leave this helpless old woman because somehow, I felt her disgrace, and just by sitting there, I hoped in some strange way to alleviate it.

"So, with blood running from both her lips and nose, the old woman retrieved another tissue and dabbed at her wounds. Anybody within a ten-mile radius would have jumped to her rescue if she had asked, but it seemed like she didn't want to escape him. She couldn't walk away. She was like an abused animal that gets so accustomed to mistreatment, it doesn't know any better."

He shook his head in disgust.

"Just like that," I snapped my fingers, "the doctor's office lost its enchantment. It stopped being my favorite place because this old couple had invaded it—my colorful dream world—and corroded it with reality.

"The tears streaming down my face might as well have been synchronized with the old woman's. I was just this scrawny little girl, but I knew somehow that every female owned that poor old woman's agony."

Mike stared at me with such intensity that I wasn't sure if he got what I was saying, or if he thought I was crazy.

"My mom threw her coat over one arm and grabbed my hand. Even as she tugged me toward the door, I stared at the lady. I kept willing her to look up, which she hadn't done the whole time we'd been there. I can still recall every contour of her face, every wrinkle in her tired, bony hands, but I couldn't tell you the color of her eyes to save my life. I caught a fleeting glance of one of the posters on the wall right before the door shut. It said, 'Knowledge is power.'

"I squeezed my eyes shut all the way down on the elevator. I was so relieved when the crisp winter air scratched my tearstained cheeks. My mom said there are sick people in the world who can only feel good about themselves by hurting other people. I promised myself I would never be one of those people, and that I would never let one of those people hurt me.

"I grew up that day. That old couple stole the last of my childhood. It's not that I didn't know about abuse, but something happens when you see it up close. I don't know. I guess that was a defining moment because when I went home that day, I wrote my first story."

"About the old couple?" he asked.

"Yeah. I needed some way to relieve the pressure, but I didn't have anyone to talk to. Even if I had gotten my mom to stop what she was doing and listen to me, I don't think I would have known what to say. So, I invented a world on paper where the old woman was a hardcore business tycoon who didn't take mess off anybody. I think, subconsciously, I made her just like my mom because she was the strongest woman I knew—still is. And I made the old man her evil husband who was out to take over her business."

I rolled my eyes just thinking about it.

"And you were only eight? You're definitely meant to be a writer. I couldn't put together an intelligent sentence when I was eight, much less make up a story like that."

I shrugged my shoulders.

"Well, anyway, that's it. That's my defining moment."

"Tell me another one," he said.

"What?" I couldn't believe he found me so intriguing.

"I could listen to you tell stories all day."

And so that's what we did. I stored the rest of the soup, fixed us a pitcher of lemonade, and we took turns telling stories. It was, by far, the best day I'd had in a long time.

When Trina walked in at 6:00 that evening, Mike and I were still sitting in the living room. He had me practically rolling on the floor in tears with an imitation of his high school football coach.

"Hi," I said, regaining my composure. I fanned away my tears. "How was your first day at work?"

"Hectic." She tossed her keys onto the table.

I wanted to ask if hectic was good or bad, but our friendship was still in a funny place. I didn't want to press her. So I just nodded.

"I stopped by to drop off some soup," Mike explained.

"Then we got to talking, and I guess we lost track of time," I chimed in.

"Uh-huh. Well, no need to explain to me," she winked.

Mike started to get up.

"Don't leave on my account. I'll leave you two to your own devices." She couldn't have made the situation more awkward if she'd stripped down to her underwear and done a belly dance. "I'm just going to get changed for Bible study."

"What time is it?" Mike asked, looking down at his bare wrist.

"It's, uh," I glanced down at my watch, "just after 6:00."

"I hate to cut this short, Gracie…" he began.

Trina raised on eyebrow. She looked at me and mouthed the word "Gracie," as if she were offended that I let him use her nickname for me.

"But I have to get things set up. People are gonna start showing up in thirty minutes."

"Oh, yeah. Don't worry about it. I understand." A deaf man could have heard the disappointment in my voice.

Trina's face softened.

"Why don't you come, Gracie?" Trina suggested.

Mike grinned from ear to ear.

"Yeah, come. You'll have fun," he promised.

I looked at Trina, who was waiting for me to answer. This was the nicest she'd been to me in days. I wanted to go. Not just to be with her and Mike, either. All their talk about praying and God had made me curious. But wasn't it just last night she'd asked me to give her space? She wanted to start exploring different areas of her life without me. I didn't want to interfere with her newfound interest in God. Even though she seemed willing to share it with me now, I didn't want her to later feel like I'd stolen it from her. I treasured our friendship too much.

"No, you know what? I think I'm just gonna stay here and do some writing."

"You can write anytime," she said.

"Yeah, but this is your thing. Remember?" I tried to remind her what we'd spoken about last night, without divulging our business to Mike.

"I remember," she nodded. "But maybe I was wrong."

It felt good to hear her say that. I hoped it wouldn't take long for her to realize that we didn't have to spend less time together in order to meet other people. I smiled.

Mike looked baffled. "So then, you're coming?" he asked, his tone a mixture of hope and hurriedness.

"No, maybe another time. But thanks for the invitation." The disappointment on their faces made me feel special.

After they'd gone, I had another bowl of soup, washed out the rest of the dishes, and took a long hot shower. I made myself a cup of tea and headed to my office. My computer was sitting on my desk like it had been since I'd moved in, looking foreign. I grabbed a paper towel and wiped away the dust that had accumulated on the screen. As I listened to it start up, I felt like I was returning home.

Spending the whole day telling stories had renewed my imagination. I didn't want to be a journalist. Real life issues didn't interest me as much as creating my own stories. As my fingers started tapping away on the keyboard, my mission in life became crystal clear: I wanted to be a novelist. Before today, I didn't have the courage to attempt such a feat. Writing a full blown tale so intriguing that people would pay to read it seemed unattainable.

But I never thought I'd meet a man like Michael or nearly lose my friendship with Trina, either.

Life, I was starting to realize, is anything but predictable. Some opportunities present themselves for a flicker of time and then they're gone, while other people and things I take for granted, assuming they'll always be there, vanish. There would never be a better time to write a novel than now.

I thought about my budding relationship with Mike and how my friendship with Trina was slowly returning to normal and smiled.

Who knows? Anything's possible.

Chapter Six

The next few months flew by. All the parts of my life that had started to fall apart were being carefully pasted back together. Trina and I were back to normal. The turning point was when I decided to let her take all the initiative in our friendship. I stayed sweet and helpful, but if she wanted to talk or go out somewhere, I made her ask. As soon as I stopped chasing our friendship, she came back to it on her own. I hadn't been to Bible study yet. Mike kept trying to persuade me to go, but I'd promised Trina I would respect her space, and I wanted her to feel like she had another source of friendship and support besides me. At first, the idea of her not being able to tell me certain things was threatening. I'd become too accustomed to dropping everything whenever she needed a listening ear or a comforting shoulder. After a couple of weeks, though, I was relieved to get a break from her daily drama. Her new job was rewarding, but dealing with emotionally stunted kids made her discouraged a lot of the time. On occasion, she told me some of the kids' stories. Mike had nothing on *them*. I even got downhearted listening to their traumas.

So, on Tuesdays and Thursdays when she headed up to Mike's place for Bible study, I relished the calm peace of my quiet loft. During those few hours, I got some of my best writing done.

My book was coming along slowly. I had sketched a blueprint of a plot and was toying around with different concepts and ideas. I found out early how much research is involved in writing a novel. But the entire process is enjoyable and I refused to lose my enthusiasm. The few times I found myself frustrated, I just shut everything off and turned my attention to something else.

Or I called Mike.

Mmmm. Mike. Ever since that night he prayed for me, I couldn't think about him or say his name without smiling. We've been seeing a lot of each other lately. Our relationship hasn't really been defined, though. I think we're both apprehensive about labeling what we have. Technically, we're friends, but I want us to be more. I think he does, too, but right now what we have is comfortable. Sometimes, when I'm out with Trina, I find myself wishing I was with Mike. It's not that I don't enjoy spending time with her, but Mike makes me feel like life's opportunities are limitless.

When I told him I was attempting to write my first novel, he was ecstatic. I felt inspired knowing he had faith in me.

"Just don't forget about us little people when you make it big," he teased, as we walked in the park across the street from the lofts. I hit him playfully in his stomach.

"Whatever," I said.

He grabbed my wrist and pulled me to him. Without saying a word, he gently rubbed my cheek and then bent down and kissed me. It was a pure and innocent attraction, one that had developed over time. Mike had pinpointed things about me that he admired—things that made him want to be close to me. It wasn't anything like I'd experienced with Don, who only wanted me to fill a void that his marriage couldn't fix. Don made me feel cheap, while Mike made me feel cherished.

As he held me close—one hand pressed against my back, the other affectionately caressing my cheek—my heart soared. When we finally parted, I was breathless and alert. The trees were taller and greener, the sky brighter, and life itself had more meaning. We looked at each other for a second. I tried to hold in my emotion until I could figure out what he was feeling, but I couldn't help smiling. Once he realized he hadn't crossed any unspoken boundaries, he scooped me up into a tight, warm hug. I buried my face into his chest and took in his scent.

"I've been wanting to do that for so long," he whispered.

"Me, too."

That happened nearly a month ago. We haven't shared another kiss, but we have other ways of showing affection. Mostly we hug or rub each other's backs. His favorite thing to do is make popcorn, rent a movie, and snuggle close with his legs stretched out on the ottoman, and my legs stretched out across his. He says he never feels better than when I'm near him. I appreciate how natural things are between us. There's no pressure, no assumptions, no expectations. We accept each other—faults and all. I learn something new about him every time we're together.

But the kicker is that as attracted as I am to him, I don't want to have sex. I've spent most of my young adulthood concentrating on men and how they perceived and treated women. For the first time, I've realized that disrespect is a two-way street. I didn't respect Don. The most that might have come out of our relationship was a couple of dinners and a few lusty nights of passion. When I felt like that's all I deserved, that was okay. But Mike made me realize I was worth more than what I could give him behind closed doors. He handled me delicately and treated me with respect. And I, in turn, respected him—for so many reasons.

I was in awe of the man he'd become after all he'd gone through in his life. I was attracted to his optimism, his honesty, and his integrity. And I was drawn to his love for God. I'd never seen a man more passionate about anything. Even though I didn't consider myself a Christian, I felt as though his Christianity made him even more of a prize. My physical attraction to him was an added bonus, but sex would only cheapen what was evolving between us.

Really, there was only one unfortunate element in my life at the moment—Don. I hadn't bothered to call him to resolve the issue of my contract, not to mention the mini-nervous breakdown I'd had in his office. For the most part, I could avoid him by checking my Caller ID, but a few times he caught me off guard. Like when he called me from his sister's house.

"Grace? Finally! I've been trying to reach you for weeks."

"Don?"

"Yeah. Why haven't you returned any of my calls?"

"Oh, things have been so chaotic around here lately. Listen, I'm in the middle of a family crisis."

"Is everything okay?"

I looked down at the red nail polish bottle and my half-painted toes. I felt so low for lying outright like that.

"I hope so, but I have to go. Someone's on the other line."

"But, wait, I just wanted—"

"Talk to you later. Bye."

Or the time a couple of days after that when he called me from a pay phone down the street from my loft.

"Grace, this is Don. Please don't hang up," he begged.

"Hey, you caught me at a bad time."

"I need to see you. I'm right around the corner."

"I'm sorry. I had a death in the family. I have to go pick up some relatives from the airport." It wasn't even a good lie, because my entire family lived in Detroit. If anyone died, I would be flying there. But he was too dense to catch that little slip.

"Well, when can I see you?"

"I don't know. Give me a couple of weeks for things to calm down. I'll call you."

"Promise?"

I ignored the question.

Other than that, most of his correspondence was through voicemail. He left me several every day. They ranged in emotion. At first, he was concerned about my well-being.

"I haven't heard from you and I'm really worried. Please call. We don't have to talk. I just want to put my mind at ease, and I can't do that until I hear your voice."

Next, he was a little offended that I couldn't find the time to return his phone calls.

"It's pretty inconsiderate for you to just rush out of here one morning and then not even bother to call and explain yourself."

Then, he was just plain ticked off.

"Look, time is money. I could have filled your 8:00 slot weeks ago. I don't have time for this, Grace. You signed a contract. I've been pretty understanding up till now, but if you don't call me and let me know what is going on, I'm gonna start charging you for all the days you've missed up to this point. You're only hurting yourself. You've probably gained back half the weight you lost, and if that's the case then you can go find someone else to waste his time on you, because I take this business seriously. Your progress and the way you look are a reflection on me and my skills. And you're kidding yourself if you think I'm gonna let you make me look bad."

Finally, he was empty without me.

"Grace, baby, I'm sorry about blowing up on you like that. I'm just frustrated. Can you understand that? I have a lot going on right now. Laura and I aren't getting along. And not knowing where you are and if you're okay is starting to drive me crazy. All I want is to hear your voice. I keep thinking about the day we spent together. You remember? We went to a movie and played pool. I'd give anything to be close to you like that again. If I did something wrong or gave you the wrong impression, just call me so we can fix it. Please call me."

And then the cycle repeated itself. I considered changing my number, but so many people had my current one. Plus, I didn't want him to show up at my building one day. At least my voicemail was acting as a sort of decoy. I knew I needed to talk to him, and that hiding behind my Caller ID and a rash of lame lies was childish. But I had nothing to offer Don, not even an explanation.

Luckily, I was still shedding pounds at a steady rate. I didn't own a scale, so I didn't know exactly how much weight I'd lost, but my clothes fit looser by the week and my slight double chin had completely disappeared. After I resolved not to go back to Don, I made up my own exercise and diet plan. The diet part was simple. I ate whatever I wanted as long as it was reasonably healthy, but I only let myself eat when I was hungry. Most of my weight gain had been due to stress. I used to eat whenever my emotions were running high, and I wouldn't stop until I felt sick. It wasn't as hard as I thought it would be to restrict myself to three meals a day and two light snacks.

In place of going to the gym, I started walking again. Mike went with me sometimes. We'd meet at my place at seven, walk for a couple of hours, and then I'd fix us breakfast. He understood my desire to lose weight, but he didn't agree with it.

"There is such a thing as being underweight," he told me once, while we were out walking. The weather was perfect—no humidity and a light breeze.

"Mike, look at me. That's not something I have to worry about."

He shook his head.

"I wish I could rewind your life and strangle whoever it was that made you believe you weren't beautiful."

"You'd have a lot of people to strangle."

"I just think people are meant to be certain sizes. You're not a small woman, Grace." He stopped walking and picked up my wrist. "Look at this." I had notoriously thick wrists. "You don't have a small frame. You're not supposed to be some one-hundred-pound waif."

"I know that. I'm not trying to get skinny. I just want to get down to a comfortable weight." We started walking again.

"Well, to be honest, I think you looked better with more meat on your bones."

"So, if I stopped trying to lose weight today and just maintained, you think I would be the perfect size?"

"I think if you gained a couple of pounds back and maintained *that* weight, then you'd be the perfect size."

"Are you trying to say…I mean, so you're not…" I didn't know how to phrase the question. Basically, I wanted to know if he was attracted to me. Luckily, he knew what I was trying to ask.

"What I'm saying is that you're beautiful to me no matter what size you are. I would be attracted to you if you were two hundred pounds or one-hundred-twenty pounds. I just don't want you to overdo it. You don't even know how much you've lost. At least go to a doctor and find out what the ideal weight is for someone your height and stature."

Instead, I got on the Internet and found a chart. I was five feet, seven inches. The average weight for my height was one-hundred-thirty pounds. All I had to do was buy a scale. I also wanted to pick up a smaller pair of jeans and maybe a couple of shirts.

The next day, Mike had to drive out to Arkansas to meet some clients and I didn't feel like walking alone. So I decided to have a leisurely morning. I read the paper, made myself a spinach omelet, and watched a couple of talk shows.

I headed out to Oak Court Mall around eleven. I walked in and out of the department stores, looking at clearance items. But after nearly an hour of browsing, I hadn't found anything I liked. I gave up on the clothes and decided to look for the scale. I located a mall map, figured out where I was, and where I needed to be. I was on the wrong floor on the opposite end of the mall. I turned around to go back to the escalator I'd passed, and standing in front of me with a shopping bag in one hand and a soda in the other was Darius.

We both froze in our tracks. It was the first time I'd seen him in months. Trina and I never went back to his house to get her things, and he never bothered to call. He walked over to me and made a weak attempt to smile.

"Hey, Grace, I thought that was you. I wasn't sure at first. You've lost some weight."

I didn't have any desire to shoot the breeze with him. In fact, if he dropped dead in front of me right then, I would have stepped over his useless, limp body and been on my way.

"I'm in a hurry," I said, coldly. "Take care of yourself."

I tried to step around him, but he held out his arm.

"Wait, Grace. Please." He looked pitiful. His shirt and pants were wrinkled and he had a five o'clock shadow. Darius was a pretty boy, like Stanley. His appearance meant everything to him. He was slipping.

"I don't have anything to say to you."

"I know. I don't blame you. I just want to know how she is?"

"Who, Trina? You're a little late. You should've been worried about her after you used her face as a punching bag and then left her locked in your laundry room. Or maybe you should've worried about how she was doing *before* you started sleeping with your boss. I don't know. Just a thought."

He hung his head and sighed.

"Okay," he said, accepting defeat. He looked deflated. I watched him head up the long corridor lined with shops on either side. I don't know why I felt bad for him. He deserved any misfortune that came to him. But he was still a friend. I grew up with Darius, and even though I hated him for what he'd done to Trina, my heart ached for him. He was obviously falling apart.

"Darius, wait." He turned around and looked at me sadly with those big, dark brown eyes. "Do you have plans?"

"No," he shrugged.

"You wanna get a bite to eat?"

"Table for two?" the lanky, auburn-haired waitress asked. She was tall with the body of a twelve-year-old. I wondered why she was wasting her time herding people to tables when she could easily be a model.

"Yes."

"Smoking or non?" I looked over at Darius. He was zoned out. I'd tried to get some input on where he wanted to eat, but he didn't care. So, I picked a quaint little Mexican restaurant across the street from the mall.

"Non," I answered for both of us. She consulted her seating map.

"Right this way," she said. We followed her to the back of the restaurant where she handed us our menus. Then she scurried off to greet the next set of patrons.

I turned to Darius.

"So, how've you been?" I asked, unsure how to start the conversation.

"Things have never been worse." He wouldn't even look up at me.

"Look, Darius. I'm not really sure what you want me to say. I think you know my opinion on the whole matter."

He nodded.

"Whatever I get, I deserve."

"You don't agree?"

"I agree," he mumbled. "But I miss her. I don't think you understand how deeply ingrained she is in my life."

"I understand. You're just as deeply ingrained in hers, but some things aren't meant to last forever." I'd decided before we sat down to discourage Darius from trying to reconcile with Trina. She deserved better, and the minute she came to terms with what had happened and locked Darius away in her past, things started looking up for her. I felt for him, but my main obligation was to Trina.

"It's not like that with Trina and me. We've been through worse. She just needs time to cool off."

I could see the sincerity in his eyes. He was in serious denial. Trina hadn't spoken to him or about him since the morning he'd hit her. That was over three months ago.

"Listen, I don't want to spread my girl's business all around, but as a friend, I'm telling you, it would best for everyone if you moved on."

Just then our waiter came over. He was a fat, pimple-covered kid with braces and greasy hair.

"Y'all know what you wanna order or do you need some more time?" he asked, with a southern drawl. Both of our menus were still closed, lying flat on the table in front of us.

"Maybe a few more minutes."

"Can I get either one of ya somethin' to drink?"

"An iced tea with lemon?" I asked.

"Alrighty." He scribbled on a notepad. "And you, sir?" His pencil was poised in the air. Don was staring out the window, absently ripping paper napkins into tiny shreds and rolling them into little balls. The waiter looked at me.

"He'll have a Coke."

"Right," he said, jotting the order down. "So, we got an iced tea with lemon and a Coke. I'll be right back with y'all's drinks."

He must be new, I thought. I'd done some waitressing in college. All the rookies made the mistake of paying too much attention to detail. The first couple of weeks, they were really uptight—tried to be meticulous. But as the weeks wore on and they realized that fast service meant more tables and more tables meant more tips, the pad and pen went out the window.

"So, she's met someone else," Darius said, putting down the napkin. I skimmed the menu's lunch specials. I was leaning toward the vegetable fajitas. If someone had told me that I would be voluntarily ordering a meatless dish at a Mexican restaurant one day, I would have bet everything to prove him wrong. I couldn't help but eat healthily. My body was taking shape and everyone was noticing. There was no food in the world that I craved enough to hinder that progress. I glanced up at Darius. He was waiting for an answer.

"I didn't say she met someone else. Don't put words in my mouth."

"Come off it, Grace. It doesn't take a rocket scientist to read between the lines."

"It's not what you think," I tried to explain. "I mean, okay, yes. She's seeing someone, but that has nothing to do with why I think you need to go on with your life and leave her alone."

Truthfully, that was a big part of it. Ronald and Trina spent just as much, if not more, time together than Mike and I did. At first, I didn't know what to think of Ron, not because he was white, but because he didn't seem to fit Trina. But over time, I got to see the two of them together—how they interacted with one another—and I realized Trina couldn't have *invented* a nicer guy. Last month, the four of us—Mike, Ron, Trina and I—started a Friday movie night. We all meet at my place at around eight, order in, and watch a couple of movies. We talk, tell jokes, and just enjoy each other's company.

"Whatever. Look, you wanna be a friend? Then don't patronize me."

"I'm not. Trina is not the same woman she was when the two of you fell out. She's dedicated herself to God and gotten a really good job. She's happy and more confident now. Obviously, I can't tell you what to do. I'm just saying that the girl you're sitting here falling apart over doesn't exist anymore."

The waiter came back, carrying our drinks on a tray. *Poor guy*, I thought, as he teetered up to the table, trying to keep the glasses from tipping.

"All ready to order?" he asked, setting the drinks down.

"Yes. I'll have the vegetable fajitas with no mushrooms and no sour cream." He scribbled my order, speaking every word as he wrote it.

"And you, sir?"

"Just another refill on my Coke," Don answered.

"Okay, your orders should be out shortly." The waiter stuck his pad in his apron, tucked the tray under his arm, and headed back to the kitchen.

"So, she likes her new job?"

"Yep. I've never seen her more excited. She's working with troubled kids."

"What, like a therapist?"

"Yeah."

He nodded his head slowly.

"Good for her. Doesn't surprise me, though. That's what she's always wanted to do."

"The job stresses her out sometimes, but you know Trina. She loves a challenge."

"Where's she working?"

A few years ago, Darius had gone to the temp agency where Trina worked and caused all sorts of problems. They'd had a fight and she wouldn't return his phone calls. He insisted that the agency knew where she was and he refused to leave until someone told him. Actually, she and Arlene had gone to Chicago for the weekend. But all he knew was that nobody was answering the phone or the door. The agency had to call the police and have him removed from their property.

There was no way I was going to tell him about Home Sweet Home.

"Look, the point is that she's finally doing something for herself."

"Who's this guy she's seeing?"

"Nobody you know."

"What's his name?"

I shot him a cynical look.

"You know I'm not about to tell you, so why are you asking?"

"What difference does it make if I don't know him?"

I guessed just a first name wouldn't hurt anything.

"Ronald."

"Ronald? Sounds like a loser."

Yeah, like Darius is the name of champions.

"Well, he's not. He's a nice guy, and he does right by her."

"I don't care!" He slammed his hand against the table. "I don't care who he is or what he's like. Trina and me, we have a history. Nobody can touch that."

"Be honest with yourself. Do you think your history has been mostly good or bad?"

He rolled his eyes.

"Every relationship has troubles. Getting through all our bad times together made us stronger. We love each other."

"I see you don't plan on answering my question, but that's okay because you know what the answer is. I'm just gonna break it to you straight. I've known you for a while, and I've known Trina my whole life. Quite frankly, I don't think she loves you anymore."

Part of me regretted saying it because I wasn't one hundred percent sure it was true. But I *did* know she would never go back to him—ever.

"Come on, Grace. You expect me to believe that? You can look at your own life and know that's not true."

"What are you talking about?" I resented how Darius was turning the conversation onto me. Shifting the focus—that was always his specialty.

"You can't tell me that if Stanley walked through that door right now and asked you to give him a second chance, you wouldn't take him back in a heartbeat."

"Yeah, well, you're wrong."

He's just trying to throw me off guard.

"Whatever. You and old dude called it quits, what, four years ago?"

"Three," I corrected him.

"And you still talk about him every chance you get."

"That's not true, and you know it."

"Please! You compare every guy you see to him. If we sat here long enough, you'd start telling stories about the good old days when Stanley did this and Stanley did that."

My ex-boyfriend bore no relevance to the topic at hand.

"First of all," I said, doing my best to sound authoritative. "The only reason I'd ever compare another guy to Stanley is that he's the only boyfriend I've ever had."

Don and Mike popped into my head. What label did they fit under?

"If you say so," he said, facetiously.

"And second," I continued, ignoring his cavalier attitude. "I don't think what Stanley did to me was half as bad as what you did to Trina."

His head flew back in bitter laughter.

"Don't kid yourself. Cheating is cheating. It's all the same."

"No," I said, looking him dead in the eye. "My ex-boyfriend's unfaithfulness does not even begin to compare to you dragging your girlfriend away from the only home she'd ever known, treating her like a virtual slave, sleeping around with your boss behind her back, humiliating her, and then sucker-punching her the minute she found the strength to stand up for herself."

That knocked the smugness out of him.

"I don't need to hear this right now. Do you think she's the only one who's suffered over this?"

Did he think I cared?

"I lost my job, Grace. After Trina pulled that little stunt with Janet's husband, she had my desk emptied and my voicemail disconnected by the time I got to work the next day. I'm about to lose my house. I poured everything I owned into that house and now it looks like I'm going to have to go back to Michigan. Do you have any idea how humiliating *that* is?"

"Sounds like a personal problem to me," I answered, sourly.

"Great. That's just great." He leaned back in his chair and folded his arms across his chest. "I come here thinking you're going to be a friend, but you've already picked your side."

"It has nothing to do with sides. I'm your friend, Darius, but you were wrong.."

"I never said I wasn't. I know I made a mistake. Do you have to keep rubbing it in my face?" His volume was rising.

"What do you want me to do?" I asked, in a hushed tone. "Do you want me to run over to Trina and beg her to forgive you? Do you want me to try and convince her to go back to you? Make her believe that you're the best she can do?"

"It's a thought."

"Well, you can forget it."

"Why?" He whined.

"Because I would be lying. I don't want to see Trina with you anymore. You've damaged her in too many ways. You'll never appreciate her like she deserves. I don't think you know what to do with a woman like Trina. She's too good for you."

"Right. So it was all me, then. She never did anything wrong the entire time we were together?"

"Of course she did. You're bad for each other. The only difference is that Trina's finally opened her eyes and realized it."

"So, that's it? You're not going to help me."

"If I thought anything good would come out of it, I'd be out there trying to play Cupid right now. But that's not going to happen."

"You know, I pretty much knew it was over when she didn't call. She always calls after every fight, no matter what."

I thought back to Trina's reaction the day I picked her up from the house. She was hurt, but after we talked and she got some sleep, her whole attitude changed. I was surprised by her strength. Darius was right. After a disagreement, she would usually spend most of the day trying to talk herself out of calling him. It never worked. It was like they had this magnetic pull that forced her to go back. Somehow, she'd broken free of that pull toward Darius, and I was proud of her.

"You never know, it might be for the best," I assured him.

"I'm glad I got rid of her stuff."

"What do you mean, you got rid of it?" I remembered how he'd thrown all her clothes out on the lawn. Trina was so adamant about staying away from the house and Darius, she was willing to give up everything she'd left over there. I assumed that one day, when she was detached enough from the situation, we'd go retrieve anything she still wanted.

"I threw out some of it and gave away most of it."

"When you say most of it, you don't mean *everything,* do you?"

"Yeah, everything is gone. I don't know, I just didn't wanna keep looking at her stuff—too disheartening."

"But what about her bed?"

"Salvation Army," he answered casually.

Trina had spent every last penny she had on a beautiful mahogany sleigh bed from the Bombay Company. It was a housewarming present for Darius and her.

"It's the first bed that's going to be *ours*," she'd told me. "I want it to be special."

I couldn't believe him.

"How could you do that?" I asked.

"Do what?"

"Do you have any idea how much that bed cost?"

"Hey, I figured if it was that precious to her, she'd have picked it up sooner. What was I supposed to do with it? Drag it back to Detroit?"

He was serious. The longer I looked at him, the more repulsive he became. I couldn't wait for the food to come so I could hurry up and leave.

"You've got a lot of nerve."

"It's not the end of the world. Didn't you say she had a big, new, fancy job? She should be able to afford ten of those beds by now."

The money wasn't the point. Yes, the bed cost her more than she could afford, but it was the principle. That sleigh bed was the first big, substantial thing she'd ever bought for herself. It was the first thing she could truly call her own. And now somebody else, who has no idea what it's worth, is sleeping in it.

I wish I had known earlier. I would have saved the bed for her even if I had to buy it back from Darius. Trina deserved that bed. She'd earned it. I always thought it would fit perfectly in the smaller bedroom—the one that I used as an office, where Trina had been sleeping. I started mentally rearranging my furniture. My office was sparsely decorated. I hadn't been spending much time in there, so there was no incentive to fix it up. There was just my desk, a chair and my computer, all of which would easily fit in the corner of the living room or even better, in my bedroom.

I bet there's a Bombay Company here, I thought to myself. *And I bet they're still selling that bed.*

I looked at my watch. It wasn't even one. She and Ron were supposed to be having dinner after she got off work. If I hurried, I could probably get everything done before she came home. My blood started bubbling with excitement as I planned the rest of my day.

Our waiter came and set my food down on the table. It smelled delicious, but listening to Darius's nonsense had ruined my appetite.

"Anything else I can get you?"

I looked at Darius. He had retreated into his own little world as soon as it sunk in that I wouldn't try to persuade Trina to go back to him.

"Just a doggie bag and the check."

I drove out to Winchester Mall and sure enough there was a Bombay Company. The bed was sitting in the middle of the showroom. It was adorned with a bright white comforter and lots of fluffy, ornate pillows—a bed fit for a princess.

"Can I help you?" The sales associate was an older woman who wore elegant wire-rimmed glasses and her hair pulled back into a tight bun. She had on a stylish black business suit and open-toed heels. Her nametag read *Gladys*.

"Yes, I'm interested in this bed." I pointing to the beautiful sleigh.

"What size?" she asked. I made a map of the room in my head and measured the wall space.

"A queen would be perfect."

"Okay, let me check and make sure we have it in stock."

"While you're at it, could you see if you have everything that's on the bed in stock also?"

"Everything?"

"Yeah, the comforter, the sheets, the dust ruffle, the shams, the decorative pillows—everything."

"That's not a problem, but if I can just make a suggestion. Some of these pillows are really overpriced." She spoke in a conspiratorial whisper. "You'd be able to find the same type of pillows and get the same effect if you went to a linen store."

I tossed the idea around for a second.

"I'm sure you're right, but I'm gonna stick with what you have displayed here. I'm trying to furnish a room for a friend," I explained. "And this is exactly her taste."

"There are matching night stands and dressers, if you're interested."

"May I see them?"

She walked me to the front of the store. I picked the taller dresser because it had more drawer space and would fit nicely between the two windows. I also picked two nightstands, a regal, antique-replica chair, a big mirror and two large framed pictures of roses. The paintings matched, except that one rose was closed and the other was open. I was going to hang them over her bed as a symbol of how much she'd blossomed.

"Will that be all?" Gladys asked.

"I think that's going to do it."

"Okay," she looked down at her notes. "Just give me a second." She hurried off and disappeared behind a door that read, "Employees Only." A few minutes later she returned.

"It looks like we have everything except the pictures." My heart sank. "But if you want, I can sell you the ones on the floor at a discount."

"Great! Let's do that."

I followed her to the register and held my breath as I waited for the total.

"And how will you be paying for all of this?" she asked.

"Credit." I dug out my wallet and handed her my charge card along with my license.

"Thank you, Ms. Naybor," she said, swiping my card. "It'll just take a minute for that to go through."

I nodded.

"Now about delivery. I know this is going to sound crazy, but I need all of this delivered to my loft by this evening."

She looked at me as if I'd just told her I was about to rob her blind. She was going to need a little persuasion.

"Ms. Naybor, that's just not possible. You see, all our trucks leave in the morning. They load up the day before deliveries are scheduled."

I looked around the store. Except for me, it was empty. In fact, the entire mall, for the most part, was deserted. There was no way every last one of their delivery trucks was tied up. I decided to call her bluff.

"I understand what you're saying, but the friend I was telling you about? She's being flown in from South Carolina. She's dying of cancer," I lied. "It was sort of last minute, and I need to have a place for her to rest. This is her favorite store, so I came straight here. I want to surprise her when she arrives, but more importantly, she needs to have a place to lay her head."

"I sympathize with your situation, but there's nothing I can do."

"Listen. I just spent nearly three grand in here. Surely, you can manage something."

She bit her lip. I used to hate it when my mom coerced people to do what she wanted by mentioning how much money she'd spent or donated to their company. I swore I'd never do it, but I was desperate.

"I'm sorry, I don't see a solution."

"Okay, then. I understand. I guess you can just credit the money back to my charge card." I opened my purse and pretended like I was searching for my wallet. "I'll have to find a store that'll be able to deliver today."

"Well, let's just see if there's any way we can work this out." She reached under the counter and pulled out a white, three-ring binder. I knew she would fold. She wasn't going to give up that commission without a fight.

"Great." I zipped up my purse.

"What's your zip code?"

"38103."

"Is that midtown or downtown?"

"Downtown."

"The gods must be shining on you today," she said, with a smile. "I have a truck due in for reloading at three and he'll be making two stops in Harbor Town, which is right near you—just over the bridge, in fact."

I looked at my watch.

"What time should I expect him?"

"In light of your special circumstances, I'll make you his first stop. So, you can expect him between four and six."

It would be tight, but I'd be able to pull it off.

The moment I got home, I changed into some old clothes and started moving furniture around. I ended up putting my desk and computer in a small nook in my room, next to one of the windows. Next, I mopped the floors and cleaned the windows. I didn't want them bringing new furniture into a dirty room.

I was done with everything by four o'clock. I poured myself a glass of ice water and flopped down on the living room couch, covered in sweat and dust. I took a gulp of water as the phone rang. The Caller ID listed the number as "out of area."

"Hello?"

"You don't know how good it is to hear your voice." It was Mike.

"Hey, you! How was your meeting?"

"It went okay. I'm on my way home now."

"But I thought you weren't going to be in until around eight."

"That was worse case. Things went smoothly. We let out early."

"Good. I can't wait to see you."

"How was your day?"

I thought about my relaxed morning. About Darius, and lunch, and about Trina's surprise. Since Mike was coming home early, he could help me hang the pictures, arrange the furniture, and get my extra mattress set out of the building's storage. Everything was falling into place.

"My day was really good. I'm doing this thing for Trina."

"What thing?"

"It's a surprise. I was going to try to do it all myself, but since you're on your way, I could use your help."

"Sounds intriguing. You know I'll do whatever you ask, but first can we eat something? I'm starved."

Grocery shopping was on my to-do list, but I'd gotten sidetracked and if I left now, I'd probably miss the delivery truck. My own stomach growled. I hadn't eaten anything except that omelet this morning. I'd thrown the fajitas out because they'd been sitting in my trunk and I didn't like the way they'd started to smell.

"My refrigerator is kind of bare right now."

"How bare?"

"Down to condiments."

"Me, too. We're pathetic."

"Let's order in. I can have it set up by the time you get here."

"What about Ron and Trina? You think they'll resent us for eating without them?"

"No, I forgot to tell you. It's just gonna be us tonight. She and Ronald wanted to spend a romantic evening out. I'm not expecting them until later."

"So we get to spend time alone?" The anticipation in his voice was adorable.

"Yeah, just you and me and a movie, if you want."

"Okay, how about this? You order the food and I'll pick up a couple of movies."

"What do you feel like eating?" I asked.

"I'm in the mood for something spicy."

"Thai?"

"That sounds good. What do you feel like watching?"

As much as I couldn't wait to spend a romantic evening with him, I wasn't in the mood to watch a romantic movie. He didn't watch horror flicks and I couldn't stand suspense.

"A comedy?" I suggested. "I'm too tired to think. I want to watch something that'll make me laugh."

"You got it," he said. "I'll see you in a half hour."

Lately, when we're hanging up, I want so badly to tell him that I love him. It's almost an involuntary urge. A couple of times, I had to bite my tongue to keep from blurting it out. Mike is such a great guy, he'd probably play it off without embarrassing me, but I would be mortified if he didn't say it back. I know he has feelings for me, but I don't know if he's in love with me.

I could still hear him breathing in the phone. He was such a gentleman. He refused to hang up the phone before I did.

"See you in a few."

Mike, the Bombay Company, and the delivery guy from Taste of Thailand all showed up at the same time. I answered the door in my robe, my hair wrapped in a towel.

"What's going on?" Mike asked. "I've been out here knocking for five minutes. Is everything okay?"

"I'm sorry. I spent the last couple of hours cleaning and I wanted to take a shower before you got here."

"These guys are here for you, too," he said, pointing to a short Asian man carrying a big brown, paper bag, and a tall white man carrying a clipboard. I dashed to the dining room table and retrieved the money I'd set aside for the food.

"$23.16, right?" I asked the Asian guy.

"You got it," he nodded.

I handed him $28.00.

"Keep the change."

He handed Mike the food and left. I turned to the tall white man who'd been patiently standing out in the hallway.

"You're from the Bombay Company?"

"Yes, Ma'am. Here to deliver..." he looked down at his clipboard. "One queen-size sleigh bed, one dresser, two nightstands, one chair, one hanging mirror, two paintings and an assortment of linens and pillows. That sound about right?"

"That's everything." I grinned.

Mike had a peculiar look on his face.

"Is this all for Trina?" he asked.

"Yeah, she's gonna be so surprised." I clapped my hands in excitement.

"If you don't mind me saying, I think it's a mighty nice thing you're doing," the delivery guy said. "It's rare these days for people to be so good to one another. I just hope that if I ever have to stare my last days straight in the face like your friend, I'll have someone as good as you to help me out."

Mike looked at the delivery guy and then back at me. Gladys must have relayed the fib I told her. I jumped in before Mike could ask any questions.

"Well, it all goes into that room right there." I pointed toward my ex-office. "Are you going to move everything yourself?"

"No, ma'am. I got another guy outside sittin' with the truck. Do you happen to know if this building has a service elevator?"

"Yes, it does," Mike answered. He handed me the food. "Why don't you go ahead and finish getting dressed? I'll show him where it is."

I started toward my room when I remembered the mattress and box spring down in the basement of the building.

"Oh, wait! Do you think you could bring up the mattress set I have in storage?"

"I'm sorry, ma'am, we're not authorized to move anything that doesn't come from our store. It's against our policy."

I rubbed my forehead in frustration. All I wanted to do was get everything moved in and situated as quickly as possible so I'd have a chance to relax with Mike.

"Are you positive you can't bend the rules just this once?" I asked, in a puny voice.

"Well," he wavered. "Since it's for a good cause, I think we can make an exception."

Mike looked bewildered.

"I'm sure you'll explain everything later," he said, heading out the door. I smiled sheepishly.

I changed into a pair of plaid drawstring pajama bottoms and a white tee shirt. Mike went upstairs to change out of his suit. I carried the food, two plates, and silverware over to the living room coffee table. The deliverymen set up the furniture and for an extra twenty bucks apiece, they hung both pictures and the mirror, and cleared out the trash.

"Thank you so much," I said, as they were collecting their tools. "I could have never had it all ready in time if it weren't for you."

"Don't mention it. Feels good to do something like this for someone else. You know, someone who really needs it," one of them said. "All we need is your autograph right there." The other tapped his finger on the signature line of the receipt.

I signed, thanked them again, and let them out. And then leaned against the door. Everything was silent. Mike would be down any second. I had just enough time to admire Trina's new room.

It was gorgeous, even nicer than mine, breathtaking. The furniture fit perfectly. The bed looked exactly how I'd seen it in the store—plush and inviting. Trina had spent most of her life sleeping in a bunk bed Arlene had bought from Goodwill for thirty dollars. Almost everything she owned as a child was secondhand. I knew she would be beyond excited when she saw the room.

I heard Mike come in. He looked great dressed in a pair of dark blue sweats and a black tee shirt. He'd pulled his dreads up, which drew even more attention to his chisled face.

"Are they finished?" he asked.

"Yep, they just left."

"How does it look?"

I grabbed his hand and led him to the room. He flipped on the light.

"Whoa," he murmured. "It's unbelievable."

"I know!" I was proud of myself.

"She's gonna love it."

"I hope so."

"You're amazing," he said, turning me to him. We were still holding hands. "That's what I'll call you from now on."

"What?"

"Amazing Grace." I laughed and shook my head. I couldn't even look up into his eyes, he was so beautiful.

"I'm not amazing," I said to the floor. "Trina deserves this. Anyone who knows her can tell you this doesn't come close to what she's entitled to."

He hooked his index finger under my chin and gently lifted my face so that our eyes met.

"You're amazing to me." His voice was soft and deep. He leaned down to kiss me, passionately this time. His arms closed around my waist at the same time I wrapped my arms around his neck. He pulled me closer. He was like everything I always wanted, but never thought I deserved. I didn't know it was possible for a kiss to make me feel so complete.

When we finally parted we were both out of breath.

"I didn't know good boys kissed like that," I teased.

He smiled.

"Gracie, I want us to be together." For a split second I thought he meant sexually, until he clarified himself. "Just you and me. I know we haven't talked about this before, but I don't want to see other people. You're the only woman I want."

"I feel the same way," I said, rubbing his cheek with the back of my hand.

"So it's just you and me?"

"Just you and me," I promised.

He kissed my nose. "Food?"

"Yes. My stomach's about to start digesting itself."

We spent the evening feeding each other, laughing, and kissing. He was different than any man I'd ever dated. He handled me with such gentle care. With Don, the only way I could determine if he liked me or not was through his physical affection. If it weren't for his wandering hands and his eager, sloppy kisses, I don't think I would have ever known he was attracted to me. But it was different with Mike. I could look into his eyes and tell that he felt something for me. The way he smiled at me and took the time to brush my hair out of my face, how he held me and put my comfort before his own.

I was drawn to him from so many different angles. I loved to hear him speak. I could sit around all day and pick his brain apart about anything under the sun. He was more poignant and intelligent than I'd given him credit for. His opinions and beliefs made sense and his life had value, worth and meaning. He was as close to perfect as a man could get.

I remembered an article I'd read once about the "Perfect Body Myth." Some noted psychiatrists got together and did a study on fifty college kids—twenty-five males and twenty-five females. First, they asked each person to describe the perfect body and of course got fifty different answers.

Next, they ran a series of psychological tests to determine each student's level of self-esteem. The results ranged from blatant conceit to utter self-loathing.

In the third step, they picked the five kids who were the furthest away from their own ideal body types. One kid was severely obese, another had acne. All five thought that if they became the exact opposite of who they were, their quality of life would improve.

The psychologists worked for one year to help the kids achieve their goals. Drastic measures were taken. Three of the five students were successfully transformed into what they had described as their ideal body types.

The doctors then asked each of those three students, once again, to describe the perfect body. Each of the transformed students described almost the exact opposite of what they now looked like.

The experiment concluded that there is no such thing as a perfect body. People we look at every day and admire and wish to be like, are all looking and admiring and wishing to be like someone else. The perfect body doesn't exist. It's a myth that more people than not get duped into chasing. The trick is for every individual to learn what's perfect for them.

I decided the same conclusions could be applied to men. There is no such thing as a perfect man. Women hold out for the dream guy they've invented in their heads. They complain about one man's attributes and then seek out another who's the exact opposite and discover he's not right, either. Stanley and Don were my mythical men—exact opposites and both wrong for me. But Mike, he's my happy balance between what I want and what I could never have hoped to expect. I could reinvent myself a hundred times over and he would still be perfect for me. He'll always fit.

I glanced over at the wall clock. It was just after eight. Running around all day must have taken its toll on me because I found my eyelids getting heavy. Mike and I were watching one of the movies he'd brought over. His feet were propped up on the coffee table and my head was resting in his lap. He was massaging my back, which wasn't making it any easier for me to stay awake.

Trina's key turned in the door and she flipped on the lights. "Oh, sorry, guys," she said, when she saw us on the couch. She turned the light back off.

"No, it's okay," I said, perking up. I didn't want to tell her about the room. I wanted her to walk in and be surprised.

"How was dinner?" Mike asked.

"Nice." Trina smiled over her shoulder at Ronald.

"That's good. I put your mail in the office," I said, trying to coax her into her new bedroom.

"Cool. I'll get it later."

"One of the letters looked important."

She cocked her head and looked at me out of the corner of her eye.

"I'm not expecting anything important. I'm sure it's just a bill."

A chuckle escaped Mike. I could tell by the smirk on his face that he found the whole situation hilarious.

"So, what're we watching?" Ron asked, taking off his coat.

"Trina, why don't you put that in the office for him?" I asked.

"Oh, don't worry about it, Grace, I'll just drape it over the chair," Ron said.

"No. Let Trina hang it in the closet so it won't get wrinkled."

"Grace, are you on drugs?" Trina asked.

"Of course not."

"Well, why are you so fidgety?"

"I'm not. I just want you to hang the man's coat in the closet. Is that too much to ask?" I snapped.

Mike burst out into a thunderous laugh. Trina and Ron exchanged worried glances.

"Is this some sort of inside joke?" she asked, annoyed.

"Would you please just go hang the coat up in the office?"

"Why?"

"Just do it!" I shouted. She snatched the coat off the chair.

"You've lost your mind, little girl." She huffed down the hall.

I jumped off the couch and could hardly wait to see her reaction. Mike stood up next to me, the suspense killing us both.

"Be patient," he whispered.

Ron looked confused.

"Oh, my God!" she screamed. All three of us ran down the hall. Trina stood in the doorway with her hand over her mouth, her eyes wide. She'd dropped Ron's coat on the floor. "What is this?"

"It's your bedroom," I announced, proudly.

She took a few steps into the room.

"Is this...is this *my* bed?" she asked.

"Yes, and no. It's exactly like the one you bought from the Bombay Company, but it's not actually the one you bought."

"I can't believe it. It's so beautiful. Look at all these pillows! When did you find the time?"

"It's amazing what people will do when they think you're dying," Mike blurted out.

I'd told him everything over dinner. He didn't condone my lying, but he understood why I'd done it.

"What?" Trina asked.

"Nothing." I gave Mike a stern look. He winked at me.

"Oh, but Gracie, where's *your* stuff?" she asked.

"It fit perfectly into my room."

"I don't know what to say," she said. Her eyes began to fill with tears.

"Well, you can say you like it," I suggested.

"Are you kidding me?" She had a huge smile plastered on her face. "I love it!"

"Good. You deserve it."

"You know what else I love?"

"What?"

"You!" And with that, she pummeled me to the floor and started planting kisses all over my face. Mike and Ron stood in the doorway, laughing hysterically.

By nine o'clock, all four of us were situated in the living room watching a movie. I looked over at Trina and Ron. He sat on the floor with his back propped against the loveseat and she sat between his legs, her back propped against his chest. They looked so content. Mike and I sat on the sofa. This time, my feet were on the coffee table and his head rested in my lap. I twirled one of his dreadlocks around my finger. At that moment, my life felt full, in a way it never had before. There was no one and nothing else in the world that I desired.

Chapter Seven

My novel wasn't coming along as well as I had hoped. Creating the plot and developing the characters came easily to me. But when I actually sat down and attempted to start the first chapter, only garbage came to mind. For two straight weeks, my routine was the same. I'd go for a walk, take a shower, make myself breakfast, and then sit and stare at my computer for an hour or until I got so frustrated. I couldn't stand it. I was beginning to lose faith in myself.

"Maybe you're trying too hard," Mike suggested, as he massaged my shoulders. I still hadn't told anyone else that I wanted to make the leap from children's books to novels.

Frankly, I didn't care what my mom thought about my writing career, but I also didn't want to sit and listen to her drone on about the grass always being greener on the other side. She'd probably sigh and say something like, "You're an adult, so I can't tell you what to do, but one of these days you're going to learn that everybody isn't meant to do everything. Just think before you leap, that's all I'm saying."

And Trina, God love her, wouldn't understand how much it meant to me. If I told her, she'd just downplay it and say something generic like, "I know you're talented. If you put your mind to it, I'm sure you'll do great."

By default, Mike was stuck listening to me whine about my writer's block. But he took it like a champ. I'd never met anyone with so much patience. *I* even got tired of pouting and complaining about my dry spell, but night after night, he let me vent as much as I needed to.

"How can I be trying too hard?" I asked.

"I don't know. I'm just saying that sometimes you can over-think an issue—give it too much significance and obsess over it till you psych yourself out."

"But this *is* significant," I whimpered.

"I know, baby, but sometimes things have to happen in their own timing." I loved when he called me pet names, especially "baby" and "angel." He'd been giving me nicknames since we decided to date exclusively.

"That doesn't make any sense. Look at my life," I said, throwing my hands up. "I don't have anything else to do. I spend my days exercising and screaming at my computer. If now is not a good time to write, then when is? After I've been stricken with carpal tunnel and need a magnifying glass to read?"

He laughed.

"You're being a little intense, don't you think?"

"It's just that a few months ago when I decided to write this book, I had all these big plans. I thought I was going to be one of those lucky people who manages to write a bestseller in three weeks and then retires."

I was exaggerating, but my disappointment was genuine.

"Come here," he said, pulling me into his warm arms. "Everything that's meant to happen, will happen in time. You have to wait on the Lord."

"I'm sure God couldn't care less about my novel."

"Now, that's where you're wrong. He blessed you with the gift to write and has placed a desire in you to write, so you're going to write. It just may not be time yet."

I wanted to believe him. The idea that my inability to produce anything worth reading was due to God's timing and not my own inadequacies was encouraging. But the truth was, I didn't know if I believed in God. I hadn't been to Bible study with Trina and Mike, but I did go to church with them a couple of times. It didn't do anything for me. I listened to the sermons and watched people fall out in tears and run up and down the aisles. Whatever it was they were experiencing, I could tell it was real. But I still didn't know if God actually existed, or if people just needed to believe that He did.

Still, I didn't discourage Mike from talking about Him. Mike had overcome tremendous odds to get where he was, and I knew he drew his strength from his faith in God. But I was a woman of logic. I believed the earth was round and the moon controlled the oceans' tides, but only because there was proof. God, on the other hand, came with no proof. I couldn't see Him, I couldn't hear Him, and I certainly didn't feel His love for me. Mike told me once that half the battle of being a Christian was finding the will to have faith in God.

"There are moments when things look dire and hopeless," he admitted, one Sunday afternoon over lunch. "You look at your circumstances and wonder where He is and how He could leave you so alone. That's when you have to make a choice. You can panic and do things in your own power, you can get mad and throw your fist up at Him, or you can just let go."

He threw his arms up and leaned back.

"Let go?" I asked. He nodded.

"When you're exercising real faith, it almost feels like you're being irresponsible. That's something Earl told me once." I gave him a quizzical look. "Okay, say you're months behind on your house payment, your car's about to be repossessed, and you don't have any money to buy groceries, but you've been tithing every week, even when you didn't have it to give."

"Okay," I said, letting his analogy sink in.

"You could get mad and curse the Lord, stop tithing, and quit reading your Bible. Or you could trust that God is not a liar and keep going like you always have—keep praising, keep believing. If you choose the latter, I guarantee He'd bless your socks off." He spoke with such passion, the veins in his neck protruded.

Over the months, he'd recounted numerous occasions in his life when he thought all was lost and then at the last minute, God delivered him from a bind. But after each of his incredible stories, I thought of Earl. Where was God when that truck driver decided to get drunk and slam into Earl's car? What kind of God would let that happen? Or what kind of God would let women get raped or children be molested? I wanted to believe in something greater than myself—to know that someone or something all-powerful was out there watching over me. But I still had questions. I still needed proof.

"Well, if it's not time to write," I said, trying to give God the benefit of the doubt, "then what am I supposed to do?"

"Can I tell you something?" He sat on the couch and pulled me down on his lap.

"I suppose," I said, playfully.

"I think this whole thing is more about you being bored than about writing a bestseller."

"I'm not *that* bored."

The truth is I had the *TV Guide* memorized. I spent most of my days watching television and napping. Trina and I didn't see each other as much as we used to. I left for my walks before she got up and by the time I returned, she was gone. She worked until the evening and lately, instead of coming straight home, she went to Ronald's.

Mike was busy, too. *Life Sketch* was in the process of expanding and buying out a couple of firms. The negotiations required him to travel a lot. There were entire weeks when our only communication was by telephone.

"I can see your mind churning," he said. "What're you thinking?"

"I *am* that bored!" I grabbed my hair as if I were going to rip it out. He smiled and kissed my neck.

"It's not that bad," he soothed. "All you have to do is find something productive to occupy your time."

"Like what?"

"I don't know. Volunteer at St. Jude's or go take a couple of classes."

Candy striping was out. I hated hospitals and thanks to my grandparents, I was allergic to old people, but taking some writing classes might not be such a bad idea.

"That's a thought," I said. "Creative writing courses might be just what I need to inspire me."

"You should call around and see," he prompted. "What do you have to lose?" He was such an encouragement, but even more than that, he believed in me. I stared at him in amazement.

"What?" he asked, smiling.

I shook my head.

"I love you." I said it without thinking. Before I could weigh my words—before I could be certain that he felt the same, I got caught in a moment of personal bliss and it just slipped. His smile faded and he narrowed his eyes. I would have given anything at that moment to turn into a lamp or a piece of lint—to be anywhere in the world other than in my loft, sitting on his lap.

"What did you say?" he asked. I avoided his gaze. My face felt hot. I lowered my head and rubbed the back of my neck.

"Uh, nothing," I said, hoping he really hadn't heard.

"Grace," he said firmly. "Look at me."

My heart was pounding so hard, I was certain he could hear it. I looked at him.

"What did you say?" he asked again.

I closed my eyes and bit my lip.

"I said, 'I love you'."

He didn't say anything. I opened one eye and peered at the serious look on his face. *Oh God, what have I done? Just take me now*, I pleaded silently. I felt a sob catch in the back of my throat. It was obvious he wasn't going to respond. I didn't know what was more devastating—my embarrassment, or the fact that he didn't love me. I stared at my hands, resting in my lap.

"I'm sorry," he said, quietly. "I couldn't hear you. Could you say that again?"

I glanced up to see a slight smile on his face. Did he find this amusing? And then I realized he was teasing. Relief passed through me, I cleared my throat, and looked him in the eye.

"I love you," I said a third time. He nodded and his smile grew wider.

"Say it again," he whispered, pulling me closer.

"I love you."

"Again." He stretched his neck out so that our faces were only inches apart.

"I love you." My voice was thin, but I kept my eyes locked on his.

And just before our lips touched, he whispered, "I love you, too."

It was drizzling outside when I woke up the next morning. My mood matched the weather. Mike was going to New York until Saturday. It was only Tuesday. He promised to call me as soon as he landed and every night while he was away, but knowing that I couldn't touch him or see his face for five days made my stomach sink.

"Absence makes the heart grow fonder," he said, before he left.

"Yeah, yeah." I refused to cheer up.

"Hey," he said. I glanced up at him, my bottom lip practically dragging the floor. "I love you."

My heart fluttered. I cracked a smile. "I love you, too." He gave me a delicate kiss on the cheek and was gone.

Five days. I sulked to the bathroom. What would I do today? It was too wet outside to walk and I was too disheartened by Mike's leaving to try to write anything. I thought about the classes he'd suggested. It was late August, so the semester had probably already started. But like Mike said, I had nothing to lose. I dried off my face and headed to the kitchen phone.

"Please hold while I connect you," the operator chirped. After two rings, I was greeted by the University of Memphis's automated phone service. The series of prompts finally directed me to the Registrar's Office.

"Registrar's Office. This is Carol, how may I help you?"

"I'm interested in attending the University."

"Have you submitted your application for review?"

"No, but—"

"Well, you've got the wrong office, hon. Let me transfer you to Administration. They'll help you with admissions."

The phone went silent.

"Administration, Mary Ann."

"I'm interested in attending—"

"Have you submitted an application for admittance?"

"No."

"That's the first thing you have to do. I can send you an undergraduate application, or you can pick one up."

"Oh, I'm not an undergrad."

"So, you already have a four-year degree?"

"I have a BA in English."

"Well, ma'am, you've called the Office for Undergraduate Admissions."

"No, I didn't," I informed her curtly. "I was transferred to you by the Registrar's Office."

"Uh-huh. Let me transfer you to Graduate Admissions."

"Wait—no, I'm not interested in—hello?"

Silence again. My patience was wearing thin. I gripped the phone and tried to calm myself.

"Graduate Admissions. This is Barbara, how may I assist you?"

Here we go again.

"I'm interested in attending the University, but not graduate school."

"Okay, but this is the Office for Graduate Admissions."

"I realize that. Undergraduate admissions transferred me before I had a chance to explain my situation."

"Bless your heart!" she exclaimed. "Well, tell me what you're trying to do and we'll direct you to the right place."

Finally! I felt my exasperation waning. "I graduated with a BA in English from Michigan State, but—well, for some personal reasons, I'd like to attend a couple of writing courses at the University of Memphis."

"Okay. So, you're not applying for an undergraduate or a graduate program?" she asked.

"No. I only want to take one or two classes. Refresher courses."

"Hm. Hold on and let me check something."

I heard the phone click, but instead of silence, classical music played on the other end. A few minutes later she returned.

"You'll need to apply for guest admission. If you're accepted, you'll be allowed to attend for one year on an audit basis."

"Audit?"

"Yes, you won't be taking the classes for a grade or for credit hours. Like you said, you want to attend for personal reasons. The only way you can do that is if you audit the classes. You'll be expected to attend and participate, but you won't earn credit. The classes will never show up on your transcript."

It sounded like a perfect arrangement to me.

"The Administration Office can help you with a guest application."

Transferring again.

"Administration. This is Susan, could you please hold?" *Click*. The clock struck ten. Twenty minutes later, I was still holding. My irritation began to climb. Being on hold got under my skin, even when I didn't have anything else to do. So what if as soon as I hung up, I'd crawl into bed and sulk until Mike called? Somewhere, Susan the receptionist was gossiping and finishing her morning coffee.

Maybe this wasn't meant to be. My finger reached for the hang-up button.

"Thank you for holding. How may I help you?"

"I'd like to apply for guest status—if possible, for this semester."

"Are you a transfer student?"

"No."

"Is this for next spring?"

"It could be," I said tentatively. "But, I'd like to try for this semester."

"Miss, the fall semester started yesterday."

My heart sank.

"So, it's too late?" I asked.

"Not technically." My ears perked up. "We're in the middle of late registration. If you came in now, I could process your application by this afternoon. Do you have Internet access?"

"Yes."

"Good. That'll be the fastest way for you to enroll for classes."

"Sounds like a plan. When should I come in?"

"If you can make it here before noon, I can run your application through on my lunch break."

"Thank you so much," I gushed. She gave me the address for the Administration Building and a few sketchy directions. I threw on a pair of jeans, a long-sleeved tee shirt and my sneakers. My clothes were too big. It was bittersweet. I'd shop for smaller clothes later. For now, I pulled my hair back, grabbed my purse and an umbrella, and headed out the door.

By two that afternoon, I was officially a guest student at the University of Memphis.

"You're almost all set," Susan reassured me. Over the phone, her squeaky voice was innocent and unpretentious. I was expecting her to be a young, white girl with pigtails and a retainer, but in fact, Susan was a heavyset black woman in her forties. She handed me my receipt.

"Almost?" I asked.

"You'll have to go to the Bursar's Office for an ID card. And you'll need to swing by Public Safety to register your car."

It was pouring rain. Running from building to building and standing in long lines didn't appeal to me.

"I can't do that tomorrow?"

"I'm afraid not. You can't register for classes until your ID number's in the university's system. And you won't be issued an ID number without an ID card. And if you park on campus without a sticker, you'll get a ticket."

"Looks like there's no avoiding it then." I sighed. She smiled sympathetically.

"You should be in and out in less than an hour. Things don't really start to get chaotic until Friday—that's the last day to register, the last day to drop and add classes without penalty, *and* the last day to get a free ID card."

"Somebody wasn't thinking," I criticized.

"Honey," she laughed. "You're preaching to the choir." She gave me a map of the university and highlighted the fastest routes to the Bursar's Office and to the Public Safety Building, which were on opposite ends of the campus.

"One more thing," she said, handing me a stack of pamphlets. "You'll need these to help you through the online enrollment process. The site can get confusing at times. If you can't navigate it, just view the classes that are still available and then call STRIPES to register over the phone."

"Stripes?" I'm sure I looked confused.

"STRIPES is our phone enrollment system."

I sighed and couldn't help but wonder if I'd bitten off more than I could chew.

"Don't worry." She smiled. "You'll get the hang of it." She looked down at her watch. "You might want to get a move on, though. You have quite a trek and both offices close at four."

Susan lied. I wasn't in and out in no time. Both offices had long lines that didn't move. By the time I'd gotten my student ID, I only had twenty minutes to get across campus and register my car. Instead of trying to walk it, I drove. But when I couldn't find a parking spot, I created my own space on the grass. There were two cars and an SUV parked on the sidewalk alongside me.

I'd made it just in time. An employee locked the door behind me.

"Unfortunately, you'll have to make do with the general lots," said the young man behind the service desk. He pulled out a map and circled all the areas labeled, "General."

"If you'd registered your car a couple of weeks ago, you might have been able to get into a lot closer to the building where you're taking your classes. Like here, or here," he said, pointing to random spots on the map. "Those cost fifty dollars a semester, but like I said, we're all sold out."

"I'll just take what you have." I filled out a form describing the make and year of my car and handed him my driver's license. Fifteen minutes later, my car was registered and I was done. It felt good to spend the day doing something productive. I was starting to feel proud of myself until I saw a pink ticket resting on my windshield—ninety dollars for illegal parking.

I left my wet shoes in the front hallway when I got home. "Trina?" I called out.

Wishful thinking! On a *short* day she was home before ten. I was happy for her. Ronald was a good man and her future was looking brighter than ever. I just missed spending time with her. It's funny how our relationship had evolved over the past few months. We'd become less of a support base for one another and more like silent partners. She and I had hit a comfortable rhythm in our friendship and while we'd always be irreplaceable in each other's lives, we'd matured and learned to find happiness in other people and other things.

That reminded me of Mike. He should've landed in New York hours ago. I picked up the nearest phone and dialed voicemail. Mike's smooth voice filtered through the receiver.

"Hey, baby, it's me. I'm at the Waldorf Astoria and I'm missing you like crazy. I can't wait for Saturday. Listen, I have a couple of meetings scheduled for this afternoon and then I have a business dinner at six I can't get out of. If you get this message before then, I'd love to hear your sweet voice." I grabbed a pen and scribbled down the hotel phone number.

I flopped onto the couch, wet clothes and all, still clutching the phone. *Mike makes life perfect. I don't deserve him.* I sat up to listen when the second voicemail played back.

"Hey, it's me again. I almost forgot." He paused for a few seconds. "I love you." The clock read 5:08. Maybe I could still catch him in his room.

I dialed the number I'd written on the note pad. The phone rang once, and I asked for room 1650.

"And the name of the guest?"

"Michael Cambridge."

The line went quiet for a brief moment before ringing. I held my breath. After the fifth ring, I knew I'd missed him. I hung up and slumped into the cushions.

I tried his cell phone, but it was turned off, and I didn't feel like leaving a message. Instead, I peeled off my wet clothes and took a warm bath. Then I started a load of laundry, nuked a Lean Cuisine, and tried to register for a couple of classes online.

Susan was right about the University's website; it didn't make sense. One prompt led me to another, which led me back to where I started. So I took her advice. I clicked on the icon that read, "Class Availability," and then clicked on "English." The listings of literature courses made me nervous. English Lit courses were the one part of my major requirements that I loathed when I was in college. I had hated being forced to read long, drab, overanalyzed books in a short span of time, only to pick them apart for meaningless symbolism. Those classes took the joy out of reading.

Luckily, as I continued to scroll down, I discovered more and more writing courses. Where should I start? I didn't need the basics. My grammar was impeccable and I had no problem putting together sentences and writing essays. But I also didn't want to overestimate my skills. I didn't want to walk into a class and be completely lost or feel inadequate. Too bad the course listings didn't come with descriptions.

What the course titles lacked in description, they made up for with quantity. I had dozens of writing courses to choose from, everything from introductory poetry to advanced screenwriting. I decided to play it safe. I picked one class called "Imaginative Writing." It met on Monday, Wednesday, and Friday afternoons from 2:00 to 3:50. I'd already missed the first day of class, but I wasn't going to stress over it.

The second class was called "Intermediate Dialogue." If I was going to write a novel, I figured, I needed to brush up on my dialogue-writing skills. That class met Tuesdays and Thursdays from 11:00 to 1:00. It was only offered to upperclassmen, honor students, and people like me, who were just auditing.

I felt a quiver of anticipation run through my hands as I picked up the phone and dialed STRIPES. Again, Susan was right. The automated enrollment system was crystal clear. I'd registered for both classes in less than fifteen minutes.

My nervousness surprised me. Nearly ten years had passed since I'd first stepped foot onto a college campus. By anyone's standards, I was a full-fledged adult. Still, my stomach was tied in knots as if tomorrow would be my first time as a student of higher learning.

I fished through my purse for the map Susan had given me, then got back online to find out which buildings my classes met in. They were both in a building right off the corner of Patterson and Central. There were no general parking lots nearby, but a parking garage was across the street. I wouldn't mind forking over a dollar an hour since my classes only met a couple of hours a day.

I rummaged through my desk and found a notebook that was practically empty. I didn't have a book bag, so I threw the notebook and a couple of pens into the biggest purse I owned, then I headed to my closet to find an outfit.

"This is stupid," I chastised myself out loud. But that didn't stop me from digging through my wardrobe like a wild woman. It wouldn't have been so difficult if all my clothes weren't three sizes too big. I was starting to look scruffy when I went out. Even the new jeans I'd bought a few months earlier looked baggy. *Give it up, Grace. You're gonna have to go shopping*. I made a mental note to stop by the mall sometime that week.

At nine, Trina still wasn't home. I really wanted to talk to her, but my eyelids drooped as I watched the news. I turned off the television and felt my way, in the dark, to my bedroom. I tired to imagine what it would be like tomorrow—going to class with all those young people. Suddenly, I felt very old.

Before I let myself fall into sleep, I said a little prayer. *God, if You really care like Mike says You do, please make this experience worthwhile. Introduce me to people I would have never otherwise met. And help me use what I learn to write the best book anyone's ever read. Amen.*

The phone rang at a quarter to midnight. I was so startled, I dropped my cordless and had to fumble to turn on the lamp to find it. My heart pounded as I focused my eyes and pushed the talk button. My first thought was that, had something happened to Trina?

"Hello?" My voice was panicked.

"Gracie?" Mike sounded alarmed by my alarm. I was about to respond when Trina picked up.

"Hello?" she croaked, her voice deepened with sleep. Immense relief washed over me as I realized she was in her room—safe.

"It's for me," I told her.

She hung up.

"Gracie?" Mike asked again.

"Hi, Sweetie." My dismay had turned to wide-awake joy.

"Hey, baby. I would have called you sooner, but I just got back. Is everything okay?"

"Yeah, everything's fine. The phone just startled me."

I would've called you sooner, but everything ran long."

"You can call me anytime—day or night. You know that."

"Yeah, I know." He grew silent.

"What's wrong?" I asked.

"Nothing. I just miss you, that's all."

"Aw. I miss you too. How was your day?" We sounded like newlyweds.

"Blessed. Everything went smoothly. Looks like we'll break ground on the new office sometime at the end of this year."

"That's earlier than expected. Is that a good thing?"

I was at a loss when it came to business stuff.

"Yeah," he said. "The sooner, the better."

"You sound tired." I said.

He let out a sigh.

"I'm exhausted. But I had to hear your voice tonight. If I'd known I was going to miss you like this—"

"One day down and only four more to go," I tried to encourage.

"You sound chipper," he noted. "How was your day?"

"Wonderful!" I exclaimed. "You're talking to an official student of the University of Memphis."

"That's great. I'm proud of you."

"I'm really excited," I confessed. "My first class is tomorrow at two."

"You'll have to tell me all about it when I get back."

"I will," I promised. "Guess what else I did."

"What?"

"I prayed."

He'd been encouraging me to pray for weeks. I felt awkward talking to God out loud, but I loved to hear Mike pray.

"Good girl. What'd you pray about?"

"Nothing really," I said, suddenly embarrassed. "Just that He would make my classes a worthwhile experience. You know, learn things that would really impact my writing, and help me meet people who would change my life."

"Well, if you have faith and stay right, I know He'll answer you."

"I hope so."

"Well, angel, I wish I could talk to you longer, but I'm beat and my first meeting's at 8:00."

"Okay." I tried not to sound disappointed.

"I'll talk to you tomorrow. You can tell me all about your return to academia. I love you."

"I love you, too."

Chapter Eight

The campus looked small and manageable enough on the map, but when I pulled onto Patterson, twenty minutes before class, everything felt different. I drove in circles for ten minutes before finding the parking garage. The first available spot was on the fourth level, and then it took forever to get my bearings because I accidentally exited the back of the garage instead of the front.

By the time I found the classroom, I was late. All eyes were on me as I rushed into the room. The professor raised an eyebrow.

"Yes?" he asked, snottily. He was an older black man, fairly tall with large lips. He wore a brown sweater vest over a tan button-down shirt. His glasses sat on the brim of his nose and his beard, which was streaked with gray, was trimmed to perfection. The yellow eyes, puffy face, and distended gut didn't match his otherwise tidy appearance.

"Sorry." I sat down at the first empty desk.

"You must be my audit." He sounded disinterested as he picked up a pen. "What's your name?"

"Grace Naybor." His hand froze above his notebook. He shot me a frightened look.

"I'm sorry, what did you say?"

I cleared my throat.

"Grace Naybor," I repeated, a little louder.

He stared at me, his mouth agape. I shifted uncomfortably.

"Um, yes, of course. Thank you," he sputtered, regaining his composure. "Ms. Naybor, punctuality is expected in this class."

"I know, I'm sorry."

"No need to apologize. Starting Monday, I'll be locking the door promptly at two. There are no exceptions to the rule."

I nodded. He was a little anal-retentive for my taste, but I was still going to make the most of the situation.

"See me after class, and I'll give you a syllabus."

All through his lecture, he kept looking at me. It was strange and embarrassing. Regardless, I enjoyed his teaching style. He spoke with passion and conviction. If he'd been published, I would love to read his work.

I was disappointed when he dismissed us at ten to four. I had seven pages of notes and my hand ached, but I could have listened to him through the afternoon and into the night. Our first assignment was to write a three-page dialogue between two people. We were to concentrate on evoking a specific emotion. Half the class would read their first drafts for critique on Friday and the other half on Monday.

"If you want it to be a dramatic dialogue, fine," he said. "But make it really dramatic—soap-opera dramatic. Don't be afraid to go overboard. Overindulge, if that's what it takes. I want it to make our hearts stop." He pounded his chest in order to bring home his point. "I want these walls to shiver. Same thing applies if you write a comedic dialogue. Make it really funny. Not just giggles or chuckles. I want to fall out of my seat. I want to laugh so hard my stomach aches. Now, here's the catch," he said, looking over at me. "Your characters have to be the antithesis of each other."

A girl in the back raised her hand. "Can you elaborate on that?"

"Your characters must be complete and utter opposites. You could have a nine-year-old black girl and a ninety-year-old white man. Or you could have a homophobic male and a flaming lesbian. I don't care, as long as they're opposites. I want your characters to play off each other. It's essential to good creative writing. And remember, no settings, no thoughts—just pure, simple dialogue. Is everyone clear?" A low rumble spread through the class. "Good. I'll see you on Friday."

The once-quiet classroom grew noisy as students hurriedly scattered.

"Ms. Naybor?" The professor called over the clatter. "Can I see you for a moment?"

I shoved my notes into my bag and made my way to the front.

"I'm glad you were able to join us today."

"I really enjoyed it."

"I could tell." He handed me a printout and smiled. "Here's your syllabus."

"Thanks," I said, folding it and tossing it into my bag.

He hesitated a moment before speaking again.

"May I ask why you are auditing this class?"

Should I tell him about my non-existent novel?

"I wanted to take a few writing courses. You know, refreshers. But I've actually already graduated with a BA in English. So, the only way I could get into the University was by auditing my classes."

"And where did you matriculate from?"

"Michigan State." He removed his glasses and started to wipe the lenses with his handkerchief. He appeared to be slightly anxious.

"You're from Michigan?"

"Yes."

He stiffened.

"This might seem like a strange question, but is your mother's name Cherie?"

It was my turn to be nervous.

"Yes."

He smiled, but it seemed forced.

"My Goddness," he said, more to himself than to me. "Look at you."

"I'm sorry?"

He shook his head in disbelief.

"How's your mother?" he asked. "Does she live here in Tennessee?"

"Uh, no. She still lives in Michigan. You two were friends?"

"Something like that," he said. "I tell you, it's a small world."

"Yeah, it is."

"How are Doria and Mearl?"

Okay, he and my mother must have been close if he was on a first name basis with my grandparents.

"Alive and ticking."

He chuckled.

"Listen, I'd be glad to give you mom's phone number. She'd be happy to hear from you." I didn't even know his name or their history, but I figured putting him in touch with her couldn't hurt.

"I don't know," he hesitated. "She must be a busy woman."

"I'll give it to you anyway." I ripped out a piece of paper from my notebook and jotted down her number. "You might change your mind."

Instead of going home, I stopped at a little shopping area off Summer Avenue, on a mission to buy some clothes that fit. There was a funky little boutique I'd been to with Trina months earlier, back when they didn't carry my size. They hadn't changed, but my size had, so I was sure I could find something to wear. I wanted to get away from my jeans and tee shirt look. The weather was warm and I was in the best shape of my life. I was ready to splurge on something colorful that would show off my figure.

A blast of cool air hit me as I walked into the store. Right away I spotted a red sundress with spaghetti straps that I had to have. I pulled out a size fourteen.

"Would you like me to start a fitting room for you?" the pleasant looking sales associate asked.

"That would be fine," I said, handing her the dress. She looked down at the tag and then back at me.

"Sugar, this dress will swallow you whole." She hung it up and grabbed a smaller size, stepped back, and looked me up and down. "Yep, a size ten should do you."

I looked at her like she'd lost her mind. I don't ever remember being a size ten, not even when I was ten years old.

"Are you sure?"

"Trust me, I'm never wrong at this sort of thing."

I shrugged and selected several more dresses, a few skirts, some tank tops, and a couple pair of capris. I wasn't planning to buy it all; I just wanted to see how they fit.

I was blown away by the woman in the mirror. I looked like women I'd envied my entire life—only better! My arms were toned, with just the right amount of definition and no flab. My stomach was virtually flat and my love handles had completely disappeared. I had a waistline! Not to mention my calves, which were nice and shapely. I gawked at myself as I tried on outfit after outfit.

"How are we doing?" the sales associate asked.

"Perfect," I answered. I was beside myself, I felt lightheaded.

"Was I right about the size ten?" she asked.

"Oh, yeah. Right on the money."

Nearly an hour later, I walked out of the shop with everything I'd tried on plus a couple pair of shoes. My arms were saddled down with bags. I didn't know if I'd make it to my car. I put everything down to search for my keys and found them at the bottom of my purse. As I bent down to gather up my packages, someone called my name. I looked up, and there was Don coming out of Baskin-Robbins, waving a waffle cone stuffed with two scoops of green ice cream.

"Hi," I said. He didn't look as good as I remembered. I realized I wasn't attracted to him anymore. It could have been his risqué behavior that had turned me off, or maybe it was that I had a Prince Charming in New York waiting to talk to me. Whatever the reason, Don seemed unworthy of my time.

"I can't believe my eyes! You look great!" he said.

Just then a pudgy woman with braids came out of the ice cream shop and hooked her arm around Don's. He looked irritated. "This is Laura," he said, blandly. "My wife."

I was taken aback. She looked so ordinary. Don had portrayed himself to be such a Rico Suave that I expected his wife would be some runway model look-alike. Instead, she looked like me when I was heavy.

"Hi!" I said to Laura. "It is such a pleasure to meet you. Don talks about you all the time."

Her look of uncertainty lifted and she smiled broadly. She had a beautiful smile.

I left my bags and walked over to shake her hand. Don looked like the sky was falling. The anxiousness in his eyes was priceless.

"This is Grace." His introductions were uneasy.

"Hi, Grace," she said, giving me a warm handshake.

"She's so pretty," I said, turning to Don. I wanted to make the encounter as unnerving as possible.

"Oh, thank you," she blushed. "So, how do you and Don know each other?"

"I'm one of his clients at the Y," I said

"Well, that's debatable," Don interjected. "Grace hasn't been in to see me in almost four months."

"I've been so busy," I lied.

"Why are you wasting your time at the gym?" Laura took a lick of her ice cream. "You look great!"

She was so sweet. My stomach flipped thinking about the date Don and I had shared. How could I have ever stooped so low?

"Thanks," I said.

"I tell you what," she continued. "If I had a body like yours, I wouldn't be spending all day at the gym pumping iron and sweating."

"Well, how do you think she got that way?" Don's tone was rude. "I can promise you it wasn't by eating ice cream." He looked down at her and pursed his lips. She lowered her cone and gave a tiny embarassed nod. How could he disrespect her like that?

"Please, girl," I said trying to override his degradation. "Don't listen to him. I couldn't live without my scoop of Cookies and Cream every night.

Actually, I lost weight by going for long walks every morning. My eating habits haven't really changed that much."

"Really?" she asked, looking hopeful.

"Yep, exercise and moderation are the keys."

"Don's been trying to convince me to lose some weight," she said, looking up at him through the corner of her eye. "But it's easier said than done."

I smiled sympathetically.

"I know what you mean. But, ironically, once I started losing weight, my boyfriend told me he liked me better heavy."

Don's eyebrows furrowed. He took his arm from Laura and shoved his hands in his pockets. I'd said it on purpose; I wanted to get him back for Laura's sake. *Serves you right, you big jerk*!

"See there, baby," she said, playfully bumping up against Don. "Some men like thick women."

He grunted and rolled his eyes.

"Well, it was a pleasure meeting you." I gave her a hug.

"Likewise." She hugged me back, taking care not to drip ice cream on me.

"When will I see you?" Don asked.

"I don't know. I'm taking some classes at the University of Memphis. My schedule's changed. I'll call you when things calm down."

Once in my car, I decided to give in and drive out to the mall. I still needed to buy a scale so I could see how much weight I'd actually lost. I knew I'd have to face rush hour, but anything was better than sitting at home—alone.

I found a station that played my kind of music and sang along to the radio as I made my way across town in bumper-to-bumper traffic.

The mall was just as empty as the last time I'd been there. On my way to the nearest department store, I passed a nail shop. The neon sign read, "Walk-ins Welcome." I looked down at my feet. My toes were hidden by gym shoes, but I knew they looked rough. *What the heck*, I thought, turning back.

"What you want done?" a small Asian woman asked as I walked in. Her accent was so heavy, I could barely understand her.

"You want acrylic?"

"I want a pedicure," I said.

"No manicure?" I looked at my fingers. My cuticles were a mess and each of my nails was a different shape and length.

"Okay," I shrugged. "I'll have a manicure and a pedicure."

"Good," she said, smiling kindly.

"You pick color, ok?" She pointed to an entire wall of nail polish. I picked an earthy, burgundy color.

"Come sit here." She led me across the room to a big leather chair. There was a porcelain basin attached to the bottom of it. "Take your shoes off and put feet in here." She turned the water on and the basin began to fill. She added a soap that created a load of suds. "I be right back." She scurried behind a door labeled, "Employees Only."

I laid back and stretched my legs. The water was warm and soothing. A few minutes later, she returned carrying a stack of white towels and a Caboodle. She turned the water off.

"You can turn chair on," she said. I couldn't understand her, but I didn't want to be rude.

"Oh, uh-huh." I nodded, hoping my reaction matched whatever it was she had said. She shook her head and reached for the side of my chair. She pushed a button and the chair began to vibrate.

Oh! Turn the chair on, dummy, I scolded myself, silently. "Thank you. That feels great."

"No problem." I closed my eyes as she started to massage lotion into my foot and leg.

"Hey." She tapped my knee. "You come over here for manicure." I must have fallen asleep, because when I looked down, my toes were perfectly painted and my feet felt soft and clean. "Be careful," she warned., as I stepped down from the chair. "Don't bump your toes. Paint still wet."

She gathered up my socks and sneakers and walked over to a small table in the front of the shop. I waddled behind her, sat down, and put my hands in the small bowl of tepid water she'd supplied.

"You want same color on fingers?" she asked, holding up the polish she'd used on my toes.

"Sure." She filed, buffed, and snipped. She made the whole process look like second nature. She didn't speak or look up once.

"You pay now, okay?" She meticulously applied two coats of polish after I handed her a check. I held my hands out and admired her work.

"You're good," I said. "It's the best manicure I've ever had."

She looked flattered.

"Good. You come back."

She plugged in the miniature fan that was sitting on the table and pointed it toward my hands.

"You wait ten minute for it to dry."

I nodded. She took her utensils, the towels, and her Caboodle to the back. After fifteen minutes, I lightly touched one of my fingers. It was dry. I slipped on my socks and shoes.

"Hello?" I called, wanting to give her a tip. There was no response, so I left a five-dollar bill on the table.

I felt like a queen as I ventured into the mall. It had been a long time since I'd pampered myself like that. I looked down at my hands—dainty and feminine.

I got a few catcalls as I made my way down the wide corridor lined with stores. It was a nice feeling to be admired, but I didn't pay them any attention. My heart belonged to Mike, and no man could undo that.

I found the scale I wanted in no time. I was so excited about being a size ten that I didn't even wait to get home to use it. I unboxed it and weighed myself right there in the department store. I almost choked when I saw that I'd lost over forty pounds.

"Ma'am, do you plan on buying that?" The sales woman was blatantly annoyed. But I didn't care; I'd lost forty pounds, dropped to a size ten, and met the man I was quite possibly going to marry. She could have called security and had me thrown out, and I still would have been over the moon.

You bet I planned on buying it.

I couldn't wait to check my voicemail. It was past seven; I was certain Mike had called. Sure enough, I had five messages.

"First message," an automated voice blared into my ear.

"Hi, baby, it's me. I'm still at the office. I have twenty minutes before my next meeting. How was your first day in class? Everything you hoped for and more? I'll talk to you later."

Second message. I bet it was Mike calling again to say, "I love you." I held my breath and waited.

"Grace, this is your mother. You do remember me, don't you? I couldn't tell by the way you *don't* call. I haven't heard from you in over a month. Call me; we need to talk." That was an unpleasant surprise, to say the least.

Third message.

"Grace. I'm not kidding. I need you to call me. I'll be home all evening. I expect to hear from you tonight."

Even long distance, she'd found a way to boss me around.

Fourth message. If it was her again, I was going to throw the phone.

"Hey, angel, it's me," Mike said. "I'm done for the day. Call me at the hotel—I don't care how late. I just want to hear your voice. I love you."

He sounded tired. If he were with me, he'd lay his head on my lap and I'd massage his temples while we talked and watched TV. I missed him. Saturday seemed so far away.

Fifth message.

"I'd appreciate it if you called me tonight." It was my mother *again*. There was a short silence. "Please, Grace. It's important."

A pang of guilt shot through me as I hung up the phone. I was torn. The only person I wanted to talk to was Mike. I wanted to hear about his day—even though I probably wouldn't understand half of what had happened. I wanted to tell him that I loved him and hear him say it back. But there was desperation in my mom's voice and as much as I wanted to strangle her at times, she was still my mother. I loved her—in my own warped way.

I dialed her number. She picked up on the first ring.

"Hi, Mom." Even *I* could hear the dread in my voice.

"Please, don't sound so excited."

"I've had a long day," I said.

She laughed. "Doing what? Channel surfing?"

"Now I remember why we don't talk often."

"Oh, Grace. It was a joke." It was too late. My defenses were up and they weren't coming down until the conversation was over. It was each woman for herself.

"What is so important that you've been calling me practically every hour on the hour?" I tried to hurry along our discussion.

"I'm coming to see you."

"What? Why?" My pitch rose a notch.

"What do you mean, 'why'? Because I'm your mother, that's why."

"I thought we agreed that you wouldn't subject me to your presence at *least* until Thanksgiving."

"Excuse me?" she snapped.

I'd gotten under her skin. I knew I was wrong, but it gave me pleasure to knock her off her high horse sometimes.

"I'm sorry. Did I say subject? I meant *grace*. I thought you weren't going to *grace* me with your presence until the holidays." My words dripped sarcasm.

"Take down my flight information," she ordered, ignoring my last quip.

"I'll get it later." I wasn't in the mood.

"No, you'll get it now. My flight gets in tomorrow morning at 10:30."

"You're coming *tomorrow*?"

She had too much gall for her own good.

"Yes." She didn't even realize that she'd crossed a line. "Is that a problem?"

"Well, yeah, as a matter of fact, it is. You didn't even ask."

"The last time I checked, Grace, I didn't need to ask my daughter for permission to attend a meeting in Tennessee."

"If it's a business trip, why can't you stay in a hotel? The Peabody's right down the street."

She slammed something on her end and exhaled loudly.

"You are picking me up and I am staying with you. End of story. Now write down the information! No more lip."

I knew that tone. It was her I-brought-you-into-this-world-and-I can-take-you-out tone. Her I'll-smack-you-into-next-week tone—the tone that made me, a fully-grown, self-sufficient woman, grab the nearest piece of paper and writing utensil I could find.

"Okay, I got it." I said.

"Read it to me."

I bit my lip to keep from cursing.

"I said I got it—can we just leave it at that?"

"I'm not going to ask you again."

I repeated the information.

"Sounds good," she said. "Okay, sweetie, I'll see you tomorrow. Don't be late."

I didn't respond. She hung up. My eyes filled with tears as I tossed the pencil and pad onto the floor. I hated dealing with my mother. Just that quickly, she'd ruined an otherwise delightful day.

I thought back to my Intermediate Dialogue class. I still had no clue what angle I was going to use for my first assignment. It was going to be a fun challenge. Professor…Professor…what was his name? I grabbed my bag and fished out the syllabus.

Professor A. Harris. I wondered why he didn't give out his first name. I tried to guess what it might be. *Angus, Arthur, Adam*. It didn't matter. Whatever his name, he seemed like someone I could learn a lot from. I realized I'd forgotten to tell Mom about him. I'd let her know tomorrow. I wasn't going to call back and chance another round of her snippy, belittling remarks.

She had a lot of nerve inviting herself to my place out of the blue. Because of her, I was probably going to miss my class tomorrow. There was no way I could pick her up at 10:30, get her back to my place, and be in my seat by 11:00. I sank, despondently, into the couch.

I had to call Mike.

"Hello?" he sounded groggy.

"Oh, honey, are you sleeping?"

"Not really. Just resting my eyes." I smiled.

"Go to sleep, we'll talk tomorrow."

I heard the mattress springs creak as he shifted his weight.

"How was class?" he asked, ignoring me.

"Fine."

"Uh-oh. That doesn't sound good."

"No, class was great. I really like the guy who's teaching it." I wanted to tell him about the clothes and the scale, but talking to my mom had zapped my energy. Good news would have to wait.

"Then why do you sound funny?" he asked.

"My mother's coming tomorrow," I spewed, and then burst into tears.

"Shhh. Grace, calm down." He sounded incredibly alert for someone who'd just been cat napping.

"I-I'm s-s-so mad at h-her."

"It's not that bad," he said, after coughing. I'm not sure how, but I could hear him smiling.

"Y-y-you th-think this is f-f-funny?" I sobbed.

He took a deep breath and tried to control himself, but a laugh escaped his lips. Within seconds he was cackling so hard he dropped the phone.

Despite myself, I smiled. I wanted to be mad at him, but I couldn't. Just hearing his deep, throaty laugh lifted my spirits.

"I'm sorry. I'm sorry," he said, regaining his composure. "Gracie? Baby? I'm sorry."

I giggled. "Thanks for the sympathy."

"You feel better? You know I'll support you as much as I can."

I realized how silly I was being.

"I'm used to her," I said, wiping my tears on my shirt. "You're the one who's gonna need the support."

He chuckled.

"What time is she due in?"

"10:30 in the morning."

"I tell you what," he said. "I'll leave my cell phone on. If at 10:35, she starts to get on your nerves, call me."

"But what if you're in a meeting?"

"You're more important," he said softly. My elation started to return. He always knew just what to say.

"I miss you," I confessed.

"I know, but I'll be home soon."

Home. He equated *me* with *home*. Everything was going to work out. My mother could come and try her best to rip to shreds the life that I'd created for myself in Memphis. She could magnify my flaws and try to make me feel like a little lost girl. But I knew who I was and I had a home—home was in my heart. Home was Mike. Home was a place where I was untouchable and where the world fit into the palm of my hand.

We talked for an hour. He told me about his meetings and the unexpected direction in which things were moving. I could hear the worry in his voice. It was the first time ever I'd heard him dispirited.

"Baby, before you go, will you pray for me?" He sounded defeated.

"Over the phone?"

"Yeah. It doesn't have to be anything fancy."

"I don't know, Mike. I'm not good at praying."

"There's no such thing as being good at praying." I stayed silent. "Please, I need you."

I felt my neck grow warm. Prayer seemed like such an intimate thing—something that should only be experienced between "the prayee" and God. I was about to decline when I remembered the night he prayed over me—the night he brought me roses. I wanted him to know that I had his back the way he had mine. Even if it meant putting aside my pride and fumbling through a prayer.

"Okay," I conceded. "What am I praying for?"

"Just that God's will be done with the expansion and that He'll grant me the strength and wisdom to accept whatever happens."

"Um. Okay." We both grew quiet. "Ready?"

"Yeah. You can start."

"Dear God," I began. "Mike's had a long, tiring day. He's worked so hard to build this company and now things are looking shaky. Mike wants to do whatever You want him to do. Please show him the next steps he should take."

"Yes, Father," he whispered.

"And wherever You're leading him, please give him the wisdom and the strength to follow."

"Yes," he agreed.

"Amen." It was an abrupt ending, but I couldn't think of anything else to say.

"And, Father," he added. "We want to lift up Grace and her mother to You. Please bless their time together, and bind those spirits of confusion and dissension that come between them. These things we ask in Your precious name. Amen."

"Your prayers are so much better than mine," I said.

"I don't think so. That prayer you just prayed was the best I've ever heard."

"Whatever!" I laughed.

"I'm serious."

"What made it different from the millions of prayers you've heard?"

"It came from you."

Nervous about my mother's arrival, I tossed and turned all night. By seven o'clock the next morning, I'd given up on the idea of sleep and had gone to the kitchen to fix a bowl of cereal.

"Morning," Trina said. She was sitting at the dining room table in her pajamas, reading over some papers. I hadn't seen her in two days.

"Hey, stranger." I grabbed a spoon out of a drawer.

"Look at you," she said, taking off her glasses and massaging the bridge of her nose. "You're wasting away."

I rolled my eyes.

"And what are you?" I asked. "A size five? I'm not a bettin' girl, but if I had to put my money on which one of us might waste away first, I'd bet on you."

"Ha, ha. Very funny," she said dryly. "I'm serious, Gracie. Are you sure you're not taking this whole weight loss thing too far?"

"I'm not even trying to lose weight anymore," I said, sitting down with my bowl of cereal. She gave me a skeptical look. "I swear."

"Did you buy that scale like Mike suggested?"

"Yeah."

"And?"

"And, what?" I asked, trying to avoid the inevitable.

"How much, Grace?"

"I dunno." I shoved a spoonful of bran flakes into my mouth. "A little over twenty pounds." I'd cut the number in half so I wouldn't have to hear her nag.

"Hm. That's not too bad. But don't drop anymore, okay?"

I raised an eyebrow. I didn't want to make a promise I wasn't going to keep.

"We'll see. So, guess who's going to be here in less than," I looked at the clock on the wall, "four hours?"

"Mike."

"Nope. Would you like to guess again?"

"Not really."

"My mom."

Trina's jaw dropped and her eyebrows sprang up in surprise.

"She called me yesterday and told me," I said, giving her a look that added *So typical*.

"Should I make myself scarce?" she asked.

"Girl, please! You live here. She's gonna work around us, not the other way around."

Trina smirked and grabbed my hand. "We'll make plans—she can't annoy you if she doesn't know where you are. Right? When does Mike get back?"

"Saturday morning."

"So, you're virtually in the clear. You can come to Bible study with me tonight and then Friday it'll be just me and you—girls' night out."

"What about Ron?" I asked.

"He'll be okay for one night by himself."

"Well, at least something positive's coming out of this," I said. "You've finally roped me into Bible study."

She bit her lip. Guilt was written all over her face.

"Actually, there won't be much roping needed," she said, sheepishly. "Our Bible study is going to meet here tonight."

"Here as in *where*?" I asked, copping an attitude.

"Don't be mad," she pleaded, squeezing my hand. "Mike asked me last week when he found out he was going to be out of town. I've been meaning to ask, but I can't ever catch you. You're all over the place these days."

"No," I corrected her. "*You're* all over the place. I'm where I've always been—here." I pointed at the ground.

Her face fell. "Is that a no?"

I didn't have the heart to let her down. "No, it's not a no." I sighed.

"Thank you, thank you, thank you." She was beaming as she shuffled her paperwork into a neat stack. "I'm gonna leave my phone on for you today. If you feel like you're about to lose it, call me."

"What about work?" I asked.

"Don't worry about it. You're more important."

Those were Mike's exact words. I was touched to have two people who cared so much about me.

"You'll get through this," she promised, heading to her room.

I hope so.

I spotted her as soon as I pulled up to the Northwest terminal. She was wearing a bright red business suit, matching red heels, and dark sunglasses. Her hair was pulled back into a tidy french twist and her makeup, as always, was flawless. She only had one small suitcase and her purse—no laptop, no briefcase. She sure wasn't here on business.

Her face brightened the instant she saw me drive up. I wasn't expecting such a warm welcome

"Oh my word!" she gasped, as I popped the trunk and stepped out of my car.

I was wearing one of my new sundresses and a pair of flip-flops.

"Hi, Mom," I greeted her.

"Turn around, turn around. Let me look at you," she said, grabbing my elbow and twirling me. I caught a skycap looking at us through the corner of his eye.

"Okay, that's enough." I pulled away from her grip. "It's not that big of a deal."

"Not that big a deal? Grace, you look like a different person."

A smile of satisfaction crossed my face.

"Yeah, I guess I do."

I heaved her suitcase into the trunk.

"Your trainer must really be working you hard," she said.

Oops, I thought. I never bothered to tell her that I'd stopped seeing Don. Come to think of it, I hadn't told her about Mike, either.

"Actually, Mom, I haven't gone to the gym in months. I've just been walking in the mornings and watching what I eat."

"But, I thought you bought a year's membership."

"I did, but some stuff happened, and doing it my own way worked out better for me," I explained.

She snatched off her sunglasses and gave me a disapproving look.

Here we go.

"That's a waste of money," she said. "If you commit to something, stick with it. It's a sign of integrity. You're constantly starting things and not finishing them."

"Well, technically, I *did* finish," I said flippantly. "You said yourself I look like a different person."

She shook her head.

"That's irrelevant. And quite frankly, the fact that you don't see how wasteful you're being really disturbs me." I got into the car and fastened my seatbelt. She sat down in the passenger's seat. I decided to drop the topic.

Getting into a fight within the first five minutes of her arrival would only make the next few days even more unbearable.

The ride home was quiet. I was itching to call Mike or Trina, but there was no way I could vent with her sitting right next to me. Instead, I popped in a CD and tried to relax. As I exited the interstate, she turned down the music and positioned herself so that she was facing me.

"Grace." I could hear in her tone that she wanted a truce. "I don't want to fight with you, honey." Something was seriously wrong. She almost never called me honey.

"Then don't," I snipped.

"I'll try my best. I promise."

"Me, too." We drove the rest of the way in silence.

She was impressed with the loft. "It's spacious," she said. I put her bag down in my room and gave her the grand tour.

"This is Trina's room," I said, swinging open her door.

"My, my. Look at this. She's done quite well for herself."

There was no reason to tell her that I'd furnished the room. I didn't want to hear her make accusations that Trina was a leech. The only reason she hadn't blown Trina's moving in out of proportion was that I'd told her Darius was abusive.

"So, you'll stay in my room." I sat down on the couch.

"Where are you going to sleep?"

"Right here," I said, patting the cushion next to me.

"Nonsense," she dismissed the idea with a shrug. "I'll sleep on the couch. I don't mind."

"Since when?"

"Come on, Grace. Give me a break. I'm trying to be accommodating."

I rolled my eyes.

"Mom, please. Save it for somebody else. I know you too well. I'll sleep here and you'll sleep in my room, and everyone will be happy."

"Have it your way," she said, throwing her arms in the air. "I'm going to change."

She emerged a few minutes later, wearing a blue jean skirt and a pink knit top. She looked nice in casual clothes.

"So what are we going to do today?" she asked.

"What do you mean? I thought you had a meeting."

"Oh. Well, that's not until Saturday."

"You have a business meeting on Saturday?"

Who did she think she was fooling? We both knew she wasn't in Memphis on business. I don't know why she decided to come and ruin a perfectly good weekend, but here she was. Ten minutes into our truce, and she was already beginning to irk me.

"I have to go," I said, grabbing my purse and keys.

"Where?"

"I have this thing I have to do." I didn't feel obligated to tell her anything, and especially not unless she told the truth about why she'd come to Tennessee.

"Well, can I go with you?"

I didn't have anywhere to be. I just wanted to get away from her for a while.

"I won't be long," I said, ignoring her question. "Make yourself at home." I walked out the front door before she could argue.

My Imaginative Writing class let out in fifteen minutes. It would take me that long just to get to campus. I sat in my car and tried to think of something to do. I thought about Professor Harris's class. I didn't have to read my dialogue until Monday, but it wouldn't hurt to get an early start on it. With Bible study tonight, my mother to deal with, and Mike coming back on Saturday, today might be the only day I'd have to sneak away and write.

I didn't get home until three that afternoon. Writing turned out to be a dead end. My mind went blank every time I looked at the computer screen. So I people-watched. Forty minutes later, I hadn't written a thing, but I could describe the librarian to a tee, and I knew that the guy sitting at the desk next to me had read twelve pages and was sneaking Cheetos from his backpack.

Eventually, I gave up and went to a movie. It was a drama about a kid who had cancer. He wanted desperately to find his biological mother before he died. She'd walked out on him and his father to pursue a singing career when he was just a baby. I felt like I had a similar story, minus the cancer. Turns out his mother had died of an overdose shortly after she split. It was a heartbreaking story that made me appreciate my own mom a little more.

I felt guilty leaving her alone all day. On my way home, I stopped and picked up some Chinese food—cashew chicken, and pork fried rice—her favorite. *Be nice*, I ordered myself, as I put my key in the door.

The strong smell of ammonia hit me as I stepped into the loft.

"Mom?" I called.

"Yes, sweetie?" She came out of the kitchen wearing rubber gloves and holding a sponge. Her shirt was wet and she was sweating.

"What are you doing?"

"I wanted it to be a surprise." She smiled. "I decided to do a little light spring cleaning, everything was so filthy." My mother didn't clean. She was the type of person who hired people to do housework, water the plants, and balance her checkbook. I wasn't sure how to respond.

"I brought you food," I said, holding up the bag.

"Mmmm. I'm starved. But we'll have to wait a little bit for the floor to dry."

I stared at her in awe.

"I'll put the food in the dining room."

"What'd you get?" she asked, following me like a puppy.

"Your favorite."

"Thank you, Grace. You didn't have to do that. I could have just whipped something up here."

I laughed. "You cook now, too? I never knew you had a domestic side."

She gave me a sly look and grinned.

"You'd be surprised what this old bird can do. People change." She took off the gloves.

Who was this woman?

She opened the cartons, grabbed a pair of chopsticks at the bottom of the bag, and dug right in. That was so uncharacteristic of her. My mother's always believed that civilized people eat off plates with silverware. When I was younger, she wouldn't even let me eat a slice of pizza out of the box.

"Mm, Grace, try it," she said, handing me the other pair of chopsticks.

I grabbed the carton of cashew chicken and tried to pick up a spear of broccoli. I couldn't get it. Chopsticks were not my forte.

Mom chuckled. "You'll never get it like that." She put down her own chopsticks and positioned my fingers. "Okay, now try."

I managed to pick up the broccoli that time, but halfway to my mouth, it slipped and landed in my lap. She laughed. I would have laughed, too, if I hadn't been wearing my new dress.

"I hate these things," I said, tossing the sticks aside. I patted at the stain with a napkin.

"It'll come out," she said, gently. "Let me get you a fork." She ran to the kitchen and seconds later was back with the fork.

"Thanks." I speared a piece of chicken and popped it into my mouth.

"Do you remember when you were little and you stuck your fork in an electrical socket?" she asked, smiling.

"No."

"Oh, it was *so* funny."

"I almost electrocuted myself and that's funny?"

"It was priceless," she said, switching cartons with me. "Your grandmother and I were setting the table and we had you locked into your highchair. All of a sudden we heard this zap and all the lights flickered. You started laughing and when we looked over at you, your hair was standing straight up."

She was so amused she could hardly finish the story. Her shoulders bobbed as she laughed. Her eyes were older and her roots were turning gray, but she was just as beautiful as she was ten years ago. I smiled.

We sat and talked long after the food was gone. It was the first time in years that we'd communicated without bickering. I learned something new with every story she told, and I enjoyed listening to her reminisce.

By 6:30, the loft was packed. At least thirty people were crammed into my living room. I leaned against the wall and watched everyone chitchat. Mom had changed her shirt and was standing next to the TV talking to a woman.

Apparently engrossed in what the stranger was saying' she sipped her bottled water and nodded her head enthusiastically. Ron sat on the couch talking to an attractive blond guy. I felt completely out of place.

"Okay!" Trina shouted. The room fell quiet. "It looks like everyone is here, so let's get started." All eyes were on Trina. "First, I think we should thank Grace, my best friend and roommate, for letting us use her beautiful home. Where are you, Gracie?" I raised my hand, hating to be in the spotlight. To my surprise, the room burst into applause.

I smiled. She motioned for me to come over. I squeezed by a heavyset woman and stepped over a couple of people sitting on the floor and joined her at the front of the room. "Many of you may not know this," she said to the group. "But Grace is Mike's girlfriend."

"Ahhh," was the collective response. I watched as they turned to one another and whispered. I wasn't sure if they approved until I heard one woman who looked to be about my age say, "Figures. She's gorgeous."

"So, now that you've been introduced," Trina continued. "Why don't we get things rolling with a word of prayer? Gracie, would you do the honors?" My palms grew clammy. There was no way I could pray in front of all these people. Mike loved me, so I knew that whatever spilled out of my mouth, I'd still be an angel to him. But these people were strangers. They bowed their heads and closed their eyes, expecting me to say something. I opened my mouth but nothing came out.

I looked over at my mother. She gave me a peculiar look that said, "I didn't know you knew how to pray." I looked at Trina. Her eyes were closed. Before I could fully panic, the phone rang.

There is a God.

"I'm so sorry," I said. Everyone's eyes popped open. "I really have to get that. I'm expecting an important call." I excused myself, and dashed to my bedroom.

"Hey, beautiful."

"Mike? Your timing couldn't be more perfect!"

"Why, what's going on?"

"Trina's holding Bible study in my living room and she asked me to pray."

"Ooo, baby, I'm sorry. I forgot to tell you that I asked her to take over while I was gone. It just seemed like the most logical solution since you only live a few floors below me."

"It's okay. I was surprised at first, but everyone's really nice."

"Is your mom there?"

"Yeah, and it's the weirdest thing. She's been so helpful today. She actually cleaned the loft."

"That's the power of prayer." I'd forgotten about our prayer the night before. Just then someone start singing. A minute later, the rest of the group joined in.

"Speaking of prayer," I said. "Did mine work?"

He chuckled. "Well, I signed a contract to break ground in December, so I guess it did. But I have even better news than that. I'm on my way to the airport, and I should be home in a few hours."

I squealed with excitement.

"You're not playing around, are you?"

"Nope. Everything's been signed, there's nothing left to negotiate, so there was no need to stay. I had my secretary change my flight. My plane doesn't get in until after midnight, but it's better than Saturday, right?"

"Come straight here," I demanded.

"Can I at least take my luggage up to my place first?"

"No," I responded, playfully.

"You're the boss. Do me one favor, though? Go to Bible study."

Bible study turned out to be very entertaining. I was surprised by the group's openness. The lesson for the night was on mercy—how God showed the world mercy by sending Jesus to die for our sins, and how we, in turn, need to show others mercy. I thought about my mom and how callous I was with her at times.

After Trina finished teaching, she took prayer requests, and then we sang a couple of songs. I didn't know the lyrics, but I listened and watched. Some people cried, and others closed their eyes and raised their hands. I was sad when nine o'clock rolled around and the crowd started thinning out.

Ron was the last to leave. Trina gave him a kiss and promised to talk to him in the morning.

"Well, Trina," Mom said, picking up a couple of abandoned paper cups. "I really enjoyed that."

Trina smiled. My mother rarely had anything nice to say to her.

"I'm glad," she said, cordially. "What did you think, Gracie?"

"I liked it," I answered, and I meant it. "Maybe I'll go again next week."

"I want to know who Mike is," Mom said, "and when do I get to meet him?"

Trina feigned a yawn. "Look at that. It's late. I should get ready for bed." Without looking back, she went to her room and closed the door.

"So?" Mom asked, waiting for an answer.

"He's my boyfriend, and he gets home late tonight. You'll meet him tomorrow," I answered.

"He's not a bum, is he?" After what happened with Stanley, I couldn't get mad at her for asking.

"No," I said. "He owns his own company."

She tilted her head. "Are you sure?"

"Yes, Mother. I'm positive. *Life Sketch, Inc.*"

"Didn't they do your illustrations?"

"No. Their waiting list was too long." I wasn't going to tell her what really happened.

"Well, I'm impressed. You've finally met someone worth something."

"Our relationship has nothing to do with money."

"Good," she said. "Because that's not the type of worth I was talking about."

I sat in the darkened living room and waited for Mike. I was wired. Just before one in the morning, he knocked. He looked like an angel standing there in his white dress shirt and slacks. His coat jacket was draped over his arm and his suitcase was leaning against the wall.

I threw myself into his arms and let him squeeze me tight.

"Mmmm," he moaned. "Miss me?"

"You have no idea."

He stepped back and looked into my eyes.

"Yes, I do."

I stood on my tiptoes and kissed him. He placed his hands on the small of my back and pulled me into him. We kissed passionately—frantically. I let my hands move across his chest and then to his soft, warm neck. I could have kissed him forever.

Suddenly, the lights flipped on. We broke apart and I whipped around. My mother was standing in the living room in her satin robe—wide awake, her makeup still on. She hadn't been asleep; just like me, she'd been waiting for Mike.

"Oh, I'm sorry, honey," she said. "I got hungry."

I shook my head and smiled.

"The kitchen's that way." I pointed.

"You must be Michael," she said, ignoring me.

"Mike," he said. He handed me his jacket, walked over, and gave her a warm hug.

"Oh, aren't you sweet?" She patted him on the back. "I'm Cherie, Grace's mom."

"It's nice to meet you."

Just then Trina emerged from her room wearing a pair of flannel pajamas. She, too, was wide awake. She tried her best to look surprised.

"Hey, Mike! When did you get back?"

"About an hour ago."

She gave him a hug and a peck on the cheek. I tried not to laugh. It was obvious what was going on. My mom couldn't wait to meet Mike, and Trina couldn't wait to watch my mom meet Mike.

"What are you two doing up so late?" I already knew I didn't have a chance of getting any alone time with him.

"I told you," Mom answered first. "I got hungry."

The liar. Between the two of us, we'd eaten enough Chinese food to feed five people.

"I just wanted a glass of water,"Trina said.

"To tell you the truth, I'm kind of hungry, too." Mike said. He looked at me apologetically. Luckily, my cupboard was stocked and my refrigerator was full.

"I can make us all breakfast,"Trina offered.

All three of them looked at me and waited for permission.

"Okay," I said grudgingly.

"I'll help you," Mom said, tugging Trina toward the kitchen. Mom couldn't wait to drill Trina for details about Mike and me.

"How do pancakes and omelets sound?"Trina called over her shoulder.

"Perfect," Mike answered. After they disappeared, he scooped me into his arms. "Where were we?"

We kissed again. This time it was calmer, more sensual. His right hand glided up and down my back. I melted into his arms and lost myself in the pleasure of the moment. He pulled away abruptly.

"Grace, we need to stop," he said. I laid my head on his chest, and he kissed the top of it. We'd never discussed the issue of sex, but I wasn't crazy. I knew Mike had no intentions of sleeping with me unless we were married. So far, it hadn't been an issue, and I wasn't going to make it one. I respected him for wanting to hold out. In a day and age when most guys were self-proclaimed "players," a man like Mike was a gift.

"Look at me." He tilted my face up to meet his gaze. "You know I love you."

I nodded.

"And you know I've never been attracted to anyone more than I am to you." I nodded again. "I want you, Grace—in every sense of the word. But I need to do this the right way, as husband and wife. Our time will come."

"I know, sweetie." I gave him a peck on the cheek. "We'll wait as long as it takes."

"Grace, for goodness sake, let the man breathe," my mother nagged.

"How long have you been standing there?" I asked.

"Long enough to know you snagged a good one," she said, with a wink. She walked over to him and hooked her arm through his. "So, Mike. What do you like in your omelet?"

We ate pancakes and omelets and talked until four that morning. I was exhausted by the time I curled up on the couch, but happy that Trina, Ron, Mike, Mom and I had made plans to have dinner later that night at Mike's.

In the several months that we'd been together, I'd never seen Mike's loft. He never invited me up, and I never asked to go. I didn't think much of it, since I figured his looked just like mine—only masculine. Still, I was excited to see where he fell asleep every night, how he decorated, and what was in his medicine cabinet. As far as I was concerned, it was all a part of getting to know the mysteriously perfect man who'd stolen my heart.

Chapter Nine

The first three presenters were horrible. I was embarrassed for them. I don't know if they didn't prepare or if they didn't understand the assignment, but their dialogues were stale and trite.

The first guy used the idea that Professor Harris had given us in class two days prior. He tried to write a comedic dialogue between a ninety-year-old white man and a nine-year-old black girl. While he fumbled through it, I couldn't decide if I should feel sorry for him or be offended.

He made Laquisha, the black girl, out to be the quintessential uneducated, going-nowhere-fast stereotype. The old man said devastatingly cliché things like, "Help! I've fallen and I can't get up." Even worse than the actual dialogue was the way the presenter acted it out. What's more disturbing than a southern white boy trying to portray a rough, black chick from Crenshaw? I'd never heard the word "ain't" pronounced so awkwardly.

The second guy tried to write a dramatic dialogue between God and Satan, except it wasn't dramatic—it was boring. He basically just quoted Scriptures. Most of his three pages described setting, which was exactly what Professor Harris told us not to do. His idea had a lot of potential, but it was obvious he hadn't put much effort into the assignment.

The third presenter was a short, dumpy girl with wild, curly hair. She wore thick-framed glasses and a greasy tee shirt. I knew her dialogue would be bizarre even before she took her place behind the podium.

"This piece is entitled, 'That's the Way I Like It,'" she began, in a deep husky voice. The dialogue that followed was nothing short of pornographic. It was a steamy discussion between a closet freak librarian and an illiterate janitor. As the characters' conversation became more risqué, people shifted uncomfortably in their seats. I couldn't wait for it to be over. When she finished, Professor Harris opened the floor for discussion and critique, but nobody had anything to offer. I was sure he was going to rip her apart just like he'd done her predecessors, but to my surprise, he liked it.

"That's what I meant when I said to evoke an emotion," he lectured. "The minute she opened her mouth, I saw shock on half your faces. If you want to write, you have to take risks. You can't expend energy trying to be politically correct or afraid to offend. Controversy is a premium—it hooks people whether they want to be hooked or not. Well done."

I sat through seven more dialogues, all of which were mediocre. In order to draw an emotion from the class, I would have to find an angle that was personal and familiar. I would bet money that the Porn Writer really was a wanton sex kitten like the woman in her story. In the same way, I needed to tap into something that was a part of me—something that, in real life, made me feel the emotion I wanted the class to experience.

When I got home, Mike and Mom were sitting in the living room drinking tea. It was a disarming sight, to say the least.

"Hey, baby," Mike said. He put his mug down and reached out for me. I dropped my bag and went over to give him a peck.

"How was class?" Mom asked, sipping her tea.

"It was okay."

"Just okay?" Mike looked up at me. "What happened to all that enthusiasm you had?"

"I'm still enthusiastic," I said flopping down next to him. "I just have this assignment due on Monday and I'm stumped."

"Did you try talking to Professor—Professor, what's his name again?" he asked.

My mother put her teacup down and smoothed out her skirt.

"Professor Harris. And, no, I didn't bother talking to him about it. I'm sure his advice would be counterproductive."

"Why? Two days ago you said he was brilliant."

"I still think that," I said. "But he's acting weird around me."

"He acts weird around you," Mike echoed. "Are you sure you're not being paranoid?"

"Yeah, I'm pretty sure. It was only my second time in his class, but I feel like I make him nervous or something—like he's afraid of me."

My mother cleared her throat.

"I'm sure you're reading too much into it," she said quickly. "You know," she said, looking at Mike, "Grace has always had a flare for the dramatic."

If I was on fire and screamed for a cup of water, my mother would think I was being melodramatic. It's as if she didn't want me to voice my opinions. Sometimes I think her life would have been a lot easier if I'd been born a mute. I opened my mouth, preparing to say something snotty, but decided not to. I wasn't going to let her goad me into showing Mike my ugly side. Instead, I leaned back into the couch and propped my feet up on the coffee table next to her tea. It was an act of silent rebellion. She pursed her lips and glared at me. Mike didn't seem to notice.

"Grace, don't you think it's inappropriate to have your shoes on the table when your guests are trying to enjoy tea?" she asked, barely masking her irritation.

"Not really." I folded my arms across my chest and rested my head on Mike's arm.

"Well, I do," she huffed.

"If it bothers you so much, move your cup." I glared at her, my voice dry and daring.

She glanced at Mike. She wouldn't squabble in front of a prospective son-in-law, would she? Still, being my mom, she had to have the last word.

"I raised you better than that."

"That's funny," I retorted. "I always assumed that one had to be around in order to raise a child."

She rolled her eyes, which fueled my rising anger.

"I see you haven't matured much since you moved away." She shook her head in disgust. "Same nasty attitude."

"Only when you're around," I spat.

"I find that hard to believe."

"Thank God what you believe doesn't really matter."

"Let me tell you something," she started. She leaned forward, her index finger pointed at me. Her sweet, reserved tone turned cold and forceful. More than anything, I knew, she was infuriated with me for embarrassing her in front of Mike.

"Please spare me," I begged dramatically, cutting her off.

"Come on, Grace. That's enough," Mike said. I lifted my head off his shoulder and looked at him.

"Why are you scolding me?" I asked. "She's being just as rude."

"Yeah, maybe. But she's your mother."

"So I'm supposed to let her bite my head off and publicly pick apart and criticize every statement I make?"

"No one's biting your head off," my mom snapped. I glowered at her.

"The point is, I think you're being a little childish. You're blowing things out of proportion," Mike said.

"That's the understatement of the year," my mother sneered.

My neck grew warm with a mix of emotion. I was angry—mostly with my mom. Why was she so ornery? And why did she make it so impossible for me to get along with her? It's as if she made deliberate efforts to undercut my feelings and minimize my accomplishments. When I was younger, before I found other sources of love and acceptance, I ached with the desire to be good enough for her. All I wanted was to make her proud—to be who I had to be to gain value in her sight. For years I worked tirelessly to prove that I was worth backing—that it was okay for her to be proud of me. But in the end, it was to no avail. And now, sitting in my home, watching her sip tea and smirk with the satisfaction that Mike had taken her side, I loathed her with a hate that scraped my soul and made my fingers tremble.

And Mike—this was our first fight. I wasn't happy that he'd called me out in front of my mother. I probably *was* being childish, but couldn't he see that the fight was a two-way street? Didn't he hear her call me immature and dramatic? Didn't he see how she baited me and took pleasure in getting under my skin and making me feel insignifigant? Even if I was wrong, whose side was he on? He was supposed to be my man. If he had a problem with how my mom and I dealt with each other, fine. But why would he undermine me in front of her?

I looked back and forth at the two of them. I felt double-teamed—taken again by my mother and betrayed by Mike. What could I say? Instead of arguing my point and making the situation even worse, I took my feet off the table and reached for my bag.

"Whatever," I said, shaking my head. My voice was thick with hurt. I got up, ready to escape to my room.

"Gracie." Mike took hold of my wrist. I snatched my arm loose without looking back at him and walked away.

"See what I mean?" my mother said. "Drama—all day, every day."

I imagined myself smacking her. Or even better, booking her on the next flight back to Detroit and then throwing all of her stuff into the hallway. Instead, I closed my door, tossed my bag on my bed, and headed to my closet to change. If I had my druthers, I would've crawled under my covers and cried until I fell asleep, but that would be too much like the old me. I was stronger than that now. I wasn't going to let her rule me anymore.

I'd slipped into my new floral print skirt and was looking for a shirt to wear with it, when I heard a light rap at the door.

"I don't feel like talking," I snipped. "I'm not—"

"Gracie?" It was Mike. Before I could cover up, he walked into the room. His eyes widened as he caught a glimpse of me. I dashed into my closet.

"I'm not dressed." I said from behind the closed door. I slipped into my chambray halter.

"Wow," he whispered, giving my outfit the once-over. "You look beautiful."

I made a futile attempt not to smile. "Flattery won't fix this."

He snapped out of his trance and gave me an apologetic look. "Please, don't be mad."

I wanted to forgive him, but he'd crossed a line. He was going to have to suffer a little.

"Look, I don't want to talk about it right now."

"Are you going to carry it around and let it fester? We might as well get it out and resolved, instead." As usual, he was right.

"Will you at least close the door?" I asked. When he turned back to face me, I stood with my hands on my hips, waiting for an apology. He held out his arms; I shook my head.

"I'm really upset with you, Mike. It's going to take more than a hug and a few nice comments for us to get over this hump."

He pouted, opened his arms up wider, and looked absolutely adorable. I sidestepped my self-control, walked over, and gave him a hug. He held me close, and caressed my back and shoulders.

"I love you," he said.

"I love you too, Mike, but—"

He kissed my shoulder. "But what?"

"But you really—"

He kissed my neck. "I really what?" he asked.

"I just don't appreciate–"

He tenderly kissed my jaw. "Don't appreciate what?" he whispered.

I smiled. He was slowly breaking me down, and he knew it.

"You know what," I said.

His lips brushed my chin. "No, I don't. Explain it to me."

Before I could speak, he kissed my mouth, and in seconds I was lost in his nearness. My hands ran through his dreadlocks and caressed his neck. His quick, eager breaths let me know how much he wanted me—as much as I wanted him. It was almost more than I could bear. Suddenly, I became aware of his strong, masculine hands on my skin and at that moment, more than anything else, I wanted to feel his body, too.

Before I knew it, I'd slipped off his shirt and dropped it to the floor. He didn't protest or back away.

Still kissing him, I took a few, careful steps backwards until my heel hit the foot of the bed. I reached behind me with my left hand and felt for the mattress. In one swift motion, I backed onto the bed and gently pulled him down on top of me. We both moaned simultaneously. *Is this it? Are we really going to do this?* I hadn't been with a man in a long time and to say that I didn't want to experience that kind of intimacy with Mike would be a boldfaced lie. But I wasn't a virgin, and he was. While the experience would be special, it could never mean as much to me as it would to him. He'd saved himself for that certain someone—for his wife. And I knew how much he wanted his first time to be on his wedding night.

At first, I thought he was joking when he told me, about a month ago, that he was a virgin. I mean, come on. It's almost impossible to find a sixteen-year-old boy who's a virgin, much less a man in his thirties. But he wasn't kidding.

"Don't you have, you know…desires and urges?" I asked.

"Yeah, of course. Give me some credit, Gracie, I'm not a robot. You of all people should know. Can't you tell how attracted I am to you?"

"I know you want *me*, but we've only been together a few months. What about the thirty plus years I wasn't around? Aren't guys really hormonal in their teens and twenties?"

He laughed. "Men are hormonal from puberty until the day they die."

"So how have you managed to stay steadfast for so long?"

"You can't miss what you've never tried."

I rolled my eyes.

"I don't buy that. I was curious about sex way before I lost my virginity. The desire for sex is an animal instinct. You can't tell me people don't crave it before they actually experience it."

"That's true," he agreed. "But it's not like I had sex and then was constantly aroused by the memory of it. It's something special that I know I'll experience eventually and that's enough for me right now. I refuse to let the thought of it consume me. And besides that, it's a sin. The Bible specifically says that sexual immorality, which includes premarital sex, is like desecrating the cross."

"I don't know," I shrugged. "Don't you think that's kind of harsh? How can sex be a sin if it has to be done for procreation?"

He shook his head.

"Sex isn't a sin," he corrected. "God created sex. He wants us to have sex—lots of it, and He wants us to enjoy it, just not outside marriage. Casual sex breaks His heart. Sex was meant to be something exclusive between a man and his wife. It's the greatest form of intimacy two people can share, and it binds them. If you think about it, the concept of sex parallels the concept of marriage. When two people get married, they become one. They're bonded by love, trust, and commitment. It's the same thing with sex. When a man and a woman come together, they become one body." He laced his fingers together to emphasize his point. "They're joined, and whether they realize it or not, their bodies make a promise to each other."

"I don't know," I said, trying to take it all in. "Didn't you say a sin was a sin? That no sin was worse than any other sin in the Lord's eyes? So back when you robbed Earl and Lani—that was a sin."

"Right." He nodded and waited for me to go on.

"So, you won't have sex before marriage because it's a sin, but you'll rob people?"

He chuckled and kissed my forehead.

"I wasn't a Christian when I broke into the shop. I was a kid in survival mode. I wasn't thinking about God, I was just trying to find a warm spot where I could crash."

"Yeah, but surely you've sinned since then. If premarital sex isn't any worse than say...lying, why is it that you've lied, but are determined not to have sex?"

"It's hard to explain," he sighed. "A sin like lying can be subtle—sometimes, I don't even realize I've done it until I go before the Lord in prayer. But sex is different. It takes thought, time, effort, and emotion. I can't accidentally make love to a woman. Don't think sex doesn't tempt me. It does, but at the same time, it's something special to me. My virginity is a gift to my wife."

"So you *have* been tempted?"

"With you? Every day."

Up until that discussion, I never realized what a serious and precious act sex was. My mother had sex the first time out of curiosity, Trina did it out of rebellion, and I did it because I thought I loved Stanley. I never thought about it being wrong, and I certainly didn't know I was throwing away a gift for my future husband. For the first time, I wished I still had my virginity. How special it must be for husband and wife to experience sex together for the very first time. It all made sense.

Now, lying on my bed, passionately kissing Mike, feeling the weight of his body on mine—I didn't want to have sex. I loved him with all of my heart—more than I'd ever loved anyone, and that's exactly why I wasn't going to let it happen. In the heat and intensity of the moment, we wanted each other, but when it was over, I knew there would be a wedge between us. He would feel angry and disappointed with himself, I would feel dirty, and our relationship would be sullied. It wasn't worth it. He meant so much more to me than one steamy afternoon. I couldn't offer him my virginity, but I could make sure that our first time together, if it was ever meant to be, would be done the right way—in the future, on our honeymoon. Like Mike said, he was only human. Not having sex would take an effort on both our parts.

I pulled away. He looked at me in bewilderment. "Sweetie," I said, breathlessly, "we need to stop."

He gazed into my eyes for a few seconds and then got up and sat down on the bed next to me. For a minute, I thought I had offended him. He leaned forward, put his elbows on his knees, and started to rub his temples. His shirt was still off and I watched his back muscles flex.

"Grace, I am so sorry," he said, after an uncomfortable stretch of silence.

"Sorry? What for?" He didn't answer. I sat up and squeezed his shoulder. "Mike, look at me."

He hesitated before turning around and looking into my eyes. I knew he was ashamed, but his humility only made him more desirable.

"I love you so much," I said. "I never knew I could want someone as badly as I want you. Everything about you appeals to me. But if we do this now, we'll never forgive ourselves."

He smiled and nodded slowly. "I know."

"We have all the time in the world. Neither one of us is going anywhere. If it's meant to be, it'll happen. And it'll happen the right way."

Without saying anything, he got up, retrieved his shirt from the floor, and slipped it back on. Grabbing my desk chair, he placed it beside the bed and sat down.

"Come here," he said. I rolled off the bed and perched myself on his knee. We sat in silence, me resting my head against his shoulder and him stroking my hair.

"Thank you," he said, the words rumbling through his chest like tranquil thunder.

"For what?"

"For loving me so much. You didn't take advantage of a weak moment. If you hadn't stopped us, we would have made a huge mistake. This," he said, tucking a strand of hair behind my ear, "is all new to me."

"What? Being in love?"

"Yeah, but it's more than that. It's being in love with someone I never in a lifetime thought I would have. It's thinking about you whenever I'm not with you, and forcing myself not to stare at you whenever I am. But most of all, it's wanting you so badly, in a way I've never really wanted any other woman before, and not being able to have you like that."

"But it won't be like this forever. Besides, after this weekend is over, you may decide that being with me is not worth dealing with my neurotic mother."

"That reminds me," he said. "I think you owe her an apology."

"What? You can't be serious." I jerked my head off his shoulder and stood up.

"Why do you do that?" he asked. "Why do you physically push me away whenever I say something you don't want to hear?"

"I didn't push you away."

"You got defensive and moved over there. Would you rather me not tell you when I see you doing something wrong?"

"No."

"Then why are punishing me?" He was genuinely hurt.

"I'm not," I said, with a little less attitude.

"Okay, then come back over here." Grudgingly, I baby-stepped closer to him, but I didn't sit down in my original position.

"There, are you happy?" I asked.

He shook his head. Before I realized what was happening, he wrapped his big arm around my waist, pulled me to him, and gave me a long kiss.

"Now I'm happy," he said, holding me close. "Grace, just because I point out things you do wrong, doesn't mean that I don't still love you, and it doesn't mean I think less of you. Everyone has baggage."

"Yeah, everyone except you," I said, placing my head back on his shoulder and nuzzling my nose close to his neck. "You're practically perfect."

"You know that's not true." He leaned back to look at me. "Obviously, I'm not perfect; otherwise you wouldn't have gotten mad at me out there."

"I wasn't mad," I admitted. "I was embarrassed."

"By what I said?"

"Well, yeah. I felt like you two were ganging up on me. I'll be the first to admit that I say things I have no business saying to her, but why did you have to call me out like that?"

"Because you were wrong."

"But so was she."

"But she's your mother."

"That's not fair, though. I'm not made of steel. The comments that come flying out of her mouth hurt, too. Why were you on her side?"

"It has nothing to do with sides. She's your mother and you should respect her. Period."

"Yeah, but what about her respecting me? You're acting like this is all one-sided."

"No, I'm not. I don't know everything that's gone on between you two, but it's obvious she's really hurt you over the years. Don't think I haven't noticed her words and actions. But she loves you and you love her."

"What makes you so sure?"

"She wouldn't be able to upset you like she does. If she didn't matter to you, she wouldn't affect you. But the first negative thing that flies out of her mouth, as you put it, sends you reeling into a tantrum."

"Aha!" I exclaimed. "So, you admit she's a nag."

"Yeah, she's a pretty critical person. And to tell you the truth, I think that's why you have such extreme reactions when I give you the slightest little criticism."

"You think?"

"Yes, but that's not how it's supposed to be. I'm yours and you're mine. If anyone should be able to tell you the truth, it should be me. And I expect the same from you."

"But there's a time and a place. There's nothing more humiliating than being chastised in front your mother."

"You're right. I should've left well alone and talked to you about it later. I just hated hearing you spat back and forth like that. I know she gets on your nerves, but you only get one mother. I think you might be taking it for granted that you have her."

I thought about Mike and all the foster homes he'd been in and out of. If it hadn't been for the miracle of Earl and Lani, he probably never would've known what it meant to be loved. I hated to admit it, but my mother and I were a family. If I ever lost her like Mike lost Earl, my world would go into a tailspin.

"So we'll make a deal," I suggested. "I'll make more of an effort with my mom and the whole taking criticism thing, and you'll be more careful about when and how you say stuff."

"I can handle that," he smiled. We sealed our pact with a kiss.

An hour later, Mike and I were on our way to the grocery store. I tried to make peace with my mom by inviting her along, but she insisted she had to make some important phone calls regarding Saturday's meeting.

"Some of us work for a living," she said. Immediately, I tensed with frustration. Odds are she didn't mean to be offensive, but nevertheless, I was offended.

"Okay," Mike jumped in. "We're gonna get going. Dinner's at seven; just take the elevator to the sixth floor and you'll be there."

Neither one of us were culinary geniuses, so Mike borrowed a few of his mom's recipes. The idea was to impress everyone without killing ourselves. But just to ensure that our attempt at a decadent, charming meal for five didn't fall through, we had a backup plan which involved a rush delivery from the gourmet restaurant down the street and a store-bought peach cobbler. If everything went well, though, we planned to serve crab cakes and stuffed mushrooms as appetizers, apricot chicken, roasted potatoes, and creamed spinach for the main course. And for dessert, a double-layered mint chocolate cake.

"How hard can it be?" I asked, picking up an armful of bags from the backseat of Mike's truck. "I mean, you roast a couple of chickens, throw some potatoes into the oven and voila, a three-course meal."

He laughed. "Yeah, we'll see."

He grabbed the remaining groceries and we headed up to his loft. I'd been dying to see Mike's place. I've always believed that a woman could gather all necessary knowledge about a man from two simple sources: his shoes and his home. I wasn't big on brand names or designers, but the fact that Mike's shoes were always clean told me he was a reasonably tidy person. Now, after all these months, I was looking forward to finally seeing where he lived.

"I'm nervous," I admitted, as we waited for the elevator to come down.

"About what, cooking?"

"No, about finally seeing your loft."

He grinned.

"It'll be my first time seeing where you call home."

"It's nothing special."

"It probably looks like my loft, only decorated all tacky in black and white, but I'm still excited to see it."

"Now, that hurts," he said, gripping his chest dramatically. "Why does my place have to be tacky? Do I need to remind you that despite my keen business sense, I'm an artist by trade? Let's let the loft speak for itself."

The elevator doors opened. We stepped inside and he stuck his key in an obscure little slot in the elevator wall and pushed six.

"What's that for?" I asked, pointing at the slot.

"To get to my tacky loft," he teased.

I could barely stand still as I watched the numbers climb. When we reached his floor and the doors opened, I almost dropped my groceries. Instead of the customary beige hallway lined with birch doors, I was standing outside of a long vestibule lined with fascinating, one-of-a-kind artwork. The marble floors gave the loft a formal, traditional feel, but just beyond the foyer, his living room had modern, straight-lined furniture and more funky art on the walls.

"Oh, my God," I gasped. "You have the penthouse."

"Come on, the kitchen's this way," he said, leading me to the left. "Try not to trip over your jaw."

I put the bags down on the island and looked around the room in awe. The ceilings had to be fifteen feet high.

"This is amazing."

"Go ahead," he said. "I can baste the chicken and start on the appetizers without you. Go on and snoop around."

"Please!" I said, looking innocent. I opened the nearest grocery bag and unloaded its contents. "I would never intrude on your privacy like that."

"If you say so."

"I mean, what would that say about me?"

"That you're a curious girlfriend. And curious isn't bad." He grinned.

"Well, in that case, maybe a little snooping is okay."

There was no point in trying to pretend I wasn't fascinated. I'd hung around some wealthy people in my lifetime, but I'd never seen a place like this. Besides its size, the loft's most striking feature was the living room wall, which was comprised of floor-to-ceiling windows. My home was bright, but nothing compared to Mike's. We had a similar floor plan, but instead of two bedrooms, one on either side of the living room, he had four. One of the rooms to the right of the living room was used as a library. He had custom bookcases built in, complete with an attached ladder that slid from one end of the room to the other. I thumbed through one of the shelves. There were several devotional books, a couple of Bibles, some art books, a range of classic fiction, and two huge anthologies of poetry.

The second room was set up as a complete home gym. On one side, he had a treadmill, a Stairmaster, two different types of stationary bikes and a rowing machine. On the other side was a full set of free weights along with several different weightlifting machines. *That explains how he stays in shape*. I walked across the hall to look at the bathroom. It was pristine, with a nice-sized garden tub and a separate shower. Of course, the first thing I wanted to check out was the medicine cabinet, but there wasn't one. I peaked inside the drawers and the cabinets underneath the sink. There was a box of Band-Aids, a bottle of hydrogen peroxide, and some cleaning products. It was the guest bath, and was easily double the size of my master bath.

The other two rooms, which were to the left of the living room, were his office and his bedroom. Mike's office was amazing. It was creatively divided into two parts. On the right, he'd set up a couple of desks, each with computers and complicated, hi-tech looking equipment. Not one thing was out of place. Hanging above the desks was a big, flat-screened television. I'd only seen those on TV. I'd always blamed my aversion to technology on my creative side, so the fact that Mike was both an artist and a technology buff showed just how intelligent and well-rounded a person he truly was.

The left end of the office was in drastic contrast to the right. In one of the corners, there was a large drawing table covered with all sorts of papers and across from the table were three easels, each with canvas paintings on them. One of the paintings looked like the beginning of a portrait and the other two were abstracts. Leaning against the walls were stacks and stacks of sketches, drawings, and paintings, at least a hundred of them. Mike had made a comment once that he hated feeling more like a businessman than an artist. When did he find the time to create these?

"When I started *Life Sketch*," he'd said, "I swore I wouldn't let the logistics of the business steal my love of the craft. For a while, it was easy. We had a handful of clients, but almost overnight, the business exploded. We had artists knocking on our door looking for jobs and agencies ringing us day and night looking for artists. Before I knew it, I was spending twelve-hour days shuffling through heaps of paperwork and smoothing out all the kinks. I'm not complaining. I know I've lived a blessed life and that I'm using the business to serve the Lord. I guess I'm just scared I'll wake up twenty years from now and regret the man I've become."

But I could look around his office and see he had nothing to fear. The room was indicative of the type of person he was—neat and orderly in some respects, and wild and artistic in others. He hadn't sacrificed his love for drawing; he'd successfully meshed it with his business sense and created an innovative concept, serving tens of thousands of people.

The master bedroom was the size of three of my rooms combined. In place of the black bedroom set I was expecting, he had expensive-looking, dark cherry wood furniture. His four-poster, king-sized bed was adorned with a plush, beige comforter and huge, fluffy pillows. Hanging on the wall above were two large, framed, black-and-white photographs. One was of an older white man sitting in a rocking chair. His head was thrown back in laughter and his eyes were closed. The other showed an elderly white woman delicately smelling a rose. Had Mike taken them? I studied them for a few moments and then walked across the room and peaked inside his top dresser drawer, which was pretty organized. I flipped on the light to his walk-in closet. It was almost half-empty. On the left were his business suits and on the right were his casual clothes. His shoes were neatly lined up against the wall and his laundry basket was tucked into a corner.

Next, I explored the master bath. Like the other bathroom, it was sparkling clean. He had a Jacuzzi tub that was big enough to hold six people and his shower had built-in benches and two showerheads. Next to his linen closet were Jack-and-Jill sinks, and in the corner just above the mirror was a mounted television. These drawers contained soaps and colognes, razors, shaving cream, and other assorted toiletries.

I went back into his bedroom and reclined on his bed. It had a nice, firm mattress, and the pillows were cloaked in his scent. I looked up at the ceiling and tried to imagine myself living there—what it would feel like waking up next to Mike every morning. As much time as we spent together, there were so many things we hadn't experienced—so many things I didn't know about him.

"Don't you look comfortable?"

I propped myself up on my elbows. Mike was standing in the doorway with a lopsided grin plastered across his face.

"Sorry." I started to climb down.

"No, stay," he said kicking off his shoes and flopping onto the beautiful suede couch in front of the window. I joined him. Gingerly, he placed his head on my stomach. I toyed with one of his dreads and watched as his head rose and fell with the rhythm of my breathing.

"I could really get used to this," I said, sighing with contentment.

"Me, too."

"This place is gorgeous. I can't believe Trina. All this time she's been coming here for Bible study, and she never once mentioned how incredible it is."

"And she calls herself a best friend!" His hot breath tickled my bellybutton.

"The library is amazing," I raved. "And with your gym, I don't have to go on those long walks anymore."

"You can use it whenever you want."

It was sweet of him to offer, but I'd probably never come to his place to work out. I'd grown to love my morning walks, and I'd die before I let him see me a sweaty, smelly mess.

We were silent for a few minutes. "I like your office, too. You have one of those flat TV thingies."

"So, that's what you call it," he teased. "All this time I never knew."

I popped his head playfully. "I looked at some of your drawings, the ones stacked against the wall. They're really good."

"Those are old—mostly college projects. You can have one if you want."

"Are you serious? I know exactly which one I want!" I squealed.

He lifted his head and looked at me.

"It's the picture of the three little black girls praying." The picture was so life-like that when I first saw it, I was taken away by its detail. He captured the girls expertly, from their plaited hair down to their clasped hands

He inched up and rested his head against the couch cushion.

"Those are my sisters." He waited for me to say something, but I was too stunned, so he went on. "When child services came to pack us up, the social worker told me I was going to be placed in a separate home because I was the oldest and the only boy. Even as a little kid, I knew I wouldn't see them again. It was just this gut feeling. So I ran to my mom's room and grabbed that picture out of her nightstand drawer. I loved my sisters—still do, and I wanted to make sure I never forgot what they looked like. I had this whole elaborate scheme to go get them as soon as I found us a good home. But as I got older, it dawned on me that it was never going to happen. I took that picture with me everywhere, and at night I'd stare at it for hours and cry."

"Have you tried to find them?"

"For years. I hired private investigators, searched the Internet and old documents. But this happened over twenty years ago, back before records were filed in computer databases. They only had paper copies, and the agency that handled our case closed before I turned eighteen. So I never had a chance to petition for the documentation on my sisters and me. After running into dead end after dead end, I gave up—put it in the Lord's hands. If it's His will, one day it'll happen. Over the years, the corners of the photo turned yellow and the edges started to tatter, so I decided to sketch it—every strand of hair, every eyelash. It took four months."

"It shows," I said, caressing his cheek. "It's beautiful."

"I'm glad you like it. It's my mom's favorite, too. Good pick."

"Are you crazy? I can't take that. Not now that I know how much it means to you. You should keep it."

"No, I want you to have it. I'll have it framed for you and then we can hang it in your living room. You need some art in there. The walls are stark."

"I don't know what to say. Are you sure?"

"Of course. You saw it in the office—it's just collecting dust."

"Thank you so much," I gushed, leaning forward to give him a kiss. That's when I noticed a strange smell, a sweet stench. I sniffed Mike's shirt. It reeked.

"Why do you smell like putrid baby food?" I asked.

"Oh yeah, that," he said in disgust. "I had a small mishap with the apricots."
"What kind of mishap?"

"Well, the recipe said to sauté them on low heat for twenty minutes. But I figured if I put them in the microwave, we could have them done in half the time."

"So what happened?"

"They exploded."

I closed my eyes and shook my head, trying desperately not to laugh. *Classic*!

"I thought we agreed to call your mom with our cooking questions before we did anything rash."

"It seemed simple enough." He looked pitiful.

I wondered how much of his personality and mannerisms came from his biological mom and what he picked up from Earl and Lani. We were hoping Lani could come for dinner, but she'd already made other plans.

"Are you sure your mom can't come?" I asked for the hundredth time.

"Yes!" he answered, in playful exasperation.

"Okay, okay. I won't ask anymore. It's just that she lives two floors below me, and I still haven't met her. I don't even know what she looks like."

"She's right there," he said, pointing toward the wall behind his bed. I looked up at the two pictures I'd been admiring earlier.

"Oh!" I said, my hand involuntarily covering my gaping mouth. I walked to the foot of the bed so I could get a better look. "Earl and Lani."

"Yep." He stood and joined me.

"They're...well, they're..." I couldn't think of a tactful way to say it.

"White." he said.

"Well, yeah."Their race didn't make a difference, but I'd just assumed they were black.

"Does that bother you?"

"Not at all," I said, my gaze never leaving the pictures. "I'm just surprised."

"Why?"

"When you told me about this loving couple willing to take a chance on a scrawny black kid who tried to steal from them, I assumed the couple was black. I just figured that the only way two people could have such compassion for someone they didn't know was if they shared a common denominator with that stranger—like race." I cocked my head to the side and continued to stare at the pictures.

"That's true for the average person, but not with Christians. That's the beauty of putting Christ first—you realize He's the only common denominator that matters. His love for the world is the ultimate tie that binds us all together."

I wasn't sure what he meant by God's love connecting the world when millions of people didn't believe in Him and millions more relied on "higher powers" like Allah and Buddha, but I nodded. Whatever or whoever it was that enticed Earl and Lani to take Mike in and give him a permanent home, complete with love and support, had to be powerful and supernatural. I don't know if I would have had it in me to do what they did.

"You want to know something else that binds you and me together?" I asked, gazing up at him.

"What?"

"We have dinner guests coming in a few hours and nothing to feed them but apricot purée."

His face fell. "Whose idea was this, anyway?"

"Yours."

"Next time I suggest that we cook anything for anybody, slap me," he whimpered.

"I'll do that, but in the meantime I'm gonna salvage the apricots and start on the chicken." We were running short on time and I knew that Mike and I could easily waste the rest of the day talking, and subsequently have nothing to serve for dinner.

"What do you want me to do?" he asked, catching my decisive tone. He stood at attention like a little soldier waiting for his orders.

"Well, first things first. Go change your shirt. You reek!"

By all accounts, dinner was a success. Mike and I soaked in the "ooh's" and "ahh's" we received as Trina, Ron, and my mom arrived and admired our elegant spread. *I* was even impressed, considering we'd spent half the afternoon talking and kissing and the other half scurrying about adding little finishing touches.

"I didn't know you had it in you," Mom said. With her, it was as close to a compliment as I was going to get.

"Thanks." I gave her a quick, stiff hug. An expression of curious surprise crossed her face. My mother and I were never big on physical affection, but after my talk with Mike, I resolved to lose the attitude, sweep my bitterness under the rug, and make the best of my relationship with her.

"How come you don't cook like this at home?" Trina jabbed, taking her seat next to Ron.

"Please! Never again," I swore. "This was way too much work."

"Even with your handy assistant?" Trina asked, nodding in Mike's direction.

Ron chuckled. "I can only imagine how helpful Mike was," he said, a sinister grin spreading across his face. "Between drooling over Grace's every word and filling the glasses with ice, I'm sure his day was jam-packed."

We all laughed.

"Hey now, be nice," I chastised playfully. "Aside from blowing up a pound of fruit, Mike's help was invaluable."

"Thank you, baby."

"He blew up fruit?" Trina asked, an amused expression on her face.

Mike hung his head.

"This I have to hear," Ron said, reaching for the potatoes.

Trina tapped his hand. "Who wants to say grace?"

"I will," Mike offered. We held hands and bowed our heads. "Father, thank you for this food You've so graciously put before us and even more than that, thank You for letting Grace and me live through the experience of preparing it." I smiled as our guests erupted into stifled snickers. "Please bless our conversation," he continued. "And thank you for affording us this opportunity to get together and enjoy each other's company. In Jesus' name we pray, amen."

"Amen."

"So," my mom said, spearing a chicken breast and then passing the platter to Mike. "You were about to tell us how one blows up fruit."

Chapter Ten

My mother's charm and charisma blew me away last night. Over the years, I'd seen her lather up hoity-toity CEOs and other overpaid, under worked muckety-mucks, but never had I seen her so personable around regular people—people from whom she had nothing to gain. She was the life of the party, a role I didn't know she could play. Mike, Ron, Trina, and I were wide-eyed the entire evening, listening to her recount hilarious tales of college, men, and motherhood. I always knew she had a way with words, but she was acting like a totally different woman.

After each story, we'd all grip our stomachs, wipe away our tears, and then—like little kids—beg for more.

"Oh, I've been talking all night," she said, polishing off her second piece of cake. "I don't want to bore you."

"No, please!" Ron pleaded. "You're anything but boring." We all nodded eagerly, unable to hide our anticipation. She glowed from the attention.

"Are you sure?" she asked, looking at me intently.

"Positive," I said, with a reassuring smile. Armed with my blessing, she launched into an even funnier, wittier story than before, flooring us with yet another one of her life experiences.

At one point, she volunteered to help me clear away the dishes and serve the coffee. Once in the kitchen, she set down the empty plates she was carrying and gently grabbed my elbow. I placed my dishes in the sink and turned to face her.

"Grace, I'm having a great time," she said. Her words were earnest. My heart fluttered.

"Good," I said, squeezing her shoulder. "I'm glad." I started to turn back toward the sink when she tugged at my elbow again.

"I'm not just talking about this evening. I've really enjoyed being here these past couple of days."

I studied her face—her body language. She seemed vulnerable, as if with those few words, she was attempting to apologize and offer me a previously guarded part of herself—perhaps a portion of her softer side, perhaps a piece of her heart.

"Thanks, Mom. That means a lot."

"I love you, Grace. I know I haven't always shown it in the ways you've expected, but I do love you, more than life itself."

Tears filled my eyes. It's not that my mom had never told me she loved me before. She had—many times, but never with such conviction. It was always said in passing—three obligatory words with universal meaning, but lacking in feeling.

I wanted to say the same words back, as powerfully and truthfully, but for some reason I couldn't. I loved her and she knew it, but the words stuck in the back of my throat like thick molasses and refused to budge. I nodded and tears trickled down the contours of my face and dripped carelessly off my chin.

"Promise me you'll never forget that," she ordered tenderly. "No matter what happens between us, promise me you'll always remember that you've been my one, true joy and that I love you." Her voice caught and she averted her eyes.

"I promise."

She reached up and wrapped her arms around my neck. This time the embrace was warm and genuine.

"I'm glad you came," I admitted, as we separated and dabbed at our tears.

We got home around midnight. I would like to have stayed longer, but Mom insisted she needed to get some sleep for her meeting.

"Stay, Grace. I'm a big girl. I think I can get down to the third floor by myself."

I tossed the idea around for a second, but decided it would be selfish of me to send her back to the loft alone, even if it was in the same building.

"I'll tell you what," Mike said, sensing my reluctance. "Go home with your mom, get some sleep and tomorrow, say, around nine, I'll bring over coffee and croissants for the three of us."

"What am I?" Trina asked, one eyebrow raised. "The ugly stepsister?"

"Okay, coffee and croissants for the four of us."

"Sounds good, but what time do you have to be at your meeting?" I asked my mom, who was patiently standing by the door.

"Don't worry about me," she said, with a wave of her hand. "Someone's coming to pick me up."

"Okay," I shrugged. "Then it looks like this is goodnight."

I gave Ron a quick hug.

"Thanks again," he said. "Dinner was great."

While everyone else said their good-byes, Mike gave me a long hug, and then we piled into the elevator and headed home.

By eight, I was up and still as shocked as I was last night. I was amazed by the depth of my mom's love for me, and how knowing her love nourished me in ways I never realized I needed. This morning, as I tiptoed around the loft getting ready for my walk, I wasn't just in awe of my mother's heartfelt confession. I was taken aback by my current circumstances and how they came to be.

My life had taken crazy, unexpected turns lately, starting with my move to Memphis. Who follows her best friend across the country? Even though it had almost cost me my friendship with Trina, I was glad I did it. If I hadn't, I never would have met Mike, and Trina never would have met Ron. I wouldn't be back in school or forty pounds lighter. I'd still be in Michigan, miserably fat, locked up in my room, afraid to step out and make something more of myself.

In under a year, I'd morphed into a new woman. I had a wonderful man and for the first time ever, I didn't have to contort myself to fit into someone else's world. Somehow, everyone just automatically fit into mine. The mere thought had me smiling as I headed for the park.

My walk was spectacular. I hadn't realized how heavy the air had been all summer. Twenty minutes into my jaunts, I'd become accustomed to tying my sweatshirt around my waist and pulling my hair up into a bun, while sweat drenched my neck and back. But summer had quickly turned into fall, and the notorious Memphis humidity was dissipating with every passing week.

I took the grass-trodden path that paralleled the Mississippi River. Every few steps, I raised my face to the sky and enjoyed the soft, crisp wind caressing my cheeks and nose. I watched the barges move slowly through the murky water, leaving behind massive ripples that grew into calm waves, which eventually vanished altogether. I walked briskly, keeping a quick pace, and enjoyed the warmth of the sun when it peeked out from behind the clouds every now and then. I so enjoyed the walk that I was surprised to see the end of the path up ahead.

Instead of going home right away, I walked across the street and bought a bottle of water from a street vendor and found an empty bench.

Two small birds hopped around the sidewalk, pecking at anything that resembled a crumb. Every once in a while, they'd stop, crane their necks, look around and then go right back to pecking. Their breakfast was interrupted when two men covered in sweat and panting heavily came jogging around the corner. They nodded at me and said "good morning" as they passed.

Shortly after, a young man strolled by with a cute little boy toddling beside him. They were walking slowly, stopping periodically to share a croissant and a carton of juice. Mike was supposed to bring over breakfast at nine. I looked down at my watch. It was a quarter to ten! I jumped up and walk-trotted home. My mom had probably already left for her meeting and Trina was probably still knocked out. Images of Mike standing outside my door carrying an armload of coffee and pastries made me hasten my pace to a run.

No one was waiting for me as I stepped off the elevator and turned my key to open the door. If I was lucky, Trina had heard him knocking and let him in.

"Hello?" I called. Trina, Mike, and Mom were sitting in the living room, stone-faced. No one greeted me or even smiled.

"Who died?" I joked. Trina bit her lip. Mike remained quiet.

"Where were you?" Mom asked, cautiously. "I woke up this morning and you were gone."

"I know," I said glancing around the room for Mike's promised croissants and coffee. "I decided to go for a walk. I didn't want to wake you."

She nodded and looked at Mike and Trina, who in turn looked in every direction but mine. Their peculiar behavior was starting to panic me. Mom opened her mouth to speak just as the toilet in the guest bathroom flushed.

"Who's that?" I asked. Mike looked at me with a worried expression, but no one answered. "What's going on?" My voice had an edge to it this time.

The bathroom door opened, and a familiar puffy face emerged. "Professor Harris?" He froze and shot a worried glance at my mother. Nobody offered an explanation. "What are you doing here?"

"Uh, well," he cleared his throat. "Your mother invited me."

I recalled my first day in his class, when he'd said he and Mom were old friends. My heart resumed its normal beat as I pieced things together.

"So, this is your Saturday meeting?" I asked my Mom.

"Well, I was hoping that it could be *our* Saturday meeting."

"I don't understand," I said, looking from Mom to Trina, then to Mike, and finally to Professor Harris. It was clear they were hiding something, and the tension in the room was thick.

"I don't understand," I repeated.

"Gracie," Mike said, speaking for the first time since I'd arrived. "Professor Harris—Anthony Harris—is your father."

I don't have any memories of my father—not his touch or his smell, not even his voice. My father existed only in a handful of pictures and a few recycled stories, told so frequently by so many different people, I couldn't even be sure which version was true. Everyone in my mom's family held a different opinion of him. To my grandma, he was a no-good deadbeat after a good time. According to my grandfather, he was just a boy pretending to be a man. And to my mom, he was nothing more than an unfortunate mistake.

Of all the different descriptions of my father, only three things remained consistent: he was an alcoholic, he loved jazz, and he smoked two packs of cigarettes a day. They're insignificant little details that didn't set him apart from all the other vodka-chugging, Coltrain-listening, tobacco-sucking masses, but they were all I owned.

Who is my father and what is he about? I don't know if he prefers McDonald's over Burger King, what his thoughts are on the rising cost of health care, if he has any other children, or if he believes in God. But I've always respected his decision to leave. Maybe I needed to pump him up in my mind—make him more than he was capable of being. Or maybe it was my way of living without hate in my heart. Whatever my reasons, deep down, I always felt he was a good man who'd extricated himself from a situation before he made it any worse.

At one point, my parents were happy together. I've seen pictures of them back in the day. They both had tight, puffy Afros and huge smiles on their faces. There's one snapshot, my favorite, where they're leaning forward and gazing into each other's eyes. It looks like they're about to kiss. I've never seen my mother look so vibrant. For as long as I can remember, she's always had a curt, businesslike manner about her. I used to assume that she didn't know how to have fun—that her diligent work ethic was ingrained in her. My uncles still tease her to this day about getting beat up when she was a child because she asked the teacher for more homework. When I saw that picture, though, I realized she had a lighter side—a side only my father had managed to wrestle out of her and because of that, I knew he couldn't be all bad. There had to be more to him than people were willing to see.

The situation with my father was not unique. He disappeared for most of my mom's pregnancy. Then, a couple of months after I was born, he reappeared and promised to make us a family. But things got complicated. My mom went back to work and wanted him to stay home and watch me. She made more money than he could ever hope to earn and it seemed like the most logical arrangement. But he didn't want to be a house-dad. His pride told him that he was supposed to be the provider. He got frustrated and started drinking. By the time I was a year old, he was guzzling cognac by day and abusing Mom by night, until one winter morning when he dropped me off at my grandma's and never came back. Mom says she hasn't heard from him since—not once.

"I couldn't tell you if he was dead or alive, married or single, crazy or sane," she told me when I was a teenager. "He made the choice to walk out. I didn't ask him to leave."

"Yeah, but you moved us clear across the city right after he left. He could have come back—realized he made a mistake," I argued.

She sighed. "I waited for him for a year before deciding to pick up the pieces and move on with my life. I had *you* to think about. Besides, Grandma and Grandpa's number and address have stayed the same for thirty years. If he'd wanted to find us, he could have. Sometimes, we have to accept the truth for what it is—stop hoping against reality."

But now, standing in my living room watching him watch me, I was angry. It was easy to love him—to forgive him—when he was just a nameless face, someone I could pity. But he wasn't some alcoholic, panhandling on a street corner somewhere, incapable of raising a child. He was a college professor, well-spoken and educated. He wasn't the lowlife I'd pictured over all these years. Instead, he was a deadbeat who'd walked away from his responsibilities. A jerk, who'd left behind a living, breathing person he helped create, and had started a new life—an easier life—without so much as a backward glance. His strange behavior in class, my mother's sudden trip to see me—it all made sense.

I don't know what they were hoping for, maybe a touchy-feely reunion, complete with teary eyes and runny noses, but it wasn't going to happen. He didn't have a right to be in my home. He chose to leave, and I made peace with his decision. I'd set aside the feelings of failure and inferiority that came along with abandonment and carried on with my life. If I hadn't walked into his classroom a week ago, he would have gone on pretending I didn't exist. It wasn't my job to make him feel better about himself, and I was going to show him that I could shove him into a closet and throw away the key just as easily as he could. I owed him nothing.

"Why did you bring him here?" I questioned my mother coldly.

"I thought it would be best to get together and talk."

"Best for whom?"

"Grace," she pleaded. "Don't be angry. This isn't easy for any of us."

"Yeah, I'm sure it took a lot out of the two of you to plan this little ambush."

"We didn't plan this," Professor Harris jumped in. I rolled my eyes and shot him a nasty look. "I'm telling you the truth," he insisted. "I wouldn't lie to you."

"You can't be serious!" I shouted. "Who do you think you are? Do you actually think I'd put any stock in what you say?"

His eyes grew wide and he stepped back, stunned by my sharp words.

"Maybe this was a mistake," he said, turning to my mom, who was nervously shifting her weight from one foot to the other and wringing her hands.

"Grace, he's your father," she whispered, a glint of desperation in her eyes.

"He is nothing." I whipped around to face him. "Do you understand that? You made a choice a long time age to walk out and you don't get to renege. If you had any kind of integrity, you wouldn't be here. You would've treated me like any other student and gone on with your pitiful little existence. This," I said, flailing my arms around wildly, "proves you're nothing more than a selfish coward."

"Gracie, don't," Mike urged gently. He and Trina were still standing in the living room, caught in the crossfire of my family's feud.

"How do you want me to react, Mike?" I asked. "What do you want me to say? You want me to say everything's okay—that all's forgiven?"

"No, I just don't want you to say something you'll regret."

"Well, that shouldn't be a problem because as far as I'm concerned, this conversation is over."

Professor Harris inched closer and closer to the door.

"I'm sorry you wasted your time coming to see me. I'm sure you had the best of intentions, but I just want you to go away."

He looked at me through his wire-rimmed glasses. Out of the classroom, the same gray hair and wrinkled hands that gave him a semblance of wisdom there made him look old and tired here.

"I can't make you listen," he said quietly. "But I promise you, there's more to this story than you know."

"That may be, but I'm not interested," I said, raising my chin in defiance. He nodded and slumped his shoulders—a clear mark of a defeated man.

"If you ever change your mind, you know where to find me."

I stood across from him, my face cold and stony.

"Cherie," he said to my mother. "I'll talk to you later." She nodded and shrugged her shoulders apologetically. And just as easily as he'd entered it, my father exited my life for a second time. We all stayed quiet for a moment after the door closed. Silence descended, and I felt all three of them looking at me through the corners of their eyes, carefully trying to evaluate my state of mind.

"Grace," my mother said. I held my hand up and silenced her before she could start.

"You had no right," I said icily.

She sighed. "I'm sorry."

I knew she meant it, but I was too angry to listen. I just wanted to be by myself. I blew by her into the safety of my room and slammed the door.

I spent the rest of the morning and most of the afternoon brooding. Part of me wanted someone to chase after me, to rush into my room, to kneel down by my side and tell me I did the right thing. But it didn't happen that way. Instead, everyone cleared out and left me to stew by myself. I wanted to blame someone—Professor Harris, my mom—but all three of us were suffering. Professor Harris hadn't expected me to walk into his classroom any more than I expected him to step out of my bathroom. Even if my mom had found a better, less obtrusive way to break the news, I was still going to have to dismantle the wall of anger I'd erected over the years. The talk I had with my mom the night before was a start, but now that my father was involved, the same old feelings of confusion and disarray came creeping back. I didn't want to be hard or unforgiving. It took a lot of time and energy to harbor grudges and that wasn't the way I wanted to spend my time, that's not the person I wanted to be.

So I wrote. I grabbed a legal pad and a pen and I scribbled furiously, filling page after page. I created a nameless character and recounted my childhood through her. The words flowed effortlessly and the emotion that took shape was raw. All of my frustration, my rage, my dread—I confined it to the page and sealed it with my tears. And by the time I heard a light rap at my door, I'd completed two chapters of my first novel and had started the third.

"It's me," Mike said.

"Come in." He carried a brown paper bag from our favorite Italian restaurant. The aroma wafted across the room and made my stomach growl.

"I thought you might be hungry," he said, placing it on my desk next to my computer. He stood in front of the window, nervously shifting his eyes around the room, waiting for me to say something. I put down the pen and pointed to the chair parked at my desk.

"Do you want to sit?" I asked sweetly. He carried it to the foot of my bed and sat down. "What're you thinking?" I asked, sitting Indian-style, and turning so that we were facing each other. His eyes moved slowly over my face.

"I'm thinking I'm sorry this happened to you, and I'm even sorrier that I couldn't help you."

"You think I was wrong?"

"Gracie, I've never had to experience anything like this before. My opinion doesn't matter."

I took his hand. "It matters to me."

He sighed. "You weren't given fair warning. You didn't know he was the reason your mom came to Memphis. If you'd known, the reaction you had would have been kind of heartless. But it was a surprise, and it wasn't even private. You were cornered and your defenses went up and that's normal."

"But I shouldn't have called him a selfish coward."

Mike grinned. "You could have left that part out."

"So you're not mad at me?" I asked. His eyebrows furrowed. "You left without saying goodbye. I thought maybe you were disappointed with how I handled the situation."

"Come here," he said, spreading his arms. I crawled out of bed and sat on his lap. He cupped my face in his hands and raised my chin until our eyes met. "This isn't your fault. You didn't cause this."

"I know."

"Do you really?" he asked, rubbing my cheek with his thumb.

"At first, no. I wanted to blame someone and being the dysfunctional casehead that I am, the first person on my list was me. But that didn't feel right, because I didn't do anything. It's just something that happened and nobody knows why, right?"

"Right."

"Wrong!" I exclaimed, a huge smile spread across my face. Mike looked at me as if I'd lost my mind.

"What do you mean?"

"I mean, I think I know why this is all happening." He released my face and tilted his head to the side.

"Tell me." I handed him the two legal pads I'd already filled. He flipped through the pages, which were covered, back and front.

"What's this?"

"I'll give you one guess." The bed shook as I bounced with excitement.

"Your book?"

I nodded vigorously, my eyes wide. I must have been glowing.

"It's only two chapters, but that's something, right? That's not too shabby for an afternoon's work."

"You did all of this today?" He flipped through the pages.

"Yeah. I was lying here kind of stunned, unable to control all the thoughts and emotions running through me. So I just started jotting everything down and this is what I got. And it's good, Mike. It's better than anything I ever thought I could produce, because it's real." I held my hand over my heart, pledge-of-allegiance style.

"What's it about?"

"Me, except that I haven't really come up with a name for the protagonist yet. But it's definitely my life on those pages, without sounding freakish and tragically flawed like I'd always perceived myself to be. It's interesting—I'm interesting! It reads like fiction—like a book you'd take to the beach or curl up on the couch with on a rainy afternoon."

"And you think your dad inspired you?"

"It has to be. Otherwise, how do you explain this?" I slapped the note pads that Mike was still holding.

"I don't know, but I'm happy for you."

"For once, I made something good out of a bad situation. And you know what else? This is what I'm supposed to do with my life. I'm so hyped, I could do cartwheels. I was never this excited about *Simon and Eddie*, never felt this much—"

"Joy?" he offered.

"That's it! Now I feel like I have a whole new purpose and direction for my life." I was talking so fast, my breath came out in short, airy spurts.

"So what will you do about your father?"

"I don't know," I confessed. "I've imagined this day for so long—what I would say, how I would act, even what I'd wear. But it didn't unfold anything like I'd hoped. And I'm the one who messed it up."

"You didn't mess anything up."

I groaned.

"Yeah, I did. I had myself convinced I was okay with him leaving. I told myself he had a reason—that there were two sides to every story and somewhere in between was the truth. But the minute he showed up to tell his side of the story, I chewed him out and sent him on his way." He nodded, but didn't speak. "I promised myself I wouldn't play the martyr," I continued. "I didn't want to be the typical scorned daughter, to drag baggage into my adulthood, but I did. I'm not sure I can let it go, but I'm starting to see that I can use it. I'll never be able to pretend it didn't happen."

"No one expects you to pretend he didn't leave," he said slowly. "He just wanted a chance to explain, to say he was sorry, and to see if there was any chance of rebuilding."

"You think I should give him a chance."

"That would be ideal, but in your case, I don't know if it would be realistic or even healthy. If seeing him opens up wounds inside you, maybe it's not a good idea."

"But what about forgiveness and respect?"

"I was talking about your mom when I said that. She was there—a constant in your life; she raised you. He wasn't there, and it damaged you in ways you didn't even realize."

"Should I leave things the way they are?"

He shrugged. "Whatever you decide to do, you need to forgive him. You don't have to shove aside twenty-eight years of pain and invite him back into your life. But you do need to accept the situation and really, truly move on. If you don't do that, you'll always be bound by this part of your past."

"I get what you're saying. I just don't know if I can do it right now."

"What about your mom? She feels terrible."

"She should."

He gave me a stern look. "She loves you. Bringing him over here wasn't the smartest route, but she didn't mean to hurt you. She cried for hours."

I bit my lip. A flood of guilt swept over me.

"Trina and I took her to my place. She was so upset she could hardly speak. We prayed over her and tried to convince her to come back down, to talk it out, but she insisted on checking into a hotel."

I hung my head and covered my face with my hands. "Why would she do that?"

"She was scared to come back. She messed up—she's embarrassed. She's staying at the Peabody." He dug a crumbled scrap of paper from his pocket. "Here's the number."

A sob swelled in the back of my throat. Mike pulled me to him.

"I don't know how to fix this," I admitted.

"Call her; invite her to church tomorrow."

"She doesn't go to church," I whimpered.

"That's not the point She's leaving on Monday, right? Don't you want it to get resolved before she goes?"

I nodded, my head still resting on Mike's shoulder. The thought of my mother in a hotel room, distressed over me, made my heart sink. I wanted to hop in my car, check her out, and bring her home with me. But that type of overt, ardent emotion wasn't expressed between the two of us. Mike was right; church was probably the best way to get the recovery train rolling.

"I'll invite her," I consented. My stomach made a hideous churning sound. "But first, can we eat?"

She wouldn't come back to the loft. Mike tried coaxing her and I tried begging, but she insisted on staying at the hotel.

"I need to be by myself for a while. I need a quiet place to clear my mind and think." She exhaled loudly, sounding weary and unhappy.

"But don't you think we need to talk?"

"Not yet, Grace. Okay? I can't." Her tone was firm, but laced with regret.

Mike nudged me. "Church," he whispered.

"Will you come to church with us tomorrow?"

"I don't know; church was never really my thing."

"Church is for everybody, Mom. And besides, that's not the point. Tomorrow's my last chance to see you—to talk face to face. Please, Mom."

"Okay."

I breathed a sigh of relief. "We'll pick you up at 10:30."

I hesitated a few seconds before saying *I love you*, and then realized she was already gone.

My mother looked uncharacteristically ragged when she stepped off the elevator and into the lobby fifteen minutes late. Her slacks were wrinkled, her blouse was misbuttoned, and her hair was matted to her head. She forced a smile when she saw me.

"I'm sorry about the time."

"What happened? Didn't you set your alarm clock?" I held the door open for her and pointed to Mike's SUV across the parking lot.

"I didn't get much sleep," she shrugged. "I was a little disoriented this morning, that's all."

"Well, get prepared to wake up," I said, trying to stay cheery. "I think you're really going to like this church."

"Why's that?" she asked, sounding disengaged.

"It's not what you'd expect church to be like. No boring hymns or bland sermons. They've got great music—a full orchestra, the works. And the people are really friendly."

"Sounds like an experience." Her flat, uninterested behavior startled me. If there's one thing my mom was sure to have, it was an opinion. But since yesterday's fiasco, she'd lost her trademark spunk. I grabbed her wrist and stopped her just short of Mike's truck.

"Mom, are you okay?"

"Yeah," she said, taking a step forward. Dark bags circled her eyes. "I'm just tired."

"Well, we don't have to do this. Mike can take Ron and Trina and we can stay here." She shook her head.

"It's not that kind of tired." Before I could ask her to explain, the passenger door swung open and Trina stuck her head out.

"We really gotta go if we're going to get seats," she said, looking apologetic.

"Mom, you take the front seat," I offered. Without a word, she climbed into the truck next to Mike. Trina gave me a questioning look. I shook my head and shrugged.

We arrived at church just as the choir was walking down the aisles. Like five little ducklings in a row, we followed one of the ushers to our seats. My mom clapped half-heartedly through the praise and worship hour, standing and sitting as the worship leaders instructed. I studied her out of the corner of my eye. She was going through the motions, but I couldn't tell if she was getting anything out of it.

She watched in bemusement as dozens of people—old and young, black and white, male and female—ran and danced in the aisles. My breath caught when I noticed her left foot tapping to the music. She began mouthing the words to the songs, which were projected onto huge screens on either side of the stage. Before I knew it, her whole body was swaying to and fro. She looked looser—livelier.

By the time the offering baskets came around, her old glow was back.

"Do I have to be a member to give?" she asked Mike in a loud whisper. He shook his head and grinned, obviously pleased by her fervent interest and participation. She rifled through her purse and dug out a twenty-dollar bill.

The message was on God's undying love for us. I listened as Bishop told how God sent Jesus to earth for the sole purpose of being crucified.

"Don't take those words lightly," he warned. "Did you hear me? I said do not take those words lightly."

A few members shouted in agreement.

"Amen! Preach, Bishop!"

"Let me ask you something," he said, addressing the entire congregation. "How many of you have kids?" About eighty percent of those present raised their hands, including my mother. "Now, I know I don't even have to ask this next question, but I'm gonna throw it out there anyway."

"Ask, Bishop," one woman exhorted.

"Do you love your kids?"

A low rumble spread through the crowd as people nodded and mumbled expected answers like, "yes," and "of course."

"You would do anything for them, wouldn't you?" Again a low rumble. "You'd protect them at all costs. Jump in front of a speeding car, take a bullet if it meant keeping them safe. Am I right?" Most everyone nodded; a few people clapped. "Come on now," he shouted. "Let me know if I'm right."

The sanctuary erupted into thunderous applause.

"You're right, Bishop!" He nodded slowly and paced the stage.

"That's what I thought. See, I don't know about you, but my children—who, by the way, aren't even children anymore—are my heart's delight. Always have been, always will be."

My mom reached over and squeezed my hand.

"Now, let me ask you all another question."

"Ask, Bishop!"

"Would you sacrifice your child to save me or someone else from sin?" The murmuring congregation quickly died down to a hush. "Look at your neighbor," he instructed. I looked to my right at Mom. "If you had a daughter or son and your neighbor lied to his or her boss or coveted his friend's wife or murdered someone, would you put your precious child—your baby, your flesh and blood—on the altar to keep your neighbor from going to hell?"

"No!" someone up front shouted.

"Not in this lifetime!" another person yelled.

"Well, God loved us so much that He sent His only Child—His only one—to earth to die, so that we might have a chance to go to heaven."

"All right now!"

"He sent His only Son to die for you and me. Don't take those words lightly. Imagine your son or daughter. It doesn't matter how old they are, because they'll always be our babies, am I right?"

"Mmmm," my mother nodded.

"Imagine your child hanging naked from a cross high up in the air for all to see. Imagine your baby being beaten with whips this wide." He held his thumb and index finger about five inches apart. "With all sorts of sharp objects, like nails and rocks, wedged into that leather, so that each time the whip landed on His back, it ripped His skin open and left gaping slashes."

Some individuals shook their heads, while others shifted uncomfortably in their seats.

"Now imagine those heartless guards beating your child relentlessly until his or her back was nothing more than a bloody, fleshy mess. Now, after all of that, your baby is forced to carry his own cross miles and miles on his bloody, mutilated back in the sweltering heat. And once he reaches his destination, he's nailed by his hands and feet on this slab of wood, and posted up with no clothing for people to mock him while he dies. Are you picturing it? Can you see your child?"

A low rumble spread through the crowd. Random sniffles could be heard throughout the sprawling sanctuary.

"Imagine precious hands and feet, covered in blood. Envision your child hanging there, struggling for breath minute after minute, hour after hour, until lungs finally collapse and he or she passes away. Now, was it worth it? Was it worth watching your child being tortured and killed so that you," he pointed to one random person in the front row, and then another, "or you, or you, wouldn't go to hell?" He let the question sink in. "Well, I'll tell you what. God felt everything I just described, and as painful as it must have been for Him, it was worth it, because He loves you that much. He loves you more than you love your neighbor, more than you love your kids, more than you love yourself. Wake up! Wake up! Wake up!"

The words rang through my ears.

"Salvation is a gift. It's a gift that nobody—nobody—deserves. You don't earn it, it isn't owed you. It's a gift—a present that sits there until you choose to receive it, open it and make a conscious decision to give your life to Christ. Won't you come to Jesus? He's waiting for you right now with open arms."

"Amen! Thank you, Jesus." Many people were standing, wailing openly.

"Come to Jesus," Bishop started to sing. "Come to Jesus, come to Jesus just now. Just now. Come to Jesus, come to Jesus just now."The choir stood up and hummed the tune as the piano played softly. " If you don't have a personal relationship with Christ, and you desire to, I want you to step out into the nearest aisle and walk down to the front. Don't worry about the people around you and what they think. There's so much at stake. You just follow that voice inside you and come on."

Amazingly, people started filing down the aisles—some were alone, others were paired off. I began to applaud with those who were seated.

"That's right, come to Jesus. Some of you may be sitting down, too ashamed to come forward. You think Jesus' love couldn't possibly extend to you, but I promise that it does. Remember, no matter how far down the wrong path you've gone, it's never too late to turn back. He's always willing to forgive you and offer the gift of eternal life. But it's up to you to repent. Don't turn His gift away. Set aside your doubts, cast down your worries, and come to Him now. Some of you are tired. You can't make it on your own strength anymore. Don't you think He knows that? Bring your burdens to this altar and hand them over to Jesus. He'll save you."

The choir softly sang. "He will save you, He will save you, He will save you just now. Just now. He will save you, He will save you just now."

Nothing could've prepared me for what happened next. My mother—tears streaming down her face—squeezed past me into the center aisle and walked forward. I sat there stunned, my mouth agape. Mike, Ron, and Trina stood and clapped wildly. What was she doing?

"That's right, Sister," Bishop said as my mom made her way down front. "Come to Jesus." The greeter gave her a warm hug and began to talk to her. She nodded and as the greeter spoke, Mom's shoulders began to heave dramatically as she sobbed into her hands.

Twenty minutes after church let out, she came walking down the hallway, armed with a Bible and a stack of pamphlets. She looked just as rough as she did earlier that morning—her pants were still wrinkled, her hair was still in disarray—but she was beaming. The cloud that had settled over her yesterday was gone. Her eyes were sparkling, her skin was radiant, and her smile was broad.

Trina rushed over and gave her a long hug. "I'm so happy for you."

"Thanks, sweetie."

"Congratulations," Mike said, and planted a light kiss on her cheek.

"How do you feel?" Ron asked.

She took a big breath and thought about it.

"Lighter," she giggled. *My* mom, Cherie Naybor, giggled. Mike, Trina, and Ron all laughed knowingly, and as ridiculous as it was, I felt suddenly envious. It was as if they were all part of an exclusive club, and I was the odd man out.

"We should go celebrate," Trina said.

"I'll take us all to lunch—my treat," Mike offered.

"Sounds good to me," Mom said. "Grace?"

"Uh, yeah, sure. I could eat."

"I'll go get the car." Mike headed for the door.

"We'll go with you," Trina said, grabbing Ron's hand. It was plain as day that they were making themselves scarce for my sake.

Once they'd gone, Mom turned to me. "What're you thinking?"

I shrugged. "Nothing."

"Come on, Grace. Talk to me."

"I guess I just don't understand why you shut me out yesterday. You wouldn't talk to me. You'd barely even look at me, but you practically spilled your heart out to a bunch of strangers in front of more strangers."

"I'm sorry that I made you feel as though I was shutting you out. I didn't mean to."

"Well, what did you think you were doing when you ran away to a hotel room?"

"Yesterday was hard on everyone, not just you. Grace, I know it seems like I should be immune to everything that brings down the average person, because I'm your mom, but I crack and break just like everyone else. When you father called, it opened up a can of worms I'd sealed years ago. I started to evaluate our relationship, my life, my accomplishments—and I wasn't proud. I crumbled before I even got on the plane."

"But nothing's really changed."

"Yes, it has," she said with a smile. "Every word the Bishop preached today was exactly what I needed to hear. I'm one of those tired, weary people he was talking to. I've lived life in my own strength and what do I have to show for it? A daughter who hates me and a big house."

"Mom, I don't hate you."

"But you did. There was a time when I'd look into your eyes and all I saw was contempt. I made you unhappy and was too selfish to acknowledge it."

"There were a lot of reasons why I was unhappy," I argued. "So does this make you happy?" I pointed to the Bible tucked under her arm.

"It frees me."

"What did they do once they took you in the back?" I asked out of curiosity.

"Well, we said the Sinner's Prayer. I repented—you know, asked God to forgive me of my sins and invited Jesus into my heart. Then they encouraged me to join a church in Detroit and get into a Bible study."

"Are you really going to do all of that? What does all this mean?"

"Yeah, I'm going to do it," she said with a content grin, "because I'm a Christian now—a believer. Things are going to change for the better. *I'm* going to change, because I have hope."

Chapter Eleven

Over the winter months, I dedicated the majority of my time and energy to my emerging novel. Most days I'd wake up around 8:30, roll out of bed, put on the baggiest, comfiest sweats I could find without resorting to my dirty laundry, and be power-walking by 9:00.

I'd walk and think until my mind was empty or my legs gave out. I didn't time myself or set any goals. I relieved myself of self-imposed restraints by not wearing a watch and not mapping out a course. Each day was something different. I followed my feet, sometimes for hours, perusing the streets of downtown Memphis.

After my walk, I'd run a hot, steamy bath complete with exotic bath beads and vanilla scented candles. I used to hate baths, but lately I'd found them relaxing—almost indulgent. Showers were too hasty—lather up, rinse off, and hop out as quickly as possible. But baths required a certain level of pampering—a certain level of self-appreciation.

Bath completed, I'd slip on something comfortable and head to the kitchen to eat. My dwindling appetite was definitely a contender for the world's eighth wonder. I used to live to eat. Food was my comfort—my security blanket. After a bad day, a large pepperoni and onion pizza with extra cheese and a pint of Haagen Dazs chocolate, chocolate chip ice cream was like coming home. In the process of losing fifty-four pounds, I found myself constantly slapping my hand and telling myself "no." But now, foods that appealed to me four months ago no longer called my name. Mike thinks it's because I'm no longer using food as a cure-all. Instead of delving into a hoagie or eating a pound of Oreos, I sit down at my computer and write.

I was on a literary roll. The book was good and from the time I sat down in front of my computer to the time I went to sleep, it consumed me. The characters, the dialogue, the setting—all of it transported me to another time and place.

But like anything else, progress and growth came at a price—and the price was Mike. The distancing started slowly. I didn't want to be around anybody. I told Mike I wasn't feeling well and that I needed to spend some time alone to figure out the rest of my book, and he respected that. At first, we talked to each other some mornings and most evenings, but I began to decline his invitations to go out or come over. The book was only part of it, though. I could have easily worked Mike into my schedule, especially since I'd dropped the two classes I was taking to avoid seeing my father.

Part of the problem was what happened during my mom's visit. She and I never really got a chance to talk about my dad or her episode at church— both topics that hung in the air like ripe fruit, ready to be picked. Neither of us was willing to take the initiative. So we left them dangling awkwardly above our heads. I wasn't angry; I just didn't care to be bothered. I felt a strange separation from those around me, as if I was staring at them from the other side of an ever-widening gap. I pretended everything was normal and blamed my inaccessibility on fatigue and menstrual cramps.

Mike wasn't hard to convince. He accepted it, and waited patiently for me to come around. It was my mom and Trina who hounded me relentlessly about my sudden penchant for solitude. So I lied. I told both of them that Taylor and Dotson, the publishing house for *Simon and Eddie*, advanced me for three more stories and that they wanted the edited drafts no later than Thanksgiving.

"That's great, Grace," Mom said. She sounded genuinely excited, which was odd considering she'd never taken an interest in my writing before.

Trina, on the other hand, was skeptical.

"How can they just call you up and tell you what you have to do and when you have to have it done?" she asked. "If you don't start telling people where to get off, they'll walk all over you."

I'd rejected her pleas to go out to dinner three nights in a row and she was projecting her frustration with me onto Taylor and Dotson.

"It's not like that," I tried to explain. The whole thing was a big fat lie, but I was too deep into it now to turn back. "This is my livelihood. There are disadvantages to being a writer, just like with any other profession. Most of the year, I sit around and ride on my royalties, while everyone else trudges to work from nine to five. But now, it's time for me to get busy—earn my living."

"Yeah, but you're tucked away in your room all day working. You need to have a life. They can't expect you to write twenty-four hours a day."

"Don't be ridiculous." I was itching to get back to my computer, but there was no way that Trina was going to let me cut this conversation short. "I don't write twenty-four hours a day. I take lots of breaks; you just aren't here to see them." She looked at me, her eyes at half-mast. She wasn't buying it.

"What about the weekends?"

"Trina, gimme a break," I huffed, flopping down on the couch. "I don't question you about how you spend your days because you're grown and—"

"Being grown has nothing to with it," she said, cutting me off. "I'm worried about you, Grace. Moderation is the key to everything—even work."

"Writing's different," I countered. "Some days I'll write twenty pages and other days, I'll only write two. It's not this controlled process that you're trying to make it." She looked at me long and hard until I fidgeted.

She shook her head. "Nope, I'm sorry. It just doesn't make sense This whole pensive, melancholy phase doesn't sit right with me."

"I'm not melancholy," I corrected her. "I'm cerebral. Why is that so hard for you to understand?"

"Because you've been writing for a living since we were in college, and never once has it torn you away from your life like this. You went to school full-time, wrote full-time, and still maintained your friendships and your relationship with what's-his-face—"

"Stanley," I interjected.

"But now look at you. You don't have time to do anything but write? It doesn't make sense."

"It's my life," I snapped. "It only has to make sense to me."

"Fine, Grace," she said throwing her hands up. "You want me to back off—give you some space? I can do that, but what about Mike?"

"What about Mike? I talk to him every day."

"Really? *I* talk to him every day and half the time he's moping around because he can't reach you."

She was right. Lately, I'd been screening my calls, trying specifically to dodge him. I wasn't trying to be mean. It's just that I hated having to come up with excuses why I didn't want him to come by and cook me dinner or swing by Blockbuster and pick up a movie. I didn't take pleasure in hearing his disappointment day in and day out. I still loved him. He was my heart, but something had snapped inside of me, and I had to get the book done. For the moment, it was my source of purpose—my reason for getting up every morning.

Mike wouldn't be able to understand that. He drew his strength and validation from God, but it didn't work like that for me. Mike, Mom, Trina—they all had their faith. Jesus was their reason for being. But He wasn't mine, and it divided us. I couldn't expect them to empathize with me. As the weeks bled one into the next, the book claimed me piece by piece, until I had nothing to offer anyone or anything else.

I went from talking to Mike once a day to twice a week. I'd be the first one to admit it was selfish, but it was also necessary—almost a default mode of self-preservation. And as much as it pained me to hear that he was upset, I couldn't apologize for what I was doing.

"Look," I started. "Mike's had to go on extended business trips halfway across the country. It's not like I haven't spent my fair share of days missing him."

"Is that what this is? You're trying to prove your job is as important as everyone else's?"

I rolled my eyes.

"I'm not trying to prove anything. I'm working."

"But that's my point, Grace. Most people take breaks—days off, weekends, vacations—" She wasn't going to let it go.

"My whole life's been a vacation, Trina. Up until a couple of months ago, I sat around and did nothing, while you and Mike and the rest of the world earned a living. Did it ever occur to you that I hated those long, boring days? I need to feel useful, to know I'm pulling my own weight."

"Are you kidding?" she asked, her eyes scanning the room. "This is all yours. How could you feel like you're not pulling your own weight?" Her forehead wrinkled. "Are you having financial trouble? Because if you are—"

"Okay, you know what? I don't want to talk about this anymore. Taylor and Dotson is expecting three edited stories by mid-November. They've already paid me the money. I have to deliver the goods. I'm not broke or struggling or strapped. I love you and I love Mike and hopefully by the holiday, things will slow down. But until then, I'm under a deadline and you're just going to have to respect that."

She didn't respond. I'd probably stepped on her toes, but if I was lucky, that would be enough to squash the issue for a while. I got up, prepared to get back to my book.

"Grace, wait, I don't want to discourage you. We're all worried about you, that's all. You hang around in sweats all day, glued to your computer. You don't want to talk to anyone or do anything—and that's just not like you, deadline or not."

"I'm okay," I assured her. "Really, everything's okay."

That conversation was a month ago. Since then, I've started leaving the loft around the time she comes home from work. She was bound to test the subject again and I chose to avoid it. Sometimes I sit in my car and brainstorm, some days I go to the park or a restaurant. It doesn't matter, as long as I'm alone and writing. I've completed over two hundred pages of my novel. The faster I finish it, the sooner I can send it off, breathe a sigh of relief, and make everyone— including myself—happy.

Today was Tuesday. Trina wouldn't be home until after Bible study, which gave me several more hours to work. The skies were dark and it looked like rain, so I skipped my walk and settled into the couch with a mug of apple cider, a printout of chapter thirteen, and a red pen. My goal for the day was to finish editing what I'd already written.

By three in the afternoon, I'd managed to read through two chapters, editing as I went, and was quite pleased with the results. Mike called twice, but I couldn't bring myself to talk to him. He didn't leave a message.

At half past six, I fixed myself a Lean Cuisine. My legs were stiff and my neck was sore, but the day had been productive. I stretched out my arms and rolled my shoulders to relieve some of the tension. As I waited for my food to warm, someone knocked on the door. I considered not answering it, but gave in.

"Who is it?" I didn't sound pleasant.

"Don." Neither did he.

"Uh, this really isn't a good time. I'm busy."

"When aren't you?" he asked, rudely. "Open the door, Grace."

I ran my fingers through my hair and scoured my brain for believable reasons why he couldn't come in.

"Just a second." I walked to the front door and opened it just wide enough for me to peer out. He was wearing his "YMCA Staff" tee shirt. "What're you doing here?" I asked. "You really should've called first."

"I have called—nonstop. You never pick up." He must have been all of those "private" calls I'd been receiving.

"I haven't been home," I lied. "My life's kind of hectic right now."

"Yeah, I bet." We stood in silence on opposite sides of the door. "So, are you going to let me in?"

I closed my eyes and tried to stay calm. *In and out in five minutes*. I stepped aside.

His expression quickly changed from annoyance to shocked concern. "What happened to you? Have you been eating?"

The microwave went off with perfect timing.

"Yep, that's my dinner calling as we speak."

"How much weight have you lost? You look sick—undernourished."

I rolled my eyes.

"Did you come here to bother me about something that's none of your business?"

"I came to ask you what you want me to do with the money you paid for my private instruction. Do you want me to refund it, or put it toward your general membership?"

Between my long walks and dwindling appetite, I no longer had use for a gym. But if I took the refund, Don would lose his cut—a tidy sum—and that wasn't right either.

I shook my head. "Why don't you just keep it?"

"It's over four hundred dollars."

I shrugged. "Consider it a generous tip."

"What's happened to you?" he asked again. "You look so…so miserable."

"You wouldn't understand." I was tired of trying to explain my state of mind and reassure people that my life was hunky-dory. If I looked as bad as Don said and acted as strangely as Trina claimed, people would make their own assumptions, regardless of what I said.

"Try me."

I left him in the front hallway and headed to the kitchen to get my glazed chicken. He followed.

"It gives me a headache to talk about it, and I already feel like I've been run over by a bus." I transferred the contents of the small plastic tray onto a paper plate, got a fork, and walked back to the living room.

"Have you been eating these every day?" he asked, pointing to my less than appetizing dinner.

"Yeah, why?" I shoved a forkful of rice into my mouth.

"Those frozen dinners are really high in sodium, which makes you retain water. That's probably where your headaches are stemming from."

I looked down at the tiny portion of food. The measly appetite I'd managed to work up was quickly waning.

I put the plate down on the coffee table in front of me.

"I didn't mean to ruin your dinner," he apologized.

"No, thanks. That stuff about the sodium, it's good to know. Maybe if I stop eating them, I'll be able to write without my head pounding."

"So that's what you've been up to," he said, with a sly smile. The fact that he thought he'd extracted vital information grated on my nerves.

"Did you need something else, or are we through?"

"Since you asked, I'm curious what happened between us that day—in my office."

"Listen, whatever happened is in the past."

"And what brought on this sudden change of attitude?" I stared at him in amazement. Our current situation was anything but sudden. He was even denser than I'd originally suspected.

"I don't know," I said facetiously. "Maybe the fact that you're married?"

"You've always known my situation," he said calmly. "I never hid Laura from you. Why do you have a problem with it now?"

He was talking as if he and I were a couple—like I was his mistress.

"Maybe I'm being too subtle for you. I thought months of avoiding your phone calls would be enough of a hint, but it looks like I'm just gonna have to lay it out for you."

"Please do."

His untouchable, airy attitude irked me beyond belief.

"There's no hope for you and me. I have a conscience and you have a family. End of story. I don't know why you're so determined to hang onto me, but the nitty-gritty of the situation is that I've moved on and so should you."

"I think you still want me. I can see it in the way you look at me. Don't let Laura scare you off. We're getting a divorce. I just need you to give me a little more time."

"Believe what you want to believe. Just stay away from me. I have to get back to work now. You need to go."

"You don't even want to be friends?"

I shook my head adamantly.

"I have enough friends. Really, I just want you to go."

I picked up the paper plate, carried my cold dinner into the kitchen, and tossed it in the trashcan. When I came back, he was still sitting on the living room couch.

"Here," I said, heading to the front door. "I'll show you out." Slowly, he got up and walked over to me.

"I'm sorry it has to be like this," he said.

Before I could respond, he swooped me into his arms and started to kiss me. At first, I was too stunned to react. He crushed me against his chest and forced my lips apart with his teeth. I tried to pull away, but he put his hand on the back of my head and pressed my face into his. I couldn't free myself from his strong grip. I tried to scream, but my cries for help came out as muffled shrieks. When I stopped resisting, he released me. I stepped back in horror, ready to pound the mess out of him, or die trying.

And that's when I saw her—Trina—standing in the doorway with her mouth agape and her eyes flaring.

"What're you doing?" she gasped.

"It's—it's uh. Um, it's not what you think," I sputtered.

"Who is this?" she asked me, but didn't wait for an answer. "Who are you?"

"I'm Grace's personal trainer."

She looked at me in disbelief. "Don?"

"Trina, please, this is worse than it looks."

Her eyebrows shot up. "It doesn't get any worse than this."

"No, Grace is right," Don stepped in. "You have the wrong idea."

"Shouldn't you be at home?" she spat. "With your wife and child?" Don looked panic-stricken.

"And you," Trina said, pointing at me. "What about Mike?"

"Who's Mike?" Don asked.

I closed my eyes, amazed at how rapidly the cards were stacked against me.

"Grace's boyfriend of the past year. But she didn't tell you about Mike, did she?"

She turned to me.

"Apparently, you've been too busy sneaking around with this loser to tell anyone the truth," she said.

I glared at her. "You're way out of line."

"No!" she shouted, her anger boiling. "*You're* out of line."

My eyes began to well up with tears.

"Go ahead, cry." Trina seethed. "You should be crying. You should be ashamed of yourself! I'm ashamed to even know you."

"Maybe I should go," Don said cautiously.

"No, please. Don't let me interrupt your dirty little rendezvous." She turned on her heels and headed down the hall to the elevator.

"Trina, wait!" I ran after her. "You've got it all wrong. This isn't what you think. I didn't do anything."

She jabbed the up button and spun around.

"You are such a liar! You've been hiding out here week after week worrying all of us to death, when really you were skulking behind closed doors with another woman's husband. It's like you're incapable of treasuring anything worthwhile. You never deserved Mike, you don't deserve to live in that beautiful loft, you don't deserve to write books, you don't deserve your wonderful mother. You didn't even deserve to meet your father. Do you know why?"

I didn't answer.

"Do you know why?" she screamed.

Tears streamed down my face.

"Because you live in this fantasy world. You have tantrums and pout when things don't go your way. You speak to people any way you feel. And you use people—good people like Mike. You have everything and deserve nothing." She stepped into the elevator. "You think your messes don't stink. Let me tell you, they're rancid."

Part of me feared the worst—that Trina would relay to Mike her misinterpreted version of things. I kept quiet for a couple of days and tried to assess the damage. Trina wasn't speaking to me, wouldn't even look at me.

"Trina, can we talk?" I asked last night, when she was fixing herself something to eat. She rummaged through one of the drawers, pulled out a spatula, and said nothing.

"Okay, fine." I said. "I'll talk and you listen."

She snatched a plate out of the cupboard and banged the door shut.

"The other day with Don—it's not what you think."

She rolled her eyes.

"No, please, listen to me. He came over here out of the blue. I was just as shocked as you were."

She slammed the skillet down on the stove.

"Trina, please! I asked him to leave and he kissed me."

She grilled her sandwich, one hand on her hip.

I wanted to know what she'd told Mike, but asking would seem like an admission of guilt, and I wasn't guilty. I watched her in silence. She was stubborn, but this was more than her iron will she was displaying—it was disgust for me that stemmed from a callous prejudgment, and it hurt.

She put her sandwich onto the plate, placed the skillet in the sink, and breezed by me toward her room.

"Trina, I love Mike, more than you know."

She whipped around—her expression cold, her eyes stony.

"You know what?" I stood there, afraid of what she was going to say next. "You aren't capable of loving anyone but yourself. Anyone dumb enough, naïve enough or—in Mike's case— in love enough to let you into their lives, will pay for it sooner or later."

A full week had gone by, and I hadn't heard from Mike. I tried calling him several times over the weekend, but I got no answer. By Tuesday, I was too upset to even write. My only chance to see Mike was Tuesday and Thursday evenings, when he hosted Bible study. Those were the only times he gave the elevator free access to his loft—otherwise, I'd need a key.

I sat around all Thursday afternoon, rehearsing what to say, but it sounded so contrived. *Just tell the truth. Trina may not have said anything. You could be freaking out for nothing*.

At a quarter to seven, I stepped onto the elevator and headed up to Mike's place. There were a handful of people milling around the living room and some more in the kitchen. Trina and Mike were nowhere in sight.

"Hey! You're Mike's girlfriend. Grace, right?" I turned to face a cheery woman, squat with blonde hair and gray eyes. Her smile was picture perfect, but her face didn't ring a bell. She must have recognized me from the night Trina held Bible study at our place.

"Do you happen to know where Mike is?" I asked.

"Yeah, I think he's in his room."

I made a beeline to his room and found the door closed. I took a deep breath and knocked.

"Who is it?"

"It's me, Grace." He didn't reply. My breath caught and I heard the thud of my own heartbeat. "May I come in?"

Again, a long silence. I heard his footsteps and then the door cracked open.

"I'm not dressed and I'm running late. Can this wait?" His eyebrows furrowed in irritation. He could barely look at me.

"No," I answered.

He glared at me, his jaws clenched. He opened the door and stepped back so I could enter. He walked into his closet wearing slacks and an undershirt, and emerged in a black sweat suit. He pulled his dreads back with a rubber band and slipped on a clean pair of socks. I hadn't realized how much I'd missed him.

"Look, I don't have time to stand here," he said curtly. "What do you want?"

"You're upset," I pointed out. Granted, it wasn't the smoothest way to get the conversation rolling, but I was nervous and it was the first thing that came to my head. His face was hard and uncaring.

"I don't have time," he said, sitting down to tie his shoes, "for these stupid little mind games you like to play."

"Mike, nothing happened! The guy came over. I asked him to leave, but he wouldn't go."

"So you thought you'd sleep with him and send him on his way," he said nastily.

"What? I never—I would never..." Trina told him that I *slept* with Don? She had no basis—none whatsoever—to think or say anything like that. She made a shotgun assumption and relayed it to Mike as the gospel truth. Mike would be hurt and angry just thinking that I'd kissed another man, but I couldn't even imagine what he was feeling now that he believed I'd had sex with someone else. No wonder he was being so rash and cruel. All of our talks on virginity and virtue came flooding back to me. I remembered the time in my room when I stopped things from progressing forward.

"You would never what?"

I couldn't decide what was more upsetting—the fact that he'd gotten the idea I'd given myself to another man, or the fact that he believed I could be that low.

"What kind of person do you think I am?" I asked, ignoring his question.

He rubbed his temples for a minute and stood up.

"I don't know and I don't care."

"You're being irrational and judgmental." I was on the verge of tears.

"You think so? Maybe if I'd been a little more rational and judgmental eleven months ago, I wouldn't be in this predicament."

"And what predicament is that? Being in love?"

He shook his head and looked me up and down with an expression of utter disdain.

"This wasn't love," he said icily.

An indescribable pain pierced my chest. I was speechless.

"Not for you, anyway. It couldn't have been."

There was a knock at the door.

"Mike," Trina called. "We're all set." She popped her head in. A shadow crossed her face when she laid eyes on me.

"Are you okay?" she asked Mike.

"Get out of here," I ordered, with more authority than I felt. She arched one eyebrow and stepped into the room.

"Cheating doesn't make you tough," she said, folding her arms across her chest. "So unless you've taken some boxing classes to go with that mouth of yours, I suggest you watch who you're talking to. Don't let the clothes fool you, little girl. I'm still good 'ole Trina, born and raised on the streets of Brooklyn, and I don't take attitude off of anyone—especially you."

"I'm tired of you and your lies!" I shouted. "I'm through with you, period!" I took a couple of steps in her direction, my hand balled into a fist. Trina looked at me, eyes wide. I knew she could beat me up. I'd never been in a physical fight before, but I was a woman with nothing to lose and she knew it. There was no punch, kick, or slap that could equal the blow she dealt when she told Mike I'd slept with Don.

Mike grabbed my wrist and pulled me back.

"Give me a second," he requested.

Trina looked at me, this time with a twinge of fright, and nodded. He dropped my hand once the door closed.

"So, what? You're going to fight everyone now? This isn't Trina's fault; it's yours. At least she cared about me enough to be honest."

There was no point in trying to argue. He'd had a week to let his imagination run wild. Combined with my failure to call and my distant behavior over the past couple of months, there was no convincing him that I was faithful. I scoffed.

"Yeah, well, I'm glad you find this funny. At least one of us gets a laugh." He shook his head. "I should've known better."

"What does that mean?"

He shrugged. "This is all my fault."

"It's nobody's fault, because nothing happened."

"I should've known better. I shouldn't have gotten involved with you. This is what I get for playing with fire."

"How is being with me like playing with fire?"

"You're not a Christian, Grace." He pointed back and forth between the two of us. "We're unequally yoked."

"We're what?"

He rolled his eyes. "Maybe if you'd pick up a Bible once in a blue moon, you'd be more familiar with the term."

I was stunned. "Please don't talk down to me."

"Un-e-qual-ly yoked," he pronounced each syllable slowly, his voice dripping with sarcasm. His patience, which I'd assumed was limitless, was wearing thin. "When one person is a Christian and the other one isn't, it's called being unequally yoked, and the Bible expressly forbids it. The minute I realized you weren't saved and had no interest in coming to the Lord, I should've walked away. But there was something about you." His face grew softer for a second. "Or at least I thought there was. My heart fell for you before my mind could fully register the consequences, and this is what I get."

"But I didn't do anything."

"And you know the worst thing?" he asked, ignoring me. "There's someone who's even more affected by this than I am. His wife—not to mention his daughter."

I fumed. Trina had depicted me as some sort of home-wrecker, out to destroy lives.

"Mike," I pleaded, tears running down my cheeks. "I'm telling you, it's not what you think."

"I don't care," he said with a cold shrug. "It's not my problem anymore."

"So what're you saying? It's over?"

He grabbed his Bible off the nightstand and flipped off the light in the closet. "Answer me!" My voice was loud and shrill. "You owe me at least that much." He scowled at me.

"I don't owe you anything. And I'm telling you to go away."

My heart stopped beating, I stopped breathing, I stopped living, and everything was quiet, like the passing of a storm's eye. In slow motion, I watched him walk by me, the sound of his heavy footsteps pounding in my head, and leave the room—leave my life—without so much as a backward glance.

Chapter Twelve

I finished it—my novel. It's printed out, all 362 pages of it, and sitting on my desk. There was no one to tell, no one with whom to celebrate or get excited. Trina stopped coming home the night I told her our friendship was over, and when I tried to call Mike several days after the fight, his number had been changed. Don stopped calling. And my mom? Well, Christian or non-Christian, work still came first. I seldom heard from her. I was alone, in a way I'd never been before. This time, I was completely by myself, in mind, body, and spirit. Everything was quiet.

I was hurt more than anything. The two people closest to me had cut ties over something that never happened. What could I have done differently? For starters, I wouldn't have pushed Mike away, even if it meant never finishing the book. I would have taken breaks—lots of them. I would've even gone out to dinner with Trina. And I never would have let Don into the loft. If I hadn't opened the door, none of this would have happened.

Eventually, my regret turned to anger. I reversed the roles and put myself in Mike and Trina's place. Even on a bad day, I never would've done what they did to me—assumed what they assumed. And *Mike* had pursued *me*. I wasn't even interested in him in the beginning. He brought me roses and Nyquil and his mother's precious chicken soup. I was just living my life, minding my own business. All his talk about me being "the one," about how he never in a million years expected to fall so hard for someone—only to tell me later that he should have known better than to ever love me. Suddenly, I wasn't good enough for him because I wasn't a Christian. If being a Christian means judging people you love and throwing them to the curbside, then he could keep his Christianity. I'd be better off on my own.

The only thing that saved him a little in my mind was that Trina had probably fed him a lot of bologna. I knew, firsthand, how convincing she could be. I don't think she did it maliciously. Odds were, she really did think that the kiss between Don and me was consensual. But what made her think we'd had sex? And why would she tell Mike that unless she knew for sure? I hated her. She didn't used to be so self-righteous—she used to be the most tolerant, understanding person I knew. She used to have a rough exterior, but inside, she was soft.

Now, it's the opposite. She looks like this sweet, refined businesswoman on the outside, when really she's as hard as a rock. And she didn't get like that until she started going to church. It seemed like the deeper she got into God and Bible study and Christianity, the more intolerant she became. How easy it must be to commit every sin under the sun, claim to find God, and then condemn others for their wrongdoing. I gave her a place to stay when she got evicted from her apartment. I paid her tuition when she lost her scholarship. I went to her classes and took notes when she was too hung over to wake up. I rescued her from Darius, and gave her a place to stay—rent-free.

And now, after all my years of giving, I'm not worthy of anything? I don't deserve Mike? I don't deserve my mom? Without all that stuff I don't deserve, she wouldn't be where she is today. I was serious when I said our friendship was over. Even if I managed to set the story straight and reconcile with Mike, I would never let Trina back into my life. She'd burned me for the last time.

Now, three weeks after losing Mike, my anger had turned into depression. It was a heavy, oppressive sadness that left me limp and unable to get out of bed. I closed my shutters, blocked out the sunlight that I used to enjoy and slept throughout the day and half the night. I didn't shower. I barely ate. I kept my eyes closed and tried to pretend I wasn't in pain. The phone never rang; there were no knocks on the door. Nobody cared, nobody was trying to find me, and so, gradually, I lost myself.

I woke up at two in the morning to rumbling thunder and bright flashes of lightening. I was covered in sweat, my hair was stuck to the nape of my neck, and my bed sheets were damp. I looked over at my desk. My novel was still sitting there, ruthlessly reminding me of what I'd gained and what I'd lost.

I climbed out of bed and went to the bathroom. My reflection startled me. I'd lost a lot of weight—too much weight. My eyes were sunken with large, dark circles hanging beneath them. My cheeks, which had always been round and plump, were now sharp points. My collarbone protruded, making me look emaciated, and my fingers were bony and wrinkled. I stared at the woman in the mirror. Her eyes were sad and she looked barely alive.

Ashamed of what I'd become, I turned away from myself. I fished around my medicine cabinet and pulled out a bottle of extra strength Tylenol. Carefully, meticulously, I counted out fifty pills. If life was content to beat me up, I'd go ahead and finish the fight. I had nothing to hold onto—no ray of hope, no light at the end of the tunnel.

Ten minutes later, I was dressed in a pair of jeans that I had to hold up with a belt, and a sweatshirt that draped loosely over my shoulders and hung down to my knees. I put the pills in a sandwich bag, poured myself a thermos full of water, and left my loft.

The rain was falling hard, and it stung my face as I walked across the street and sat down on one of the park benches. Downtown Memphis was deserted. There was only me, the rain, and my solution to a hopeless situation. I pulled out the bag of Tylenol and stared at it. How did it come to this? Even in the worst of times, I'd loved life, and I'd never considered killing myself. Why did things seem so bleak now? Maybe if I just had someone to talk to, someone who would listen to my side—the truth—and help guide me out of this dark maze. The only person I could think of was my father.

"If you want to talk, you know where to find me." His words rang in my ears. I didn't *want* to talk, I *needed* to talk. And if he rejected me, I decided, then I would come back and finish what I had started.

Back at the loft, I sloshed to my room and got onto the Internet. I looked through the University of Memphis's faculty directory for his name. It gave his office and home numbers, but no address. I scribbled down his home number and went to the White Pages online. I typed in his name and number in the boxes provided, and just like that, I had his home address. It was a street I'd never heard of, so I went to Mapquest.com and got driving directions.

Five minutes later, I had his address and was in my car, speeding in the rain toward the man on whom I'd shown no mercy, hoping against hope he'd have mercy on me.

"I know it's late," I said apologetically. My father was standing in front of me wearing a burgundy robe and black slippers. His eyes were bloodshot. "I just, um, I just wanted to stop by. You know, since it's been a while."

I shrugged my shoulders and timidly glanced up at him.

"How did you find me?" he asked.

I shivered in my drenched clothes. "You'd be surprised how easy it is to find people these days."

There was no denying he was my father. We had the same big cheeks and little ears, the same dark skin and almond-shaped eyes. In class, I'd only known him as my professor and that day in my loft, I was too blinded by my anger to really study him. It was amazing to stand in front of the man responsible for half of my genetic makeup and see myself in him.

"Does Cherie know you're here?" he asked.

"Uh, no. I don't think so. We're allowed to spend time together without her around, right?"

"Yeah, of course," he said slowly—cautiously. "Is something wrong?"

"Um, well...yeah, I think so." My voice cracked and my chin started to quiver. "I was, uh, at home, you know, and I uh, I couldn't sleep. I haven't slept in a while and my thoughts they just...I don't know, they're so loud." I couldn't get the right words out, and I bounced from one train of thought to the next. He waited patiently for me to go on. "All I wanted to do was finish writing it. Everybody needs purpose. I had to write it. I was selfish and look what's happened to me." The tears stung as they slipped out of my sore, red eyes. "Everyone's turned on me."

"Come in," he said, wrapping his arms around my shoulders. "Let's get you dry and then you can tell me all about it."

I talked for what seemed like hours. I told him about the novel, about Trina, about Don, about Mike. I poured my heart into his hand and waited for him to filter out all of the impurities and hand it back to me whole and renewed. He listened intently, a look of worry etched on his face, and handed me tissues every few minutes.

I finally told him about the park and the Tylenol.

"Where are the pills?" he asked.

"In my sweatshirt." Without another word, he walked over to my wet clothes, which were draped over a chair, dug out the plastic sandwich bag and walked down the hall. A few seconds later, I heard the toilet flush. He came back to the living room and sat down next to me on the couch.

"I wish you had come to me sooner."

I shrugged. "I called you a coward in front of everyone. I told you to go away. I didn't think you'd want to see me again."

He rubbed his jaw with his big, dark hand and closed his eyes. He looked like he might cry.

"Grace, there hasn't been a moment when I didn't want to see you. You're my daughter. I've loved you since the day you were born."

"But—but you left us. You left *me*."

He shook his head. "Like I said before, there's a lot you don't know."

"What's there to know?"

"I didn't walk out on you. Your mother left me. You might not believe me, but it's the truth. You can confirm it with your mom."

"So what happened?"

"Your mother and I had an arrangement. I was messed up back then—I had problems. We decided it was best if I stayed away."

"You were a drunk," I blurted out. His gaze dropped to the floor. "I'm sorry. I didn't mean for it to come out like that."

"You're right," he said, looking me in the eyes again. "I had a problem with alcohol. Cherie hung in there with me, but it got to be too much. I was out of control. She had to make sure the two of you would be okay. Grace, listen. You've probably got a bunch of nasty ideas about me, and it's true that I abandoned you in a way by choosing drinking over being a father. But I've always loved you, and I never wanted to be without you for so long. Whatever Cherie said, she thought it was in your best interest at the time. But you're grown now, and you should know the whole story—if you want."

"Okay," I said quietly. "I'm listening."

He took a deep breath and sat back.

"Cherie never loved me. Your mom's always had a need to be in control, and that makes it hard to fall in love, to succumb to it. You have to be willing to accept all the twists and turns love brings, and dance to the music of your heart." His eyes were closed and he was swaying his arms as if he was conducting a symphony. "Our time together was real—magical. I wanted to marry her—I wanted to spend the rest of my life with her. But every time I proposed, she had a new reason why it wasn't a good time."

"Every time?" I asked. "How many times did you ask?"

"Oh, I don't know—maybe five or six."

"That's tenacity for you," I said, with a laugh.

"Well, I don't know if I was tenacious or just out of my mind," he confessed. "But she wasn't ready. Eventually, she got pregnant, and things took a turn for the worse. I'll never forget when she told me. I'd been trying to reach her all week, but she wouldn't return my phone calls. I left roses on her front porch and a love letter in her mailbox, but she refused to talk to me. Honestly, I thought she'd dumped me and was waiting for me to take a hint." He chuckled at the memory of it. "Then one night there she was, standing outside my mom's house, waiting for me. She wasn't crying, but her eyes were all puffy, kind of like yours," he teased. "Before I could get a word out she said, 'I'm pregnant and I'm having an abortion.' Some mess about it being her body and her decision. 'I'm not asking for your permission, I just thought you should know.' And then she was gone."

"Sounds just like her." I shook my head in disgust.

"Don't say that," my father reprimanded gently. "It was a hard thing for her. In a way, I think getting pregnant shattered her illusion of control. Deciding to have an abortion was her way of regaining charge of the situation."

"Well, she obviously didn't go through with it," I said, ignoring his attempt to justify my mother's selfishness. "So what happened?"

"Your grandfather called me the day before she was scheduled to go to the clinic. He told me plain and simple, 'We don't have abortions in this family, son. Now, if you consider yourself a man, you go do right by my daughter.'" He imitated my grandpa's deep voice perfectly. "So, I did. I took off work and went to the clinic with her."

I smiled. "You *do* know that's not what he meant by 'Do right by my daughter,' don't you?"

"Of course, I do. But I wasn't going to make Cherie have you if she didn't want to. I felt like supporting her decision was the right thing to do. Besides, I knew she wasn't going to go through with it before we even walked into the building. She couldn't sit still. In less than thirty minutes, she'd flipped through every magazine in that place. And when they finally called her back, she was shaking so badly that the nurse told her they couldn't start the procedure until she calmed down. Then she started bawling, and she didn't let up for two hours."

He laughed and slapped his knee. "I said, 'That's it, Cherie, get up. You're not having an abortion. We're gonna have this baby.' She didn't argue with me, either. Just grabbed her purse and walked out the door. We went and celebrated at this old mom- and-pop diner around the corner from where she stayed—ate two burgers apiece. That's the last I ever heard about an abortion. After that, she got so excited about having you that at times I thought she was on drugs."

"Excited about having me? Please!" I snorted at the very idea. "*That* I would've loved to see."

"She was, I promise you. Everywhere we went, she bought you things—stuff you wouldn't even be able to use for the first few years of your life. And when she had a girl, man." he said, with a nod of his head. "She was ecstatic. I think she bought all the pink stuff she could get her hands on."

He gazed off into the distance like he was reliving the whole experience in his mind. His smile faded.

"We moved in together, and that's a hard thing to do when you're accustomed to living alone and by your own rules. Cherie went back to work and I stayed home with you. Now, it's not that I didn't love you or enjoy spending time with you, but a man feels a responsibility to his family. I wanted to go work, too, bring in some money and feel like I was needed. But every time we talked about it she said I would never make enough to support the three of us and I'd be more useful at home. The days seemed to get longer and everything felt dreary. And then with one sentence, it all fell apart."

I leaned forward, hanging on every word..

"I came home one evening with you, after the two of us had spent all day at the park and on a ferry ride. You had to be almost one by then, and we'd had a good time. I was surprised to see your mom sitting in the living room when we got back. Man, was she mad. She asked why I hadn't cleaned the house, why this was dirty and why that wasn't washed. 'If you're going to sit at home all day, the least you could do is keep the house tidy.' I'm telling you, I saw red, and I laid it out for her. I said 'Listen, I'm tired of this arrangement. This is my daughter and you're my woman and I don't have any business sitting here babysitting, while you're out supporting me. I'm going back to work. You have two options. You can find her a day care or a nanny, or *you* can stay home with her. But you're not running me anymore.'"

"I'm sure that didn't go over too well," I guessed. My mother was bossy. *She* demanded and instructed. It was never the other way around.

"No, it didn't. I'll never forget what she said next. It haunted me for years." I held my breath. "She told me that I could stop trying to be father of the year because you weren't even mine."

"What?" I asked, suddenly dizzy.

"She told me she'd been with another man around the same time, but when he found out she was pregnant, he split. We didn't have all the paternity tests you have nowadays. So, I had no way of being sure. There's nothing worse than falling in love with a child, and then hearing something like that. All of a sudden, I couldn't touch you—couldn't look at you or stand to hear you cry."

"Are you telling me you're not..." I let my sentence trail off and my voice quaked.

"No, honey," he said, patting my knee. "A few days later, she admitted she lied."

"Why would she lie about something like that?"

"Why does anyone lie about anything?" he asked in return. "I don't know what was going on in her head, but the damage had already been done. She'd planted a seed of doubt in my mind, and I couldn't look at her the same. I started going out more—drinking a lot. First, I drank just to loosen up a little, and then I drank to forget things and eventually, I'd drink until I couldn't move. I'd stumble home at all hours and pick fights with her. I wanted her to be as unhappy as I was. I didn't know that she already was.

"Then one morning she told me she was going to work, that she wanted me to drop you off at your grandparents' house, and that if I was still in the apartment by the time she got back, she was going to call the police and have me physically removed."

"Just like that?" I asked.

"Yeah. She said I was the biggest mistake of her life and that she wasn't going to watch me ruin her daughter. I packed my stuff, dropped you off with her parents, and went back to my mother's house."

"How could you just let me go like that? If you loved me as much as you say you did, how could you walk away without a fight?"

He let out a deep sigh.

"If I'd thought I was the better parent or that you were in any sort of danger staying with her, I would've fought to keep you. But you have to understand, I couldn't stay sober for more than a couple of days if my life depended on it. And I didn't have a job or my own place. Even as a drunk, I had enough sense to know that Cherie was right."

"How was tearing me away from a loving father the right thing to do?" I asked indignantly.

"Grace, I know you can't see your mother's logic on the matter, but she did the right thing. It wasn't Cherie's responsibility to keep us together, it was mine. I could've stopped drinking and bridged the gap between us, but I didn't even try. You're what? Twenty-eight—almost twenty-nine?" I nodded "Well, I've only been sober for nine years. That's almost twenty-one years of your life that I chose booze over fatherhood. Your mom knew what she was doing, and she did it for you."

How could I agree? I think I would be a different person—a better person—if he'd been around, even if it was just through phone calls or letters. I wouldn't have spent so many years wondering what was wrong with me, or why he didn't love me enough to stay. But whenever I tried to place the blame on Mom, he defended her by beating himself up even more. He shouldn't have to dissect his past and serve his pride to me on a silver platter. He'd told me his side—given me enough of an explanation. How could he have lived with a woman who wouldn't let him work and denied that he was the father of her child whenever he crossed her? Any person with a decent level of self-respect would have walked.

I should know. Most of my life I've been subjected to my mother's condescending attitude and insinuations. She's always had a way of skinning a person down to the bone, one humiliating layer at a time, while making sure nobody got close enough to shred her dignity in the same way. If my dad felt like he had to leave, I respected his decision. I'm sure it wasn't easy living with an alcoholic, but I still wondered if Mom's ultimatum hadn't been selfish. She'd stripped me of my right to have a father and she'd stripped my father of his right to have me. It might have been different if she'd been a loving, involved parent, but she wasn't. I couldn't help but wonder if she made him leave to make her own life easier. She was young and ambitious. Her life was already on hold because of a baby. The last thing she wanted was a man dragging behind her.

"So that's it? You went on with your life and she went on with hers? You didn't call? You weren't even curious about me?"

He smiled sweetly.

"No, no. I called regularly—sent checks too. After a little while, we tried to work out a visiting schedule. I was supposed to pick you up from day care on Fridays and take you home on Sunday afternoons. But I always got tied up. Parties, friends, bars—they all got in the way. I pushed her too far, took advantage of her willingness to work with me. When you were two, she told me not to call or come around until I stopped drinking. She promised to send letters and pictures, but she didn't want anything from me, including money, until I straightened up and flew right."

"And you never heard from her again?" I asked.

He smiled and disappeared down the hall again. When he came back, he handed me two large photo albums.

I opened the big blue one. On the first page, there were two pictures with captions neatly placed beside each other. The notes were in my mother's handwriting.

The first photo was of Trina and me at an amusement park. Mom had taken us for my thirteenth birthday. The caption read: *Grace and Trina at Cedar Point*. The second picture showed me at age eight, standing on a stage playing the violin. I was wearing shiny Mary Janes and frilly white socks. *Grace at her first recital/competition. She won third place*. I flipped through the rest of the album. My mother had sent him pictures from nearly every milestone in my life. She captured moments that I didn't even think she cared about—graduation, prom, birthdays. There was even a picture of Stanley. On the last page of the album was a photocopy of my first *Simon and Eddie* cover.

"Wow," I said, flipping through the neatly kept scrapbook.

"Yep." He poked his chest out proudly. "I've kept everything she's ever sent me."

I was flattered.

"Flash forward twenty-one years," I said, setting the albums down. "You got it together—sobered up. What happened?"

"I went back to college, got my Master's in English, and I've been teaching for about five years now."

"No, I mean what happened with the arrangement? Why didn't you come find me?"

He sighed. "Sobriety is more than just not drinking. It's a mental state. The slightest upset could throw me off. That's something I learned in my meetings—I'll always be an alcoholic, but it's a choice not to get drunk. I needed time to get my life back on track. The last thing I wanted was to be in your life and cause you turmoil. By the time I felt ready to give it a go, you were a full-grown adult, publishing books, and making a way for yourself. I was scared. I kept asking myself, 'What does she need me for now?' But I guess God had other plans."

I made a face. "God had nothing to do with it."

"How do you explain how we met? Four different professors teach the class you signed up for, and you ended up in mine. If that's not God, what is it?"

"Coincidence? Fate? Destiny?"

"Can your old man give you some advice?" he asked. "Don't punish God for someone else's mistakes."

"What do you mean?"

He looked at me closely.

"You've tied Mike and Trina's harshness to their Christianity, but I'm telling you it's not so. They were wrong, no two ways about it. And even if they had been right about you and Don, their reactions were wrong. But *Mike* and *Trina* are acting like that, not God. Being a Christian doesn't make you perfect. You still sin—you still make mistakes. You're condemning many people and a whole belief over the stupidity of two people. It's like when a black man robs a bank and people assume that black men are all thieves. You know better than that."

"This is different."

"It's no different. Don't judge God like Mike and Trina judged you, or like you judged me."

"It's too much to think about right now," I said, yawning. Faint rays of sunlight were beginning to sneak through the blinds.

"You're tired," he pointed out.

I nodded. "I guess I should go."

"No," he said firmly. "I can't let you drive home like this. You're already half asleep. You'll stay here."

"Are you sure?" I wasn't going to argue. My head was swimming, and the last thing I wanted to do was drive back to my cold, empty loft. "I don't want to put you out."

"I have three bedrooms and a pullout couch. You're welcome to any of them."

I chose the small bedroom right across from his. The mattress looked inviting. I changed into the large flannel shirt he gave me and snuggled deep under the covers. The last thing I saw before my eyelids drooped shut was the clock on the nightstand. It was six in the morning.

"Grace? Grace, wake up." I tried to open my eyes, but my lids were too heavy. There was a blurry figure in front of me. I blinked a couple of times and waited for my vision to straighten itself out. My father held a plate and a glass of orange juice.

"What time is it?" I asked, my voice raspy with exhaustion.

"It's almost eight."

"Just a few more hours," I groaned.

"It's Thursday," he informed me. "You slept all yesterday and through the night. I think you need to get up and eat something."

Slowly and with much effort, I hoisted myself to a sitting position and propped my back against the headboard. My head and my limbs felt heavy.

"There you go," he said, placing a plate of French toast on my lap and handing me a fork. He put the glass of juice on the nightstand and sat down on the edge of the bed.

"Are you feeling any better?"

"Um, I don't know," I said, still disoriented. "I think so."

"Good. You had me worried."

I took a bite of the breakfast and closed my eyes as I savored the mix of syrup and butter and sweet bread mingling in my mouth.

"Mmmm, this is good." My stomach growled.

"Eat up," he said. "I can make you more."

He was wearing a pair of dark blue jeans and a white Polo shirt. It was the most casual I'd ever seen him dressed.

"I'm not going in to work for the rest of the week. I told them I had a family emergency."

"I'm sorry," I apologized. I was disrupting his life.

"I'm not," he said. "I want you to stay here with me for a few days." I stopped eating, my fork in midair. "You don't have to. I'm just worried about you and I have to admit, I like having you around."

"But I've been asleep most of the time."

"Even so," he said, smiling. "Even so."

"Okay," I consented. Maybe a different environment would give me a brighter perspective.

"I was thinking we could go through your novel. See exactly what it is you have."

"Seriously?"

"Yeah, why not?" My dad was a smart man. I knew by the way he spoke and the way he taught. There was plenty he could contribute.

"I'd love to," I gushed.

"Take your time," he said, getting up. "I washed your clothes. They're in the closet. When you feel up to it, run home, get the book and a few more clothes, and come on back."

I polished off every last bite of French toast, changed into my jeans and sweatshirt, and drove home. My heart raced as I pulled into the parking lot. Mike's SUV was parked in its usual space. I wouldn't know what to do if I ran into him. The front lobby was empty as I stepped into the elevator.

I entered my loft and stood still for a few minutes to make sure Trina wasn't home. It was quiet. The door to my room was closed and taped onto it was a typed letter.

To Whom It May Concern:

> *I, Trina Calloway, am giving my thirty (30) day notice to the aforementioned. I will be taking only those items that I have personally brought into said place of residence. All such items will be removed by November 15.*

I rolled my eyes, tore the note off the door, crumpled it, and dropped it on the floor. *Thirty-day notices are only pertinent if you actually pay rent*, I thought nastily. I grabbed my gym bag, emptied its contents onto my bed, and packed enough clothes to last me through the weekend. I put my novel into a box and grabbed my keys. I couldn't wait to get out of the loft, which had come to feel more like a prison.

I decided to call my mom so she wouldn't have the National Guard out looking for me. I put my bag down, grabbed the phone, and dialed her number. She picked up on the first ring.

"Well, this is a first," she said cheerily. "You hardly ever call me."

"I just wanted you to know that I won't be home for a few days. I'm going to be over—" I caught myself mid-sentence. I wasn't sure what to call him.

"Over where?"

"Anthony's."

She was quiet for a moment.

"Anthony—as in your father Anthony?"

"Yeah."

"I don't know what to say. Does Mike know?" she asked.

"Actually, Mike and I aren't together anymore."

"What?" she gasped. She sounded as if I'd killed someone. "When did that happen?"

"It's been several weeks now."

"Why are you just now telling me?"

"I would've told you sooner if you'd called me, but I haven't heard from you in almost a month."

"I'm sorry, Grace. I've been so busy with work and—"

"Don't worry about it," I cut her off. "These things happen, right?"

"I suppose. Such a shame, though. I really like Mike. He's a good guy." Her words were like salt in an open wound.

"I have to go," I said.

"Wait. Have you already talked to your father?"

"Yeah, Mom. And now I know the truth. What do you want me to say? That I agree with what you did?"

"I want to hear your thoughts."

"I understand why you told him to stay away. But I can't say I would've done the same thing if I were in your place. Honestly, I think you were selfish."

"I was," she admitted quietly. "I didn't know what else to do. I wish I'd known the Lord back then. I would have handled things so differently."

I was sick of hearing about God. Everyone was always giving Him credit when He tended to be a day late and a dollar short.

"Whatever," I sighed. "That was then and this is now."

"Don't bottle up your feelings, Grace. Have you talked to Trina about your dad and Mike?"

The conversation just kept getting worse.

"Things are complicated," I said. "Trina and I, we..." I sighed. "She's moving out soon. It's time for us to go our separate ways."

"What's going on, Grace? This sounds more serious than you're letting on."

No. It was serious two nights ago when I was sitting in a thunderstorm ready to take my life. Now, it's just sad.

"I'm your mom. You should be able to talk to me about anything."

"I *could* talk to you about it. I just don't want to."

"Sweetie, let's not push each other away like this anymore." That was easy for her to say, now that her life was on track. But when she was feeling down and out, she ran away to a hotel and shut me out completely.

"I'm not pushing you away," I lied. "I just don't feel like getting into it right now."

"Okay." It sounded like she was giving in. "Listen, now that I have you on the phone, there's something I've been meaning to tell you."

I impatiently checked my watch.

"Can it wait?"

She sighed. "It's something that's been pressing on my heart."

As much as I appreciated our rare, but beautiful, mother-daughter moments, I didn't want to get emotional. I'd spent the better part of the month drowning in turmoil, and I finally felt like I could breathe again.

"Can we talk about it tomorrow?"

"I'll be on a plane to California all day tomorrow, and I won't be back till early Sunday morning. It's important, Grace."

I started to get irritated. I couldn't count the times I needed to tell her something important, only to be brushed off for her next meeting. Now I was supposed to drop what I was doing?

"Mom, I'm late. If it's *that* important, put it in a letter." It came off harsher than I intended.

"Okay," she said, audibly hurt. "I'll talk to you when I get back. Have fun with your dad."

I wanted to apologize—set my keys down, pull up a chair and listen to everything she wanted to say. But my pride wouldn't let me.

"Later."

The four days I spent with my dad changed my life forever. He was such an interesting, complex person, full of ideas and philosophies. Just like in class, his intelligence beguiled me. His words were powerful and packed with meaning. So when he suggested that I file a complaint concerning Don, I listened.

"You need to let someone know what type of person he is. You're a strong woman, but what if he had preyed on someone younger and weaker? The outcome could have been much worse than a kiss." I hadn't thought about it that way. "The Y employs him to instruct its customers, not to harass them. Even if you don't want to do it for yourself, do it for all the other unsuspecting women who are liable to fall into his trap."

"I don't want to go back there."

"You don't have to. We can write a formal letter to the Director, and let him know that you've also sent a letter to the District Manager. Trust me, they'll take action."

The thought that Don believed he'd gotten away with something had plagued my mind. Maybe Dad was right. Maybe writing a complaint letter would force someone to discipline Don.

We drafted a long letter explaining, in detail, everything that happened. Just sending it off made me feel lighter, like I could finally close that chapter of my life.

The rest of our time together revolved around my book.

"I can't say it enough," my dad said, putting down another chapter. "This is impressive, Grace. Really, I didn't know you were this talented."

"Thanks," I said. My face flushed with embarrassment and excitement. "Do you think it's publishable?"

"Are you kidding? Not a doubt. I'd like to make some suggestions and tune up the mechanics and then, if you'll let me, I'd like to send it to a couple of literary agents I know."

"Oh, but I already have an agent."

"I just want to see what they think, maybe get some tips on the best publishing houses to send this to," he said, tapping the pages on the coffee table. "You don't want just anyone to publish this novel. With the right marketing and the right editors, this could be big—bigger than anything you've imagined."

His words of encouragement sent me soaring.

He made me breakfast every morning and I made him dinner every night. Even when we were sitting in silence—him reading my book and me watching TV—it was nice to be in his company. I felt like a little girl around him, but in a good way. He loved me and accepted me, and I wasn't alone anymore. He took off work to be with me—to make sure that I was okay. Nobody had ever done that for me before.

Sunday morning, we went to his church. It was more conservative than Mike's church, with a smaller congregation, but I enjoyed the people and the message all the same. I found myself dreading the end of my stay. He had a class Monday afternoon and I'd taken up every second of his time since Thursday.

"I hate the idea of going home. This was such a nice escape."

"You can come back anytime. As a matter of fact, that is now officially your room," he said, pointing down the hall. "If you're not doing anything tomorrow afternoon, why don't you come to my class?"

He didn't have to twist my arm.

"And then we'll have lunch—talk about what direction you want to take with your book."

"You're on."

"Good," he said. "Now, come give me a hug."

I thrust my arms around his neck and planted a kiss on his cheek. He wrapped his arm around my waist and squeezed for all he was worth.

"Thank you," I whispered.

"No, thank *you*."

Chapter Thirteen

I was dressed in my pajamas, pink with tiny rainbows speckled all over. It was dark out and I was lying on the side of a busy highway. I tried to get up, but I was caught in something—something sticky. I wrestled my neck free and glanced down at my feet. I was suspended a few feet off the ground, entangled in a huge spider web.

I hate spiders! *I thought to myself. I tried to twist and turn my way to freedom, but the more I fought, the more entangled I became.*

"This isn't working," I said aloud. "I need help." I screamed to the cars speeding by on the busy road. They must not have seen me. Car after car zoomed by without even slowing down. "This is hopeless."

Out of the corner of my eye, I spotted something big and black crawling toward me. The spider, easily twice my size, bounced and shook the web as it inched my way. I held my breath, petrified. My life is over, *I thought. I closed my eyes.*

"What're you just lying there for? Move! Move! Move!" I heard a voice shout. An elderly man stood above me.

"I can't," I whimpered. "I'm stuck."

"No, you're not. Take one step at a time." The spider, spooked by the old man's presence, stopped a few feet short of me. It watched me carefully through its wet, beady eyes, but didn't move.

"Trust me," said the old man. I lifted my left foot, and with some effort, managed to wrench my whole leg loose. The web made loud snapping sounds as I freed the rest of my body. The old man held out his hand and helped me to the ground. I dusted off the remnants of the web, which were no longer sticky, but were dry like cobwebs.

"It's a long way back to town." the man said. "If you need a ride, my house is just down the way." He pointed to a purple and gold house, not twenty feet from us.

I followed behind him, but after my first few steps I had to stop. My feet were too sore to walk. He waited while I emptied my shoes, which were filled with rocks.

I put my slippers back on and walked with him the rest of the way to his house. It was bright inside and much bigger than it appeared from the road.

His kitchen cabinets had no doors. On the counter were several blueprints.

"Getting new cabinets?" I asked.

"Only new cabinet facings," he said, "the insides are just fine. This is my daughter—"

A woman my age—and familiar looking—appeared out of nowhere.

"I know you!" I exclaimed. I hadn't seen Kaye since high school. She was popular then, a girl all the girls envied. Now, though, she was a long-lost friend.

"I have some things to do," the old man said. "You girls get acquainted until I return."

He disappeared into thin air.

"I have a surprise for you," Kaye said, unfazed by her dad's disappearance.

She floated over to the far wall, which was hidden behind a rich, lavish curtain.

"Ready?" she asked.

I clapped my hands in excitement. She pulled back the curtain, and revealed a massive collage, composed of scores of pictures. Trina was in the center photo wearing her blue cap and gown. My freshman English teacher, Mrs. Long, was there, along with my grandparents, cousins, coworkers, and everyone else who'd played a significant role in my life.

"This is so amazing. May I—may I touch it?"

"Sure, it's your life."

As I reached up, one of the pictures came loose and fell to the floor.

"Oh, no!" Kaye shouted.

"It's okay, it's okay," I tried to console her.

"No, I wanted it to be perfect," she said, shaking her head. "I'll fix it—just give me a second."

She laid the picture flat against the wall and began to pound on it in an effort to make it stick.

"Stop, Kaye," I begged. But she continued to pound furiously on the wall. The thuds grew louder and louder until I stepped back and covered my ears.

"Grace! Wake up!" I opened my eyes. I was in my room. A faint stream of light peeked from underneath the shutters. My sheets were wrapped all around my body, and my duvet was on the floor. I was sweating profusely and disoriented from sleep.

"Grace!" Trina shouted. She pounded on my bedroom door. "For God's sake, wake up! You have a phone call." She sounded groggy and irritated. I shook my head and tried to get my bearings. "Grace!"

"Okay," I said. My voice was raspy—inaudible. I swallowed. I heard her heavy footsteps as she tromped away, back to her side of the loft. I took a deep breath and looked around. The bright, red numbers on my clock read 7:02.

Who in the world could this be?

"To whom am I speaking?" A woman's voice filtered through the receiver. She was curt and formal.

"*You* called *me*," I said, an edge to my voice. "To whom am *I* speaking?"

"I need to speak to a Ms. Grace Naybor."

"This is she." I hoped for her sake that she wasn't a telemarketer.

"My name is Deirdre Coleman, and I'm calling from AmeriSpan Airlines."

"It's seven o'clock in the morning," I snipped.

"Are you the daughter of a Ms. Cherie Naybor?" she asked.

My heart skipped a beat and my ears began to ring. I suddenly felt very alert.

"What's going on? Who is this?"

"Ms. Naybor," she said calmly—too calmly. "We need you to come down to our offices as soon as you can."

I swung my legs over the side of the bed and switched on the lamp standing next to my nightstand. My stomach dropped. "What's happened?"

"Ms. Naybor, please stay calm—"

"Don't tell me to stay calm!" I shouted. My hands shook uncontrollably. "Don't do that. Airlines don't call people at seven in the morning for nothing. Tell me—just tell me."

"Ms. Naybor—Grace—there's been an accident."

My breaths came in shallow puffs.

"Flight 727 departed out of LAX at approximately 1:20 Saturday morning, and crashed en route to DTW about fifty minutes after takeoff. Your mother was a passenger on that flight."

"Wh-where is she now?" I stammered.

"There's still a search team out. They've been working around the clock and—"

"Where is she now? Where is she?" I shouted.

"Due to adverse weather conditions and the fact that it was a water crash—."

"Where is she?" I screamed. "Answer me! Where is my mother?" My voice bounced off the walls and made my chest vibrate.

"At this moment, it looks as though there were no survivors."

I went numb. The words echoed in my head. *No survivors*. I lowered the phone from my ear.

"Please, Grace, let me send a car to bring you to the airport offices," Deirdre's tiny voice said. She sounded far away—in another time and place.

"Grace?" Tina knocked at the door. "What's going on? Why are you shouting?"

"Ms. Naybor, are you still there?"

I'd spoken to my mom just a few days ago. She was fine—she was happy. She was very much alive.

"I want to talk to you about something," she'd said. "It's really been pressing on my heart."

I'd cut her off. I wouldn't listen. This had to be a dream—a sick nightmare. *It's not real*, I told myself. *This isn't really happening.*

I hung up on Deirdre and dialed my mom's home number. It rang five times and then her voicemail picked up. I listened to her cheery voice inform me that nobody was available to take my call at the moment.

"Mom?" I called. "Mom, this is Grace. Please call me when you get this message." My voice was unsteady. "Mom, it's just past seven in the morning, where are you? Maybe you're asleep."

Fat tears streamed down my face. "Mom?"

"Grace?" Trina knocked on the door again, her voice more urgent. "Unlock the door."

I didn't want her in my room, didn't want her near me. We hadn't spoken in months. She'd caused an irreconcilable rift between Mike and me. She lied, threatened me, and treated me like a gnat to be swatted away.

I hung up and dialed my mom's business phone. Again it rang and rang until her voicemail kicked in. The reality of the situation was starting to hit me.

"Mom," I pleaded. "Please, Mom. Please. Call me. I don't care what time it is. Call me as soon as you hear this."The words were deep—throaty and muffled in sobs. A wave of sorrow swept over me. I hung up the phone.

"Grace,"Trina knocked on the door again. "What is going on?"

The phone rang. I took a sharp breath and prayed that it was my mom returning my calls.

"Ms. Naybor?" It was Deirdre.

I felt as if someone had punched me in the gut. There was no air in my lungs and I struggled for breath. My body tingled. The room seemed smaller and my heart was beating so fast I was having chest pains.

"Ms. Naybor, are you all right?"

Was I all right? What kind of question was that? What kind of person called people to tell them their loved ones were dead and then asked a question like, "Are you all right?"

"Grace, I need you to talk to me," she said.

I looked at the phone cradled in my hand. I didn't want to talk to her. I didn't want to talk to anyone but my mom.

In one swift movement, I threw the phone across the room and it smashed against the door and broke into pieces.

"Grace!"Trina shouted. "What was that?"

She pounded on the door. I didn't answer her. Instead, I picked up my clock, snatched the cord out of the wall and threw it also.

"Grace, please open the door,"Trina pleaded.

She jiggled the knob. I staggered over to my television. Without hesitation, I pushed it off of its stand and crashed it to the ground. Sparks flew up in the air as it smoked.

"Grace!" Trina screamed, now frantic.

The phone rang in the living room.

"Hello?" Trina answered. "No, this is her roommate, what's going on?"

I picked up my lamp, and holding it like I would a baseball bat, I knocked down my bookshelves.

"Oh, my God," I heard Trina gasp.

My head throbbed as I chucked my stereo and speakers across the room. I don't know what I was thinking. I smashed, broke, destroyed everything I could get my hands on. Trina had said I didn't deserve it anyway. I demolished my computer, my mirror, my books and CDs. I screamed and cried and threw things until I was panting and drenched in sweat. By the time I stopped, the floor was a sea of rubble and my left hand was bleeding.

There was a knock at the door, and a voice.

"Grace?" It was Mike. "Grace, can you let me in?"

I ignored him and turned my wrath on the contents of my closet. I flung shoes, bags, hangers all over the place. What clothes I had the strength to rip, I ripped. Tears, snot, and spit ran from my face, down my chin and neck.

Mike kicked open the door with a loud bang, and the first thing I saw was his foot in midair. Then Mike and Trina stood next to each other, pity and worry written on their faces.

Trina brushed past Mike and rushed toward me. Who did she think she was kidding? Anger, hatred, and bitterness sprang out of me like water from a fountain. I glared at her, my nostrils flaring. Just as she got within striking distance, I hauled off and slapped her across the face with a strong, heavy hit that sent her head flying to one side. I shook the sting from my hand.

"Get out," I ordered, my jaws clenched.

She stared at me in horror, holding the side of her face. Tears sprang to her eyes.

"Get out!" I screamed at the top of my lungs. "Get out!"

"Gracie," Mike said, approaching me cautiously. He reached out to touch my shoulder, but I slapped his hand away.

"D-don't touch m-m-me," I shrieked. "B-both of you get out! G-g-get out, now!" I picked up a stray shoe and hurled it at Trina. She dodged it.

"I h-hate you!" I screamed at her. "I hate you, d-do you h-hear me? She's gone! Y-y-you said I didn't d-d-deserve her and n-now she's gone!"

Trina's face crumpled as she realized what I meant. The day she saw Don kiss me, she told me I didn't deserve anything I had in life, including my mom.

"I'm so sorry, Grace." Her chin quivered and tears trickled down her face.

"Keep your apologies." I seethed.

The phone rang again. Trina left the room.

"Grace," Mike stepped closer. I swung at him, but missed. He grabbed my wrist and pulled me to him. "Easy," he whispered.

"D-don't touch me," I cried. I punched him in the chest with my free arm. He didn't flinch.

"Okay," he whispered, and pressed me to him, pinning down both my arms. "It's gonna be okay."

"It's n-n-not gonna be okay!" I shouted. I tried to wrestle myself from his grip but it was no use. "It's not gonna be okay."

He stroked my hair and back. My body began to go limp as I stopped resisting and allowed myself to succumb to the tragedy that had just befallen me. My shoulders heaved violently as I sobbed.

"Ssshhh," Mike soothed. "I'm here."

"Why?" I wailed to no one in particular. "I d-don't unders-s-stand why."

He held me tightly—firmly. The warmth of his breath brushed the top of my head. And despite myself, I felt safe. My knees buckled. Mike slid with me to the floor. His back was against the wall, my body leaned helplessly against his. I'd never experienced such an immense sadness in all my life. I didn't know anyone could feel that much anguish—that much misery.

I let go and cried. I cried for myself. I cried for Mike. I cried for Trina. I cried for my dad. But most of all, I cried for Mom, who died a horrible death. I wondered if she was scared, if she was thinking about me, if she felt any pain. And I lamented because I knew she went without knowing how much I truly loved her. Mike stayed with me. He held me and rocked me and whispered words of encouragement. And I cried. I cried even after the tears stopped spilling out of my eyes. I cried until all I could do was moan. I cried until my eyes finally closed and everything went black.

When I woke up, it was late afternoon. I was tucked into bed with the covers pulled up to my chin. There were hushed whispers coming from the other side of my closed door. A vision of Trina's face, shocked and stunned from my cold slap, flashed into my mind. I waited for regret and shame to follow, but I felt none. My mother's death hadn't changed the pain Trina had caused; if anything her actions and words were magnified. The same thing went for Mike. Suddenly, my feelings for him—our relationship—took on a different meaning. He didn't matter as much as he used to—nothing did.

I had perspective now.

Someone had cleaned the room. The clothes, shoes, books, and CDs that I'd strewn all over were nowhere in sight. My computer, which I'd pushed off my desk and then kicked repeatedly, was sitting neatly in the corner. The screen was cracked in several places and it was dented on one side. The broken television had been removed and all of the glass had been swept away.

I rolled to my side, prepared to go back to sleep, but when I closed my eyes, I saw my mother's face. She was smiling in her quirky sort of way. Her eyes were sparkling; her hair was down. She looked vibrant. I felt a sinking sensation in the pit of my stomach as I pictured her panic-stricken, her fingers gripping the seat in front of her as her fragile body bounced violently about the cabin. My eyes stung with a batch of new tears. There were so many people to call—so many arrangements to be made. I became weary at the thought of it all. Where would I find the strength? I wiped away my tears. My hands were clammy.

Feeling myself slipping, I took several deep, calming breaths and tried to pull it together enough to call my dad. He'd know what to do. I sat up slowly and reached for my phone, but it wasn't there. That was the first thing I'd thrown. I hung my head in frustration and dread. If I wanted to talk to my dad or anyone else for that matter, I was going to have to leave my room.

Trina, Mike, and Dad were all sitting in the dining room eating bagels and drinking coffee. Their conversation came to an abrupt halt when I entered the room. All eyes were on me. I combed my fingers through my hair in an attempt to smooth it out.

"Hey," I said softly. The word came out as a whisper.

"Hey," Mike said back.

"Are you hungry?" Trina asked, cautiously.

I ignored them both and looked up at my father.

"I was just about to call you." With all my screaming and ranting, I must have overworked my vocal chords. My voice was hoarse and my throat hurt.

"Trina and Mike called me early this morning," he said, walking over to me.

I met him halfway and fell into his embrace. He held me—cradled me for a minute, kissed my forehead—and then pulled away.

"What do you need?" he asked. "I don't want you to worry about anything. I'm here. Just tell me."

I bit the inside of my cheek.

"Um, I'm not sure what to do next." My shoulders stiffened as a sob welled up in the back of my throat. "I, um, I have to make arrangements." My tears rolled freely down my face.

"Don't worry about that. I've got it under control."

"What about Grandma Doria and Grandpa Mearl?"

"Grace, honey," he said, wiping the tears from my face. "They already know. Don't worry about it. We'll get it taken care of."

"Who will?"

"I will. We'll take it one day at a time. Okay?"

I squeezed my eyes shut and shrugged my shoulders.

"I feel so lost."

"You're not lost," he said tenderly. "I'm here. I'm not going anywhere. You've got me and a lot of other people here to support you."

"He's right, Gracie," Trina chimed in. "If there's anything you need, I'm here for you."

I turned to her, my jaw set.

"You've done enough. Just leave me alone."

She scooted her chair away from the table and stood up. I waited for her to charge at me or storm off, but she just hugged herself and swayed.

"I owe you an apology," she said.

"We both do," Mike said, standing next to her in agreement.

I looked at them, baffled. Where had this come from?

"I know it wasn't my place," my dad interjected. "And I apologize if I crossed any boundaries, but I told Mike and Trina everything that happened—the truth."

"You didn't have to do that."

"Yes, I did. You weren't going to stand up for yourself and it was eating you alive. I felt like as your father, as someone concerned for your well-being, I needed to let them know what really happened."

"You told them everything?" I asked.

"Everything. That's the only way the story was going to get straightened out."

"Grace," Mike said, coming from around the table toward me. I stepped back. It was an involuntary reflex. He stopped cold when he realized that I didn't want him to come near me. "I just want you to know how sorry I am."

"I'm sorry, too," Trina said.

"You're sorry?" I asked, my blood boiling. "I don't want your apologies. What I wanted was for you to tell the truth."

She lowered her eyes.

"I have blame in this too," Mike said. "I could have sought out the truth for myself—not been so quick to judge."

"Oh, trust me," I said glaring at him. "You aren't out of the woods on this one. You and I both know that you should've known better. I've lost my faith in you. In fact, your *only* saving grace is that you were fed bad information."

"Don't do this now," my dad advised. "You've got enough stress to deal with. You can talk this out another time."

"No," I shook my head, keeping my gaze fixed on the two of them. "Now is as good a time as any."

First, I turned my wrath on Trina. "You think my mom's death erases all the drama and heartache you've caused? Is that it? You think that after months of you treating me like a trespasser in my own home—a home in which you stay for free—that I'm gonna cower back to you so that you can subject me to even more humiliation and pain down the road? No thanks, I'll pass. You're nothing more than a pretentious little troublemaker." I spat in her direction. "It's over between us. You don't exist to me."

Trina exhaled deeply.

"And you," I said to Mike. "You seem so forgiving, so understanding, so tolerant at first glance. But when trouble hit, you turned on me just like that," I snapped. "And even worse, you threw your Christianity in my face. You should've *known* better. Being with me is like playing with fire. So unless you're a pyromaniac, you have no reason to apologize, right? I'm too dangerous to take a chance on, so you say."

"Grace, you have every right to be angry with me." Trina said. "I messed up."

"You messed up?" I asked incredulously, my voice rising a notch. "You didn't mess up—you lied."

"I didn't mean to lie. The whole thing with Don—I-I was upset with you and hurt for Mike."

"You were hurt for Mike? That makes all the sense in the world," I said sarcastically. "You were hurt for Mike, so you told him that I slept with another man. I get it now."

My voice was saturated in feigned delight, but my face was cold and stony.

"I made a bad assumption," she tried to explain. "I saw you guys kissing and I remembered how excited you were about Don when you first started going to the Y. Then you started disappearing on us—locking yourself away, not answering the phone. I don't know—I put two and two together."

"And two and two equal me being unfaithful to the man I loved?"

"I was wrong," her voice quaked. "I've never been more wrong about anything in my life."

"A few hours ago, you were confident I was a cheating home-wrecker. How can you be so sure that I'm not now?" I asked, facetiously.

"Professor Harris explained a lot of it," she said, her head hung in shame. "You know, the kiss, the novel, the pills...everything."

"So if my dad hadn't taken up for me, things would've stayed the same, right?" She bit her lip. I asked Mike the same question. He backed away, but I stared at them, determined to get a response.

"Grace, honey, let it go for now," my dad came to their rescue. "You're upset; we can all see that. Don't misdirect your emotions."

"I'm sorry," Trina said again, her voice a whisper. "What can I do to make this up to you?"

I looked at her, our entire friendship passing before my eyes. We'd been through so much together. There were times when it felt like she was a literal piece of me. I had very few memories that didn't include Trina and for as long as we'd known each other, I'd never been able to picture my future without her. But all journeys come to an end. As I watched her looking at me with those puffy, sad, pleading eyes, I felt nothing. It could've been that the death of my mom overshadowed losing Trina's friendship, and that maybe, later on, I'd realize our relationship was still worth something. But at that moment, I knew that my life, my future—or at least my near future— no longer included her.

"Nothing. This isn't even worth trying to fix. It's beyond repair. I'm done."

My dad and I flew to Detroit on Wednesday. The funeral was held the following Monday. She'd been gone for one week, and the reality wasn't any less cutting. My coping reflexes hadn't yet kicked in to shield me from my motherless state. I wasn't able to pinpoint a reason or some grand purpose for why it happened. Memories, stories, thoughts—none of it consoled me or rescued me from my permanent state of shock. I was just there—smiling, nodding, and pretending I wasn't hollow inside—pretending my mind and body were in sync.

People came in droves. Old secretaries, coworkers, distant family members, and close friends, they all came—some of them from other states—to say goodbye. The ceremony was beautifully done—tasteful. Because her body had not been recovered, I decided not to have the traditional casket. Instead, we gathered photos of her from every stage of life, and had them blown up and displayed on large gold stands. Surrounding the pictures were fragrant, colorful flowers and in the middle of the entire arrangement was a podium, where people would be allowed to come forward with their fondest memories and thoughts.

My Grandma Doria wasn't crazy about my idea.

"What about the Reverend, the sermon, the choir, the eulogy?" she asked. "People are expecting to attend a funeral."

"I'm not all that concerned about what people are expecting," I told her. "She was *my* mother."

"Now hold on just a minute," my grandpa said in his deep, gruff voice. "She was our daughter, you hear? She meant a lot of things to a lot of people. Everybody's hurting here, Grace."

"I just don't feel right about sticking an empty box in front of a congregation and acting like she's there. Why not put out the pictures? Let people see her in her true form. Let them leave with a better understanding of who she was and where she came from."

"Why can't we do that the traditional way?"

"We can," I said with a shrug. I didn't have the strength to argue. "Do what you want. I just thought maybe we could leave people with a brighter memory of her."

"We'll do it however Grace likes," my grandma said, giving my grandpa the evil eye. "We don't need a casket to put Cherie's memory to rest. It was just a suggestion. Pictures and flowers will do just as nicely."

I sat in the front row, my grandparents to the right of me, my dad to the left, and listened as one person after another told the rest of us something great about my mom—things I never knew. The sanctuary was packed; every pew was filled. People were standing against the wall and sitting on the steps. I didn't know half of those who spoke, but I could see that my mother meant something to each of them—that she'd somehow managed to touch every individual on a personal level.

One of the first to speak was Trina. We hadn't spoken since the day before I left Memphis, and even though I no longer considered her a friend, I respected the fact that she came to the funeral.

"I'm not related to the Naybors, but I'm a close friend of the family, particularly with Grace."

She glanced at me nervously, as if she was afraid I would challenge her statement, right there in front of everyone. I didn't bat a lash.

"I was there the day Ms. Naybor gave her life to Christ. I don't know if many of you knew that she was born again. We're all dealing with this tragedy in our own ways, but the thing that's helped me most is the knowledge that she's in paradise with Jesus."

I crossed my arms and willed her off the stage. My dad patted my knee.

"Maybe knowing that will help some of you, too. Thank you."

Arlene, Trina's aunt, went up next and sang a touching hymn, "It Is Well." Even my dad, who'd remained composed throughout it all, cried. Then a stumpy white man took the podium and told a hilarious story about my mom in grad school. I lost count of how many people spoke. The funeral was scheduled to last only an hour, but nearly two-and-a-half hours later, there was still a line down the aisle. We listened respectfully to all of them. Some made us cry, others made us laugh, but in the end, I think people were able to walk away with some closure.

The last person to speak was Grandma Doria.

"I'm so glad to see so many people here today," she started. "Many of you I know, some I haven't seen in years, and others I haven't had the opportunity to meet. But we're all here today to pay homage and lay to rest my beautiful baby girl. There's not much I can say that hasn't already been said. We'll all miss her, but she lives on inside each and every one of us. And those of us who are the Lord's can rest easy knowing that Cherie's soul is safe in heaven, and that someday we'll see her again. Cherie leaves behind one daughter, my grandbaby, Grace, who has turned out to be an exceptional woman. And though you may not know it," she said, speaking directly to me, "you've always been and forever will be the apple of her eye."

The crowd dispersed slowly, like sand through an hourglass. Countless people passed down my aisle to pay their condolences and then headed up front to admire our beautiful arrangement of pictures and flowers. Forty minutes later, the sanctuary was empty. My grandparents, who were holding family hour at their house, had already gone to meet the onslaught of guests. My dad and I sat silently next to each other, his arm wrapped around my shoulder.

"Ready to go?"

I shook my head. "Not yet. I just—I want to be alone for a minute." I sounded apologetic.

My dad had been so helpful over the past week, not to mention the days leading up to Mom's death. I didn't want him to feel like I was unappreciative.

He nodded understandingly. "Take your time. There's no hurry."

"Thanks, Dad." I wrapped my arm around his neck and gave him a hug. He walked down the long aisle and out the door.

All I could think as I stared at the picture in front of me was how beautiful Mom's smile was. As a child, I used to wonder if she wore dentures—that's how perfect her teeth were. Looking at that smile now just made me sad. It's such a small, simple word, isn't it? I was shocked to realize it encompassed everything I felt. I was sad my mom was gone and that I was never going to find out what it was she wanted to tell me the day I cut her short. I was sad Trina and I were no longer friends and that our time together ended so abruptly. I was sad I'd finished writing my novel—that I had nothing else to throw myself into, nothing to relieve the pain. And I was sad that Mike, one of the most important people in my life, turned out not to be the man I thought he was.

I was so deep in thought that I didn't realize someone had walked into the building, until I heard footsteps just a few feet away. I turned around expecting to see my father, but it was Mike.

"What're you doing here?" I asked, wiping my tears on my sleeve.

"I flew in last night."

"You didn't have to."

"I wanted to. Your mom was a special woman. The service was nice."

"Well, thanks for coming," I tried to sound as gracious as possible. "There's a family hour at my grandparents' house. You're welcome to come."

"Listen, can I talk to you for a minute?" he asked.

I examined him in his black suit and gray tie. His dreads hung loosely around his face. His jaw was just as chiseled, his shoulders just as broad as I remembered. It had been so long since the two of us were alone together. He was still gorgeous—still charming. I slid down to make room for him at the end of the pew. He unbuttoned his jacket and sat down.

I crossed my legs and turned to face him. He took a deep breath.

"Can you ever forgive me? For not believing in you, for acting how I acted, for saying everything I said, for—"

"I don't know," I said. I was planning to let him get all the words out—to admit he was wrong. "Maybe you could help me understand how you could think so badly of me."

He shook his head and slouched in his seat.

"We were moving full steam ahead," he started. "Everything was perfect and then, out of nowhere, it's like you didn't want to be bothered with me anymore. You never wanted to go out; you didn't want me to come over. Sometimes all I wanted was to hear your voice, but you stopped answering your phone. I couldn't figure out if it was something I'd said, or done, or hadn't done. Trina was just as lost as I was. She rarely saw you and if she did manage to catch you at home, you were always locked in your room. And it seemed like you were giving everybody different excuses. You told me that you just weren't feeling like yourself and that you needed some time alone to think, but you told Trina that you were working. Nothing added up."

I nodded, taking in everything he had to say.

"So I decided to back off, give you some space. Then one day, Trina said she had something to tell me. Her story explained the way you were acting."

"But *I* tried to tell you the truth and you thought I was lying. What makes you think my dad's not lying now?"

"He showed us the novel, to prove what you'd been up to."

"So if I had shown you my book, you would have taken my word for everything."

"Well, he also showed us a copy of the complaint you filed against Don."

"Ah," I sang. "So he had tangible proof. You shouldn't have needed proof."

"I know."

"Do you really? Or are you just experiencing the clarity of hindsight?"

He shook his head. "I love you, Grace." He reached for my hand and I didn't pull away. "Ever since I found out the truth, I've been kicking myself. There were so many better ways to handle the situation. I just couldn't see past the hurt."

I didn't know what to say. I still loved Mike. There was no denying that. But the part of me that embraced people had shut down. I was too scared to give him another chance. I'd lost my best friend, the man I loved, and my mother. I didn't know if I could survive losing Mike again.

"It's okay," I slid my hand from underneath his. "I forgive you."

"I don't just want your forgiveness."

"Mike, I—" He held his index finger to my lips.

"Do you still love me?"

"Of course, but—" Before I could finish my sentence, he was down on one knee.

"Grace," he said, fishing around in his pocket. "I know we're here under unfortunate circumstances. And I know I have a lot of work to do to prove myself worthy of you again. But you're the only woman I've ever loved. You take up a bigger part of me than I ever thought possible. I love you so much." His voice cracked and his eyes filled with tears.

He pulled out a small, black velvet box and held it out to me. I took it from him, gingerly holding it in my hand for a few seconds before opening it. Inside was a beautiful, three-stone engagement ring set in yellow gold. I gasped at its size, my hand clasped over my open mouth. It must've cost him a fortune.

"Gracie." I pried my eyes away from the ring and looked at him. Tears streamed down his face and his chin shook. "I made the mistake of letting you go once; I won't be stupid enough to do it again. I want to be with you and only you," he whispered. "Will you marry me? Will you be my wife?"

I looked at Mike and then at the ring. Was this what I wanted? At one time, yes, it was *all* I wanted. But things were so different now. It's not that Mike and I couldn't get over the "Don hump." With a little bit of work and communication, we'd be right back to our old selves in no time. The problem was, I didn't know who I wanted to be anymore. Something had been missing. I'd tried everything to fill the void—weight loss, Mike, the novel—but nothing worked. I always found myself back at square one. I needed to fix my damaged parts and I couldn't see myself doing that as a married woman. It felt good to be vindicated—to know that Mike wasn't walking around with a bunch of lies in his head. But that was only the beginning. I had a long journey ahead of me.

I closed the box.

"No," I said, handing it back to him. "I can't."

He swallowed hard and looked away, his eyelashes glistening.

"Mike, I'm sorry, but it's over." He didn't move. He didn't respond. There was nothing left to say—nothing that hadn't already been said.

"I should go," I said quietly. "My dad's waiting for me outside." He continued to gaze silently into the distance. "Take care of yourself, Mike."

I gathered my purse and coat and headed down the aisle to the exit. And I left him there—crying, wounded, and on bended knee.

Chapter Fourteen

My dad had to leave on Thursday. I had to stay until Monday, when my mom's will would be executed. I hated to see him go. He turned out to be my backbone—my hero. If I could, I would've followed him anywhere. In the few weeks since we'd been reconciled, I'd turned into a "daddy's girl." My only regret, when it came to him, was that we had spent so many years apart. He was a good man and I was proud to have him as a father.

"Are you sure you have to go?" I asked. His suitcase was lying open on his bed.

"Trust me, if I could stay with you, I would. But I took most of last week off and most of this one. I have to get back to my classes."

"Can't they hire a substitute?" I whined, poking my bottom lip out.

He chuckled.

"I don't have to just get back to my students," he said. "I have bills to pay. What am I going to do if I get home and my lights have been shut off?"

"Light a candle?" I teased.

"Ha, ha," he said dryly. "You know, Grace, since you're not sure when you'll be going back to Memphis, you might want to have your mail forwarded here."

"Why would I stay here?"

"You've got a lot of loose ends to tie up. What are you going to do with your mom's house?"

"There really isn't anything for me to do until I know for sure that she left it to me. The house may not even be mine to worry about."

"But still, you'll want to go there—collect memorabilia, clean the place out. You'd be surprised how long that can take."

"Do you not want me to come back to Memphis? Because it seems like you're dreaming up reasons for me to stay in Detroit."

"I want you to live where you'll be happy—and I'm not sure that's Memphis anymore. Memphis isn't the same warm, fuzzy place it was when you first moved there. Unless you're planning to give it another go with Mike, I don't know what you're so eager to get back to."

"Well, I'm pretty sure that all hope's lost with Mike."

"Oh, I wouldn't say that. The man loves you. If you knocked on his door tomorrow, he'd be over the moon with joy."

I hadn't bothered to tell Dad about the proposal, mainly because there was nothing to tell. Mike asked me to marry him and I said "no." I left him kneeling in front of a church pew—his spirits crushed. The last thing I wanted to do was embarrass him on top of it all. Rejection was enough of a sting in itself. Spreading the story around—privileging people to our private business—would have just added public humiliation to the equation.

Who was right? Who was wrong? It didn't matter anymore. We'd both been through enough. It was time to move on. And as painful as it was, turning down his proposal was a step in the right direction.

"Mike asked me to marry him," I confessed. "And I said no."

"Okay," he said slowly, weighing his words. "Why?"

"Well for starters, he proposed the day of Mom's funeral."

"That's it?" He shook his head. "That's not a reason—it's an excuse."

I opened my mouth, ready to argue.

"Just listen to me for a second," he said, holding up his hand. "A reason is an explanation or justification for an act. But an excuse is nothing more than a pretended reason for conduct. So let's have your reason."

"What's the point?" I asked, frustrated. "The damage is done. Even if I wanted to change my mind, which I don't, Mike's gone. It's over."

"Maybe, but one could argue that you sent him away just like you did me. And look at us now."

"I don't know," I said, shrugging my shoulders. "I feel like I need to be alone right now— unattached."

"Now we're getting somewhere," he said, pushing his suitcase aside and sitting down. "*That* is a reason."

"How so?"

"Because it's a need, and needs are defined by necessity. You feel as though it's necessary for you to be alone at this juncture in your life, right?" I nodded. "Well, you can't very well do that engaged to someone, now can you?"

"What are you trying to say? Do you think I did the wrong thing?"

"I can tell you what I think, but ultimately *your* decision is the only one that matters."

"So what do you think?"

"I think you made a mistake. But I could be wrong—it's been known to happen. I'll tell you one thing, though—I don't think I've ever seen two people so right for each other. You each have weaknesses, but they're complemented by the other's strengths. You're impulsive, he's methodical. You're high strung, he's laid back. You write, he draws. You're made for each other."

I took a minute to digest what he'd said. "Yeah, we are, aren't we?"

"If your reason for turning down Mike was really based on a desire to be alone, I respect that. Only *you* know what's best for you. But if you said 'no' because you were afraid, or because you're still angry with him for what happened, then I think that a few months from now—or maybe years—you'll realize you made a monumental mistake. And then it really will be too late."

We fell silent. He resumed his packing.

"I'll think about what you're saying. What am I gonna do without all your fatherly advice?" I asked playfully. "What if I do something stupid without you here to guide me? That's all the more reason for you to stay."

"You don't give up easily, do you? That you got from me. It's the Harris genes." He smiled, and zipped his suitcase closed. "Don't forget to forward your mail, Grace—at least have your bills sent here. You don't want a Memphis mailbox full of overdue bills."

He was right. Two months later, I was still in Detroit. I don't know why, but I felt drawn to the city. It could've been that I had family in Michigan. My mom's death really created a closeness between all of us. Not everything changed for the better. My grandpa was still mean and surly; my grandma still got her feelings hurt when I didn't eat dinner. My cousins still nickel-and-dimed me for everything in my pockets. And my aunts and uncles treated me like a one-woman, pro bono babysitting service. But we were family.

I felt accepted—welcomed—something I didn't experience for months in Memphis. People called me, invited me out, and came over. I hadn't known I had so many friends. I'd spent so much time concentrating on Trina and dealing with all her issues that I rarely had time for anyone else. But now that I'd pushed her out of the limelight, I was finally able to hang out with other people—experience normal friendship, where one person doesn't constantly overshadow the other. I'd spent so many years tending to Trina's hair-trigger temper and snippy attitude, I'd lost sight of what true friendship was like.

Thanksgiving came and went. I spent the better part of the day in the kitchen with my grandma and aunts, helping them cook. I enjoyed spending time with them. For the first time since Mom's death, I didn't feel guilty when I laughed.

We made hot water cornbread, collard greens, macaroni and cheese, ribs, fried chicken, turkey, ham, stuffing, mashed potatoes, cabbage, yams, two types of cobbler, fresh boiled corn, green beans, deviled eggs, and red beans with rice. There was so much food, it wouldn't fit in the kitchen. We had to lug half of it onto the back porch.

I lost count of how many times I refilled my plate. After my second scoop of peach cobbler, I had to unbutton my jeans. It was all I could do to sit down on the living room couch without rolling off.

I watched my cousins chase each other around the house and wrestle. The men headed down to the basement, toothpicks in their left hands, pie in their right, to watch football. The women stayed upstairs, content to chat and throw their heads back in laughter.

With my belly full and my mind lazy, I sat on the couch and soaked in my environment. I let their voices, their happiness, their love seep into my pores. And for a brief moment, I let go of my worries.

"Hey there, girl," someone said from behind. It was a familiar, gruff voice.

"Hey, Grandpa," I said, opening my eyes.

"You try my ribs? How'd you like 'em?"

"They were delicious."

"Hmph," he grunted. "You ain't just sayin' that? Your grandma said they were too salty."

"Really? I went back for seconds."

"You know I love you, don't you?" he asked, out of the blue.

"Uh, yeah, sure," I lied.

"That's what I figured. Your grandma got it into her head somehow that you didn't know how much I loved you, or how proud you make me. I said, 'Doria, she's my grandbaby. How do you figure she thinks I love everyone but her?'"

"Well, you are kind of hard on me sometimes."

"I'm hard on everybody. If I don't push you, who will? I don't want a bunch of useless kids running around with my last name. I want all my grandkids to make something of themselves."

"I know."

"Yeah, *I* know you know, but I decided to come on over and ask you about it to put your grandma's mind at ease."

He patted my knee and got up. I caught a quick glimpse of my grandma, who'd been peaking discreetly from around the corner. I couldn't help but laugh. They were such an odd couple. She was so nosy—always in everyone's business. And he was so rude—always acting like he didn't want to be bothered. But deep down they were good people. And they loved me.

After my third dessert, I went upstairs and settled down for a nap. My overstuffed stomach gurgled as I snuggled deep under the covers and fell fast asleep.

An hour later, I was awakened by a knock on the door.

"Grace, phone call," my grandma said. She cracked open the door. "It's Malikah. Do you want me to tell her to call back?"

I sprang out of bed and dashed to the nearest phone.

"You sure you wasn't asleep or nothing?"

"No," I said, trying to disguise my groggy voice.

"Just checkin'. You know how black folk be. Eat a bucket full of chicken and then just be ready to fall out."

I laughed. Malikah was my older cousin—my favorite cousin. Out of all the grandkids, we were the only girls and the closest in age. She was two years older, and through most of my childhood, I'd admired her strength. Back then, she encompassed everything I wanted to be—strong, beautiful, and popular.

I used to marvel at her long legs, her full, sultry lips, and the way she could captivate a room without uttering a word. Aside from her physical charms, I was amazed by her strong personality. As a person who grew up taking orders from her best friend, I was floored by Malikah's ability to tell people where to get off. Granted, her "take no mess" attitude often bordered on callousness, but I admired her for being able to take up for herself.

She and Trina never got along, maybe because they were so much alike. When the two of them got into close proximity, it was only a matter of time before the claws came out and catty insults went flying. Most of the time, their disagreements were about me. Malikah used to cringe whenever she heard Trina order me around.

"She could at least say please."

I was so dependent on Trina's friendship, I felt it was my job to defend her.

"It's not what you think. You just don't understand our relationship."

"I get it, baby girl. You the one who don't understand. Old girl got you wrapped around her finger. Come on now, why she gotta ask you to get her some water when she standin' twenty feet from the sink? Don't she got legs just like you?"

Instead of starting an argument I had no hope of winning, I'd just nod and pretend she was making valid points. But given everything that happened in Memphis, I should've listened more closely. Maybe I could've avoided the trauma Trina caused.

"Why didn't you come over and eat with us? We had a lot of good stuff—all the fixings," I said.

"Listen to you, soundin' all country, talkin' 'bout 'fixings.' They musta got hold a you real good down in Tennessee."

"You didn't answer my question."

"I had to spend Thanksgiving with Deonté's family this year." Deonté was her husband. They got married early—when she was nineteen. The first couple of years were rocky. Malikah entered the relationship with two sons, each with a different father. Deonté fell in love with the boys and they fell in love with him. He took care of them like they were his own, which was perfect since neither of the boys' fathers were willing to step up to their responsibilities. But as soon as Malikah married Deonté and asked Trevor and Charles to sign over their parental rights so that her new husband could legally adopt them, everything came to a head.

All of a sudden, Trevor and Charles wanted to be daddies. They started playing mind games with the boys, telling them that Deonté was bad and that he was trying to steal their mommy away from them. The chaos drove a wedge between Malikah and Deonté, until finally Deonté was ready to walk.

I'm not sure how they worked things out enough to stay together, but they did, and their relationship was better than it used to be. The times I'd gotten a chance to sit down and talk with Malikah, she sounded like she does now—spunky, but tired.

"Whachu 'bout to do?"

"Nothing."

"That's what I like to hear. You goin' out wit me tonight."

"What about Deonté and the boys?"

"What about 'em?" she asked. "They over his mama house. It's all about you and me tonight, baby. Let's hit Excalibur at 7:00." With Malikah, that meant 8:00. "And wear somethin' cute. You gotta look tight if you wanna roll wit me."

I walked into the restaurant at quarter to eight. Malikah was nowhere to be found. I wasn't surprised.

"Table for one?" the host asked. He was a short Latino with slicked-back hair. He looked dashing in his all-black suit.

"No, two."

"Smoking or non?" Malikah was a chain-smoker. I thought about sitting in the smoking section, just this once. *Nope*, I decided. *That's the price she pays for being late.*

"Non."

He led me to a booth near the back.

"Can I get you a drink while you wait for your companion to arrive?"

"A Diet Coke," I said, taking off my coat. Two men sitting at the bar across the room stopped talking to gawk. I tried not to smile.

I knew I looked good, especially since I'd put on some weight. All my grandma's home cooking was starting to manifest itself on my breasts and hips. I filled out my clothes nicely. And I had fun fixing myself up to go out. It had been so long since I'd taken any pride in my appearance.

That evening, I settled on a fitted burgundy sweater and black, boot-cut pants that hugged my curves. I topped the outfit off with high-heeled boots and a stylish belt. I swept my hair up into a soft ponytail. I put on some mascara, a little eyeliner, and some lip gloss, and I was good to go.

Malikah sauntered in ten minutes later in a short "pleather" jacket and knee-high boots. My jaw dropped when I saw the miniskirt she was wearing. It barely covered her assets. I wasn't embarrassed to be seen with her—Malikah became a risqué dresser at an early age. But we were in Michigan—in November! It had to be twenty degrees outside. Still, she looked fabulous and it was great to see her.

"Wassup, girl?" she asked, pulling me out of the booth. "Lemme get a look at you." She spun me around. The two men at the bar enjoyed the free show. "That's more like it." She hugged me.

"What're you talking about?"

"You know what I'm talkin' 'bout. When I saw you at your mom's funeral, you was skinny. I ain't even recognize you."

"Yeah, I know. I lost a lot of weight."

"But you puttin' it back on. That's all that matters."

"Ma'am, may I get you something to drink?" our waiter asked, setting a napkin down in front of Malikah.

"Yeah, gimme whatever this is," she said, picking up my glass and sniffing it. "What is this?"

"Diet Coke."

Her face scrunched up.

"I don't think so," she said, sliding the glass across the table. "Malikah does not do diet. I'll have a Jambo Safari, and so will she."

The waiter waited for my approval.

"Yeah, sure. Jambo Safari it is."

"So," Malikah started. "How's Attila the Hun?"

That was her nickname for Trina.

"We don't talk anymore. We fell out in Memphis. Do we have to talk about this?"

"Might as well get it outta the way, 'cause you know I'm a keep askin' 'til you tell me."

"She lied about something she saw, and it caused a split between me and my boyfriend."

"Mmmhmm! What have I been tellin' you? Didn't I tell you it was only a matter of time? Did you get your man back?"

"By the time the truth came out, it was too late."

"He found someone else?"

"No."

"You found someone else?"

I shook my head.

"Okay, so then help me understand why it's too late."

"I don't know. I guess by the time he found out the truth, I was too mad to forgive him."

"Do he know about your mom?"

"Yeah, he came to the funeral."

"He came from Memphis to go to your mama's funeral and y'all wasn't even together?" She sat back and smirked. "It ain't over. Ain't no man in the world who'd fly here to be with you if he ain't in love with you. And you too smart to let a man like that go."

"Well, maybe I'm not as smart as you think I am. He proposed to me after the funeral, and I said no. So there's no chance of us getting back together."

"What does you not accepting his proposal have to do with y'all gettin' back together? Girl, the coward in you gets the best of you every time. First by Trina, and now you're using it against yourself. This ain't all that complicated. Do you love him?"

I rolled my eyes.

"What's love got to do with it?"

"Just answer the question, Grace."

I smiled.

"Yes, I love him."

"You wanna be with him?

"I don't know."

"Uh-uh," she said, shaking her head. "Now you know I ain't 'bout to let you cop out like that. Do you wanna be with him?"

"Yeah, I think I do, but just not right now."

"Have you told him that?"

"Not those exact words."

"Okay, what was your exact words?"

"Something along the lines of, 'Here's your ring back. Take care.'"

"Dang! Maybe you right. That's kinda messed up."

The waiter returned to the table with our fruity, very alcoholic drinks.

"The gentlemen at the bar would like to buy you ladies a second round when you're ready."

Malikah whipped around and craned her neck to check out the mysterious strangers. They nodded discreetly.

"You can tell them thanks, but no thanks."

He nodded and walked away.

"What's wrong with free drinks?" I asked.

"Girl, please! I'm married, you still in love with your ex, and the one in the tan sports coat has a high top fade. You can't trust no man runnin' round with a high top fade. That junk went out in the eighties."

I cracked up. "You're crazy."

"I know, I know," she said proudly. "But gettin' back to what I was tellin' you. If y'all love each other like you say you do, it won't never be too late."

I sipped my drink. "I'm just not ready to go fishing in that pond again. Who knows how I'll feel a few months from now? I may wake up one morning and decide I don't want to live another day without him, in which case I'll go crawling back. But right now, I'm enjoying my independence. For the first time in a long time, my life is drama-free and I want to soak it up."

"I wish I could say the same thing."

"Uh-oh," I sang. "Trouble in paradise?"

"It ain't nothin' new. Just the same old mess I been going through for the last eleven years. You wanna hear it?"

"I love listening to your problems," I joked. "It makes me feel better about my life."

"Okay, see. Now you were wrong for that."

We talked for hours, catching up on old times, gossiping about family members and mutual friends. I could be honest with Malikah—crude even—and it was okay. She didn't have any rules or standards, only that I be myself.

At one in the morning, I stumbled into my grandparent's house, slightly tipsy. I took two Tylenol and drank a tall glass of water. I climbed into bed, still dressed in my clothes, and fell asleep.

When I woke up, my head was pounding, and the sunlight beaming through the curtains didn't do anything but make it worse. I kept perfectly still, scared that any sudden movements might trigger a nasty bout of nausea.

It was almost one in the afternoon. Under ordinary circumstances, my grandma wouldn't have allowed me to sleep so late. But since my mom's death, she's backed off—given me the freedom to do what I want.

I sat up and waited for the room to stop spinning. My breath reeked and my mouth was hot and sticky. Drinking was always fun until the next morning. Last night, I felt liberated, but now, sitting in bed, wiping the mascara from my eyes, I felt like a train wreck.

My day, like every other day I'd spent in Detroit, was open. I could do whatever I wanted, whenever I wanted. Leisure felt exhilarating now, but it had driven me mad with boredom in Tennessee. The only part of Memphis I missed was my dad.

A wave of guilt swept over me when I realized I'd forgotten to call him yesterday. I took a steadying breath, hoisted myself off the bed, and teetered down the hall to use the phone.

"Grace! How are you, honey? How was your Thanksgiving?"

"It was great. Where'd you go?"

"I stayed home, roasted some chicken, and watched the game. Where's an old man like me supposed to go?"

"You're not old, Dad, you're mature."

"Is *that* what you young ones call us geriatrics these days?" We chuckled. "Do you have any idea when you might come home? I miss you, and well, I have some good news. And I have to tell you face-to-face."

"You can't tell me over the phone?"

"Yes, I could, but I'm not going to. Grace, I need you to come back." He was serious.

It's not that I didn't miss my dad. We hadn't seen each other in a long time and he wasn't up for time off until Christmas. It would be nice to see him, but for some reason, I just didn't want to go back to Memphis.

"Okay," I sighed. "I'll call today about flights."

"Thank you. I promise you won't regret it."

"Of course, I won't. I'll get to see *you*."

We hung up. Before I did anything else, I wanted to get my hands on some soap and water so I could freshen up.

"Grace?" my grandpa called from downstairs. "You got some mail down here."

"Okay, I'll be down in a little bit."

He answered me with a curt grunt.

I took a long hot shower. The water felt good as it pelted my skin. I stood under the spray until the hot water ran out. When I got to my room, there was a box sitting on my bed, addressed to me. Inside was a massive stack of mail held together by a large rubber band. The note read:

Grace,

Your mail was piling up. I wasn't sure what you wanted to do with it or if you even knew it was here. Just trying to help.

Love, Trina

I guess she decided not to move. That was more incentive to go to Memphis. I didn't mind her loafing off me when we were close, but now that our friendship was over, she had no business being in my loft. She wasn't on the lease, she didn't pay rent—she was a freeloader. I inhaled deeply and counted to ten. The last thing I needed was to let Trina ruin my day.

What is all this? I turned my attention back to the mail in my hand. I knew none of them were bills, because I'd taken my dad's advice and had my phone, credit card, and utility statements sent to my grandparents' house. I quickly skimmed over the first few letters. Most of it was junk. I was about to throw it all on my bed and leave it for later when a small, blue envelope caught my eye. At first glance, it didn't look special, but the handwriting was familiar. I sat on the edge of the bed and opened a letter from Mom.

Dearest Grace,

I wish more than anything I could tell you in person everything I'm about to write. But sometimes life doesn't afford us such opportunities. I want you to know that I love you. You are my reason for living. You are the only one by whom I measure my success. I could run fifty Fortune 500 companies, I could own ten mansions or drive hundreds of cars, but if I've failed you as a mother, then I have failed at everything.

I look at you and I am so proud of the woman you've become. Your brilliance and insight—they baffle me. Grace, you are twice the woman I'll ever be.

If I spent too much time in meetings, if I seemed too busy, please know that in the end, I did it all for you. I realize now that you've weathered a lot—more than you should have. And you did it alone. Don't think I haven't watched you—that I haven't cried for you.

I should have hugged you more. I should have opened my heart wider. While I can't take back all the years I've messed up, I can promise you that today is a new day. Jesus has opened my eyes. It's as if He's unthawed my heart and given me hope. I won't let Satan destroy us. You're my family—my baby.

Forgive me, please. Forgive me like Christ forgave you and hold my hand as we enter a new season.

I Love You Always,
Mom

I read the letter over and over again—stunned. *When did she write this?* It wasn't dated. I'd talked to her briefly four days before she passed. I tried to recount everything that was said. Eventually, it hit me. She'd wanted to tell me something that had been pressing on her heart. But I was too busy—eager to get back to my dad.

"Put it in a letter," I'd told her. Even now, I winced at my harshness. I was being facetious—just trying to say something to get her off the phone. But she took me at my word, and this was the letter. This is what she wanted to tell me. She wanted my forgiveness, that's all—she wanted me to forgive her so we could start fresh.

If I've failed you as a mother, then I've failed at everything, the letter read. I wondered if she died thinking she was a bad mother. And I marveled at how well she knew and understood me. All this time, I thought she gladly put work before me, that she preferred to be in all-day meetings rather than to be with me. But now, after her death—after it was too late—I found out the truth.

There was no one to blame but myself. If I had just taken a second to listen, we could have talked about it. I could have told her that I'd forgive her anything, and that despite my tantrums, I loved her, too. The letter—her willingness to throw away the past—is what I'd been waiting for all my life. She accepted me, she was proud of me. I mattered.

Gingerly, I folded the letter and placed it carefully in its blue envelope. And just like that, I knew how I wanted to spend my day. I was going to go to my mom's house—my house now. She left it to me. I didn't think I'd feel ready to go there this soon. Since the house was paid off, I'd planned to just sit on it until I could bring myself to put it on the market. But now I felt like I owed it to myself—to my mom—to go and collect as many memories as I could.

I threw on a pair of jeans, a big baggy sweater, two pairs of socks and some snow boots.

"Grandma," I called, as I bounded down the stairs. "I need to borrow your car."

"You leaving?" she asked. I followed the sound of her voice to the family room. She was reading her Bible. "Aren't you hungry? We got lots of leftovers."

My stomach flipped just thinking about food. "I'll have some when I get back."

"Suit yourself. Keys are on the kitchen table. But grab yourself a piece of fruit—just in case."

I smiled to myself and shook my head. She was determined to make me eat. I didn't argue, though. She meant well. I swiped a long, yellow banana from the fruit bowl and shoved the keys into my pocket.

"Okay, I'll be back in a little while."

"You get some fruit?" I held up the banana. She nodded—satisfied that I wasn't going to starve to death.

The air was crisp. I stood on the front porch for a minute—caught off guard by the bitter cold. I watched as my breath came out in fluffy, white puffs and then disintegrated. Memphis winters didn't come close to this.

My nose and ears throbbed as the frosty air began to turn them numb. My grandma's old minivan wasn't any better. The heat took a while to kick in. I sat behind the wheel, my arms wrapped around my body, and waited for the vehicle to warm up.

Five minutes later, I was making the familiar drive to Mom's. Even though I hadn't been there in over a year, every turn in the road looked the same. The streets were still cracked and dented from the harsh winters and the people drove aggressively—everyone was in a hurry. All in all, Detroit was the same slick, quick-paced city it had been before I left.

Growing up in my neighborhood had proven to be lonely. My mom wasn't sociable and there were no kids my age living on our cul-de-sac. I thought the neighbors hadn't even known who we were. But I was wrong. Many of them came to the funeral and a few of them even spoke.

I parked the van right outside the garage and walked around to the back of the house. The spare key was next to a huge potted plant, behind a loose brick. We'd kept it there for as long as I could remember.

I climbed the stairs to the deck and went in through the back so I could disarm the alarm. The house, like everything else, was the same. I walked through the kitchen and into the main foyer, my boots squeaking on the marble floors.

Sadness wrenched my chest. This is where I stood so many times and watched as Mom put on her coat and left for business trips. She never looked back. She was in too much of a hurry. I'd wait for her to turn around and give me a hug or a kiss—to let me know she was going to miss me. But she'd just tell me to be good—obey the nanny—grab her suitcase, and rush out the door. I'd watch her from the window as she loaded her trunk and down the street. It used to crush me. But it wasn't as devastating now—not now that she was gone.

Don't do this, I chastised myself. *Make this a positive experience*. I kicked off my wet boots and went up the long winding staircase to her office. The room was dark and smelled like stale coffee. I flipped on the light switch, but nothing happened. I'd had the lights cut off over a month ago. I waited for my eyes to adjust to the darkness. Then I made my way, carefully, to the other side of the office and opened the blinds. Light poured into the room.

Her big leather chair was tucked neatly under her desk. And next to her Rolodex was a framed picture of me, a headshot from the jacket cover of *Simon and Eddie*.

I picked it up and examined myself. I was so fat—even taking into account that the camera added weight. My face was as round as a chocolate Moon Pie. My double chin hung dramatically. And my shoulders were broad—too broad.

I looked like a linebacker. I shook my head, disgusted at how I'd let myself go. Instead of putting it back on display, I placed it, face down, in the top drawer of her desk.

I sat down in her office chair and spun around a few times. She always hated when I did that.

"Grace, this is not a playroom. I work here." Sometimes I'd play in the chair just to get her attention.

I was about to rummage through her cabinets when I realized there was a red light flashing on her phone. I picked up the receiver and pushed "voice-mail."

You have four new messages. First message sent September 23rd at 7:09 AM.

"Mom? Please, Mom. Please. Call me," my voice wailed into my ear. "I don't care what time it is. Call me as soon as you hear this."

I slammed down the phone, shaken by the dread and sorrow I heard in my own voice. The fear, the panic, the rage—all my original emotions came flooding back to me and knocked me back into a pit of despair. Any healing, any progress I'd made, vanished, and I was left clawing—scraping for something to hold onto.

I backed away from the desk and out of the office, afraid of what I might do. Something inside me wanted to destroy everything in the office, like I'd done to my room in Memphis. I wanted to rip up my anguish and misery, throw it across the room, and watch it smash into pieces.

Go. Just leave, you shouldn't have come in the first place. But my feet wouldn't move. I was stuck—bound in place by my own fear.

"No! No!" I gripped my head. My breathing grew shallow. My hands trembled and the walls closed in on me. Unable to make myself move—to escape my confusion, my hatred, my sadness—I dropped to my knees and wailed.

"Help me!" I shouted. "Help, me, please. I can't do this by myself." Nobody answered. The only sound was my staggered breaths and heavy sobs. "Please, where are you?" I called out to the empty house.

"I am here," something inside of me said. I gasped—frozen, unsure of what I'd heard. I abruptly stopped crying and sat quietly, convinced I was finally losing my mind. *Where? Where are you?* There was no response. I tried to think of someone to call. My dad was the first person on my list, but he was in Memphis—how could he help? Besides, I was tired of bothering him. I'd done nothing but disrupt his life, and I felt like a burden.

Trina was out of the question. Even if I could put aside my anger and pride long enough to dial her up, I wouldn't know what to say—where to go from, "Hello." We hadn't spoken in so long. And my last words to her were brash—cutting. Our friendship had been shattered into so many pieces—too many. There was no way to put it back together.

And Mike. I hadn't heard from him since the day of my mom's funeral. I thought about him often, wondered how he was doing—how he was coping. More and more, I found myself missing him and all of his quirks. But a substantial amount of time had passed since we'd seen each other. I imagined him locked away in his loft, eagerly awaiting my return, but I knew it wasn't likely. He'd probably moved on—come to the conclusion that he was better off without me, and found someone else who'd love him the way he wanted to be loved—the way he deserved to be loved.

The only person who could make it all okay was Mom. But she was gone, and I was lost. A fresh wave of tears sprang to my eyes as I began to fall into a heavy depression.

"Be still!" the voice inside of me spoke. Again, I froze and held my breath, unsure of who or what was speaking. "Ask and you shall receive."

"I don't understand," I whimpered, but I got no response. Ask for what? The one thing I wanted more than anything was to have my mom back—for her to be sitting in her office chair, chatting away on the phone. But that was never going to happen. What else could I ask?

I wanted Mike back. I missed him. I loved him. I knew that he brought out the best in me. But he was gone now, too. And even if he still wanted to be with me, I didn't know if I'd really come to terms with what had happened between us.

I wanted to publish my book and write another novel—an even better novel. I wanted to write for the rest of my life, until I was too old and riddled with arthritis to hold a pen or type. And even then, I'd find a way—invent one if I had to. But since I'd come back to Detroit, my thoughts were blocked. It's as if someone had built a concrete wall in my mind, cutting me off from my imagination. All the characters I'd created, all the plots I'd sketched in my head, were gone.

Mike, Trina, my writing—they weren't the real issue at hand. They served as Band-Aids—temporary solutions to a bigger underlying problem. I had no joy—no peace. If I did, my moods wouldn't be so driven by my circumstances. I'd tried for years to make people and things the center of my world. First it was Trina, then Stanley, then Mike, and then my novel. I convinced myself that concentrating on other people was the best way to feel good about myself. But I didn't feel good about myself. I hated almost everything about me—how everything had to be my way, how I spoke to people, and how I whined about everything.

"*I can't take back all the years I've messed up,* my mom wrote. *But I can promise that today is a new day. Forgive me, please. Forgive me like Christ forgave you.*"

"Come to Jesus," Mike's bishop pleaded. "I know some of you are weary. You can't make it on your own strength anymore. He knows that. Don't you know He knows? Give your burdens to Jesus."

"I prayed the Sinner's Prayer," Trina's voice echoed in my head. "I just confessed my sins and asked Jesus into my heart."

"He's helped me in ways I can't even explain," Mike told me.

"Ask," prodded the voice inside me. Fat tears rolled down my cheeks. I clasped my hands together and looked up at the ceiling.

"God," I began. "I may not be doing this right, but it's the only thing I know to do. I want to invite You to come live inside my heart—the way You live inside Mike. I confess I'm a sinner. I've done so many wrong things to so many people. I'm sorry. Please forgive me. Thank you for giving up Your Son to save me. I know it must have been hard, because I just lost my mom and I feel like I'm dying inside. So I'm asking You right now, if You can find it in Your heart, please help me. Take my burdens, give me peace, and show me the way to true joy."

Chapter Fifteen

My dad was sitting on a bench next to a luggage carousel, engrossed in the newspaper. I watched him for a moment; he was dressed in a pair of corduroys and a navy blue sweater vest. His legs were crossed, his wire-rimmed glasses sat firmly on his nose, and his eyebrows were furrowed in concentration. He was oblivious to the world. With my little carry-on rolling behind me, I maneuvered my way through the crowded baggage claim area and sneaked up behind him.

"Hey," I whispered into his ear. "You're kinda cute."

"I have an even cuter daughter," he said, folding his paper. He stood up and turned around, a bright smile on his face. "Look at you!"

"I know. I'm getting chunky again."

"Are you kidding? This is the best I've ever seen you look." He gave me a warm hug and then held me an arm's length away.

"What can I say? There's just so much good food to eat over there."

"I bet. Doria's always been a mean cook. So are you hungry or did she stuff you full of bacon and eggs this morning?"

"I could eat."

We went to a quaint little soul food restaurant in midtown. It was tucked away behind a pawnshop on a dead end street.

"How did you ever find this place?" I asked, as we drove around the block in search of a place to park.

"Actually, one of my students told me about it a while back. I come here a couple of times a week, mostly for dinner, though. It's too crowded around lunchtime," he said.

The restaurant had a relaxed ambiance. There were booths lined against the walls and in the center of the room was a mismatched array of chairs and tables.

"Y'all sit anywhere you want," one of the waitresses said, as she whizzed by carrying a tray of food. All the booths were full, so we took a seat at one of the tables near the door.

"If you liked your grandma's cooking, you're going to love this," Dad said. He pulled a menu from between the salt and pepper shakers and handed it to me.

"So what's all this talk about good news?" I asked, turning my attention to Dad. He looked at me over the top of his menu.

"I haven't decided what I'm going to eat."

"Dad, you're killing me here. Get the meatloaf, that's what I'm getting."

"You've waited this long, what's a few more minutes? That's what's wrong with kids these days. You've got no patience," he teased.

"Tell me!"

He laughed.

"I sent your novel to a friend of mine in New Jersey, just to see if she thought it was as spectacular as I thought it was and, of course, she did. So she sent the first few chapters to a handful of her friends in New York, and well, the long and the short of it is that Dream House Publishing *and* Crater, Inc., are interested in publishing your book."

I heard everything he said, but for some reason, I couldn't get it to register in my mind. Dream House Publishing was one of the largest, most prominent publishing houses in America. A good number of their regular authors stayed on the bestseller list and a hefty percentage of their manuscripts were turned into screenplays and sold to big-wig movie companies.

Crater, Inc., wasn't small potatoes, either. It was a smaller publishing house, with a less-established clientele, but in its fifteen years of business, it'd cranked out quite a few well-known and respected titles.

"One water and one iced tea," our waitress said, putting down our drinks. "Y'all know what you want to eat?"

"I'll have the fried chicken," my dad said.

"What about you, hon?" she asked. I stared at her in a daze. "You look like you need some more time."

"Just give her the meatloaf," my dad said, with a wink.

He dumped two packs of sugar in his glass.

"Grace, say something. Tell me what you're thinking."

"Dream House Publishing wants *my* book!" I squealed. "Do you know that their manuscript rejection rate is almost ninety-eight percent?" He shrugged. "You don't get it, do you?" I waved my fingers in excitement. "Dream. House. Publishing. Wants. My. Book!"

"I get it," he said, with a nod. "But I don't know why you're so surprised. I told you it was good!" He sipped his tea, eyeing me. "Well, do you want me to fill you in on the rest or should I wait for you to get up and dance a jig?"

"There's more?"

He reached for his coat and fished around for something in his inside pocket. Silently, he pulled out an envelope and slid it across the table.

"See for yourself."

Inside was a first class ticket to New York with my name on it. I looked up at him, wide-eyed.

"I'm going to New York?"

"Monday," he said. "Your itinerary's in there, too. Marsha Bumen, Dream House's Executive Editor and John Tipson, Senior Editor, are expecting you for brunch at the Four Seasons Hotel on Tuesday.

"I—I've never. I mean, how will I…? Please tell me you're coming with me. Please, Dad. What if I ruin everything?" My excitement waned as my old self-doubt and insecurities took over.

He laughed. "You know I can't come, Grace. And you won't ruin anything—you just need to have faith in yourself. I got your foot in the door—now the rest is up to you."

"One meatloaf," our waitress said, placing a heaping plate of food in front of me. "And one fried chicken." She set my dad's mountain of food in front of him. "Enjoy."

"Try it," Dad said, pointing at my meatloaf and mashed potatoes with his fork. "I guarantee you'll love it."

"Will you ask the blessing?"

He cocked his head to the side and looked at me in surprise. I hadn't told anyone about what happened in Mom's office or about her letter. As much as I loved my dad, I didn't know how he would react. Even to me, it sounded crazy—hearing voices in the middle of an empty house. The only person I'd ever trust enough to tell would be Mike. With all the supernatural miracles that had taken place in his life, he'd believe me.

I bowed my head.

"Dear Lord, thank you for all Your blessings. Thank you for bringing Grace safely here and for allowing us to enjoy this time together. Please bless this meal and the hands that prepared it. In Your Name we pray, Amen."

"Amen," I said, picking up my fork and laying my napkin in my lap. "Now let's see what all the fuss is about." I speared a forkful of meat and sampled it. "Not bad," I said, my mouth full. "Not bad at all." He grinned and watched me, a content look on his face.

"You're in a much better place," he said. "I'm glad to see you've let a lot of that anger go. Ever since your mom and all that stuff with Mike and Trina, you've had an edge to you. But you're different now. I don't know—freer."

I smiled as I thought about what he said.

"Yeah, I feel freer."

"Did you make up with Trina?"

"No. I haven't spoken to her at all. She sent me a pile of mail, but other than that, we haven't been bothered with each other."

"What about Mike?"

I sighed.

"No, we haven't talked either. I don't see the point."

"I do," he said, with a mouth full of greens. "You love him. What bigger reason do you need?"

"Dad," I said, shaking my head, "if I didn't think Mike and I could fix things two months ago, what makes you think we can fix them now?"

"Two months ago, you loved him, but you were angry with him. You've had time to calm down, though—time to miss him, time to think, and whether you realize it or not, so has he. Some things are inevitable. Don't let your pride get in the way, Grace."

We finished our lunches and shared a big cup of banana pudding. I listened to my dad as he talked strategy, giving me tips on how to deal with the editors from Dream House. By the time we pulled into the parking lot of my building, I was stoked.

"Remember, don't overanalyze it. Just be yourself. And if you feel panicked or you just want someone to talk to, call my office, and say there's a family emergency. The attendant will pull me out of class." He popped the trunk of his car and lifted out my suitcase.

"You want me to walk you up?" he asked.

"No, I'm okay." I gave him a peck on the cheek and a long hug. "Thanks for everything, Dad."

I took a deep breath as I slid my key into the lock and opened the door. On a Sunday afternoon, Trina should be out with Ron or Mike, but the music coming from my loft told me she was home.

"Who's there?" Trina asked, before I could even close the door behind me. Her alarmed voice was coming from her bedroom. She turned down the music.

"It's me." She peeked from behind her half-opened door. Her face lit up when she saw me. I smiled and waved sheepishly.

"Hey," she said, her tone unsure. "When did you get here?"

"A couple hours ago. My dad picked me up. We went to lunch." I threw my keys on the living room table, and headed for my bedroom, suitcase in tow.

"How was Detroit?" she asked, following a few paces behind me.

"It was nice."

"Everything settled?"

"Um, yeah, for the most part, everything's taken care of." I sat down on my bed and unzipped my boots.

"Good," she looked at me anxiously, as if she were waiting for a sign—for me to speak some magical words confirming that she was forgiven. "That *is* good, right?"

I nodded. "Yeah, of course."

"I wish you'd told me you were gonna be in today. I could've cleaned or cooked or something."

I shrugged. "I just ate and I'm leaving for New York tomorrow, anyway. So it's not a big deal."

"But you just got here," she said, her disappointment obvious. "And what's in New York?"

"Dream House Publishing," I answered, grinning.

"Dream House Publishing," she said quietly, trying to associate the name. I waited for her to catch on. "I don't get it. Dream House Publishing is—" She gasped, her blank expression turning to glee. "Your novel? They're publishing your novel?"

"Well, they're *interested* in publishing it. I'm having brunch with a couple of their editors on Tuesday. My dad told me today over lunch."

"What're you going to wear?"

I couldn't help but smile. It was such a typical female question. I'd spent two hours talking about it with my dad, and not once did the topic of wardrobe come up.

"I guess I haven't thought that far in advance. I'll have to see what fits—I've gained some weight."

"Yeah, but you look great." I rolled my eyes playfully. "Seriously, you do. I'm jealous."

"Jealous?" I asked, incredulously. "Of what? You've been tiny ever since I've known you!"

"Gracie, there's so much more to life than what size you are. Look at you—you're living your dream. You've always been lucky like that. You're one of those people who always gets it right the first time."

Me, lucky? What was she talking about?

"You decided in college that you wanted to write children's books for a living, so you did. Less than a year later, you had a series. You ran for president of the Student Arts Council and you got it. You gunned to be editor of the school paper and you got it. Senior year, you told me you wanted a boyfriend and a couple of months later, you had Stanley, and you had four perfect years with him."

I almost fell off the bed.

"Hello!" I sang. "I caught him cheating. In what world is that perfect?"

"I'm serious, Grace," she said, a catch in her voice. I stared at her in disbelief. She was about to cry. "We moved here and you got the perfect loft. You decided to lose weight and got the perfect body. And without even trying, you got Mike, the perfect man. Then, in spite of everything, you wrote the perfect novel, and now Dream House is about to publish it. But I," she continued, her eyes filling with tears. "I keep getting it wrong."

"Getting what wrong?"

"I got a scholarship—my only chance to go to college—and almost screwed it up by getting pregnant. For years, I forfeited my chance at a career to be with Darius, and he ended up being the biggest loser. I had your friendship, but took it for granted, and now I've lost it. I lost you and Mike and Ron.

"What do you mean, you lost Mike and Ron?"

"After the funeral, Mike grew distant. He cancelled Bible study about a month ago and I haven't seen him since. I've tried calling, but his number's been disconnected."

Worry crept up my spine.

"What about Ron?"

She shook her head. "I don't know. We got into a fight over you and Mike, and he said we should give each other some space. He's angry with me for causing so much trouble, and instead of listening to him, I told him to stay out of it."

"Okay," I said. "Come, sit down."

She sat next to me, our shoulders and knees resting lightly against each other. "First of all, I'm not lucky or perfect. I ran for president of the Student Arts Council and editor of the school paper because I was tired of sitting home on Friday and Saturday nights feeling like a reject. And contrary to what you may think, Stanley and I did not have a perfect relationship—nowhere near. *Simon and Eddie* was rejected four times before Taylor and Dotson picked it up. The loft felt like a prison, I lost most of my weight because I was depressed, and yes, Mike was the perfect guy, but I made a rash decision and now he's probably gone forever. So, whatever's in your head—that idealized version of my life—erase it. I'm not perfect or lucky and I don't always get things right the first time. And you haven't lost me. You were close," I gave her a playful nudge. "But lucky for you, I'm resilient."

"You *are* coming back to Memphis eventually, aren't you? If you're staying in Detroit just to get away from me, I can move out."

"Not that I'm telling you to leave, but whatever happened with that? You said you were going to be out by the fifteenth of November."

"Yeah, I know, but—well, with everything that happened, I didn't know what I should do. I mean, if you want me out, I can make arrangements. I just need a few days to find some place to go."

"Is that what you want to do?" I asked calmly. She looked at me curiously, her cheeks streaked with tears.

"Well, no, not really."

"I don't have a problem with you staying here, but I think you need to start contributing in some way. I'm not necessarily asking you to pay me rent, but maybe you can take over a few of the bills, you know? So it doesn't feel like I'm carrying you."

She smiled. "Just tell me what you want me to pay."

"We can work it out later. There's no rush."

She nodded and we sat in silence for a while.

"So what happened with Mike?" she asked. "Did you talk to him at the funeral?"

"Yeah, we talked. And he proposed."

She didn't seem the least bit surprised. "You said no. Do you regret it?"

"Not so much at first, but now I know I made a mistake."

"Are you gonna try to fix it?"

"I don't know. Are you gonna try to fix things with Ron?"

"I don't know."

"All I can do is pass on a piece of advice that my dad gave me. 'Don't let your pride get in the way of something this important.' If you love Ron, apologize, admit where you went wrong, and do whatever it takes to get him back."

She rested her head on my shoulder.

"I'm glad you came back—even if it was just for a day."

Following my own advice proved a hard thing to do, not because I wasn't willing to swallow my pride and admit that I'd made a mistake, but because I couldn't find Mike. I spent a good portion of my afternoon trying to scheme my way up to his loft. But without his key, the elevator wouldn't give me access to the sixth floor and both his phone numbers were disconnected.

Out of desperation, I went to the only person who could possibly know where he was.

"Can I help you?" she asked sweetly, taking in my appearance with one swift glance from head to toe.

"Hi, Mrs. Cambridge, my name is Grace. I know we've never been formally introduced, but—"

"Of course," she said, opening the door wider. The wrinkles around her eyes made her look even friendlier when she smiled. "Michael's Grace."

"Yes, ma'am."

"Oh, please, call me Lani. Would you like to come in?"

As soon as she closed the door, a small, furry dog bounded from the living room.

"Chewy, no!" she said firmly. The curt reprimand sounded awkward coming from her delicate voice. The dog backed off reluctantly, tail wagging.

"He's darling."

"He's spoiled, that's what he is," she said, adoringly. "Do you like apple cider? I just made a pot this morning. Sit anywhere you like, and I'll bring it right out."

I chose a comfortable recliner. Chewy felt obliged to spring into my lap. He turned around a few times, got himself comfortable, and then sat with his chin resting on my hand. The loft was the exact same floor plan as mine, but in place of my sparse furnishings, she had lots of dark antique furniture and a gallery of art, mostly encased in rich, gold frames. Her loft was much more sophisticated than mine.

"Bless your heart," she said, emerging with two mugs. "Chewy, you know better. Get down." The dog lifted his head and looked at her as if he were deciding whether or not to obey. "Chewy!" she barked. The dog leaped onto the floor and curled up by my feet.

"Here you go, sweetheart," she said, handing me one of the mugs.

"Thank you. It smells delicious."

"I'm so sorry to hear about your mom." She sat on the couch across from me. "It's a terrible thing to lose a loved one, especially a parent. I'm sorry I never got to meet her. From what Michael's told me, she was a great woman."

I took a sip of cider, and complimented her on it.

"I thought you were going to stay in Detroit for a while," she said.

"Well, I've been there for over two months, so I decided to come back for a visit. You know, check on everything."

"Ah, I see. Well, it's just too bad things happened the way they did."

I held my breath. *Had he told her about the proposal*?

"He's so trusting—too trusting, don't you think?"

"Um, maybe in some areas," I answered, trying to stay neutral until I knew what she was talking about.

"He just worked too hard to keep it all together," she continued. "One person isn't meant to carry a partnership like that all by himself."

Oh God! She knows.

"There's more to it than he's told you," I said politely. My stomach turned.

"No, he told me everything that happened, blow by blow."

Should I leave and cut my losses or try to defend myself?

"There are always two sides to every story, right?" It was a feeble attempt.

"That's true, but a contract is a contract."

"Excuse me?"

"Those weasels signed a contract with Michael. They were supposed to dismantle their companies and merge with *Life Sketch* and they reneged. I'm sure they had their reasons, but right is right and wrong is wrong. There's no gray area as far as I can see."

My heart resumed its normal pace as it began to dawn on me that she was talking about Mike's business partnership.

"You're absolutely right," I said emphatically. "So Mike's been really busy with business?"

"Busy? He's been running around like a chicken with its head cut off. Sometimes I wish he would just sell the whole thing and call it quits."

"Oh, I don't think he'll ever do that. He loves it too much."

She shook her head.

"He used to love it. Now it just drives him crazy. He hasn't been himself lately."

"Is that why he had his phone cut off?" She looked at me strangely. "Mike and I haven't talked in a while," I admitted. "I've been dealing with some personal things and we, well, I guess we lost touch."

She nodded slowly.

"Well, I hate to be the one to tell you this," she said, putting her mug down. "But Mike's moved back to New York."

"What?" I gasped.

"After the merger fell through, he felt like the only way to pick up the pieces was to be there to do it in person. His things are still here, though," she explained. "But as soon as things settle down, and he finds a permanent place to stay, he's leaving Memphis for good."

"But what about you?"

She laughed.

"I'll be okay. I may be old, but I still have a little spunk left in me."

A plan was already forming in my mind. I was going to be in New York in less than twenty-four hours. This could be my last chance to do the right thing.

"Do you have the number to Mike's hotel?" I asked. She studied me quietly. "Please, I really need to talk to him."

"Wait here," she said, getting up and shuffling down the hall. She came back holding a scrap of paper. "All I ask is that you don't make things any harder for him than they already are."

I looked at the paper. I should have known. He was staying at the Waldorf Astoria.

"I won't," I promised, assuming she was talking about his business struggles.

"It's not easy for a man to be rejected like that."

I looked up. Her gaze was strong—demanding.

"If you want him, then go get him and bring him home, but if not— then let him be."

People shoved and pushed past me as I rode the escalator down to baggage claim. I'd been to LaGuardia many times, but for some reason it seemed bigger than before. And compared to Memphis, the people were savage. The piece of paper that Mike's mom had given me was snuggly tucked into the zipped part of my purse. My itinerary said there would be a driver waiting to take me to my hotel.

Sure enough, an older gentleman wearing a black suit and sunglasses was holding a sign with my name on it. I stepped off the escalator and walked over to him.

"Ms. Naybor?" he asked, taking off his sunglasses. "I'm Pablo. Let me get that for you." He reached for my small suitcase. "If you'll follow me, I'll take you to the car."

"Just let me put on my coat."

"Certainly. Let me help you with that." He held my coat open for me as I slipped into it with ease. I followed him outside across the crosswalk and past the long line of taxis waiting for passengers. He led me to a long black limousine with tinted windows. "Watch your step," he said, opening the back passenger-side door for me.

The limo was nice and warm with soft leather seats and a stocked bar. "Not too shabby," I murmured.

"Help yourself to anything you like," Pablo said, getting behind the wheel. Under normal circumstances, I might have called my dad on my cell phone and bragged, but I knew what I was planning to do and it was zapping every bit of strength and concentration I had left in my body. "So we're going to the Four Seasons Hotel, is that correct?"

"Yes, but first I need to stop at the Waldorf Astoria."

I closed my eyes and tried to calm my nerves. The crazy, New York drivers didn't help, but eventually I managed to slow my breathing and keep my hands from trembling. Twenty minutes later, we pulled up to a beautiful, antiquated building.

"Here we are," Pablo said, getting out and opening my door. "Would you like me to wait or come back?"

"Why don't you wait? I probably won't be long."

"I'll be right here whenever you're ready."

A tip-hungry bellhop appeared out of nowhere.

"Will you be needing your bags delivered to your room?" he asked.

"No, thank you. I'm just here to meet someone." He nodded and turned his attention to the car that pulled up behind us.

I walked into the lavish lobby, unsure of which way to go. I didn't want to look like I was meandering around and get stopped by security. So I walked with authority behind a gray-haired man in a business suit and followed him to the elevator.

"What floor?" he asked.

"Fifteen." I waited nervously as the elevator beeped its way higher. Finally, the fifteenth floor. I stepped off and pulled out the crumpled piece of paper from my purse. Room 1520. My heart pounded in time with my footsteps. After a few turns, I walked down a long, carpeted corridor to his room. I heard a muffled voice coming from behind the door.

This is it. It's do or die. I took a deep breath and knocked.

The door opened and there he was, in slacks and a dress shirt, his tie carelessly flung around his neck. He was on the phone.

"Mike?" I heard a woman's shrill voice through the receiver. "Mike, are you there? Hello? Are we still on for seven?"

"I'll have to call you back," he said.

I looked down at my hands. "I'm sorry. I didn't mean to interrupt."

He'd found someone else. What did I expect? I was too late.

"What're you doing here?"

"Your mom," I said holding up the piece of paper. "She told me where you were staying."

"You came all the way to New York to see me?" His tone was even, his face expressionless.

"No, I'm here on business, but when I found out you were here, too, I thought I'd come by to see you."

He nodded. "Do you want to come in?"

I slipped past him into the beautifully decorated room.

"So," he said, sitting on the bed. "What's up, Grace? How've you been?"

"I've been okay."

"I see you've gained some weight. You look good."

I smiled.

"Thanks. So do you."

"How's your dad?"

"He's doing fine. It's exam time, so he's pretty busy."

"Have you talked to Trina about—you know?"

"I saw her yesterday. It's a process, but we've started talking things out. So…I hear the merger didn't go as well as expected."

"Yeah, something like that," he answered vaguely. "It'll get worked out."

I dropped the subject. He obviously didn't want to talk about it—not with me anyway.

"You said you were here on business?"

"Dream House Publishing is interested in my novel. They flew me up here to meet with some of their editors."

"Wow, Dream House—that's big time, isn't it? So, you're patching things up with Trina, your novel's about to break loose—things are looking up for you."

I smiled. "It's strange. When I was in Detroit, I was lonely and full of anger, and then something happened and all of a sudden, I was just me again."

"What happened?"

"I don't know what to call it. I was in my mom's house and I heard a voice-mail that I'd sent her the morning I found out that she died and it kind of spooked me, you know?"

He looked genuinely interested in what I was saying.

"I guess I started having a panic attack, but I couldn't move and I was sobbing and begging for help, and this voice out of nowhere said, 'I am here.' I know it sounds crazy."

"Why would that sound crazy?"

I shrugged.

"I don't know. You're the first person I've told. I started remembering things that you and Trina and my mom had said—even your bishop. And then the voice said, 'Ask and you will receive.' So I dropped to my knees and invited Jesus into my heart."

"You prayed to receive Christ?" he asked, with a hint of a smile.

"Well, I don't know if I did it the right way, but yeah, I think I did."

"There's no right way," he said. "As long as you prayed it and meant it. Congratulations. I'm happy for you."

We sat with an awkward silence between us.

"Your mom said you're moving to New York."

He nodded. "It's time for a change."

"That's what I want to talk to you about—change. I've done a lot of it over the past two months. Looking back, I think I might have made a huge mistake."

I felt myself losing my composure. I took a deep breath and bit my lip.

"Grace," Mike started.

"Just let me finish," I pleaded. "That day at the funeral, I was angry and grieving and hurt. I was in an emotional tailspin and I wasn't thinking clearly. You weren't the only one who got hurt, Mike. We both have blame in this."

"I know that Grace, but—" The phone rang. He looked down at it and then back at me. "I have to take this," he apologized.

"I gave you the wrong answer, Mike. When you asked me to marry you, I gave you the wrong answer."

Our eyes locked. The phone rang again. He shook his head.

"I have to get this." He picked up the receiver. "Hello?"

"Mike, what is going on?" the same shrill voice from earlier asked.

"Hold on a minute," he said, placing his hand over the phone. "It really isn't a good time for me. I've got a lot going on right now."

All I could do was nod. My pride—my dignity—had been shredded.

"Don't worry about it." My voice was thick with tears, but I managed a smile. "I can let myself out."

I picked up my purse and headed for the door.

"Grace," he called after me. I turned around. "Take care of yourself."

My meeting with Dream House Publishing's senior and executive editors went well, considering my mind was somewhere else the entire time. I nibbled on my cheese and spinach quiche and half listened to the vision they had for my novel.

"Okay. We'll have our people draw up a contract and you should receive it sometime next week," Mr. Tipson said. He was a rotund red-faced man with a hearty laugh and a bad combover.

My mind was so scattered, I wasn't even sure what terms we'd agreed to.

"Ms. Naybor, it was a pleasure meeting you," Marsha Bumen said, extending her hand.

"Thank you for the limo and the hotel. It's been a wonderful experience."

After they picked up the tab and put on their coats, I said goodbye and then headed across the lobby to the elevators. All I wanted to do was hide away until it was time to leave.

The fist thing I noticed when I stepped into my room was the message light flashing on the hotel phone. I pushed the button labeled "Voicemail."

"Hello, Ms. Naybor. I'm calling from Guest Services to let you know there's a package waiting for you at the front desk. Have a pleasant day."

I moaned. I'd just passed the front desk on my way up. I dialed extension 101.

"Front desk, this is Charlene. How can I help you today, Ms. Naybor?"

"I just received a message from Guest Services. Are you holding a package for me?"

"Oh, yes. It just arrived. I'll have it delivered to your room shortly."

I hung up, kicked off my heels and stretched across the bed. There was no point in getting undressed until the package arrived. Moments later, someone knocked on the door. I grabbed a couple of bucks from my wallet.

A young lady dressed in a black business suit handed me the envelope. Before I could give her the tip, she turned on her heels and bustled off down the hall. I held the package in my hand. It was lightweight with a slight hump protruding at the bottom. I didn't recognize the handwriting but without hesitation, I ripped it open.

Inside was a little black velvet box. My heart nearly stopped. This was either a cruel joke, or the first day of the rest of my life. I opened it, my fingers trembling, to find a familiar three-stone engagement ring set in yellow gold.

Tears spilled from my eyes. *Where was he?* I looked around the room, almost expecting him to jump out of the closet. I held the box in my hand, frozen—afraid to make the wrong move. There was a knock at the door. I rushed to open it. Mike stood there with a bouquet of red roses. I was speechless.

"Don't cry," he said gently. I flung my arms around his neck. He squeezed me to him tightly—firmly. It had been so long since we'd held each other. I couldn't remember anything ever feeling so right.

"Hey, hey," he said, tenderly pulling away. "Aren't you going to let me ask?"

I sniffled and stepped back. He handed me the roses and bent down on one knee.

"Gracie," he said, looking up into my eyes. "I love you. You're my heart." His voice caught. "And these few months we've spent apart have done nothing but confirm that you are the only one I want to be with. If you'll have me, I would cherish the honor of being your husband. Will you marry me?"

"Yes," I whispered.

He took the ring out of the box, slid it onto my left ring finger and kissed my hand. I got down on my knees, faced him nose-to-nose, and kissed him. I took in the taste of his lips. I ran my fingers through his hair and down his neck. And I relished the familiarity and comfort of his body.

"I missed you so much," I confessed. "I thought you'd found someone else. The woman on the phone—"

"April? She's my realtor. We were supposed to meet yesterday and look at some properties in Lower Manhattan. You really thought I could find someone to replace you?" He kissed my forehead.

"You said 'take care.' That usually means goodbye."

"Well, yeah, I wanted to make sure you were surprised. I didn't know how, but I wasn't going to let you leave New York without that ring on your finger."

"Where do we go from here?" I asked. "You want to move to New York. We both have lofts in Memphis, and I have a huge house in Detroit."

He shrugged and nuzzled his nose into my neck.

"The fact that the two of us are here now is nothing short of a miracle. When God's in something, He makes a way for it to happen. And I *know* that He's in this. Don't worry—I'm willing to do whatever it takes."

"Me, too," I said, toying with one if his dreadlocks.

He let out a sigh of contentment. "Then that's all we need."

As we kissed and talked, wrapped in each other's arms, I marveled at the twists and turns my life had taken in such a short time. My journey with Mike was sure to yield its share of bumps, but that was okay. I was ready for life now. The day I prayed to receive Christ was the day I stopped using Band-Aids and found the only permanent solution to all my ails and woes. It was time to stop living in my own strength. I had to lean on Jesus and walk by faith—just like Mike. Just like Mom.

"I'm so excited," I said lacing my fingers through his. "It's like sitting down in front of a blank sheet of paper."

"How does our story begin?" he asked, smiling.

"I'm not sure, but I know it has a happy ending."

"How do you know?" he whispered.

I closed my eyes.

"I just do. Some things are inevitable."

Contact Info

RyanMPhillips@excite.com